THE

SILK

PAVILION

THE

SILK

PAVILION

S A R A H   W A L T O N

BARB
ICAN
PRESS

Published by Barbican Press: London & Los Angeles

Copyright © Sarah Walton, 2022

With thanks to the publishers, editors and translators for quotation permissions:

Robert Graves, Ed: Patrick Quinn; *Complete Poems In One Volume* ('The Face in the Mirror'), Carcanet.

Carl Jung, Ed: Gerhard Adler; *Aion – Researches into the Phenomenology of the Self. The Collected Works of C.G. Jung. Volume 9, Part II*, Routledge (Taylor & Francis Group).

Arturo Barea, *The Forging of a Rebel*. English translation by Ilsa Barea. Pushkin Press.

C.G. Jung, Ed. Sonu Shamdasani; *The Red Book. Liber Novus. A Reader's Edition*. W.W. Norton & Company.

Registered office: 1 Ashenden Road, London E5 0DP

www.barbicanpress.com

@barbicanpress1

Cover by Rawshock Design

Cover photo by Roberto Nickson at Unsplash

A CIP catalogue for this book is available from the British Library

ISBN: 978-1-909954-56-4

Typeset in Adobe Garamond

Typeset by Imprint Digital Ltd

Sarah Walton is an Anglo-Irish author and founder of Soul Writing intuitive writing coaching and retreats. She also teaches MA Creative Writing at the University of Hull, is a Barbican Academy mentor and digital consultant. Her debut novel, *Rufius*, won her a PhD and was longlisted for the Polari First Book Award.

www.drsarahwalton.com
Twitter - @sarahlwalton
Instagram - @drsarahwalton
YouTube - Dr Sarah Walton

Advance praise:

'A strange, almost dream-like reading experience – a journalist lands in Mallorca but comes to fear that she is a prisoner of her own mind. Febrile and frequently disturbing, with a hint of Bluebeard to it, it put me in mind of Paul Bowles's "The Sheltering Sky" – that sense of someone who is lost but compelled to pursue the path as it materializes before them. It had me gripped right to the end.' – Mick Jackson

'Set in the small Spanish town of Deià and its beautiful Villa Rosa, Sarah Walton's The Silk Pavilion weaves a compelling story around a young British woman and her controlling, narcissistic lover, Miguel Mateo Nadal. Using fact, fiction and the historical remnants of the Spanish Civil War, she succeeds in bringing us, with honesty and empathy, this vividly told story that reveals how the trauma inflicted in one's childhood can distort the psyche, leading the individual into choosing, unconsciously, further abuse as an adult. Her novel reads like a thriller but is also very much a novel of one woman's journey of self-discovery and survival. Contemporary, relevant and highly readable. A brave and important book.' – Grace Nichols

'Sarah Walton gives us two intriguing characters who are romantically, dangerously and inexplicably drawn to each other. Lucy's gradual unravelling of the elusive Miguel leads her to discover her own hidden shadow self. An intense and enthralling read.'
– Philip Ayckbourn

Also by the Author:

Rufius
Sophia's Tale
The Soul Writer's Way

For abused children and the adults we become

When an inner situation is not made conscious,
It happens outside,
As fate
(Carl Jung)

La amnistía determinará en general la extinción
de la responsabilidad criminal

This law guarantees impunity for crimes
against humanity under Franco.

(Article 6, Amnesty Law 46/1977, "Pact of Forgetting")

FAMILY TREE

Miguel's Family: The Nadals

Great Grandfather Nadal – built Villa Rosa
Grandfather Nadal - Mateo Julio Nadal (married Sofia Valentina Nadal)
Sofia Valentina Nadal (Miguel's grandmother)
Maria Isobel Nadal (Miguel's ex-wife)

The Neighbour's Family: The Llobets

Juan Pablo Llobet – the neighbour's grandfather
Marta Alma Llobet – the neighbour's grandfather's sister & Sofia Nadal's best friend

PART 1

A Bedsit, North London

Last night I dreamt I went to Villa Rosa again. The iron gates that led to the driveway and steep grass lawn up to the house were closed to me. There was a padlock on the gate. He had not put that there. He would not have parted with the money, but made some half-baked thing himself. I called in my dream to him, *Miguel, mi amor.* Silence drowned the night. The madroño tree was lit by a single moonbeam. That old disappointment returned, that lonely grief that defined our love from the beginning.

Then, like all dreamers, I was possessed by supernatural powers and passed like a ghost through the iron gates. The driveway, overgrown. The lawn, high and unruly. His sculptures of gigantic phalli that had dotted the garden were gone. The two olive trees had grown so close together their branches wrapped around each other like some deformed, mythic hermaphrodite. The garden was overshadowed by the forest of the Teix. The mountain had invaded the garden; its menacing wall of trees that was bearable, beautiful even from a distance, had imprisoned the garden in a shroud of shadow. Nature had reclaimed what was always hers.

I looked up at Villa Rosa's salmon-pink walls, bruised with dirt and blistered with cancerous marks, like Miguel's sunspots, where the paint has flaked away – as if the house was covered with his skin.

Miguel has gone. Alarm floods my dream-body and I run the rest of the way up to the front door. A rose bush thorn cuts my hand as my urgent fingers hunt for the key behind the plant pots. I open the door with the key and let myself inside.

As only happens in dreams, time changes, location changes. I am my young self, sitting at the top of the stairs of my family's North London semi-detached looking at the front door. Waiting. Waiting for my father to return from golf. The front door swings open. In he comes. My father. He takes a golf club from the antique golf bag, an ornament in the lobby. The wildness is in his eyes. I run to my bedroom, pull the duvet over my head, curl into a foetus shape and brace myself. In he comes, barking like a dog. He beats the duvet with the golf club.

When he's finished, in comes my mother and strokes me over the duvet.

'Daddy loves you.'

I am sobbing, body arched and rigid in foetal protection, fingers clenched around the duvet so she cannot take it off me.

'Daddy loves you, darling.'

1

Villa Rosa

I stepped off the main road. *Walk down the lane to the black gates*, he'd said on the phone. I looked over the olive groves to the sea before descending into the cool shade of the lane. It was just an interview but I was nervous. How odd the writer hadn't shown up that morning after suggesting a swim in the sea. When I saw the tall iron gates at the bottom of the path a strange compulsion took hold of me and I floated trancelike the rest of the way down the narrow path with high walls of overhanging pink bougainvillea. The house was hidden from the path, but I sensed Villa Rosa pulling me into its field of enchantment. The black gates grated on gravel and I walked up the driveway as if tugged by an invisible lead.

The writer – for that was all Miguel Mateo Nadal was to me then – waited at the top of the lawn under the madroño tree. His appearance surprised me. He can't have updated his PR photo for at least twenty years. Thin grey receding hair made his forehead seem large. Skin folded like over-worn leather and a brown sunspot below his right eye made him almost unrecognisable from his photo. His shorts gave him a boyish look. Age had not changed those black eyes. Was that greed in his gaze as he watched me walk up the driveway?

His intense scrutiny threatened to throw me off balance. Confidence I'd pushed into my walk was feigned. It had disconcerted me when he'd not turned up that morning at the Cala – a small rocky cove at the bottom of the valley. More than that. A deep, dark disappointment had caught hold of me as I'd trod water and it dawned on me I'd been stood up. The high cliffs either side had thrown a dark shadow over the narrow inlet. Why suggest a swim if he did not intend coming? Back at the hostel, the only affordable hotel in Deià even in late October, reason shrugged off the shadow over my breakfast of bread and jam. As long as he did the interview what did it matter? But an irrational residue lingered. The disappointment had a strangely familiar quality to it, a particular flavour of deflation that I knew deep in my soul.

On the swim back to the rocks, to add injury to insult, I'd been stung by jellyfish. A tattoo of warning wheals whipped up my legs and were visible under my black dress.

Miguel Mateo Nadal had a reputation for being a recluse. The editor at the New York News was surprised he'd agreed to an interview, so the writer had thrown me by suggesting we take a morning swim. My disappointment was out-of-proportion. Even so, I felt unsure of myself as I walked towards him, accompanied by an inexplicable thump of fear in my chest. He could have warned me about the jellyfish! I resisted scratching my legs.

Without saying a word he leant down and kissed me, a brush of whiskers on both cheeks, as is the custom of Spanish men when they greet women. He did not smile. This intimacy not present in the customary handshake of the British and Americans meant I smelt him before we spoke. His scent was inexplicably familiar.

An involuntary voice whispered from deep inside me. *I will never leave this man.*

'Welcome to Villa Rosa.' He spoke English with a thick accent.

My Spanish stammered as I handed him the gift.

'Encantada. Chocolates, hechos a maño.'

Miguel Mateo Nadal looked blankly at the paper bag with the luxury logo. Perhaps he'd not understood me. Our emails had been a mix of English and Spanish. I wouldn't usually arrive for an interview with chocolates, but we were meeting at his house (rather than my suggestion of my hotel lobby) and a guest cannot arrive empty-handed. *Was the word bombones?*

He waved his arm in the air … in irritation at my rusty Spanish?

'Why are we speaking Spanish when I dare say I speak jolly well English?'

The crumbs of Spanish I'd digested on an exchange at the Universitat Autònoma de Barcelona were usually good enough for small talk. Why did I excuse his rudeness?

'These are for you. Handmade chocolates.'

He accepted the bag graciously when I spoke in English. 'I dare say I love chocolate.'

I waited for him to explain why he'd not turned up for our morning swim. Instead his gaze sucked me in silence.

My black dress was uneven and frayed at the hem and, in the shadow of the old house, boho chic felt more Mallorcan peasant wife. *Maybe that was it – he's Catalan and the local Catalan dialect is Mallorquín so perhaps he doesn't like speaking in Spanish?*

'I dare say we ought to have tea.'

Without waiting for an answer he disappeared into the house and returned with a tray, teapot and bowl of figs. Their red seeded centres burst from their swollen skins like delicious open wounds.

'Figs, how lovely!'

I took one and bit into it. He watched me. Pink juice dribbled down my chin. I wiped it, giggled and licked my lips. His gaze was intense. I felt incongruent, like I was destined for some more intimate role than interviewer.

I looked up at the salmon pink walls of the house, longing to enter.

There was nothing of the hospitality of the Spanish about him. Interviews were likely a thinly tolerated encroachment on his private life, insisted on by his publisher for publicity for his long awaited new novel. But his emails had been seductive, painting a picture of the tea we would share. Had I been lured to Deià?

As I watched him watching me in his Bermuda shorts and loose denim shirt, it struck me that I must look like I'm dressed for a funeral. My choice of dress felt inappropriate all of a sudden as I remembered why wizened Spanish ladies wore black when I visited Spain as a very young child – the Civil War.

I sat up straight in the garden chair and reminded myself, *I am here to interview him.* I'd read his novels in preparation for the interview. This was my first job since going freelance and I was grateful to my editor on the New York News for sending it my way. I'd only got it as everyone else was on vacation so I was determined to make a good job of it. It was also nice to be back in Europe. The language might not be the same, but I always felt more at home in Europe than America, even though I'd lived in New York City longer than I'd lived anywhere else. New Yorkers like Londoners allowed you to self-identify. I'm part New Yorker, but I'd left my learned identity on the plane.

I switched into work mode, unzipped my bag and arranged my tools on the garden table: video camera, mobile phone, microphone and a moleskin notebook.

'As I'm going to film you, if you could sit there … and I'll sit here. And if you could sign this, please.' I slid the two-page agreement (which I'd also emailed in advance) across the garden table and handed him a pen.

'What is this?' He flicked the pages away dismissively. Surely it wasn't the first time he'd been asked to sign a consent agreement.

'This gives your permission to use the interview material for publication online and in print.'

He made a low mocking sniff-cum-grunt, a sound grumpy old men make. It made me feel ridiculed and was peculiarly familiar.

Let's get this done and let me get back to sightseeing.

As if he sensed the change in me, his tone switched from curt to courteous.

'Certainly. Where ought I to sign?'

I held the page flat on the table as a breeze threatened to wisp it away.

'And what is this?' He picked up the cord of the microphone attached to my mobile phone and threw it away from him as if he were angry at it.

His sudden mood switches unnerved me. *He's not my first difficult interviewee and it's my job to put him at ease.*

'It's a microphone. I'm no expert with these things. Let's see if we can get it working.' I laughed hoping to break the tension.

His smile was a sudden surprise, like flowers and chocolates, and my tension dissolved instantly.

I uncoiled the white plastic cord.

'I'll clip the microphone to your shirt, if that is ok with you?'

Miguel Mateo Nadal sat while I walked around his chair. The side of my hand brushed against the grey hairs peeking out the top of his shirt and that same magnetism which I'd felt the house exert over me as I walked up the path tugged me again, but this time with such intensity that I became floaty and like some ethereal being in a fairy tale. My hands became nimble with the tiny clip and cord, at odds with an impatient desire to rip open his shirt and touch his skin.

'Um, these figs are delicious!' I took another fig and bit. Its sugary innards burst into my mouth, pink juice wet my chin and I munched with childlike enjoyment.

Miguel Mateo Nadal watched and smiled. My devouring the figs seemed to please him.

'They are jolly good – you ought to enjoy them.' His sugary tone encouraged me to indulge myself and I sensed him relax another notch as I took another fig.

As I sat back down a tiny red spiky fruit landed on the old wooden table. I looked up at the thick canopy shading us from the afternoon sun.

'What are they?'

Miguel Mateo Nadal sniffed and spoke like he was explaining to a child.

'This is a madroño tree.'

I'm here to interview a writer, I reminded myself and forced an officious tone as I read from my notebook.

'My first question is about the line between real life and fiction. Your new novel – which is a fascinating and disturbing deep dive into the psyche of a serial killer – is clearly not autobiography.' We'd laughed at my joke. 'But I note that all your protagonists are Mallorcan men. How much of yourself goes into your novels?'

Miguel Mateo Nadal came alive during the interview. He clearly enjoyed the self-reflection required to answer my questions.

'Um. Yes. Jolly good question. Well, I dare say one must remember that fiction is a lie which presents itself as truth … or ought one to say, fiction presents a truth which uses a lie to drive itself into the reader's consciousness …'

There was something odd about how he spoke English. It was not his accent. My time in Barcelona as a student meant I was accustomed to the sound of rolled r's and soft c's. What was not typical was his old-fashioned diction. The 1950s English of Enid Blyton novels transported me to another time. Our interview at the old wooden table under the madroño tree felt like we had fallen into a time warp.

Was I a fan? I admired his writing but found it deeply disturbing that all his female characters died gruesome deaths at the hands of their lovers. I was intrigued by his work, but I didn't view it as something outside myself. When I'd read his novel *La Esposa del Asesino (The Killer's Wife)* on the flight from New York City, I had the sensation that through the rhythm of his sentences his voice had entered me. Like a ventriloquist, the frequency of his vocal cords strummed the eardrum of my soul.

When I'd heard his voice for the first time on the phone yesterday, his tone was familiar. We spoke in English, but it was not his words and his funny Enid Blyton diction that fascinated me. A voice, I reflected as I listened to his low drone, exists without sound. It's the beat of the writer's soul drumming on the page. In the way he bent the words of his stories to his will, Miguel Mateo Nadal had divulged something of the silent beat of his being. His voice both lulled me into suspension of my disbelief, and alerted me to danger, for even then on the phone in my hotel room, a quiver of fear had entered me. His voice that day under the madroño tree sent me into a sort of trance, so that I wasn't listening to the words, but was carried along with its rhythm. It was as if Miguel Mateo Nadal had me hypnotised.

'… does that answer your question?'

His question snapped me out of my trance and I looked at my notes. The page of my notebook was blank.

'Oh, yes, thank you.'

I sipped the tea, now lukewarm. Now he was talking about his work, Miguel Mateo Nadal was fully engaged and animated. Thankfully he hadn't noticed that I'd drifted off.

'Next question. You deal with some difficult subjects. The Spanish Civil War, for example, comes up in all of your novels. Can you say something about this preoccupation?'

'The War Civil …' He trailed off, then returned. 'Brother killed brother. Its shame is concealed within families from one generation to the next. The truth is lost as the stories change. History is a fiction created by survivors. My character in *Two Metres Under* – I dare say that was the English title – she voices this collective shame from her grave.'

There was another conversation beating beneath the surface. It had started in our email exchange, in him painting a picture of our first meeting at his house in Deià. The poetry he'd borrowed from Robert Graves to describe the village had seduced, convinced me to meet him in Deià rather than Palma. I became conscious of my desire to enter the house, to explore what those salmon pink walls concealed.

If Villa Rosa were conscious – which in moments of madness I later suspected it was – and if the house had vocal cords, it would have laughed out loud as it watched our tentative dance of decorum – me asking the questions, him spinning answers littered with the language of seduction; me trying to listen professionally and making unintelligible notes in my notebook. As its shuttered windows peered down at us through the branches of the madroño tree, the house would have seen the spiky little red fruit hung like Chinese lanterns above our heads fall as a gust blew in from the sea, sensed magic on the wind as we performed the charade of the interview. Masquerade for a meeting of lovers.

'I dare say that is the Sirocco. It blows in from the Sahara. Graves, you know, Robert Graves the poet, said it made the sea in the Cala look like cat's fur blown backwards.'

Why didn't you meet me in the Cala this morning like you said? I didn't ask.

The Sirocco was impatient to hurry along the inevitable. In my sleeveless black dress I shivered and the gusts fluttered the pages of my notebook.

'Are you cold? Shall we go inside?'

'A little.' It was all I could do to stop my teeth chattering. I had said nothing of my discomfort. I did not want to break the spell.

His body, the way it rose and lurched towards the door – a lizard's walk – expected me to follow him inside Villa Rosa.

There are no more questions. It is time to leave. Do not follow him into the house. My quiet inner voice jittered with small fears that made me breathe in shallow gasps. I ignored my intuition, numbed the alarm and stepped over the threshold.

2

Grooming

Let her sway on the threshold, hesitant as a deer in her black dress. I dare say Villa Rosa will seduce her. Nobody leaves Villa Rosa untouched. How old is she? She suggested we meet in Palma, this British woman. In Palma we would have had a polite coffee. When I saw her profile on the newspaper website I knew I wanted something with her. Alessandra doesn't give me what I need. And I am a man.

'Please, come inside and have a jolly good look around.'

I like the cool air of the lobby, a mini gallery of my life. It has been a long time since the house was explored by a stranger.

She stops and stares at the painting of my grandmother. My grandmother's high-neck black dress mirrors hers, as if she's dressed in mourning too.

'My great grandfather built this house. That is his daughter, my grandmother. And the painting next to hers is of my grandfather. He was ... He died in the War Civil. I dare say it's a tragic story.'

Talk of death silences her. She glides between family heirlooms and my own sculptures. She didn't notice me stumble over my grandfather's fate. Her fingertips stroke the head of my favourite work. She won't be the first woman who's shocked when she discovers she's caressing a gigantic phallus.

'What is it?'

I like the way she moves around its polished surface, its head shoulder height to her bare shoulder, trying as minds do to make sense of its shape – like looking for faces in mountains.

'It's one of mine.'

She blushes and snatches her hand back from the statue. To cover up her embarrassment she does what many women do. Talks. Ha! I'm enjoying this. It's the first time I've not had to feign a smile for months … maybe years. And I haven't thought about the neighbour once since she arrived. The thought of him winning the court case sends a snap of rage through my brain.

'You're a sculptor as well as a writer.'

'The phallus is an object Ancient Romans displayed in their gardens.'

'Really? The Classical world fascinates me. Priapus used to ward off thieves, didn't he?'

Only a British woman could contemplate my cock as if we were at an academic conference. Desire races in my groin and I feel the old me return, the me before Alessandra castrated my drive. How to finish it, how end it? Maybe she is the answer.

I step close to the wooden phallus and sense her recoil slightly. ¡Uf! It's been too long since I played this game.

'Yes, I used to be a sculptor. I dare say I am interested in the anatomy.'

Our laughter echoes up through the house. Villa Rosa needs a woman.

'Priapus was the god of fertility. The medical condition priapism, which Robert Graves suffered from, derives from this god.'

'What's this one made of?' She's pretending she's not fazed.

'Cherry wood. It is a pleasure to work with wood. I spent hours with the chisel in the garden, shaping, smoothing, perfecting this piece. Sculpting, like writing is a slow, gradual process. You have a vague vision and watch patiently as the wood develops form, meets your vision, and if it has substance sometimes it takes on a life of its own.'

I stroke the shaft. Smooth.

Her cheeks flush and she feigns interest in the safety of a landscape painting. Her discomfort is amusing as she waits for me to lead the way deeper inside Villa Rosa.

'It's like the forbidden room in Naples Museum where they keep hundreds of phalli archaeologists found in Pompeii!' Her joke is breathy as she hurries past me up the staircase, sandals scuffing stone.

Obviously that wait was beyond her comfort threshold.

The staircase, the spine of the house winds up to the floor above. I sense her urge to keep climbing. I once had that same curiosity as a child, but she holds back like a dog on a leash. She has potential.

I walk into the kitchen and release her from polite etiquette.

'Make yourself at home. I ought to make more tea. Do you take lashings of milk?' I'd forgotten the British take milk in their tea. I like that she didn't ask for it even if she wanted it when we were in the garden.

Why's she laughing?

'No milk – or ginger beer for me, thanks.'

Ignore her silly laughter. I never understand jokes.

Floorboards creak as she wanders around the living room. Her footsteps relax me. I dare say it's a relief to have a new woman in the house. The mountain casts its late afternoon shadow over the swimming pool. I must get this kitchen windowpane fixed.

The bastard neighbour – he must have thrown the stone up at it. I found it in the sink. A stone from my own garden!

Damn these dirty plates. No clean cups. I slam the cupboard door shut. Mustn't scare her off.

¡Uf! The clatter of the kettle on the floor tiles makes me nervous. Every time I think of him I drop things.

'Can I help?'

Sexy, how she hugs the kitchen doorframe – she's posing for me.

'How old are you?'

'You can't ask a woman that question!'

Why does she laugh? It irritates me like superfluous punctuation. I laugh too at this game. Is she alone in Deià?

'Why are you laughing?'

'I'm sorry. You sound like a character in a Famous Five novel.'

'I learnt English from Enid Blyton books when I was a child.'

'Well, Enid Blyton taught you jolly well!'

More laughter. I'd better laugh too, but it sounds forced as it echoes up the stairwell as if the house is laughing at me.

What's she looking at? The hole in the kitchen window. I rub the tea towel against the cups so violently a cup jumps from my hand and bounces on the kitchen floor. That was her fault.

'I'm 35. How old did you think I was?'

I sniff.

I'm sixty-one this year, but I am like a man of twenty. My body is strong from swimming, stronger and younger than hers.

'I dare say I saw a mature woman.' Take your time, don't scare her off. 'A beautiful, mature woman.'

Let's serve the tea. She sits in the antique blue tartan chair opposite the lounge window. I'll sit in the sofa facing her. I arrange the tray on a little table and hand her a cup of tea. Why's she putting the teacup on the floor by her feet? I don't like that.

'Where do you live?'

'New York.'

She's not mentioned a man and her embarrassment at my sculptures ... I dare say it's a long time since she's had sex.

As I question her I adjust my posture. I was not aroused when she interviewed me – her gaze was so intent, laser blue eyes piercing into me as I talked. Clearly I'm interesting, but now I'm aware of my body's needs. I like the way she answers my questions honestly as she folds and refolds her black dress. She has that porcelain skin I like. Fragile. Smashable. My turn to interview her.

'Where did you learn Spanish?'

I like this investigation when I first meet a woman. As she talks about studying in Barcelona, parties, friends, with a prompt here and there, a version of me comes alive as I relive her life through her memories, digging into every nook and cranny.

'You're like the Spanish Inquisition!'

'What?' Rage snaps on my tongue.

Her smile disappears as she senses my anger. 'It's just an expression. You ask a lot of probing questions.'

Force a smile, Miguel.

'I dare say I do. You interest me.'

That pleased her. Silly girl – the Inquisition would have marched her to the mirador and pushed her off the cliff onto the rocks of the Cala.

She pulls her black dress further down over long tanned legs.

'Do you have any family?'

'I was married once.'

'And now?'

I don't like these personal questions. It makes me feel guilty.

'I can't follow everything you say.'

'Sorry, I'll speak slower. Are you in a relationship now?'

'Why does it matter?' That was too curt. She recoils back into the seat, her chin juts into her chest.

'For transparency. I'm married.'

'Transparency, I dare say, yes.' Transparency, what a ridiculous notion, but it tells me she's sensed the sexual tension in the room. I'm on the right track.

The light from the window falls like a spotlight on her. She is beautiful. I want her to sit here with me every night. I can't bear another night alone in the house and she's kept my mind off Alessandra.

'You sit very straight.'

She laughs.

'You're avoiding the question. Are you in a relationship?'

'Not exactly.'

She laughs again.

'You're either in a relationship or not.'

How to define my relationship with Alessandra now?

'Well, yes. It's complicated. It's practically over. I was seeing a woman for nine years. But it's over. Unofficially over.'

Her frown is amused.

'So it's not over.'

The plumbing! Banging again.

'Does she know it's over?'

That bang was loud. ¡Uf! The timing startles me. I imagine Alessandra can hear every word I utter. I push my paranoia away.

Another louder bang makes her jump – the cistern this time. I'll have to go into the cellar if it continues, but that will break the atmosphere. Damn guilt again.

'Tell me more about your travels.'

Impatience lurches in me. I cross and uncross my legs. I can't follow her English. Her chatter is boring me, but I'll keep asking her questions, keep her talking. The light from the window falls like a spotlight on her. I like how rigid and still she sits as if restrained under a police surveillance camera.

She's laughing again. 'I'm here to interview *you*!'

I should laugh too. I've learned to imitate other people's gestures, laugh when they laugh. That will relax her, coax her into believing we have an affinity. But she is foreign to me. British. I do not like the British. They come with their big ideas and change the landscape – like Graves building his road down to the Cala, attracting hordes of tourists who stayed and infested Deià with half-breeds.

Why has she got up to look out of the window? I must change tactics. I stand behind her and open the window, smell her hair. Coconut. I like it, not like that awful chemical stuff my ex-wife doused herself in.

'You see …' I point past her and stand closer so she'll be more aware of me than the house. '… that house there, across the valley is the house of Robert Graves. He called it Ca n'Alluny – Faraway House in Catalan. It was the British who changed the landscape of Deià. Graves came first, built a road down to the Cala. Then came Richard Branson. He built La Residencia which brought the tourist industry.'

This history of the landscape is one I've told many times before standing at this window. She is just like the others, thinks it is just for her. I am not touching her, but electricity flows between us.

'Who's that man staring up at the house?'

The bastard neighbour!

'Don't look at him.'

She looks shocked, but steps back from the window and sits down where I want her, pinned down by sunbeams. I feel calm again as she sits and imagine I control the beams of light that illuminate her face. If only I could control that bastard neighbour.

'Why don't you want me to look at him?'

My legs cross and uncross. Must keep my voice level, mustn't reveal my nerves.

'I dare say he is crazy. My neighbour. He attacked me last year.'

'Attacked you?'

She's shocked. Good, that will divert her focus back to me.

'Yes. Jolly frightening incident. They are Deià people. Peasants. When my parents were alive we used to come here, like many Palma families in the summer. It was for me like the Famous Five going to Kirrin Island for the holidays – you know, Enid Blyton?'

This was my attempt at a joke. I copied hers.

We laugh and the stone stairwell echoes our laughter.

'Why doesn't he like you?'

'I dare say he's jolly jealous. It has always been like this between Deià people and Palma people.' This is partly true. The rift caused by the war is none of her business. The old shame, it fires me up from my groin to my head.

'Well they won't like me then. I'm even more foreign. It sounds a bit like George Sand's book.'

¡Uf! That book! Must keep my legs still. She's looking at them. What that French woman wrote infuriates me. *A Winter in Majorca* is sold in every café on the island.

'Sand wrote about Valldemosa. You will have passed through the town on your way from Palma. But you must remember that Sand wore trousers at a time when women here wore skirts.'

'I see.'

She is polite, malleable. She questions, but is not so difficult to convince. I haven't enjoyed myself this much for a long time.

I'm fed up with Alessandra. It's her fault. I do not want to be in bed alone tonight. The neighbour casts a darker shadow than the mountain. And the house, it makes me anxious.

'But what happened with the neighbour?'

His friendship with the Chief of Police sealed the injustice. Fascists. Or did he pay him to be a witness, say I was lying? Why's she looking at me with patience in her face?

'On this island who you know matters.' This is no subject for foreign women; Alessandra understood, with her Italian and German roots. Change the subject. Her calm waiting reaches into me, changes my tone. 'Don't worry. It makes me anxious here sometimes. At other times I am content here. I live a solitary life, a poet's life as Graves would say.'

I must bring the focus back to us. I get up and look out the window. She stays still in her chair as if chained to it.

Dusk. The sun has fallen behind the mountain and shadow has swallowed the blue of the sea and silver-green of the olive groves. I like how a stranger makes me see my familiar view with new eyes. She is my new muse. Yes, I will convince her to stay, husband or not. Where have I got to with her?

In the dark the tartan chair's pattern has dissolved and the furniture has lost its edges. The air between our chairs has mingled as if she is dissolving into me. It's past dinnertime and I'm not hungry. She is all the food I need.

'I can't see your face. You're lost in the shadow.'

'Yes, it's jolly dark now.'

I fear that if I flick the electric light switch it will break the magic. Time has stopped its hurried tick. In the electric blue dusk, the world has paused to allow lovers a taste of eternity and I want to watch her in that chair, unmoving, focused on me forever. How unusual to be at peace with myself, no need to pace up and down, in and out of rooms as I usually do, my mind constantly in motion, irritated by every croak. The frogs are croaking but I do not care. Yes, she *must* live here with me.

'The frogs aren't bothering me!'

'I'd not noticed the frogs croaking until you mentioned it. It's getting late. I've taken up enough of your time.'

Her voice is hesitant. I like this new uncertainty. I didn't like the bossy woman who arrived, but the house, the mountain, a Deià sunset has done its work. I simply have to finish off what Deià and Villa Rosa have begun. The house wants a mistress.

'You know, when you arrived, I was watching for you. I dare say most people walk straight past, as the house is rather detached from the road, but you walked directly up to the gate as if you'd been here before.'

'I had a strange sensation when I opened the gate.'

'Like fate.'

'No, something about it was familiar, like I'd been here before … in a past-life or something.'

I don't care about her New Age talk, but it might be a way in. I like watching her sitting there, so unsure – wanting to leave and stay at the same time. I feel a rush in my groin, holding her in the chair by invisible black silk ribbons. My gaze grips hers.

'Maybe Villa Rosa is your *future*.'

I can almost see the picture her mind has painted of her in her peasant dress walking through Deià olive groves in this insupportable Arcadia. Now I have her. Now we need to touch.

'May I hold your hand?'

I lean forward and take her hand. Its fragility makes me feel powerful. I could crush her hand in my grip, hear her bones crack. That I could is enough to stir my passion. She watches my hand as it caresses her palm, transfixed.

'The skin. It is important that the skin of two people matches. I dare say ours is a perfect match, don't you think?'

I can feel the space between us dissolve. She belongs to Villa Rosa.

3

Desire

I wanted to laugh when Miguel sank from the sofa, walked on his knees across the lounge floor towards me and took my hand in his. It was ridiculous. More Monty Python than *caballero* and I didn't need a knight, but his absurd display of chivalry seemed sincere. I did not laugh. The moment to escape was gone. It was the moment when the last orange-purple shards of sky dissolved behind the mountain, when I remembered that I had a husband. I felt unable to do anything apart from go along with wherever he was leading me. Had I been hypnotised by his deep baritone, his fingertips tracing lines on my palm? A small voice urged me to laugh, to break the spell, but I had lost the power over my vocal cords. I was muted by a compulsive curiosity.

'You have two lifelines. I was once told by a fortune-teller in Valdemossa that is the sign of a split personality, a life that can dart off suddenly in another direction. I have the same. Look.'

He held out his palm.

He'd been hidden in shadow, his back to the window as he talked, lulling me deeper into a state of paralysis. His voice was so familiar. I had a sensation of being a child again, being read a bedtime story.

The whole time we'd talked the sensation of the smoothness of the wood statue in the lobby remained on my fingertips as if it were me he was working on with his chisel.

Something inside me had become so unsure – wanting to leave and stay at the same time. I'd never cheated. I'm not a cheat but I'd stayed too long and as the colour bled out of the day, freewill had been bled from me. It seems a weak and foolish statement, but it was as if a power greater than myself had stepped in and I no longer had control over my destiny. *Maybe he's right? Perhaps this is what fate feels like.*

'Our skin is a jolly good match.' A low, barely audible groan came from within him – more of a growl, something not quite human, and it flared life into something deep and dormant within me.

Miguel's hand – long, dark hairs on the back of olive skin as he turned my palm upwards like a palm reader – was also familiar to me.

I felt the walls of the house close in around me in the semi-darkness, its presence entwined with Miguel's, as if both were drawing me into their embrace.

This is a man who needs a woman. There's no woman here, not if those dishes are anything to go by. What an old-fashioned notion. I hated the thought, but it crept up on me like the desire to wash up the pile of dirty dishes in the kitchen, to play at being the woman of the house. *In NYC we have a cleaner as I'm no domestic goddess and neither is my husband.* I thought I knew myself.

'This is fate. I dare say you came here to meet a man, not to interview a writer.'

The spell almost broke as he rose. His knee crunched. He stooped like an old man, and I vaguely remember stopping myself from helping him. For a moment I thought it odd that he had not offered me any food. How long had we talked in the darkness? A pang of panic rose up against the paralysis. *He's twenty-five years older than me. A stranger. What am I doing here? I'm married!*

I rose with him as if I were a cog in a huge old cartwheel that was rolling down the Deiàn hillside with no will of my own. I remember his mouth tipped down towards mine and my head tilted back. There was a moment of intense repulsion, at him or perhaps myself: *I can't do this.* Our cheeks brushed. His stubble, the familiar smell of him. *Perhaps this is what fate feels like – familiar, like déjà vu.* A large age spot on his neck sent another wave of repulsion through me, but the weight of the wheel was too heavy. Instead of fighting it, I put my weight into pushing the wheel to its inevitable destination. Another inner voice, not quiet like the voice of my intuition, but insistent and determined; the voice of something primal, desperate, determined to survive, ordered me: *Close your eyes, don't look at the mole; just get to the other side.*

Down the stone stairs, to the bedroom on the ground floor he led me. I had a sensation of stepping further back in time as the room can't have changed since the house was built. Sparsely furnished, wrought iron bed, white cotton sheets damp and the walls gave off the musty smell of old plaster, which put a wheeze in my lungs.

'It's damp in here.'

He said nothing. His eyes were on me like cold fingers as I undressed.

He was quicker than me. He stood in his boxers, white against his tanned legs and I tried not to look, in that state of suspense on the cusp of seeing what is kept hidden.

I let down my hair. As it fell and bounced against my naked back, I had the odd sensation that I was sitting on the edge of our marital bed on our wedding night and I hesitated, nervous, preparing to perform my duty for the first time. *Ridiculous, bloody ridiculous!* Celibacy did this. Seven years of it. I threw off my bra, lay back on the bed, arms stretched above my head, hair splayed on the pillow. Just this one night – to remember how it feels to be a woman.

Miguel's dark eyes looked down on me as he knelt on the bed. I sensed that it was not the first time that those same eyes had surveyed my body. Cock in hand, he stared at my hair.

'I dare say I thought your hair was short.'

Was that a flicker of doubt in his eyes?

'I'm jolly nervous. My polla is nervous.'

'Polla?' Slang for penis, I guessed as I watched him touch himself.

He did not answer.

'Don't be.' I said it softly and an ancient part of my being stirred, long hidden under long skirts and bound by hair twisted tight into hairpins. I sensed Miguel could satisfy my darkest desires, uncoil a dark lust.

As we moved, a part of me displaced itself from my body and hovered above our marital bed, an entwined hermaphrodite, witness to our lovemaking from the ceiling. This was a continuation of our interview. Miguel's eyes, black as a moonless night, locked into mine. My husband closed his eyes when we made love. My husband. I pushed the thought of him away. Tomorrow I would leave and forget it ever happened. There were three of us in the bedroom that night: Miguel, me and a silent witness, the part of me who recorded the scene to memory. Fodder for my return to celibacy.

Afterwards, Miguel played with my hair like a new toy. I lapped up the attention. There I was on the other side of repulsion. I'd pushed past it and on the other side was the body of a man so familiar ... the dryness of his skin, its olive tone.

'Your hair is jolly nice.'

Coarse grey hairs on his chest, firm for a man his age. I pushed the thought of my husband – in slippers, belly flab belted in dressing gown, head in New York News – from my mind.

A rumble of something vibrating up through the floorboards from below clicked me back into the present.

'What's that?'

'I dare say it's the plumbing. It is ancient.'

I stretched over his chest to check my watch on the antique chair next to the bed.

'It's 2am. I should go.'

'Stay the night.'

Too late to go back to the family run hotel on the other side of the valley.

'They'll think I'm a *puta,* the family who run the hotel.'

We laughed. Mine was a wry laugh. Again I pushed the thought of my husband away. There was something else different the other side of repulsion. Now I was a cheat. It was a disappointing, tarnished feeling.

Miguel got up and went to the bathroom next door. His polla swung between his legs with a curious familiarity – the way he walked around naked, its swing, made me feel like I knew him. Again, that uncanny feeling of déjà vu. I thought back beyond my husband to previous lovers, then stopped myself. What was the point of remembering?

Miguel did not apologise for his impotence halfway through our lovemaking as some men might have. After starving for seven years, crumbs were nourishing.

Before getting back into the bed he stooped to kiss my nipple.

I shivered.

He pulled the sheet over me.

'It's too damp to sleep in here.' I did not add that I felt like someone was watching me, my own conscience perhaps, but I did not like the downstairs bedroom, the hollow knock and hiss of the cistern under the house as it responded to the flush of the chain from the bathroom next door.

Something lingered in the air that first night, something deeply disturbing – its presence seeped up into the bedroom.

'Is there a room under here?'

'Just the cellar.'

'Can we sleep somewhere else? It's damp here.'

'I dare say it's less humid upstairs.'

I followed Miguel up the old stone steps, past the kitchen, up another flight to a spacious bedroom.

'This used to be the attic.'

Why didn't he take me up here in the first place?

The skylight was open to the night. Owls hooted across the sleeping village, ancient echoes swooped in from the mountain and I caught myself falling into a fantasy where Villa Rosa was my home.

4

Exhibitionism

I woke in the super king size futon in the converted attic. I woke not into the house of a stranger but as if I were in my own bed. Miguel kicked open a shutter with his foot and a single sunbeam, laser hot, crossed the bed and touched my arm. Muscular legs for a man of his age. The sunspot was still there on his neck, but it no longer repelled me. I had arrived on the other side of repulsion.

Miguel went into the en suite. Again I was transfixed by his polla swinging between his legs. Strangely familiar, as if I had been with this man all my life and watched him walk to the toilet every morning. The sound of him pissing aroused me. It was as if Miguel had flicked on the switch of my sexuality. I hadn't felt this alive since I was in my twenties.

I don't think we said a word to each other that first morning. Miguel went about his daily routine as if I were not there. My teeth wanted my toothbrush to de-fur but it was back at the hotel.

He kissed me on the bottom stair by the kitchen. My lips clamped together in case my breath smelt.

'Cariño, can you help me open the shutters?'

It felt premature, presumptuous for him to call me darling.

He turned to me. 'Do you mind if I call you Cariño? Do you know what it means, darling?'

'I love it.' My voice irritated me. I sounded like a loved-up teenager.

We walked round the open plan first floor flinging open shutters of the kitchen, dining area and lounge area near the fireplace where we sat the night before.

The sun seemed to pull them open as I released the latch. An unspoilt Eden sloped down towards the little triangle of turquoise sea. George Sand dissed the islanders, but she too fell in love with the landscape.

He joined me at the window. The short stubble on my shaved bare legs stood on end like a dog with its heckles up.

'Graves said Deià is already-painted.'

The light in Deià has an unusual quality as if the sun is young. Mornings vibrate with a freshness that made me think I was the first human on earth and climate change, mass extinction, and war happened elsewhere, in some apocalyptic, far away dream.

'Shall we go for a swim, Cariño? I dare say the sea is calm today.'

His no-show the day before made me scratch my leg. In England a few waves wouldn't put me off, but if you live in a place where the sun shone most of the year, I guess you got fussy.

'Cariño, what's this? You are hurt?'

He knelt down and touched the pink wheals on my leg.

'Medusa. How do you say in English?'

'Jellyfish. It's nothing. It was from the swim yesterday.' I didn't want to make a fuss, but he could have warned me about the bloody jellyfish.

'Come.' He took me by the arm and pulled me towards the stairs. 'We will bathe it.'

I followed him downstairs to the bathroom next to the room we'd been in the night before. He sat me on the toilet seat, dabbed antiseptic on a cotton wool ball and explained how if one was stung by a jellyfish to take a credit card and drag it across the skin to remove the poison.

'There is usually a flag out to warn you if there are medusa in the Cala.'

I didn't say I'd seen the flags but had no idea what they meant as he'd stood me up. The disappointment was still sharp, but post sex contentment eclipsed the dark feeling.

'I dare say that will be jolly fine soon. Now, I want to take you somewhere.'

Those black eyes, how they breached some inner boundary as he knelt at my feet.

'No medusa?'

We laughed and the plumbing clanged as Miguel flushed the cotton wool down the toilet. That banging again, it was coming from the depths of the house, out of sync with the flush.

After the night at Villa Rosa the little hostel seemed different. I dashed through the cool lobby and upstairs, grabbed my swimming costume and brushed my teeth, still high on the heady aftermath of sex.

A sensual pulse hummed inside the car as it swung round the hairpin bends and every hair on my legs and arms tingled as if a ghost were running its fingers through them.

'You're used to these hairpin bends.'

'Do you drive, Cariño?'

'Yes.'

'I dare say you could drive here with practice. What do you think?'

'It would take more than just practice. Balls too.' I laughed as we swung another sharp corner. *Why would I need to drive here, unless he's extending the invitation?*

'This is the road to Soller. During the war the trucks with the soldiers used to pick up the women of Deià going to the market in Soller and sell them sugar ... how do you say? Black market sugar.' Miguel's jaw clenched and the tone of his voice vibrated with rage.

He pulled over, tight to the mountain and did a U-turn so the car was facing the way we'd come, on the opposite layby at the edge of the cliff.

'We park here and walk to Lluc Alcari.'

Miguel was nervous. He dropped his bag and his straw hat flew off and landed on the narrow gravel layby.

'Lluc Alcari means house of the forest. I dare say the Arabs named it. There is mud, you know. Mud is good for your skin.' And he mumbled incomprehensibly as if he were trying to hide something.

As we walked off the road into the tall pine trees and down steps hewn into rock, he went dead silent, the corners of his mouth drooped and all youthfulness disappeared despite his shorts. Repulsion returned as I tuned into the large, ugly sunspot on his neck and I found myself talking incessantly. For silence is disconcerting in Mallorca. Even in the day, with the road above us, the solid block of silence was oppressive. My chatter also disguised my discomfort as it dawned on me this strange man was leading me into the woods alone.

Where's he taking me? He led and I followed like a child enchanted by a fairytale piper, down the rough-cut steps of the wild, craggy coastline. Down we went. Him, sure-footed as a goat. Me, stumbling. He stopped and offered his hand at certain points, but his face was a frown and the deep lines of age made him look scary, a modern day Pan, that goat-god the Christians shamed into the darkness and called Satan, and Blake did not blame, but revered for facing the soul's shadow. Literary nonsense, I thought then, but later I knew it to be my intuition trying to tell me not to trust him. Instead of listening to my fears, I disguised my unease with chatter. I talked about his books, asked him questions about his life, his family. He was preoccupied. Looking back, he was rarely present.

'Your mother must be very proud of you.' I forced cheerfulness into my voice – a skill I'd learnt in New York City. Londoners find a suspicious scowl more natural. It's probably more authentic, but perhaps that's due to the drizzle.

'What?' He frowned and looked surprised to see me, then gathered himself. 'I dare say I don't know. I give her my books, but I don't think she reads them.'

Murder, sex, paedophilia and child abuse, men slapping under-age girls round the face with their cocks. A Catholic woman born in the 1920s would not want to comment on that even if she had read it.

A tattered rope had been strung between two pine trees at a steep step down. I grabbed it to steady my footing. Miguel was too distracted to notice.

'My ex-wife found my books humiliating.'

'What about your girlfriend? Did she like your books?'

'She read them. I don't know if she liked them.' Irritation quivered in his voice. It was the same tone as last night when I asked if he was single. I set myself the task to read all his novels, including the ones that had not been translated into English.

We were nearing the bottom of the rock staircase and the sea was visible, cool blue between the trees. On the rocks, some white and craggy and others smooth like enormous pebbles, men and women were dotted around like bronze statues. A woman with a perfect tan stretched her arms up into the sky and two perfect pinecone breasts rose. Topless beaches are common enough, but as we approached I noticed that she was completely naked. And shaved. Her friend too. In fact all the humans on the rocks were naked. I had a sensation like in a dream when you cannot quite understand what is going on, but you go along with it anyway. Miguel seemed oblivious to the naked people. My Britishness was in a state of prude confusion and so I acted as though it were completely normal to me.

'Do you come here often?'

'Not so much. I dare say used to. Not so much now.'

Why hadn't he warned me that we were going to a nudist area? What if I hadn't been comfortable with that? I pushed the confusion aside – public nudity must be perfectly normal to Mallorcans, living as they do in the heat. But the Spanish had struck me as more reserved, unlike Scandinavian and German tourists. I'd thought that nudist beaches in Spain were a Northern European import. *Don't be coy*, I reprimanded myself. *I don't want him to think me a prude and we're not going naked.*

I undressed, timid. I may have been naked with him all night, but shyness descended as I took off my shorts and trainers and left them on the rocks.

'You don't need your top,' he said. Where had I heard that before? His voice sounded like it was speaking to me across time. *You don't need your top – there's not enough to cover up –* that echo again – my father's voice layered on top of Miguel's like a Victoria sponge, with me sandwiched in the middle. The red jam of shame returned with those words. The humiliation belonged to my teenage self, but I kept my bikini top on just as I did that summer's day on the beach with my father.

Why is Miguel looking through his bag like an old lady who's lost her glasses? He made a performance of taking everything out. Then put it all back in again.

'Wait for me, Cariño. I only have one pair of goggles. I dare say there are medusa here.'

I thought he'd said there weren't any medusa here? I waited for him at the edge of the rocks. The sea, dark, deep and cool splashed my feet.

What's he doing? If he's forgotten his shorts, he must have realised by now.

'Have you forgotten your swimming trunks? You can wear your boxers.'

He shrugged, walked to the edge of the rocks so everyone could see his awkward striptease and walked back to the bag, cock swinging between his legs and started rummaging again. I tried to look away, but was fascinated and confused by this display. My intuition told me he knew all along he hadn't packed his trunks.

He handed me a pair of goggles and I climbed off the rock into the sea after him as he led the way around the rocks, pointing at medusa underwater as we swam, but my only focus was his polla swimming ahead of me, a hypnotist's pendulum. His exhibitionism repulsed me, but somehow drew me in like the repulsion I'd felt when we first kissed. Confusion mingled with a craving that made my head swirl in the silence of the underwater rock pools.

This was his world, not mine. However unfamiliar it was to me, there was something so mysteriously familiar about it – the sensation of being led into his world, accompanied by repulsion and excitement – but like a word in a foreign language which you cannot quite pronounce on your tongue, what was driving me deluded me. Like water people in a watery world with watery rules and a grammar I did not understand, I followed him further out to sea, round rocks, into quiet coves hidden from the land.

Did I think of my husband walking home after a long day in the office on a sidewalk covered with fallen leaves, ignorant of my betrayal? The Fall. That's what Americans call Autumn. I pushed thoughts of Autumn and my husband to the back of my mind. It was inconceivable that I was married. Looking back from the cold light of clarity is like watching a character in a novel. Perhaps that is all I was, a character at the mercy of the author. In less than twenty-four hours Miguel had painted a picture of a future for me, and I was hurtling towards his vision.

After our swim, I had a sense of freedom as we wound round the mountain back to Deià, but something inside me was changed, as if swimming with Miguel had initiated me into some foreign cult, an underwater heresy. A reverse baptism.

Miguel held my hand and drove one-handed. Vertigo, as I looked over the edge of the cliff, mingled with new feelings inside me. I was silent, breathing in the present, pregnant with something inexplicable and highly addictive.

'I dare say I'll cook a parmigiana for dinner. You ought to join me.'

'A man who cooks!'

'Spanish men cook.' He smiled. He was more relaxed. That relaxed me.

'I'd love to.'

But I needed to get the editor a draft of the interview by tomorrow. The shot of freelance reality sobered me.

'Can you drop me at my hotel? I have to do some work.'

'Yes. So do I.'

We agreed he'd collect me from my hotel at 6pm.

His car pulled into the tiny lane that led to the hotel. He leant across the gear stick and kissed me with the promise of sex.

'Cariño, bring your things when I collect you. Stay at Villa Rosa.'

The newspaper had paid for five nights but returning to the hotel felt odd, like staying in a hotel in your hometown would be odd.

The few hours I spent alone in my hotel room drafting the interview made me feel more solid, and I shook off the trance I'd entered into. I was exhausted after our swim and glad to have time alone, but something deep inside me was lonely for him – an insatiable, inexhaustible loneliness that only Miguel could quench.

Miguel

5

Seduction

Her legs are tanned, not Celtic pink. Her skin's olive like mine. I hover my foot over the break as the car rolls down the slope of the high-walled lane, past the bougainvillea so I can watch her face as we approach the house. ¡Bueno! That expectation in her expression as she looks up at the pink walls – Villa Rosa has done its work. She's under its spell – as I'm under hers. It is a long time since my mind has been so free. I've hardly thought of Alessandra since she arrived. She cannot leave. The hours I waited for 6pm to arrive made me agitated. What if she changed her mind? She cannot. I need her.

'Cariño, can you open the gate please?'

She knows my gaze is on her. She opens the gate like she belongs to the house. ¡Bueno! I touch the accelerator and the car crawls up the drive as she walks through the garden looking at my giant phalli sculptures.

As I get out of the car and reach behind the rose bush pot for the key a shudder courses through me at the memory of her touching my statue in the hallway yesterday.

I have the urge to pick her up and carry her over the threshold like a new groom. That swim this morning has invigorated me. I feel like I'm forty again … twenty, even!

Fine lines on her forehead crease with worry.

'I ought to carry you over the threshold, Cariño.'

Her laughter is nervous. I like that she is less sure of herself. And she liked that idea – being the wife of the house.

Where to put her case … on the rush-bottomed chair in the room next to the bathroom? But her clothes should be in the wardrobe. My breath shallows with impatience. She will submit to Villa Rosa's charms.

¡Uf! The kitchen's a mess. Piles of plates, forks with food dried hard between the prongs and flies everywhere. And the shopping's still in bags. ¡Uf! So much to prepare! But she's here now. Why am I doing all this? Unpacking is her job. And the cost! Good food is essential for seduction, but it's an expense I could do without.

'Cariño, can you help me?'

Her body hugs the doorway. How can she be so relaxed and free? ¡Uf! She's in holiday mode.

'Can you put this in that cupboard?'

She follows where I point – at a tin of chopped tomatoes. Her obedience calms me.

'And can you put the shopping away, Cariño?'

'I don't know where you put things.'

'Wherever you think it ought to go. I'm no good at these things.'

Now I must get out of this kitchen and leave her to it. It will be good for her to get to know the kitchen. That's how my mother used to stand at the sink, vacant, staring out over the olive groves. What's she doing with the water?

'No, no, no! Don't put the water down the plughole. Give me the bowl. It goes outside – don't let the neighbour see.' Her brow creases. Must keep my irritation out of my voice. I grab the bowl, open the kitchen door and chuck the dirty water onto the shrubs.

I like that she jumps, skittish like a lamb when I snatched the bowl.

'Why are you throwing the water outside?'

'They measure the waste water as well as how much you use.'

'But surely it won't make much difference.'

'I've measured it. It makes a difference, Cariño.'

Why does she look amused?

'I'm going to make parmigiana. Can you help me, Cariño?'

It's like training a puppy. The anxiety's back ... maybe I should take my pills? She'll learn. I see how she watches and follows, trying to deliver on the small tasks I give her, concentrating on what goes in which cupboards.

'Slice the aubergine like this, Cariño, and soak them in oil. No, not like that. Like this.' She will learn.

'Miguel ... maybe we should just go out for dinner.'

'Why, Cariño?'

'Well you clearly don't enjoy cooking.'

Flash of panic. What's she saying? Candles! Cupboard under the stairs ... I must have candles. I run out of the kitchen and rummage through old boxes. My knees, cold tiles and worn kneecaps. But I'm like a young man in all other respects.

'Candles! Where have I put the candles? We must have candles!'

What's so funny? I wish she'd stop laughing at me. She should be better than this in the kitchen at her age. The British can't cook.

The candles. ¡Gracias a Dios! I sound like my grandmother! I remember her panicking on summer evenings, looking for candles. They were afraid of the night. That's when the Dragons of Death would come and take away the men.

'Cariño, can you help me lay the table, please?'

No oil? 'Don't forget the oil, Cariño.'

'Can you stop directing me please, Señor Director de la pimiento!'

Hands on hips. That stance reminds me of my grandmother … and mother too.

Table set, wine poured, candles lit, food served. The view will do the rest.

She has something … the way her body slouches against the balcony wall … something breakable. Something irresistibly fragile. The way she draws towards my hand, like a dog eager for strokes makes me want to chain her to the balcony and have her beg for scraps from my plate. She's cured my impotence! I just wish she wouldn't talk so much.

'I dare say we should eat before it gets cold, Cariño.'

Hand hovering over her arse, I guide her to the table, serve the parmigiana and put an olive in her mouth.

'For you.'

I like how she sucks my finger, turns her head to look out over terrace upon terrace of olive trees, their ancient mangled branches black against the electric blue sky.

'I've never seen such a clear, starry sky, not even when I was in the Arizona desert last year. The stars seem so close – they hang over our dinner table like a garland of glittering diamonds.'

She's pleased with her clichéd simile. Something inside me relaxes. Deià seduces everyone.

'I dare say I've never seen so many stars either.' I recall saying these exact words to Alessandra.

Take her hand. I should account for my anxiety.

'You see how I am, Cariño – jolly anxious to make everything perfect for you. I dare say I've never felt like this before. It's fate. You are my destiny.' I kiss her palm.

She looks like she's holding back laughter.

'I'm being serious, Cariño.' Her expression changes, becomes serious.

'Shall we eat?'

'This is delicious. You really can cook.'

'Yes, Spanish men can cook, Cariño.' She likes to eat.

My chair legs scrape on the terracotta tiles as I shift closer so our bare knees touch. I'm hungry after all this effort, but I must make her feel my focus on her. She's invisible to her husband. I will make her feel seen … then she'll be mine.

'I like your lipstick. I don't usually like women who wear lipstick, but you apply it so well. Come here, Cariño.'

I pull her onto my legs like I would with a child. We're just going through the motions, but I feel suddenly alive like her energy, her excitement is feeding me. It was like this with Alessandra … in the beginning.

'You have beautiful eyes.'

'I thought novelists avoided clichés.' She's laughing again.

'I dare say cliché works sometimes.'

'Yes, I suppose so. But how do you know when to incorporate cliché? You achieve just the right balance in your novels.'

'That's an interesting question, Cariño. My rule is a maximum three clichés in a novel. No more.'

I'm enjoying this – Alessandra wasn't interested in my views on novel writing. A burst of irritation distracts me. Alessandra was so prescriptive. Why all the rules? I could write about this and not that. She wrote about her fascist grandfather, one of Mussolini's minions, in her own novel so why did it upset her when I wrote about him?

'It's up to me what I write about.'

'Sorry – I don't follow you – are you still talking about clichés?'

She looks confused. I lost my focus. Back to her – when my attention diverts from her she craves it. ¡Bueno!

'Who are you talking about?'

'Nothing, Cariño. I was talking to myself.' Back to her. Alessandra is my past.

'Look, Cariño – a shooting star.' She smiles as we look up at the stars. That distracted her. 'There's another … and another. I've never seen so many. Deià can do that, surprise you when you least expect it.'

'Ooooo! The sky's so beautiful here!'

Her childish excitement is irritating in a woman her age, but it makes her more malleable, so it pleases me. No, it displeases me, but it excites me.

'Deià is a special place, Cariño.'

Her face lights up like the wattage has increased in her smile. Tonight she will fall in love with a Deiàn sky and tomorrow she won't want to leave. She's so alive, her arms around my neck, her smell, lips so close we share the night air between us, the corners of her rosebud mouth upturned in wonder and I feel something of her wonder, her enthusiasm, which I once had as a child, rub off on me. She cannot leave.

'That's the first time I've seen your teeth when you smile.'

I close my mouth.

'Really? Are my teeth ok?'

'You have a handsome smile.'

'It's you, Cariño. You make me smile. I dare say I haven't felt this happy for a long time.' That's true. And it surprises me.

Her laughter doesn't annoy me this time. She will be my muse. My mind melts back into the landscape. The outline of the olive trees is like a child's two-dimensional paper cut-out against the moonlight. It fills me with the same wonder I had when my grandmother was alive.

I can see her now – my grandmother – dressed in black for my grandfather. Did the Dragons of Death come on a night like this? It would have been this time of year. My gaze moves directly to where they took him, to the mirador. I cannot see it from here, but I see it in my mind's eye. Strange that I went there as a child to have a sense of independence, to read Enid Blyton novels and wank at the spot where my grandfather had been pushed from the cliff. Or did he jump? I was always alone with my shame, excited and afraid by the thought of being caught wanking up there at the old execution point.

'Live here with me, Cariño. Stay at Villa Rosa.' I whisper it into her ear. She's painting the picture in her mind, seeing herself dining on this balcony under a sky full of shooting stars for the rest of her life.

She frowns and her voice sounds like a mother explaining something to a child.

'I would love to, but I have a husband. I have to return to New York.'

I wince. Why did she have to go and say that? Husband. The word is like a bullet, a cannonball in disguise hurtling through the night sky, a meteorite that crashes onto the dinner table. Why did she break the spell? Stroke her hair, whisper in her ear, paint the picture of our future. 'Are you sure, Cariño? I love you, Cariño, this is our fate, our destiny, you're my muse, come to Deià. Stay, Cariño.' I can convince her.

Her back straightens and she sits up, puts her hands on my shoulders and pushes herself away from me.

'I can't just leave my husband, Miguel.'

Our eyes meet in the candlelight.

'When I look into your eyes, I feel peace. What do you feel when you look into mine?'

She looks into my eyes and her expression changes to hard and serious.

'Like I'm standing on the edge of an abyss.'

What? Why is she not playing her move as she is supposed to? Is that fear in her tense expression? Fear I can use.

'Perhaps you need to surrender to the unknown.' I fold myself closer around her, my lips to her earlobe. That's it. Her body melts into me again. After a sexless marriage sex is her Achilles' heel. Sex my hook. 'Jump, Cariño, jump into the abyss!'

We watch another shooting star and I go to work on her body, hands, fingers, lips. It is as if the night is in cahoots with me.

'I feel as though I have been here before a long, long time ago. Like I know you, Miguel.'

That's better – I have her again. My head at the low neckline of her dress, my lips gently pulling her right nipple, between kisses, I mumble, 'Surrender to the unknown, Cariño.' Her breath close to my ear, the taste of her body submitting, melting into me. She really has cured my impotence.

6
Phalli

I swung out of the hammock, strung low to the ground between two ancient olive trees and walked up the steep garden towards Villa Rosa. Spanish grass is so springy like walking on rubber.

Should have used a condom. I doubt his generation carry them and I'm married – I didn't pack with sex in mind. There's no chance I have an STI. Might Miguel? I'm still fertile, but he's well past his prime. Maybe he's infertile … he's not mentioned children. I can't imagine him wearing a condom. Must stop thinking about Miguel's cock and do some work – I have to finish writing up the interview. Tomorrow I return to reality. Celibacy, traffic and concrete skyscrapers will replace mountains.

When I wasn't with Miguel, I was daydreaming about our latest encounter, mulling over something he'd said or luxuriating in the landscape. Deià swallows you up. Yet again I had the sensation of being initiated into a secret cult, one only Miguel and I knew.

Miguel's garden was a shrine to the god Priapus. Sculptures of proud penises stood between cactuses and palm trees like stalagmites growing up from the ground. A disappointing irony that he softened at the crucial moment. The garden reminded me of the collection of ancient Roman sculptures of penises I'd seen about ten years before on our holiday on the Amalfi coast. A yellow sickly guilt stuck in my throat like mucus that's impossible to cough up, an invisible bile. I coughed, a pathetic attempt to rid myself of my conscience. Apparently Ancient Romans put phalli in their gardens to ward off thieves. It must have looked like this in rich people's gardens all over Pompeii, before Catholic sensibility hid them away in a special room in the Naples museum. Three or four red madroño berries fell onto the table as I passed by on my way to the front door. The way they splat, red raw and wounded on the table, felt like a bad omen.

I plugged in my laptop and sat at the dining table opposite the Juliet balcony with a view of the church.

He does not need to worry about thieves, I thought as I looked at the fruit bowl full of lemons he'd stolen from the neighbour's garden. *He is a thief.*

I prised my mind free of thoughts of him and forced myself to concentrate on writing up the interview.

'Cariño, what are you doing?'

There he stood before me, shorts at his ankles, cock in hand. It excited me to see him hard but why choose this moment to interrupt me, just as I had started to type? I opened my shorts and started to touch myself.

'Do you want to suck my polla?'

I didn't particularly, but sex is about give and take, so I leant forward mouth first. The skin was smooth, no lumps, no large protruding veins. Miguel was rough and pushed my head forward to steal his pleasure. The sensation of being gagged was not enjoyable. I pulled away.

No foreplay. He did not bother with that. We both preferred instant entry so that there was a sensation of him forcing his way, but within a few moments he started to wilt.

What kept me persevering? Love? A sexless marriage? On the surface, maybe. There was a far darker reason, a compulsion that drove me, which I only came to understand later – Miguel was my vehicle to confront something so abhorrent that I'd spent my whole life avoiding it. But I'm getting ahead of myself.

He used his hands to keep himself in place. It was uncomfortable.

'Turn around,' he ordered. He pumped so hard I felt close to tears at his roughness, but mysteriously I was quick to come. In the pain was an inexplicable pleasure. His softness irritated him and he muttered to himself about stopping the drugs.

'I dare say you ought to want anal sex?'

'No, I don't want to. Let's go upstairs and lay down on the bed.'

I wanted a hug.

It was that third morning in Villa Rosa that I felt the fear, knew something was not right. Another healthier woman would have responded differently to those first hints of danger and fled. It was not the rough sex, him talking to himself, but the smell of a lie. Something incongruent and slippery, which I could not quite pin down, but which pulled me in, curiouser and curiouser, like an Alice exploring a nightmare.

He opened the wardrobe for something and forgot to close it. A woman's bright floral sundress dress hung in the walk-in closet opposite my side of the bed. Why was Alessandra's dress still hanging there if the relationship was over? But I pushed aside the suspicion that he was not telling me the whole truth. I had a husband in New York City and after tomorrow I would not see Miguel again – what difference if he was lying to me? I was lying to my husband. Even as I thought this I felt the weight of destiny. I'd be back.

Miguel jumped out of the bed abruptly after making love. Usually I did not like morning sex, but I went along with what he wanted at the beginning, until I found myself wanting the same things as he did (I still do not quite understand how he changed my desires to align with his needs). He was fretting about not being able to come again.

'Relax,' I said. He went soft as soon as he was inside me. I didn't make a big thing about it. I knew that would only make it worse, and I wanted my pleasure too. He pulled on his cock like it was a badly behaved child. I helped him, whispered to him the Spanish slang words for the anatomy that turned him on – polla, coño, that he was big, but no matter what the size, it delivers very little satisfaction soft. My Priapus, who excited me with his exhibitionism, could not perform. Regardless, I was consumed by desire.

'It's the drugs the psychiatrist gave me,' he said. 'I dare say they affect my libido.'

'Why are you seeing a *psychologist*?' I corrected his language. He must mean a psychologist. Only psychopaths and nutters saw psychiatrists.

I heard him throw something into the bin in the bathroom.

'¡Uf! I'm stopping them. Why should I take them? I don't need them anymore.'

Is he talking to himself? *Sign of madness*, warned my quiet intuitive voice.

'Perhaps you should follow the doctor's advice.'

He came back into the bedroom, over my side of the bed, swooped down on top of me.

'I don't need them now I have found you.'

He kissed me all over. The smell of his body was still new, but strangely familiar to me. The age spots that had repulsed me so much only two days before did not bother me anymore. There was something familiar about him, about his stance, an aged stoop. He was old enough to be my father.

'Why were you prescribed drugs?'

'For depression.'

'Depression?'

'I took them to get off work. I couldn't stand it anymore. My agent was a bitch.'

'That's pretty extreme. Why didn't you just change agents?'

He gave me a story about his agent. It did not ring true for a man so obsessed with his sexuality that he fills his garden with statues of his cock, to choose impotence over work. His story didn't add up. But I ignored the alarm bells and refused to let a little thing like depression drugs blow my fantasy. Maybe he was right – maybe I could make him happy.

Eros is not only blind, but deaf.

7

Hermitage

Miguel was working frantically on his novel in the attic library. I stood at the open window on the floor below. I was always aware of where he was in the house as every tiny movement was accompanied by a creaking floorboard.

As I looked across the valley I replayed the words *Deià is already-painted* in my head. The hillside town was tucked behind a smallish mountain. A large mountain loomed above that and dwarfed the town to Lilliput size. Miguel had explained that Deià had been built behind the smaller mountain to protect it from being seen at sea by pirates.

Time is different in Villa Rosa. We'd spent only days together, but it felt like I'd looked out of this window over the Teix everyday of my life. Was it Miguel? The irresistible power he had over me. Or was it something about the house, about the mountain, that wall of rock that distorted time like the wall of a prison, which made me forget my life on the other side of it I'd built for sixteen years with my husband? Back then I thought it was the house, or perhaps Deià that had the treacly hold over me. I did not understand how somewhere so foreign could feel so familiar. It was as if I'd been there before.

My New Age NYC friends might have speculated it was a past-life experience. Miguel said it was a premonition of the future – he called it fate. I should have phoned a Londoner, got a grounded, but grey perspective. I didn't want to break the spell. I knew it was wrong and like a dying man savouring the taste of tobacco from his final cigarette, I drank in the landscape and that warm winter jumper feeling that felt mysteriously more like home than anywhere I'd ever lived. After tomorrow Deià would be a memory, a brief love affair. I'd never done anything like this before. I was faithful, always. Could I live with the betrayal?

'Cariño, my muse, my magic muse!'

A creak and a thump of the lid of the bureau and Miguel came crashing down the stairs like an over-excited schoolboy who'd been set free from the classroom. He grabbed hold of me, jubilant.

'My muse, I have an ending. It is you. You helped me find it. Now I know what I must do. How it ends. I dare say my publisher will be delighted.'

I laughed as he pulled me to him, kissed me; engulfed me in attention.

'I haven't done anything.'

Since I'd arrived, he'd been manic, anxious, writing with a fervour early, as if I were not there. Pacing, always pacing. *Were all novelists bonkers?*

'But you have, Cariño. You! It is you who have decided the ending.'

He stalked across the room and threw himself with unusual abandon (a gesture that was at odds with his lizard-like limbs) on the sofa, legs on the tartan cushions.

'Nine years I've been struggling with this book. Nine years, not knowing how to end it. Argh. And now I know. I'm decided. He is free. At last I'm free.'

Nine years was the length of his relationship.

I was flattered to have played some small part in his creative process, but all I'd been conscious of doing was trying to be as quiet and patient as possible while he wrote, although I craved his attention like a little girl in the mornings when he was in another world, separate from me, hunched over his laptop.

'What's the book about?'

He frowned, looked at his bare feet for a long time, and I had a feeling I'd overstepped some invisible line, broken an unspoken rule.

Miguel had been cagy about the subject matter of his novel and said it was bad luck to talk about it until it was finished. The book was forbidden territory.

'Sorry to pry. I know you said it's bad luck, I just thought that as you're finished …'

His expression changed, as swift as a lightbulb being switched on.

'Of course, Cariño, it is your story too now. You are the reason it ends the way it does … in fact I ought add you to the acknowledgements. I was going to dedicate it to …' He stopped. 'I dare say I ought to dedicate it to you, instead.' He was talking to himself again as if I was no longer there. I was torn between feeling flattered and confused. Was it his ex's name he'd stopped himself uttering?

An atmosphere of intense claustrophobia descended with the silence. All of a sudden I caught a whiff of perfume. I lifted my head to follow it – was the floral haze falling through the floorboards?

Miguel jumped up as suddenly as he'd sat down and came over to me, kissed my neck and face, lips. I melt into him.

'Let's go out, Cariño. This house, it is oppressive sometimes. Fetch your things. I'll get the car ready. I'm going to surprise you.'

I ran upstairs two at a time to get my bag and sunglasses. Carried on his wave of excitement was an undercurrent of arousal. Where was he taking me? Would we go swimming again? Next time I'll not wear anything either. What's wrong with swimming naked? I almost hoped the surprise destination was Lluc Alcari.

That smell again – stale, perfumed sweat. I followed it to the wardrobe. It was ajar. Inside hung the floral dress. It must have belonged to his ex. She was bigger than me, busty. *Where did that smell come from?* I leant forward into the wardrobe. Hot as an oven. The smell was coming from the dress. The heat made the fabric breathe as if it were alive. I shivered. It smelt like it had only just been taken off a hot-skinned woman. I had a creepy sensation that the smell had led me to the dress. Well, of course it had – I'd followed my nose. So what? Why was my heart beating so violently?

'Cariño?'

'I'm up here.'

I felt like an imposter in another woman's house, like I was spying on someone's private life, and had been deceived into thinking I was the only one there.

'What are you doing?'

'Coming.'

As I ran downstairs my jumbled thoughts made me so desperate to get out of the house I missed a step and nearly went flying. Why leave the dress in the wardrobe if the relationship is over?

'Cariño, let's go before the sun sets.'

Miguel was kissing me again. It was as if he'd become a different man. Finding the ending had released him from some creative noose.

'I want to take you to a special place. I've never taken anyone there before. I dare say you will like it.'

In his arms my confusion dissolved. Some people hide away the reminders of breakup, but maybe Miguel took comfort from having them around. Looking back now, nothing added up from the beginning, but at the time I said to myself: *Who am I to question Miguel's motivation?*

Up and up we drove, high up the wooded mountain track, so steep I felt gravity dragging me back against my seat. Branches stroked the sides of the car and scratched my arms as they reached their long needlely fingers in through the open window. It was late in the afternoon, but the temperature was rising. Thirty-eight degrees according to the dashboard.

'Is it usually this hot this late in October?'

'It can be. Some years, jolly hot, some not so much.'

'We will park there.' He nodded towards a clearing under thick trees. 'And walk the rest of the way.' I had a sudden pang of fear: *I am in a forest with a strange man.* Reason told me not to fret. What could he to do to me that I hadn't already let him?

'Where are we going?'

'Why? Don't you trust me, Beloved?'

He's not called me that before. Miguel gave me a long sideways look. The same look he'd given me the day we met when he'd bombarded me with questions. A look that made me feel exposed.

'We're going to the Hermitage founded by the mystic Ramon Llull. He was the Christian answer to Rumi, the Sufi poet.' The windows made a hum as they raised, and branches cracked under the weight of the tires as the car left the dirt track.

'Fool, why is your love so great?' Miguel blurted out.

'What?'

'The Lover answered: "Because the journey in search of my beloved is long and dangerous." That's how Ramon Llull wrote, like Rumi: a dialogue between the Lover and the Beloved.'

He parked up. The forest felt enchanted. Sunbeams criss-crossed through the pine trees. It was a relief to be in the shade, but even here it was hot. A bead of sweat trickled between my breasts. Miguel took my hand and kissed it. It felt as if we were going on a magical journey together.

We walked in silence, hand-in-hand for what seemed like a very long time. I thought forests like this only existed in fairy tales. Lush tropical plants entwined with familiar Northern European woodland greenery, but the overall effect of the foreign and the familiar was bewitching. I fancied myself as a nymph-like wood-land creature as we moonwalked on springy ferns deeper into the forest. I did not question where he was taking me and pushed away the idea of Little Red Riding Hood wolves stalking us from the bushes. It was darker here.

By the time we arrived at a large wooden door I was under a spell and knew that I would follow Miguel to the end of the Earth if he asked me. And although we were silent, I heard his voice in my ear.

'Let me not to the marriage of true minds admit impediments.'

What impediments? The same Shakespearean quote he'd whispered to me in bed.

The door was so overgrown with foliage, the old stonewall it was hinged to was invisible and it appeared as though the door was suspended by the forest.

Miguel knocked. I half expected an elf to open the door.

He whispered to me that monks lived here, under the vow of silence.

The wooden door opened slowly on silent well-oiled hinges and a bald monk with a white beard in a floor-length robe tied at the waist with a rope belt greeted us. He nodded with a grace only the silent have.

In the presence of the elderly monk, I became conscious of my cleavage and was suddenly ashamed of my low neckline. I wished Miguel had told me we were going to a monastery. Did the monk's gaze dart to my cleavage? Did he think me a whore? Did his silent gaze stir in him what it stirred in me – a faint throb of arousal? My thoughts shamed me further. Still chained by Catholic shame, I thought. Miguel would have known it. He too is a Catholic. I had the same feeling as at the nudist beach – confusion. I felt deceived. I told myself not to spoil the treat. Miguel had been so excited about this place, and so although I wished I had a scarf to wrap around my chest and bare shoulders, I pushed that thought away too, stepped over the ancient iron doorframe and followed the men into the Hermitage.

We walked through sandstone arches and out into a perfectly manicured cloister. The monk who'd let us in had drifted silently away. I hadn't noticed him go. Perhaps he'd joined the silent army of black-robed figures bent over, picking, digging, tending the gardens in a slow, methodical silence that echoed around this oasis of calm and claimed me, drawing me into its peace.

I was alone with Miguel again looking in silence at the gardens, tier upon tier of rose bushes, fig trees, all types of beans, peas and shoots in beds of upturned soil, planted in geometric rows. How hot it must be under those black robes working the land in the afternoon sun. The monks moved with grace, each with self-contained focus on his task, but toiling in unison to a melody imperceptible to our common ears. The contrast of the unruliness of the forest with nature under the firm control of men's hands – and they were all men who bent over the land – was surreal. It felt as if we had stepped through a portal into another world.

'Ramon Llull founded this monastery. Did you know of him before?'

'No,' I whispered back.

'Llull was a thirteenth century mystic. He was born here in Mallorca, but travelled most of his life. Bought a slave to teach him Arabic, founded many schools and missions.'

'What else did he write?'

'Beloved, if you know me to be a sinner, then have pity and mercy on me.'

Gliding under an archway of intensely sweet smelling roses, serenaded with the words of the mystic who envisioned this garden, made me feel as though I were layered into its history and we had been imagined here along with the roses.

'This place is magical.'

Miguel looked around as if noticing it for the first time.

'Yes, yes it is, Cariño. I dare say I had not seen it that way before.' His face lit up as he looked around and I had the eerie sensation that something of my awe had passed from me to him and he was looking at the Hermitage through my eyes. He took my hand and led me through the gardens, pointing out bushes, fruit he didn't know the English word for, nor I the Spanish so they sounded exotic: kaki, granada, albaricoque (which later I discovered were quite ordinary), and led me to a mirador with a view across the sea.

I gasped involuntarily – and I am not the type of woman to give off those annoying little gasps that tease to be the product of a tiny orgasm. But this view genuinely took away my breath. The ocean stretched out bluer than blue and the sharp cut of the rocks and the overhanging forest as it wound around the coastline was so wild, so dramatic, so full of possibility that I felt my heart expand with it. Anything was possible with Miguel.

'Cariño, I spent my life feeling trapped by the view from this island. Islands are prisons. Today I dare say I could fly.'

'I feel that too. Like I could take off from this rock and fly with that seagull across the ocean.' I pointed into the sky.

'They perform weddings here.'

'Is this where you got married?'

'No.'

An enchanted silence engulfed us again. I'd never been one of those little girls at school who fantasised about a white dress and how many tiers would stack up on my skyscraper wedding cake, but standing there, holding hands with Miguel, looking out to sea, I almost felt the veil on my head, the silent vows being exchanged between us, the silent black-robed monk bearing witness.

It was as if time itself melted the cosmos into an imaginary matrimony, and that moment now I think of it again swells within me. That was the moment our paths fused. In that moment, I had bequeathed myself to Miguel, for better or for worse.

Miguel broke the silence. He turned to me, took both my hands in his and looked down at me. I felt like his bride looking up at him.

'Cariño, will you come and live with me here in Deià?'

I do not remember if I answered.

But I was aware of a nagging voice from far, far away – *you are already married.*

My own marriage had been performed by Elvis, as a joke really, to get my Green Card. Neither my husband nor I believed in Holy Matrimony. But there I stood wearing an invisible veil on the terrace of a Catholic monastery, thick with the atmosphere of tradition, and hearing a voice inside me say, *I do.*

8

Control

'What are you doing, Cariño?' Miguel was behind me, his arms around me, lips pecking my neck.

'Washing up.'

I'd drifted into a fantasy world again standing at the sink, staring out the window, a small world. Just me, Miguel and Villa Rosa.

'Leave the plates, Cariño.' Miguel was behind me untying the old apron I'd found hanging on a hook by the kitchen door.

'Do you like ice-cream?' There was something of the Child Catcher from Chitty Chitty Bang Bang in his coaxing tone, but I needed no persuasion.

'Yes.'

'Let's go. We will eat the jolly best ice-cream in Mallorca.'

The rusty hands of the kitchen clock pointed to 8pm and the air was still muggy with the heat of the day.

'Should I change?' I was wearing shorts and a red vest with red ribbon shoulder straps I'd had since I was a teenager, a staple for trips to hot climates.

'I dare say you're fine as you are.'

The first thing I noticed about Valldemossa was the fashionable display of ceremony. These were the types of holidaying Northern

Europeans who showered and changed into eveningwear for dinner. Women wore makeup and clothes too dressy for a rustic village. Men, white loose open necked shirts that accentuated their suntans and competing colognes. Middle class tourists loitered on Deià's streets too, but we always ate at home. In Valldemossa we walked among them. I felt underdressed and like a hermit venturing into civilisation, slightly bewildered.

'This is the town where George Sand – the French writer lived here with Frédéric Chopin – wrote *A Winter in Majorca*. What did you think of it?'

His question was inquisitor-sharp and made me glance sideways at him. He looked embarrassed as he caught my look and a quiet shame seeped from him – or was it rage?

'I can't remember it very well.' That was the truth, but I also was on the alert not to offend him.

'¡Uf! It was not a very good book. I dare say to a fashionable Parisian, Mallorcans seemed primitive. The community shunned her. To them, a woman in trousers, when women here wore skirts, would have been considered a bad woman – it was her own fault. Chopin was ill. A lung problem. The winters here can be very humid and cold.'

That's the second time he's told me. I listened without comment. I did not understand why his voice simmered with irritation at a book written about 150 years ago.

The stone-paved square was typical of villages all over Spain, church on one side and little restaurants on the other. Happy families and intimate couples at little rustic wooden tables made me feel a pang of regret that I was leaving tomorrow and I'd not sampled the food or sights of the island. Miguel seemed to want to eat in every night, but I'd have loved to eat at one of those little tables. The view from the balcony at Villa Rosa is stunning. On the other hand, I'd experienced the inside workings of a native house (I could not call it a home for Villa Rosa stood detached somehow from its inhabitants), the intimacy of being more than a tourist floating about on the surface of the island. If I'd been with my husband we'd have dined at the best restaurants, stayed at the best hotels, but I'd have been looking at these couples with a different regret, with loneliness. With Miguel I'd rediscovered a lost and forgotten part of myself. He'd reminded me what intimacy is and that I am a sexual being.

Miguel guided me towards the church, but I caught sight of a maze of hot scarlet Mediterranean flowers, so took Miguel's hand and led him into the maze in the wrong direction. We nearly collided with an elderly German couple. As they passed us I caught a look from the woman that gave me a snap of reality. I saw myself as she must have seen me in my Fred Perry shorts and strappy top – I'd not even bothered with a bra. My hair was pulled back, no makeup, legs and arms bronzed from the sun. In the shadow of the night I likely looked younger than thirty-five. And Miguel? He looked older than them. Had he noticed her judgement? Miguel's gaze letched at my legs, a dirty-old-man look that made me shiver. I'm being ridiculous – there's an age gap, but it's decent. But something disturbed me about Miguel's gaze and my groin's automatic response to it. Next time we go out I'd grill him about the dress code. *There won't be another night. I fly at 8am!*

When we reached the centre of the maze, in the shadow of a bush, Miguel pulled me close to him and gave me an urgent kiss.

'Don't leave tomorrow, Cariño. Have you thought about what we spoke about at the Hermitage? Will you stay?'

'I'm married.' I didn't want to spoil our last night together, but he was right, we should talk about it. A sigh caught in my chest. 'I hardly know you. I can't just leave my husband.'

He looked confused.

'Don't you love me?'

Love. That word.

'Love has nothing to do with it. I told you, I love my husband.'

He looked like I'd slapped him. Pained then panicked.

'We are both leaving old lives behind, Cariño, starting a new one.'

What's he talking about? I never said I'd stay.

'You're not. You've already broken up with your ex-girlfriend.'

Confusion clouded his expression.

'I could have gone to her, the day after you arrived. I intended to return to my ex-girlfriend, but after that first night together, I could not. I feel you are my wife. It is not possible for me to go back, Cariño.' He looked so utterly bereft, grief-stricken. I had to face the mess I'd created back in New York, think without the hot intoxication of bougainvillea and hormones.

'How can you go back to a loveless marriage?'

'It's not loveless. We love each other, we just don't …'

'How can you live like that, half a woman? That is not a relationship, Cariño. Let us start a new life together. I'll live wherever you want. I have no family. I'm not bound to this little island. I'll come to New York.'

My head started to spin. The thought of Miguel in New York seemed impossible. He even seemed slightly out of place outside Villa Rosa, like a fisherman away from the sea. The walls of the maze hedges were not high, but I felt claustrophobic all of a sudden, a mental collision with the consequences of what Miguel was proposing.

Another couple was walking in our direction to take their turn at the centre of the maze. Miguel seemed oblivious to them, but I pulled gently at his trouser pocket.

We walked in silence past the dining couples in the courtyard of the church, towards a café with a view over the mountainous landscape. It took a while to settle in the café. My stomach was churning and although in the heat ice-cream would have been a welcome relief, I went for a green tea instead.

'You don't want ice-cream, Cariño?'

'No, I've changed my mind.'

Miguel was agitated by the staff. He seemed uncomfortable. I realised it was the first time we'd been out together in public. I felt out of place, like I'd been isolated from society for a very long time, and my speech, like Miguel's, stuttered slightly and the words came out in uneven jolts. That's how Villa Rosa sucks you in.

'What place is that in the distance with all the lights?'

I wanted to engage Miguel in the ink-blue view. Our table was furthest from the hustle and bustle. People in Valldermosa sat where they could be seen, in the thick of it. Tourists did not venture this far from the main drag of the church. Our table was perched on a crag of rock and the only other people were three teenagers, locals by the look of their Arab eyes and olive skin, who sat on the café step sharing an ice-cream, laughing as they passed the plastic spoon. Where I grew up that would have been a joint.

Did he hear me? Miguel could not sit still. He kept turning around impatiently looking back into the café.

'¡Uf! What are they doing?'

'Maybe they're making the ice-cream!' My attempt to diffuse Miguel's agitation with humour failed. I just wanted to enjoy the view. Tomorrow this would all be in the past.

'I can't believe this will all be just a memory and tomorrow I'll be back in New York City with apartment blocks for a view.'

I turned from the twinkling lights in the distance to him. 'Thank you for a very nice time.' I meant it.

Miguel looked startled, like roadkill caught in the headlights. With the sudden attentiveness of a schoolboy told to concentrate, he forgot his agitation, leant forward and took my hands in his.

'Stay. You don't have to leave tomorrow, Cariño.'

'I must go. I was honest with you. I have a life in New York.'

Why isn't he hearing me?

He looked for a moment like a doctor considering a patient's condition and protocol, then leaned back in his chair and looked at the view. I exhaled and did the same.

'You see there, those lights, that is Palma in the distance. You can't see it now, but on a clear day you can see the sea ...' Miguel talked, animated all of a sudden and I listened. The atmosphere changed and for a short while I imagined we could be a normal couple like the ones at the little tables we passed in the square.

'Cariño, come and live here with me. Why not?' He was excited, full of hope.

'Do you like your job at the newspaper?'

'Yes. I'd like to do more interviews, more travel, but yes, I like it.'

'What would be your ideal job?'

'I'd like to be a travel writer.'

'Do you like your life, with your husband. Are you happy?' He looked at me intently as if he were seeing me for the first time, realising he knew nothing about me. 'Where do you live in New York? What type of house do you live in?'

The questions came fast and he gave me little time to think. I answered. He became light-hearted, almost funny in his inter-rogation, all the time close to me, very close, his chair pulled up to mine. It was not curiosity that fuelled his questions. I had a sensation he was prying. Considering the intimacy we'd shared it felt silly to withhold anything from him.

As suddenly as it began, the interrogation stopped. He looked out over the view, the fairy lights in the distance marking out a horizon and the edge of the land we could not see. He ate his ice-cream which had melted in the heat, pensive.

'I dare say you could work here on a newspaper. I know the editors of all the major papers on the island.' He did not turn to look at me; he just kept talking as we looked out at the landscape, side by side. 'Do you think you could be happy here, with me? I live a simple life. We would write, eat, go for walks, swim together, sleep in our bed in Villa Rosa. Sometimes we would go to Palma to the opera or a show, do city things. We would change our lives. I did that once before. With you I am prepared to give it all up and do it again. I will change my life for you, Cariño.'

'I can't work on the local paper. I don't speak Spanish well enough.'

'New York then. If Deià is too dull we can leave this island. What do I care? I'll come and live with you in your apartment in New York.'

This abandon seemed incongruent with his anxiety, but it pulled me along with it like a riptide.

'I won't have a home when I leave my husband. We did a prenup.'

'A what?'

'The apartment is his if we divorce. I agreed to that when we married.'

All my husband's money was tied up in his family's trust and I was not a named party. Divorce meant I'd get nothing. And the thought of Miguel and me in New York City, rubbing it right in my husband's face, before he'd even had time to adjust made me feel sick. The idea of even telling him I was leaving him snapped me out of the trancelike state Miguel's words had lulled me into. Why did his voice have such a hypnotic effect on me?

'What?' He looked confused again.

'Americans do that. It's quite common. I don't earn enough to pay rent for a New York apartment.'

And considering I'd cheated on my trusting husband, he deserved every penny. I felt wretched all of a sudden facing the reality of my situation. In New York City my savings would last me one month at most.

He must have seen the horror in my face.

'You can rent an apartment in London. That's where you're from. Less expensive on flights. We can come back to Deià when we need to get away from the city. I dare say we will be glad of Villa Rosa and the peace.'

Looking back, he wrote our script. I just went along with it.

I heard myself say in a robotic way, 'I feel very at home here.'

It was true, I felt as if I had returned home. Was Miguel right? Was I meant to be here? What is fate? Surely fate must feel like this – familiar like I'd been here before, like I knew Miguel. Nostalgia was the sensation I had when I looked out over the landscape. A lonely feeling. Maybe if I changed my life (Miguel's words) nostalgia might transform into happiness?

There was one thing for certain: I could not return to New York as my husband's wife, not after this betrayal. My marriage was probably over a long time ago, perhaps when we stopped making love. Seven years ago. This affair was the last nail in the coffin. I was not the type of person to have affairs. I would go home, tell my husband and find an apartment share in a cheap neighbourhood until I worked out what to do. I did not want to ruin the evening by talking about money, but Miguel seemed to think I was free to leave.

'Miguel, if you are serious about this, there will be consequences for me. If we live in London or New York, I can't afford the rent on my own.' The tone of my voice was serious.

'Cariño, money is not an issue. I have money. If you really want to live in New York or London, I might have to sell some property. I have another property in Palma I rent out. I could sell that. Or I could sell Villa Rosa.'

He said this like he was agreeing to amputation. Strangely selling Villa Rosa felt like amputation to me too.

'Come and live here with me. I can support you very easily here. We could travel together. I've spent most of my life between Palma and Deià. It's time I got out. We would travel – you could write your travel articles and sell them to English speaking newspapers.'

Miguel looked jubilant, excited, full of life, the happiest I'd seen him in the few days I'd known him. It was only a few days! This was madness.

'What do you say, Cariño?'

'It's too soon. We've only just met. How can we know it will work?'

'I know, Cariño. I knew the first moment I saw you in your peasant dress walking up the driveway towards me. I love you.'

That word, again. Fear mixed with the prospect of paradise painted by Miguel. It was too soon. Of course it was, but if we were sure, and he seemed very certain, then why wait?

'What are you going to do, live the rest of your life unfulfilled? You have a chance to make a new life with me.'

A new life, here in Mallorca, swimming everyday ... maybe I could reinvent myself as a freelance travel writer and sell articles to newspapers in New York and London. The picture Miguel painted was not impossible.

In the morning Miguel stood waiting for me in the lobby like a groom at the altar.

'Flowers!'

He must have picked them when he'd put my luggage in the car.

'Can you close the gate, Cariño? I will stay in Palma for a few days after you leave. I do not want to be in Villa Rosa alone without you, so I'll lock up the house.'

I walked down the driveway with the bunch of flowers in an electric blue Deià dawn. His black car waited, hearse-like at the gate. As I walked towards it I had that feeling again, of fate. I knew I'd be back.

We were silent as we drove away. Deià slept, tucked behind the mountain. As we passed the lane that led up to the Hermitage the sky glowed orange.

'Could you pass my tea, Cariño?'

'It was so sweet of you to make us tea.'

I unscrewed the jam jar, careful not to splash myself with hot water, and on a straight stretch of road in between the hairpin bends, passed the tea to him.

As we neared Palma he tensed up.

'Are you ok?'

'That's Palma prison, on the left. Every time I drive past I feel guilty.'

I laughed. So did he, but he eyed the prison in his rear-view mirror, as if it were a stalking tiger and he did not relax until it was out of sight.

'Prisons give me the creeps too, the idea of losing my freedom.'

'During Franco's reign they used to come in the night and take the men. When the women went to collect them, they were told they were gone. Nothing more, just, "They've gone."'

I didn't know much about the Spanish Civil War, but knew it had been brutal; not a war against another nation, but neighbour against neighbour, brother against brother. What must that do to the psyche of a nation? It was not the last time I would ask myself that question.

We arrived early at the airport and finished our teas in jam jars in the car between kisses, him quizzing me about what I would do when I was back in New York City.

'You don't have to go you know, Cariño.'

Miguel switched on the car stereo. *Knowing Me, Knowing You* by Abba. Odd track, considering the situation.

'I need to talk to my husband. He is a good man. I owe him that.'

It seemed very odd to me that Miguel would expect me to have such a grave conversation without being face to face.

'How did you break it off with your ex-girlfriend?'

'I dare say it was complicated.'

He looked away but in the side mirror I caught sight of his expression. It was the same as when we passed the prison, a mix of anger, fear and shame.

'If I am going to leave my husband, I think it normal to understand your personal history.'

'It is still painful, Cariño. I will tell you anything you want to know.'

'It's ok. I understand. This is not going to be easy for me either.'

And then he began to kiss me and talk to me in Spanish. It was not the words as I do not know what he was saying, but a deep growl in his voice that set me on fire.

'Come back, Cariño. Come back soon.'

I think I groaned.

9

Golf Clubs

I woke in my marital bed with the sick thump of grief in my chest and a hangover of horror from a bad dream. Its menacing tentacles stole into my New York bedroom with the same resolve as the daylight penetrating the edges of the blackout blinds. I was alone in the bed. I remembered my husband packing an overnight bag, the quiet click of the latch as he closed the door behind him. The silence. The tears. The exhaustion. The smell of his hair was on the pillow from the nights he'd slept alone … while I was in another man's bed. The guilt. The lump in my throat, the pain in my heart. The dream. I hadn't had a nightmare since before I was married, maybe longer. The golf clubs on the staircase at Villa Rosa. I'd not dreamt of golf clubs for years.

I got out of bed, opened the window, the noise of the city on a Sunday morning. Closed the window. Triple glazing sucked in silence and I was alone with myself again and my hideous betrayal.

November rain dribbled down the floor-to-ceiling windowpane of the Tribeca café. Back in the concrete. It was only after the talk with my husband that I realised the enormity of what I'd done. In one long, painful, calm conversation, I had unravelled sixteen years of partnership. As I sat in the steamed up café waiting for my friends I replayed the show reel of those years.

Brunch parties filtered in. Usually I felt like I was on the set of *Sex and the City* when we met for our Sunday catch up, but that morning NYC was painfully real.

My husband was not rich but very comfortable. He owned the apartment, the car, paid our extortionate health insurance. I couldn't afford to live in NYC without him.

'There she is.' Miranda (my friend even had a *Sex and the City* name) stood by the umbrella stand pointing at me. Shiva and Richie were behind her. New Yorkers crammed in behind them and the three descended on me, gabbling over each other to be heard.

'When you have news, you have news!' Richie did a whole body impression of hip hop rapper-like incredulity.

'This must be the most unstrategic break-up of all time!' Miranda summed up the obvious financial impact in her usual direct manner.

'There's no reason to throw the water out with the kitchen sink.'

I pictured Miguel throwing the dirty washing up water into the garden.

Miranda pointed at her big, dark eyes with two painted false nails.

'Look at me. This is what you are going to do. You're going to call your husband and suggest you two see a couples therapist.'

'I've been suggesting that for years. Seven years. Since we stopped having sex.'

'Well try again.'

'Wait a minute, Miranda.' Shiva put her hand gently on Miranda's arm to shut her up.

'Are you saying you and your husband haven't had sex for seven years?'

Miranda, Shiva and Richie looked at me in disbelief, then at each other. The waiter arrived with our breakfasts.

'Not once?' Miranda's high pitched shock, Shiva's frown and Richie mouthing silently *he's crazy you're a hottie,* alerted me to the fact that a) I'd never shared the extent of the chastity of our marriage and b) it was clearly not considered normal even by Shiva's standards. And Shiva's a prude.

Capers were sprinkled over the smoked salmon, eggs and béarnaise sauce. My groin twanged and I was transported back to the rocks at Deià where we picked enormous capers that hung in clumps over the cliffs, Miguel's dry hand helping me climb, nimble as a goat, muscles that had learnt the craggy terrain as a child, our descent to the cove, my initiation into exhibitionism, the sun warm on my nipples …

'New York to the Virgin Mary!' Richie was clicking his fingers in front of my face like he was waking me from hypnosis.

Shiva leant over her vegetarian breakfast. 'Not once in seven years?'

'Not once. I feel like a nun. I'd prefer to be single than the loneliness of laying next to someone, isolated, confined to my body. We hug, we're affectionate, but it's like he's hugging a sister.'

'Ok, so this Spanish guy made you feel like a woman. Find some hot young guy with muscles and tattoos and have a bit of fun once in a while. Have an affair. That's what normal people do.'

Miranda rolled her eyes. 'She's not normal. She's honest.'

'Honest! I've just cheated on the man I love.'

'The only person you're cheating is yourself. Get a relationship therapist; sort it out.'

'He won't.' I felt my head shaking from side to side.

'This is NYC. Of course he'll do therapy. He's a New Yorker.'

'He won't. Aw, it was awful.' My memory replayed last night: my husband, shoulders slumped, head in hands at the dining table. His tears. My guilt. Our pain. I held back the tears, took a breath and continued. 'He agrees it's not working, but he won't go into therapy.'

Miranda leaned across the plates and took my hands in hers. 'And what did you agree financially?'

'Nothing to agree. We have a prenup. Everything's his, pretty much. He's given me two and a half months to move out of the apartment. I need to be out by January.'

Miranda stood up, put her arms in the air as if she was about to make a speech. 'She needs something stronger than coffee.' She waved at a waiter. 'Darling, bring me an Irish coffee with a generous shot of whiskey.'

The café was hectic and steamed up with condensation which made the clatter of plates and cups and saucers and Sunday brunch story-swapping noisier. I wanted one of those plates to smack me on the head, snap me out of my confusion.

The Irish coffee thawed my shock. I started to tremble.

'What have I done?'

'You've just taken your life back,' said Miranda.

'You've thrown away a perfectly functional marriage,' said Shiva.

'Is this Spanish guy going to support you?' asked Richie.

I felt like I was under attack. Unsafe.

'I don't know. We just spent a few days together.'

'Well then, baby, there's only one way to find out.' Richie was no stranger to throwing himself into romances.

'Are you crazy? Don't encourage her, Richie.'

'I'm serious. Maybe this guy's the real deal.'

I looked from Miranda to Shiva to Richie.

I didn't need encouragement. My heart was made up before I left Villa Rosa. An invisible string that joined me to Miguel, me to the house, was pulling me back. I felt sick for breaking up with my husband and the pain I'd caused, but a deeper sickness, a homesick grief, a longing for home more powerful than me was drawing me back to Deià. Choice had departed from my soul.

PART 2

Flight AF8606 – JFK To Madrid

I woke disorientated, sobbing. And remained confused for long enough to ask myself, *where am I? Am I still dreaming?*

I'm on the plane. Rows of sleeping people. It's night. Enforced plane night-time, window shutters closed, lights off. A few travellers had their spotlights on; most were asleep. The man in the seat next to me had long legs, stretched out into the aisle and crossed at the ankles, just his socks on. A locker room smell hung in the air. I crinkled my nostrils at the stale whiff, but was glad of the realness of it. I'd taken the red eye from JFK. I forced my memory to recall the flight number. This digging into my brain helped orientate me.

I touched the screen on the back of the seat in front of me. According to the digital flight path, we were over the Atlantic. Five hours and fifteen minutes until we landed in Madrid. Then I'll be just a one hour and twenty-five minute flight away from him.

Every time I closed my eyes a doomed atmosphere of premonition hung in the sleepy cabin air – along with the smell of stale socks and a nagging knowing that it would not work with Miguel.

What did I dream? A wave and a voice – something about being conscious. I switched on my spotlight, took out my mobile and wrote the dream in notes. As I wrote, the dream revealed itself.

I'd been in the Cala at Deià. A storm blew up as I stood there looking out to sea, the Sirocco wailing through my hair and past my ears.

And after that? A wave pulled me down to the seabed.

After that? Like an ancient offering from the sea I washed up on the shore of a lake. In Switzerland. A man stood peering over his wire-framed spectacles at me. It was Carl Jung.

What was the famous psychologist doing in my dream? He said something to me, which I repeated again and again like it was essential to my survival.

And Jung's words? I knew they were very, very important. My head hurt from trying to remember.

What did Carl Jung say to me?

Another snatch of the dream emerged. I tapped a little more into my mobile.

The shore of the Swiss lake lapped against the cellar door at Villa Rosa. I went round to the front of the house and walked into the lobby and up the wooden staircase towards the bedroom. There was an antique golf bag at the bend on the stairs. Had the golf clubs caused my tears? Had Miguel been in the dream?

As I sat in my seat taking shallow breaths a cacophony of emotion overwhelmed me: betrayal, loss, confusion and deep disappointment. Then I remembered. Jung's words echoed in my mind: *Make the unconscious conscious.* A knowing deep in my gut told me those words were essential to my survival. I repeated them like a mantra as I typed into my phone. *Make the unconscious conscious.*

Make the unconscious conscious.

Make the unconscious conscious.

Writing my dream in my mobile was my first step towards understanding the ocean of myself that existed beyond the shore of my conscious life. That was the action that started the long journey to wake me up. How strange that dreams are gateways to becoming conscious.

10

Can Mir Prison

The descent to the island of Mallorca is magnificent. The plane swooped round its wild mountainous, tree-thick edges down towards the plains surrounding Palma. The drama of the coastline aligned with something inside me so I was not disturbed by its wildness, but instead drawn like a magnet to it as if it were part of me, less foreign than the low grassy slopes that meet the sea on the island I grew up on. But then I am only half English and the wild part of me belongs to another island with a coastline that does not bare its white teeth when it greets the sea. Palma's Gothic Cathedral, a synthesis of eight centuries of history stands on the site of a mosque, so that anyone kneeling at the altar does so in the direction of Mecca, not Jerusalem. This to me did not feel like a paradox, but aligned with my logic that the three traditions shared the same plagiarising god, so what difference if one kneeled to Mecca, Jerusalem or Hades? Either way, the sand-yellow building demands attention. Crew approaching on Medieval ships during the heyday of the Kingdom of Mallorca must have been spellbound. A Marseille textile merchant would surely have held his breath. I held mine too as the plane zoomed in towards the medieval city.

The silent mantra played in my mind as the wheels of the plane met the Mallorcan runway with a jolt. *Make the unconscious conscious. What did Jung mean?*

November is low season and the plane was virtually empty. As I wheeled my case to the exit, I spotted Miguel before he saw me. His age struck me, his stoop. There was something lizard-like about the way his neck reached forward as he lurched towards me. For a brief moment the repulsion of our first kiss returned.

'Cariño!' He waved. There was something staged in his embrace, something over demonstrative, as if he were acting a part in a 1950s romantic movie. My judgement fell away as his scent swallowed me, his smell and the familiar texture of his skin deceived me into feeling we were somehow related, as if we had been broken from the same mould, two distinct sides of an ancient coin, now reunited, my side struggling to distinguish itself from his as if I were an extension of his being.

'I missed you, Cariño. Did you miss me?'

'Yes.' I exhaled the word, long and slow, like I'd been holding my breath the whole time I'd been separated from him.

'Cariño, Cariño, el què m'agrada de tu és la innocència.'

His breath in my ear (I only caught the word innocence), the blend of his scent, the low mumble of his voice lulled me into the submissive, sheep-like creature I became when I was with him. Like that day in the nudist cove at Lluc Alcari, I became his follower. I could almost see the invisible leash, a low, humming vibration of sexual charge collared at my groin that dulled my other senses.

'Cariño, I want to take you somewhere before we return to Villa Rosa.' Miguel leaned across the gear stick and made such a long drawn out play of kissing me as if there were no tomorrow, nowhere to go, that I wondered if we would ever leave the car park. He continued until something inside me released, submitted to his kisses and lost sight of where we were. There was only his tongue, his hands, our desire.

He pulled away and looked at me. 'At last we can start a new life together, Cariño.' I thought he might cry his expression was so sincere. Was it the intensity of all of his attention focused on me that made my doubts and guilt at leaving my husband fall away? Or was it my own delusion that Miguel's show of emotion was real?

We drove into Palma, parked on a narrow tree-lined street off the Avenida, Palma's ring road, and entered its narrow streets on foot. After the sharp nip of a New York November, the air was gentle on my skin

'Thank you. I so wanted to visit Palma last time I was here.'

He sniffed. I'd forgotten his strangeness, the unease, his anxiety.

'Palma is a very old city. The Romans were here but I dare say there's not much left from the ancient period.'

'Oh, how fascinating. I *love* this city. Do you have any books on Mallorca at Villa Rosa? I was reading the guidebook on my way here ...' I was gushing. He didn't know that I spoke at one hundred miles an hour like a babbling schoolgirl when I was excited or nervous or tired. The jetlag had kicked in. This was a mistake. I felt awkward, stupid. What had I done? Thrown away the comfort of marriage, of sinking into oneself with someone who knows everything about you for an inexplicable something with a stranger. I didn't doubt a deep connection had pulled us together, but it did not follow that we were compatible. I was trying to make conversation as it occurred to me that although we'd spoken for hours on the phone, we did not really know each other and it seemed odd to me that after all the persuasive calls and messages, the pining for me, the missing me, he didn't have anything to say to me now that I was here. He seemed distracted. 'Is everything ok?'

'Um, probably. I dare say you can look in the library.'

I should shut up and take in Palma. As I marvelled up at the buildings in silence I became aware of him looking at me. He followed my gaze, looked where I looked, gently put his hand on my shoulder to catch my attention and pointed at a church.

'That was once a nunnery.' His hand moved to my elbow, drawing my attention away. 'I need to show you something.'

He led the way and a mild impatience seeped from him as his steps sped up. 'This is the Avenida. It circulates Palma.'

He took my hand in a way that made me feel I belonged to him and we walked up the wide tree-lined avenue and he guided me here and there until we reached a large square.

'This is the Plaça d'Espanya. And that is where the train leaves for Soller.' It was the end of the line. The side of a large building stood beside the little station platform. No graffiti on the walls. A station wall like that in the US would have at least one tag. There was something eerie about the building, something in its crumbling plaster that gave off a warning. Silence, solid and impenetrable, in its blank wall.

We walked around to the front of the large building. The ground floor was a cinema. Advertising posters of the latest films were stuck on the glass doors. Next to the cinema was a kebab & pizza takeaway. I looked up at four floors of brown, plain shutters all closed to the day. The modern ground floor shop fronts were the product of a different era to the floors above. Miguel pointed to a small marble plaque fixed to the wall at the side of the cinema entrance above eye height. The plaque was inscribed in Catalan with black letters. Beneath it was graffitied a single word: AMOR.

'This was Can Mir prison. Before it was a prison it was a warehouse for wood to make furniture. My grandfather's brother was a prisoner in here during the War Civil.'

Sometimes he put his adjectives after his nouns, but I never corrected him.

'What did he do?'

'He was on the wrong side. He was a civil servant and refused to swear allegiance to Franco.'

'What happened to him?'

'They let him out. Others were not so lucky. Wives would be called, they'd bring clean clothes and be told, "They won't need those where they've gone."'

He'd told me this before. I imagined this, the women arriving with hope, and leaving as widows.

It made me remember when I was in Spain as a child on holiday with my parents. No wonder so many little old ladies in Spain in the 80s wore black. I shivered at what was hanging in the air, unsaid. What happened to his grandfather? I'd felt the heavy weight of the unsaid the first time I entered Villa Rosa after I interviewed him – what he stopped himself from saying when we stood in the lobby next to his grandmother's portrait, perhaps not wanting to break the spell.

'And what happened to your grandfather?'

'He was not so lucky.'

The silence was jagged.

'He was in the military. Too high in the military to go to Can Mir. He was sent to the Convento de Santa Clara. My grandmother said he did not suffer there. The nuns baked, they had bread and even cake.'

'The Church was in cahoots with Franco, or they were forced?' I didn't understand. Why wasn't he as lucky as the others who were locked up in Can Mir?

'Yes, the Church collaborated with Franco.'

'Did you know him?'

'No.'

'He died in the convent?'

'No.'

The silence was cold and the shadow of Can Mir loomed above us.

'This is a new one. The Council have replaced it again. The sign is stolen often.'

Who by? I didn't ask, but imagined little old ladies arriving on moonless nights to take it instead of a tombstone denied them for their fathers, brothers. Miguel continued to frown at the plaque with a demented look on his face. I wanted to pull him away from Can Mir and into the sunlight, but was rooted to the spot. I looked at the words on the plaque, some I could guess at – *presoners politics* must be political prisoners, *assassinats per ... falangistes* could be assassinated, or murdered by Falangists. I shivered at the horrors those brown shutters had hidden. I wouldn't want to sit in the darkness of that cinema.

At last he spoke.

'He died in the War Civil.'

I wondered what happened to him, but did not want to ask. Death during a war is rarely natural and I'd only be asking to satisfy my curiosity. The line of Miguel's mouth was tight, the grip of his hand around mine even tighter. I took it as a sign to not pry.

'Who is that?' I looked in the direction of a statue of a man on horseback dressed like a medieval knight. Miguel was a reluctant tour guide, but I wanted desperately to change the atmosphere, divert his attention to the sunlight in the middle of the square.

'That is Jamie the First. Mallorca used to be an empire like the British Empire. There have been many empires.' He said this like I wouldn't know that, but I ignored the patronising tone. 'The Kingdom of Mallorca stretched from Spain to France and Southern Italy.'

His grip loosened as the subject moved away from the Spanish Civil War. We left the square and walked past El Cort Inglés. The name of the department store conjured the Medieval Court of the English – a reminder that I was a foreigner in Spain. I knew so little of Spain's history, a fact driven home as we descended into a labyrinth of medieval alleys.

We walked on dry cobblestone streets with names that spoke of Palma's Medieval past. *Conquistador* conjured Spain's conquests of South America. *Passeig de Dalt Murada*, a reminder that this was once a walled city and *Carrer del Call*, the name of the old Jewish Quarter we passed through, derived from *Kahal* meaning community in Hebrew. This titbit I remembered from the guidebook I'd read two months ago before I'd met Miguel and Mallorca sightseeing became instead a tour of his world.

Courtyards whispered of Ancient Roman *atriums,* some with wells like *impluviums*. Others with Moorish staircases tiled in red, yellow and blue with earthenware pots of bright red geraniums flashed past as I tried to keep up. He walked a big city pace, not the sauntering meander of the locals.

It was like walking in a thick cloud of grass smoke. I followed, stoned on the sexual charge. Another part of me wanted to break free from its control, to say, *slow down, I want to explore,* but the cloud of desire silenced that voice. Muted, I followed in a compulsion.

'Is this the old Jewish Quarter?'

Was that an attempt at a smile or did Miguel scowl?

Curiosity pulled my gaze to peep into hidden courtyards. Dotted between ancient houses of the nobility, façades were slick with smooth new plaster, glass and stainless steel. Miguel caught my gaze.

'German house. Palma is now a German city.'

As if he'd summoned them, a sun-kissed, blonde-haired family opened the modern door and manoeuvred a buggy on to the narrow street so we had to dodge them. I returned their smiles. Miguel grunted and dropped my hand. The German family's easy friendliness made me sad – there was no space in our toxic sex cloud for lightness. Miguel hurried on ahead and mumbled to himself about his neighbour, as if he were rehearsing a conversation.

'Is everything ok? Has something happened with your neighbour?'

'What, Cariño?'

He frowned as if I'd interrupted him. Just as abruptly he remembered his manners and took my hand in his again.

'Forgive me, Cariño. I love you.'

The touch of his dry skin triggered a dormant lust in the core of me so that my skin reddened, pounding from the inside. The intoxicating cloud thickened and throbbed with desire and we momentarily harmonised and stepped in sync with the romance of the city. I had a sudden urge to push Miguel into a dark alley and beg him to fuck me against the wall. The weeks of waiting for his body had culminated in a wanton impatience. As if he sensed this he stroked my arse.

'I dare say I'm just overwhelmed to see you, Cariño.' He stopped and looked into my eyes, drinking me in. 'It's been so difficult, alone in Villa Rosa all these weeks without you.'

I reached up and touched his whiskers. Something destitute in his gaze triggered purpose in me: to love away his loneliness. Little did I then know that his thirst was unquenchable.

With abruptness he charged on, dragging me round sharp bends and alleys on my invisible leash. This sudden change added to my confusion. Where did the romance go? Like an addict I was consumed by a craving for his hungry gaze, to slow him down, recapture his attention.

'Are there any Roman ruins in Palma?'

Again he looked as though he'd been interrupted from a far more important something.

'There are the Arab Baths.'

'Oh, wonderful. Can we have a look?'

'No, Cariño.' He curled his lip and whined like a teenager being asked to load the dishwasher.

His behaviour sent my head into a spin. I'd travelled all this way, given up my marriage, my home, my security and he was acting like a petulant child. I stopped abruptly. A familiar pain tightened around my heart and grabbed my throat. I sensed its source was buried in my past. But like the patchwork hints of ancient cultures whispering from Palma's old houses, the original context of my pain was lost. As I stood in the street I felt paralysed. I wanted to speak, but could make no sense of my mishmash emotions. My gut knotted with the sensation that I had been tricked – you know it, but you can't quite work out how you know it.

'Cariño, come on! I dare say you're behaving like a child. We're not tourists.' He added, so softly, 'You live here now.'

I live here now. That should have made me feel safe, but my gut contracted and cramped like I'd eaten sour apples. Who was the child here: him or me?

Miguel was on a mission. Head down he lurched on. I tried to peek into the courtyards and make the most of this mad dash through the old Jewish Quarter: *Carrer de Mount-Sion, Carrer dels Jueus.*

'Is this the Jewish Quarter?'

'Was. In the fifteenth century they were forced to convert.'

I wanted to look up at the buildings, know more, feel the energy of the place, pay my belated respects in a way. So I dug my heels into the pavement like a dog refusing to walk on its leash.

'Cariño, please don't be jolly silly. You live here now. I want to show you somewhere.'

I live here now. I could return whenever I wanted, enjoy it alone. I carried on walking and receded into a sightseeing world of my own that was so familiar I did not realise my withdrawal.

I never did return to those streets alone.

All of a sudden Miguel yanked me into a corner shop, a sort of health food supermarket that stocked mostly German brands. His angst increased when he couldn't find the dried apricots.

'Oh no. I dare say it's a disaster!'

'Being out of stock of apricots is not a disaster.'

I asked the man when they would get more in.

'Next week – was that what he said?' I was pleased my Spanish had been understood.

'A disaster! I can't wait until next week.'

In his silent storm Miguel dragged me around several other shops until he found a bag of dried apricots.

'Ok, Cariño, let's go home.' The idea of Villa Rosa as home made my head spin. Until last week home was a brownstone apartment in Tribeca, New York City.

Jetlag kicked in and my patience was worn thin.

'But Miguel, I thought you wanted to show me somewhere?'

He looked at me blankly. Then his climate changed as brisk as a storm at sea – perhaps he sensed my irritation might turn to anger if I discovered he'd lured me into a stressed out tour of Palma supermarkets on the back of a lie that he was going to show me something.

'I dare say you think me a bit loco, Cariño? Yes, yes, of course. I remember.'

He stroked my hair to pacify me and again I felt the toxic throb of lust as he led me on my invisible leash down *Morei* – a long road, a long reminder of the Moorish city – to the steps of a church overlooking a leafy plaza where six roads converged.

My neck crunched as I looked up at the church towering above us. The short sharp snaps of breath from being dragged down streets and alleys, the jetlag, a feeling of doom from my dream, accentuated by the bloody history of the city made me feel trapped like we had reached a point of no return.

11

Confession

We entered the cool domed silence of the church. A stale reek of incense only centuries of burning creates engulfed us. The ceiling pulled our gaze upwards and we stopped and stared, throats stretched. My neck crunched again from sleeping in an awkward position on the red eye.

'This is Santa Eulàlia.' Miguel's attempt at a whisper was a deep mumble. 'Some people call it church of conversion as the Jews who could not escape the inquisition converted here to avoid being killed.'

Did the souls of those unfortunate people linger here too? I imagined their exhalations still hung in the air. My hand reached for the water font. An ancient reflex moved fingers to brow, crossed my chest shoulder bone to shoulder bone.

'You are a Catholic, Cariño?' He was surprised.

'Irish Catholic on my mother's side.'

'You're not British?' He looked confused as if I'd broken the image of Britishness that stood before him. Then a satisfied expression replaced his disappointment. 'We share a culture. That makes it easier.' I couldn't see how sharing a culture of control, fear and guilt I'd spent my twenties uncuffing myself from made anything easier.

'Alessandra was Lutheran.'

I frowned. *A Lutheran Italian?* He read my thoughts.

'Her mother was German. She converted. I dare say because she wanted to be close to me.'

His tone was cutting. His ex's conversion clearly irritated him. He'd said it was over between them, but it seemed she was still present. And there was an anxiety about him. In the hormonal rush of the few days we'd spent together on my first visit, I'd not taken much notice of it. The mention of his ex set him off mumbling to himself again. He took my arm – a little too hard as if he were directing a child – and manoeuvred me in front of him towards an altar on the right hand side of the church.

'This is the Jesus of sailor wives.' He was still mumbling, but close to my cheek. It was a trait like doctor's handwriting that meant you were not meant to understand the words, only their seductive drugging prescription. 'My mother told me this is where sailors' wives came to pray for their sons and husbands to return from war. I came here and prayed that you would return.' His voice dropped an octave, a husky-deep tone like smokers of filterless Ducados. 'I dare say Jesus heard my prayer. Thank you for retuning, Cariño.' He exhaled the crackle of words into my ear sending a shiver to my groin. It seemed highly dramatic to the English side of my sensibility, even funny, but his serious tone, the grip of his hand on my arm drew me deeper into him and tightened the leash.

As we looked up at the sailor wives' Jesus, a chorus the Lord's Prayer echoed around us in Catalan, but the ancient rhythm was so much chanted into me at an early age that I fancied my blood cells vibrated to its familiar frequency. The group had silently gathered around us so we were at the centre of the Lord's Prayer, imprisoned by its fervour. Miguel led me out of the cultish pack. Perhaps he felt hemmed in too. We resurfaced next to an ancient polished confession box.

'Why does it bother you that Alessandra converted?' A dark expression drowned his features and for a moment I was afraid of him.

'Does it bother you, Cariño?'

'No, I just wondered as you seem agitated.'

'Do you miss your husband, Cariño?'

A geyser of grief stung my eyelids.

'I'm grieving.'

Another expression dashed across his face, like he'd had a eureka moment.

'I'm grieving too.' He said it as if this had only just occurred to him and he was happy to have realised it. He looked at the confession box.

'Do you want to confess, Cariño?'

The sight of the dark, ancient chiselled wood shot a stake of fear through my heart.

'I have nothing to confess.' Although I knew that I did and the sickly taste of guilt clogged my throat.

'Cariño, come on. I'll get into the priest's side and you can go in the confessor's side.'

He must be joking!

'We both need a priest!' My voice was level; I hid how his suggestion disturbed me.

He laughed and put his hand gently round my waist.

'It will be like a new start – we leave the past. You and I. We start fresh. Just us. I dare say I haven't confessed for years, but I want us to be absolved of our sins. Let's confess together, Cariño.' He took my hands and for the first time since I had arrived, he embraced me as if he understood my vulnerability.

Inside the small box, knees to the wood and not enough room to stretch my arms in any direction but to the floor, a dark intimacy and the smell of musty dry wood overwhelmed me. The nauseous treacle of Catholic guilt caught in my throat, the shame and far worse, the mounting sexual arousal of kneeling and confessing sent my mind into a zombie haze.

The last time I'd confessed I'd been eight years old. I'd told the priest that my father hit me. The priest had given me penance: twenty Our Fathers and ten Hail Marys. The injustice held my young self in violent paralysis as I knelt on the pew and I could not perform the penance. I ran from the church screaming at my mother that I would never ever go back to church again. She calmed me and bribed me: Just do your Holy Communion – you'll get lots of gifts – just do your Holy Communion and you'll never have to go to church again. As an adult when I holidayed in Italy or Spain, I found myself sitting quietly with the old ladies dressed in black in the back rows, suspended between belonging and yearning to flee. But until this day, I'd not set foot again in the box.

The shutter slid open and through criss-cross wooden bars was the silhouette of Miguel.

'Do you remember the prayer, Cariño?'

The prayer? My mind was blank.

'Don't worry, Cariño, just tell me your sins.'

I whispered.

'Forgive me, …' My voice broke as I tried to pronounce my soon-to-be-ex-husband's name … my kind, deserted husband. I choked up. The memory of the priest who gave me penance instead of protection, the stale smell, the confusion at Miguel's erratic behaviour, and now him acting as if he were the priest … I thought we were going to confess together?

On the other side of the wooden bars Miguel was making the sign of the cross.

The tears would not stop. I wanted to leave the claustrophobia of the box, but did not want to go back into the light, into the crowd of chanting people, exposed, naked in my grief. My sobs became more violent.

'Cariño, please. It was just for fun. Shall we go?'

I took a slow breath to calm myself.

'But you haven't confessed.'

He laughed.

'I am innocent, Cariño. We are not sinners. We are, how do you say, absolved.'

'We're both sinners! We *both* betrayed our partners.'

Confused thoughts muted me. Surely he realises he betrayed his girlfriend too. He was still in a relationship the day I interviewed him. *Surely he doesn't think he's innocent?*

'Cariño, let's go. This was a bad idea. Let's go home.'

The little window shutter slid shut and Miguel opened the door to the confession box. Very gently, he helped me out. I felt as though my legs might give way. Miguel embraced me.

'We are absolved, Cariño. Forget the past. Thank you for returning.'

He looked up at the sailor wives' Jesus with a strange look of satisfaction as if through my distress Miguel had achieved what he'd brought me here for.

'I dare say this is the very spot where the Jews of Palma were forced to convert to Catholicism.'

Gone was the soft pacifying tone. His mind had darted elsewhere, to the Middle Ages perhaps. He looked up at the statue oblivious of me.

I sobbed into his jumper in confusion – Miguel was both the catalyst and the pacifier of my distress.

'Let's get the fuck out of here.'

I made a wild dash to the door, the Lord's Prayer droning on like a dark spell behind me, my escape propelled on the urgent legs of the little girl I once was.

Outside in the sunshine I inhaled fiercely, as if I'd just resurfaced from a deep dive in the ocean, and tried to make sense of what had happened.

I'd only spent five days with Miguel. That was over a month ago, but it felt like a lifetime. Hours on the phone when I was in New York – did he convince me to leave my husband or was it my choice? My heart was shot through with shock and the terrible thought that I had made the biggest mistake of my life. Another voice made excuses for Miguel's erratic behaviour – *he's just a bit odd. A writer. He has flights of fancy. You love this man and he loves you.* That strange business in the confession box – was it just his way of trying to help me come to terms with my grief and my guilt? He was making light of the betrayal with humour perhaps. Despite the inexplicable familiarity, Miguel was a stranger.

Palm trees in a dry sunny square would usually raise my spirits. Old men sitting alone on shady benches in Mediterranean countries usually gave me a sense of peace. Not today. What were they thinking? Was that peace on their faces? Or grief? A silent long ago grief. Was I seeing in them what I was feeling? Thoughts of my faraway husband fell further into my past. Behind and beyond this did I sense a more ancient grief?

'Come, Cariño.' His voice was so gentle now, like I remembered it when I first met him, with an attentiveness that was so very irresistible to me. He took my hand again.

'If you want to do some sightseeing we will do so. I am a Palma boy. I will show you around.'

I did not care anymore. I felt as though my heart had been hung out in the sun after being spun in a washing machine.

He took me back through medieval streets until we reached a very narrow street. Carrer de Santa Clara.

'I'm taking you to the convent where my grandfather was imprisoned.'

I was confused. I was certain he'd not wanted to be reminded of the fate of his grandfather. He walked slower now, as if he were stalking a ghost down the alley, holding back like a thief not wanting to be seen. His grip though, that was so tight my fingers were going numb.

'We don't have to go here, Miguel. Let's go home.'

'No, Cariño, you wanted to go sight-seeing and I want to show you Palma.'

Why here and why not the Arab Baths? But I held my tongue.

We walked into the sunny courtyard and into the small church. When we sat down I saw a woman hover as if floating – a nun in a dark robe, belted and silent. I coughed. She darted down a corridor on the right hand side of the altar. Her silence irritated me. We were alone again in the little church, which was the only area open to the public.

It was unlike him, but Miguel started to talk, like the first day of the interview, like he was reading from a book, but in his low mumble, his attempt at a whisper.

'My grandfather was brought here by my grandmother and my mother was with her, probably.' He added the word probably – was he making this up? 'They left him with his belongings and brought him everything he needed. The men in here were lucky. They did not suffer. When I used to ask my mother what happened to him, she would tell me he was the lucky one, to be in here looked after like a king by the nuns. The nuns made cakes and pastries and the prisoners had bread every day. It was their wives outside who suffered without sugar.'

I managed to loosen my hand from his grip and flexed my fingers to bring back the blood flow. I didn't want to complain about numb fingers as I sensed it was important for me to know this about him. He was opening up and I didn't want him to disappear back into his cave. Suddenly there was a sound, quiet at first, of angelic voices ... it was coming from above our heads. I looked up and saw a high wooden balcony. Invisible human voices sung and soothed my frazzled nerves.

'Are you ready to go back to Deià now, Cariño?' His breath was on my neck, hot kisses followed, stolen beneath unseen angelic voices, Catholic shame pulsed so violently through my veins I thought I would explode from the pressure of it having nowhere to go, no release.

'A good Catholic girl.' He growled it like a hungry wolf in my ear. 'We share a culture, Cariño.'

Sick as it sounds this fact pleased me.

12

Nightdress

The house had a different feel. Miguel had rearranged things. He carried my suitcase upstairs. Following him up the second bare wood staircase to the top floor was like following him into another world, an enchanted place where the rules – all the rules I'd known up to this point – were meaningless. At the bend in the staircase I remembered the antique golf bag in my dream. I blinked and the golf clubs, superimposed in the dark wooden corner, were gone.

'Cariño?' He turned. I was pleased he'd sensed my hesitation.

'Just jetlag.' I didn't want to set off his anxiety again. When we'd pulled up the driveway he'd started muttering about the neighbour being nosy and glanced about nervously.

I followed him into the spacious attic conversion with master bedroom and en suite.

'Villa Rosa is ready for you, Cariño. I've arranged everything for you. I dare say you will like it. Do you like it? It's your house now. Er, *Abajo*. Better you don't go down there.

'Abajo? Down where?'

'Er, the cellar. The staircase is broken and there's a problem with the plumbing. I need to fix it.'

'Why don't you call a plumber?'

'Yes, I dare say you're right, Cariño.'

Miguel placed my case on a large wooden chair and I gazed past him out over the olive groves that led down to the Cala, the blue sea a triangle, a mount of Venus sandwiched between fertile wooded mountains in the distance. My new view from my new home. It felt like trying to pull on a pair of ill-fitting jeans I desperately wanted to fit me.

'This is your house too, Cariño.'

He was behind me. Every hair on my body was alert to him, each cell vibrated with the need to be naked, skin on skin, and satisfy the yearning that had built up in me since I'd left him the previous month. His low mumble vibrated in my ear.

'What would you like to do? Are you hungry? Are you quite jolly, Cariño?'

Miguel's incorrect use of Enid Blyton English was endearing. My laughter released the tension that had built up in me as a result of his mad dash around Palma … or was it that as soon as I'd become anxious, he relaxed? Or had I imagined that?

I took his hand and we moved across the landing to the darkness of the bedroom. Through the shuttered window that opened on to the road, sly slits of sunlight fell in lines across charcoal cotton sheets, faded from washing. They must once have been black. A curious choice of colour for a bedroom.

The furniture had been moved and some things added, some removed. Was the floral dress still there, in the wardrobe, I wondered? I should have been touched that he'd rearranged the bedroom for me, but it was eerie. Had he, like a groom prepared the house for his new bride, or to extinguish any evidence of the old bride? Stop being fanciful, I told myself.

A painting of an African woman nursing a baby to her breast hung above the dresser. There was something insensitive about it – not the painting itself, although the scarlet of the woman's dress against the black background did create a sharp effect – but that Miguel had chosen this painting for a childless woman. We were not a young couple with dreams of making a family.

'You like it, Cariño? It makes me think of what our togetherness will create.' He seemed pleased with his choice and I did not want to ruin the moment. Once I'd settled in I'd remove it.

Miguel was wearing a faded Ralph Lauren tee shirt and shorts. His clothes were old, but expensive. His skin was the colour of summer and the white hairs peeking through the top of his tee shirt tantalised me. I remembered how my hand had brushed against them when I pinned the microphone to his shirt the day of the interview. The same electric throb pulsed through my body now.

'These drawers are for your things.' He opened the top three.

The first two were empty. In the third was a pile of neatly folded white linen.

'These are for you to wear in bed.'

I took one out, held it by the shoulders and let the starched linen unfold itself into a long ancient nightdress, the sort that might have been worn a century ago.

'What's this?' I might have laughed. I can't remember. 'It looks like your mother's!'

'It belonged to my mother ... and I dare say to her mother before her.'

I waited for further explanation, or for him to share the joke, but none came.

'Why on earth would I wear your grandmother's nightdress?'

'For easy access,' (he touched me), '... for procreation.'

'At your age!'

'Why not?' He was talking to himself again as he folded the nightdress and placed it on the dresser beneath the image of the breast-feeding woman.

He was close to me.

A sensible woman would have run from the weirdness and never looked back, but I was too much in thrall. His proximity to me, the electric urgency, the anticipation of our inevitable lovemaking overwhelmed any good sense I once had, and I ignored his creepiness. And there was something that he'd tapped into, a secret even to myself, a subterranean longing for a child.

I do not remember how we removed our clothes. Perhaps I allowed him to unbutton my shirt, or maybe we threw them off in a frenzy, but I remember the relief of him entering me and the pornographic language (which sounded softer in a foreign language) – polla and coño – the disappointment when he softened inside me, his hasty need, not caring if he was aggressive with me in his urgency to revive his polla.

I encouraged him, spoke in the language of his desires. Betrayal was part of his fantasy.

'Remember the day you took me to Lluc Alcari? There was a woman on the rocks with perfect triangle tits the same berry brown colour as the rest of her. I fantasised about her.'

'Yes?'

I painted the scene: him, her, me. He swelled.

'Turn around.'

This was not what I wanted, but part of me did not want to refuse him.

He prepared himself with his hand. His impatience was vigorous, but he was still too soft.

'Would you like another polla? Would you like to suck a polla, while I fuck you from behind?'

I didn't like the fantasy but the imposition of his fantasy on me took me to orgasm. Alone.

'Yes.'

He started to mumble to himself, preoccupied with his polla, looking at it like he was angry with it for not doing as he wished. 'Why can I not come? I'm not taking them anymore.'

Taking what? In my post-orgasm haze I had no idea what he was mumbling about.

As he walked to the en suite bathroom, I watched. Transfixed. There was something familiar about watching his polla swing between his legs, coupled with the heart clenching pain of betrayal and a soiled feeling of having been used.

He walked back into the bedroom, polla in hand. I was as shocked and fascinated by his exhibitionism as I had been at his naked swim at Lluc Alcari. He stood above me by the side of the bed.

'Do you want to suck my polla?'

I didn't. I was luxuriating in the afterglow of orgasm. I wanted to nestle into him, bury my nose into his chest and breathe him in, but I acted against my desires due to a combination of fair play (I'd had my pleasure, so he should have his) and the knowledge that rejecting him would exasperate whatever was causing his droop. So I sat on the edge of the bed and leant forward.

Slap! He slapped me around the face with it. A disturbing flash of memory of a character in one of his novels slapping a young girl in the face with his penis came to my mind. It was just fiction, but what makes authors write dark stuff like that? Instead of pulling away, I found myself colluding in his fantasy although I received no real pleasure from it, only the perversity of submitting. He was harder than usual.

His orgasm was a relief to both of us. His impatience had infiltrated me and become my own. Relief was accompanied by concern: *Are pornographic fantasies the only way he can climax?*

Miguel laughed as he came back from the en suite, pulled on his trousers and a tee shirt.

'You know, I had a feeling to lift you over the threshold when you arrived.'

I laughed at the picture he painted, saw myself in a long white dress being carried into Villa Rosa. I brushed the silly thought from my head – marriage was the last thing I should be contemplating.

He took my case from the chair and put it away in the wardrobe. A small voice inside me wanted to tell him to leave my case where it was. I had the illogical thought that if my case went into the wardrobe it would be gobbled up and I would never retrieve it, like Alice disappearing into Wonderland … like the dress. The floral dress was gone. Where had it gone and who had it belonged to?

I got up. He was not the lazing around after sex type. I wonder, looking back, if there had ever been anything tender in our lovemaking?

'Why does that chair have a hole in the middle?' Like the painting of the nursing woman and his mother's nightdress, the chair was a new addition.

'It is a birthing chair.' He lit up like a tour guide delivering a nugget of interesting historical information. I imagined generations of women giving birth in it. 'My grandmother gave birth to my mother in it. But my mother gave birth to me in our bed.'

There was something incestuous about the thought of him being born in the bed we had just made love in. Of course it must have been normal years ago, but I grew up in a transient city where people moved home as often as they changed their socks and birth was something done in impersonal hospital beds that strangers had died in. The clinging stickiness of his family line, the claustrophobic closeness, filled the gap of family in me, as if I were being glued into the generations. Long fingernails of grief at my childlessness reached up from the past. I had thought I'd come to terms with it.

His demeanour changed again. He slapped the chest of drawers.

'Unpack your things, Cariño.'

When he went downstairs I got up, went to the toilet as was my precautionary habit even though we'd used a condom.

Moisturisers and body oils had been arranged on the cabinet, women's toiletries with Italian labels. Carthusia was written in silver letters with a logo of a naked woman covered in flowers. I unscrewed one bottle and inhaled. Rose oil. I pushed away the thought of him massaging it into the skin of another woman. I won't use her oils and creams. There was something disrespectful both to me and the woman who'd stood at this mirror to apply those beauty products and called Villa Rosa her home once. I put the bottle down. I felt like a thief sifting through somebody else's toiletries. A shiver went through me, a similar sensation to the feeling I had about him wanting me to wear his mother's nightdresses. Did his ex wear his mum's nightie? *Well I'm not wearing them. Gives me the creeps.* I put the toiletries that had belonged to the woman in the floral dress in the cupboard under the sink and arranged my own products – labelled Dr. Hauschka and Walgreens – on the shelves under the mirror.

As I passed the wardrobe a breeze of perfumed sweat wafted up my nostrils. In my mind I saw the floral dress. The wardrobe was big enough to walk in. In I went. Again I had the sensation of being a thief. Is this how Mrs de Winter felt, in the shadow of Rebecca at Manderley?

Empty hangers – for my things – were at the end where the floral dress had been. My heartbeat throbbed in my ears and I felt like a victim in a horror movie as I took another step into the darkness. I inhaled, expecting to catch another whiff of stale perfumed sweat. Only the smell of washed linen. His clothes hung covered in protective plastic, more designer items, classic clothes that Anglophile Spaniards would buy: Burberry, Scottish cashmere jumpers, clothes for Northern climates. Styles fashionable in the eighties and nineties. I remembered his age. There was one new shirt hanging there with a Zara label, modern, still with starchy shop folds. Bought to match his new younger woman perhaps.

'Cariño! What are you doing?' His voice was coming from outside.

I jumped like an imposter caught out and tripped in my hurry out of the wardrobe.

'Unpacking.'

I dressed with haste and put my clothes into the drawers. A gust of wind whistled through the shutters, the curtain that divided the en suite and the bedroom danced, and a wind chime tinkled somewhere in the garden as if the house itself was welcoming me. I pushed away the dark thought of the woman who once wore the floral dress and padded around these same floorboards. *This is my home now.* I wanted to feel good in this house, but the painting of the nursing mother above the chest of drawers made me sad and lonely.

That night I slept in Villa Rosa under the delusion that I could become the mistress of the house. His dry hands pulled the yellowed-white nightdress over my head with the roughness of a mother losing patience with a disobedient child.

'I don't want to wear it.'

'I dare say the nightdress will keep you warm. It gets cold here in winter.'

'Can't you put on the heating? This damp will set off my asthma.' An icy humidity cloyed at my lungs.

'Come on, Cariño, put it on, don't be jolly silly.'

The idea of wearing a dead person's clothes made me uneasy, more so his dead mother's ... and dead grandmother before her. A lineage of death. But Miguel had a hypnotic power over me and as he kissed me from my nipples to under my armpits so gently and I felt him harden against my leg I allowed him to raise my arms and pull the nightdress over my head. His tenderness was just a way of manipulating me, but I didn't realise that then.

His mother must have been both fatter and shorter than me. The starched linen made me feel as if I were a ghost of myself, as if by wearing it I returned to an old-fashioned era when a woman's role was predefined for her. After making love he turned his back to me and I lay awake staring at the picture of the nursing African woman. In the darkness the black background disappeared and it looked as though she hovered in the air in her scarlet dress.

I lay in the silence of the attic listening to the darkness and the slow low snuffle of his breath. It was pitch black as Mediterranean houses have snug-fitting shutters, but I sensed his back to me, broad and arched over cuddling his pillow, knees hugging another pillow to cushion worn away cartilage. Miguel hadn't showered before bed and his skin smelt like sea salt and old leather. The discomfort of arousal kept me awake, but I dared not move. His grandmother's nightdress had sent him into a frenzy. A break and entry. I was getting used to the pattern – as soon as he crossed the threshold he struggled to stay hard. He'd blamed it on the drugs again, mumbled when I'd asked him what the drugs were for, then fell asleep.

13
Ghost

Although I did not know the time in the black out of the bedroom, I knew I'd not slept long. It was probably still today's side of midnight. I must have slept for I dreamt. The image of wire-framed glasses from another era was all I remembered. The room was cold, the tip of my nose numb. As the Spanish were accustomed to hot summers and their winters were damp, it amazed me that central heating had not taken off. I was glad of the nightdress. The nightdress. It creeped me out and excited my fantasy of living a simple domestic life here in the house. That fantasy started to pull me back into the dream. My eyes darted open. There was no difference between the blackness of closed or open lids, but with my eyes open the dream could not pull me back in.

What happened in the dream? The nightdress, his grandmother's nightdress, and then I remembered a snippet of the story – for stories are what dreams are made of – a dead woman in the floral dress. I knew that the dead woman was Miguel's ex-girlfriend. She was in this bedroom undressing, taking off her floral dress and pulling the big white old-fashioned nightdress, the same one I was wearing, over her head. Apart from the wire-framed glasses that was all I could remember.

Silence can usher in peace. Deiàn silence and the memory of Miguel's dead ex in my new bedroom had the opposite effect. She was alive in real life. Wasn't she? Of course she was. A shrill cry cut through my black thoughts. My body went rigid and I held my breath.

What was that? A cat being killed by a fox? Another noise, softer, more of a howl. It wasn't coming from outside. I tuned in. It sounded like it came from inside the house, low down on one of the lower floors … from underneath the house? There it was again. I stiffened. It was coming from the cellar.

The smell of old leather and sea salt smothered me as Miguel rolled over to face me.

'Cariño, can't you sleep?'

'Did you hear that noise?'

He laughed.

'You're jolly silly, Cariño.'

'I'm being serious. It sounded like a scream, like an animal trapped in a room downstairs.' I did not say what I really heard – a human cry. I did not say the cellar either as it was out of bounds. We did not mention the cellar. He used euphemisms for it: downstairs, cistern, plumbing, underneath, but mostly he just said abajo. Below.

He rolled back over and put the cushion back between his knees.

'I'm going to look abajo.' My voice sounded unhinged, urgent, disembodied as if someone else in the room, another me had spoken.

Miguel switched on the bedside light and threw his legs over his side of the bed.

'I do not want your lungs getting full of cold air. I will go and have a look, ok?'

If he were worried about my lungs surely he'd have turned on the heaters. I was suddenly aware how isolated Villa Rosa is in the winter. Not a light on in the town when we went to bed except for the eerie glow of the church lit up on its summit like a picture postcard, an unreal church in an unreal place.

As he walked past the end of the bed, a silent rage seeped from him and the silhouette of the white tee shirt he wore to bed arched on his back like a wizened old man. A twang of arousal mixed with fear in my groin. Those two feelings, arousal and fear were so closely and inexplicably combined in me.

My ears reached out to follow his footsteps. He walked down one flight, then the next and out of the house into the back where the swimming pool was, closing the door behind him. My hearing could not follow him outside. I imagined the neighbour nosing around outside. Miguel's unease about the neighbour had seeped into me and made me edgy.

There was a dart of a noise, as if something was cut short in its screech.

Did he go into the cellar? Did that noise come from there? Or outside? It was so quick and fast I questioned whether I'd heard anything at all.

Silence returned with him. A darker silence than before, like something or someone had been silenced.

He walked back across the room. His polla was slightly raised. Why is that? It disturbed me. I'd switched on the bedside lamp and I could see the tight thin line of his mouth.

'What was it?'

He sat on the bed next to me and stroked my hair in a pacifying way that was familiar, triggered a lost memory and was far from comforting.

'Nothing, Cariño.'

Can he sense my fear, is that why he's stroking my head? His tenderness wasn't tender.

'Was there something downstairs?'

'No, Cariño. There was nothing abajo.' He laughed as if I were a silly girl having a nightmare.

So my imagining him putting an injured animal out of its misery had no basis?

'But what was that screech? I know I heard it.'

'I dare say it was the jolly ghost of Villa Rosa.'

'This house is haunted? I'm not sure I believe in ghosts.'

My turn to laugh. My laugh was an out-of-tune quiver. Of all the places I've lived, it was believable that Villa Rosa was haunted.

'That is what my family say. There are many stories of things going missing over the years, shoes disappearing, strange sounds in the night.'

'But you didn't hear anything?'

'I did.'

'But you said you didn't.' My brain started to spin as it often did when Miguel said one thing one moment, then contradicted himself the next.

'I dare say I heard it, but I did not want to scare you. Don't worry, Cariño, it's probably a friendly ghost.'

He took my hand and guided it towards his polla. Erect now. I had wanted this before, but now the timing seemed wrong, inappropriate, insensitive, but I allowed him to draw me to him. Was it fear or excitement that caused my arousal? When he was hard enough, he sank into me, all tenderness gone. Part of me wanted it raw and rough, another me cried silently inside.

He flopped his head back frustrated onto the pillow. After the first few jabs he'd softened. I could feel the invisible warring parts of him, almost felt pity for him, but a rage growing inside me prevented it. What about me? Where's the love?

'If you were not so focused on the destination, you might enjoy the journey more.' I said it kissingly.

'¡Uf! You might be right. Yes, there are things you can teach me, Cariño.' He said it as though he was the sage and I a mere student who he was big enough to acknowledge had some small nugget of wisdom to offer.

'Hold me.'

'You want me to hold you, Cariño?' He sounded surprised … or was it reluctance?

His arm was bony and I was uncomfortable. It was like being embraced by a skeleton. I did not sleep, but stayed still so as not to wake him, staring at the faint shadow of the fan on the ceiling now my eyes were accustomed to the dark. That ceiling fan, his cold embrace reminded me of something lost in some far-off memory.

14

Plumbing

I couldn't hang over the loo all morning. It was the second time I'd flushed. Miguel would start getting agitated that I'm wasting water. The day before he'd complained about how long I took in the shower and mumbled about the cost. The surge and splash as my shit swirled in its familiar lavatory cyclone was separate to the gush of the torrent outside as it heaved through the narrow gauge in the rocks, from the mountain, past the house down to the Cala and out to sea. *Please go down. I don't want to flush again.*

The tiled floor of the downstairs bathroom was the same as I'd walked on in Spanish holiday lets as a child on family holidays, but these were the tiles of my home. I had to keep reminding myself, like pinching myself to check it wasn't a dream. This cold stone needs under-floor heating.

I washed my hands while I waited for the cistern to refill. It took ages. The plumbing didn't work properly. I had a sense that the sewage gathered with the slop and effluent of the centuries beneath the catacombs of the house. My hands rubbed together faster and lathered soap into a frenzied candyfloss. The thought of the cellar directly under the tiled floor disturbed me.

Floorboards creaked above my head: Miguel pacing. As he kept reminding me, Villa Rosa was expensive to run, although I had a fanciful suspicion that the real owner of the house was in the cellar beneath the bathroom, hovering under the floorboards to my boudoir. Pipes knocked as the cistern struggled to fill. Had the house heard my thoughts? I had a creepy sensation of being watched, as if Villa Rosa had a spirit, and the spirit resided in the cellar. Since Miguel told me about the ghost, it had become part of my experience of the house. Another creak. Miguel stopped pacing. He stood directly above the bathroom, above my head. Could he smell it? I quietly put the lid down to contain the whiff. That bloody cistern sounded like a hissing monster.

It's too soon to drop the pretence that I'm a fart-free angel. At least the downstairs loo has a door, not just a curtain. My reflection in the mirror frowned back at me. Grandma used to say the wind would change and fix my frown. I adjusted my expression, relaxed the worry lines. Bloody cistern! It's like that when the romance is new – the essential functions of the body are hidden behind locked doors of bathrooms. Odours, hung like heavy medieval tapestries in the air, are ignored: whiffs of melancholy farts, the garlic grief of last night's Spaghetti Bolognese, yesterday's Thai Green Curry, sniffed and unacknowledged. Memories of shared meals might be conjured in the future, remembered with sweetness. Miguel and I might talk in years to come of the succulence of last night's home-made mango chutney, the bitterness of the Kaffir lime leaves, but the waste, the leftovers of the body's absorption of nutrients, would disappear into the darkness of the earth. Never to be spoken of again. As is normal, as is the case in all houses, but Villa Rosa was different. Villa Rosa collected those culinary memories from its guests, its temporary inhabitants and filed them away in its depths, holding on and not letting go like a baby with a full nappy; like a soldier with a rucksack of trauma.

Foam suds splattered the mirror. I shook the excess water from my hands. My toes were numb from the cold tiles as I walked to the toilet and raised the seat. Damn, still there. I flushed again.

Time to sort out my face. I unscrewed the lid of the cream and inhaled the essential oils. Ah, frankincense and rose. Dr. Hauschka face cream disguised the smell of shit and pulled me into its olfactory lie. I dipped in a fingertip and the automated routine began: cream massaged into cheeks with the same dabs and strokes as an imagined generation of women standing in front of that tarnished mirror had before me, honouring the thin membrane that protects the messy workings of the body like the annual oiling of an ancient door, a maintenance routine cultivated to ward off the inevitable transmutation of time, the eventual decay and decline of the body, but an act of love too. I watched my hands apply the cream, each stroke mindful. The mirror was old and distorted my reflection as if my hands did not belong to me.

Love me. What was that? My body shuddered and the flesh wobbled on my thighs. I had the odd sensation that the house was trying to speak to me through salmon-pink walls – did that voice come from inside me, inside the plaster or up through the tiled floor? My imagination followed the idea – the spirit of Villa Rosa, trapped beneath the rot and damp of the years. I saw it dried out in the summers and luxuriating during the brief periods of tenderness when new owners tended to its needs, laying dormant as the house fell into disrepair, through lonely winters when mildew lined the walls of the downstairs rooms. I sensed it as a living presence all around me. I can still feel it now. The hairs on my arms pinged up, my skin turned to *piel de gallina.*

Enough flights of fancy! Miguel wasn't being serious when he said the house has a ghost, surely? Stories get handed along like Chinese whispers in families, the past distorted until it's unrecognisable. And the truth, that immutable invisible *nothing* that drives Shakespearean tragedy, becomes a collective truth, an inherited atmosphere passed on with the family name.

I dropped the lid back and replaced my cream pots in the cupboard beneath the sink along with the debris of previous inhabitants of the house. Carthusia was written in silver on one bottle with the logo of the naked woman covered in flowers. That same brand as the bottles in the cupboard of our en suite upstairs. Would my Dr. Hauschka pots join the debris? Is that all I was, a visitor? I sighed. I wanted to live in Villa Rosa, keep it clean, care for it, but the longing made me afraid that I might merge into the very plaster of its salmon-pink walls and disappear.

'Cariño, are you ok in there?'

My tits jumped with me at Miguel's voice. My gaze darted from the lock on the door to the closed toilet seat. I lifted the seat with the tips of my fingers as if it were a leper and peered in, breath held. Nothing: a still pool of water.

Thank God for that!

'Yes. Won't be long.'

The flush was effective, but I sensed my shit was not destined for the Cala, that the torrent would pass by this house on the mountainside. Time had gathered here. I felt it in my bones. The sorrow of whatever part his family had played in the Spanish Civil War – the women who wiped away their tears for his grandfather locked up in the Convento de Santa Clara (did he return to Villa Rosa or die there?), filthy shadows of war crimes, foul whispers and grief. Were my longings, desires, fears and pleasure also destined to join generations of memories, flushed but not disposed of in the cistern – out of sight, but gathering an invisible strength beneath the foundations of Villa Rosa?

A thump. That was definitely a thump. I felt the vibration beneath my feet travel up my body. *That cistern's likely as ancient as the house its judders are so violent.* A great, ancient cistern. I could see it under my feet (although I'd never been down there – and didn't dare after Miguel made it clear with the hard line of his mouth when he warned me the cellar was out of bounds). I imagined a swimming pool of shit, the accumulated *impluvium* of effluent beneath the house as if the very foundations of Villa Rosa refused to let go of the debris of family dinners, rationed war meals made with black market sugar, shit fossilised and petrified, until it was no longer recognisable as the waste product of a shared meal, a lonely lunch with a place set at the table for the invisible departed (an empty chair at the head of the table after Miguel's grandfather went to prison), a fig snatched from the tree in the garden by generations of children playing hide and seek before suppertime, but a thing altogether different, a metamorphosed formation that resembled the mountain itself. The pile of shit in the cistern below the house, I imagined had taken on the form of the mountain, a smaller version, a cloned replica of the barrier between Deià and the island, Deià and Spain, a wall, a fortress of defence between this fertile mountainside and the whole continent of Europe. All the laughter, tears, fears, sacrifices, love and grief of generations swollen and mutated as if it were plugging a great, yawning hole.

Footsteps. Miguel, he was coming downstairs.

'Cariño, take your time. I'm going abajo.'

'What are you doing down there?'

Why's he going into the cellar again?

'I'm going to check the cistern. I dare say the plumbing is broken.'

Yes, of course, he would have heard the noises too. *Something's wrong with the plumbing. Simple explanation. No ghost.* I splashed cold water on my face as if I was waking myself up after a long, deep sleep. *Damn it, what made me do that? Now I'll have to reapply my face cream. Why doesn't he call a plumber?*

15
The Cala

Our days found their rhythm. He'd rise early with the caw of the crow, baa of sheep and other animal noises, swing his legs out of bed without so much as a kiss. I'd dilly dally behind him in my slumber. Tea (not coffee) was brewed – another Anglophile quirk. He ate standing up in the kitchen wearing a very old apron. By the time I came downstairs the table was laid with my breakfast: honey from the Arab quarter in Palma and his homemade jams.

I took to walking down to the Cala for a swim in the mornings. I noticed Miguel didn't like me doing anything on my own. Although he slept in sub-zero temperatures, he was completely paranoid about catching a cold. That morning he really didn't want to swim.

He was looking into the distance out of the dining room window when I dashed downstairs, bikini under my jeans, as the sun was so intense. A swim before breakfast or I'd spend the whole day in a slumber. I knew how my body was here. If I didn't get the blood circulating in the morning, my brain would be foggy all day and my body would go numb from sitting in the chill of Villa Rosa. Miguel's stingy approach to the heating meant eighteen degrees was the highest he'd allow it to go to all day.

This morning there was a book on the table by my plate. I picked it up. An image of a woman in 1950s style and apron was on the front cover, mixing bowl in her hands with a Stepford wives grin. The book was slim, greasy, tattered with age and splashed with oil and other ingredients. I put it back down. Was this a hint? I wasn't a cake-baking kind of girl.

Perhaps it was the recipe book that drove my determination to swim, or maybe it was the sight of the Cala from the window, a triangle of distant blue, the dawn throwing pink shadows over the steep cliffs either side of it. I yearned to submerge myself in the ocean.

I took a banana from the fruit bowl and stuffed it in my bag.

'Ok, I'm off. Thank you for breakfast. I'll eat it when I get back.'

I gave him a quick peck on the cheek as he didn't lean towards me.

'I dare say we will catch a cold today, Cariño.'

'You don't have to come.'

I wanted to go alone. I was used to having my own space with my husband. We lived busy city lives and this country lifestyle would take some getting used to, however much I loved Deià. I dashed past Miguel to the downstairs bathroom where our goggles hung to dry on hooks.

'W-w-wait, Cariño. Are you sure, Cariño?' There was a teenage whine in his voice, but I had to get out of Villa Rosa. I'd not left the house apart from to help him gather firewood in the grounds and a swim the week before. I caught the irritation in his tone, but I had to escape. I couldn't breathe – I needed to shake the deep, dark shadow of sleep from me.

'Ok, Cariño.' He caught hold of my arm – too tight with his fingernails – and pulled me to him, kissed my face, my neck. 'Or we could go back to bed.' He knew the power he had over me, but even his kisses didn't seduce me that morning. They were just a bribe to get what he wanted, divert me from what I wanted.

I slipped free of his grip and dashed to the front door.

'Ok, ok. You really want to swim, Cariño?' He stood in the lobby next to his enormous phallic sculptures and slouched on one hip like a belligerent teenager.

Screw him. I'm going swimming. I fumbled about opening the door. Locked! I gulped.

'Did you lock us in?'

'I always lock the house at night, Cariño.'

'Why?'

'The neighbour.'

He's paranoid.

'Do you think he'll attack you again?'

'Maybe.'

'Where's the key?'

'Ok, ok, you really want to go?'

I started jangling through the keys on hooks by the door. I wasn't repeating myself.

'Wait here. I'll collect my things. It's better you don't go alone.'

'Why?'

'Because you have to pass through his land. I have right of passage as his house belonged to my grandfather before the War Civil.'

He stroked my hair as if I were something precious, as if I too were in danger of being attacked.

'He won't do anything to me.'

'You're part of Villa Rosa now, Cariño. He wants the house. He tried to take it from my grandmother after my grandfather was gone, during the war. The neighbour, his grandfather was a Nationalist, one of the Dragons of Death. He resents anyone who lives here.'

'But that was generations ago.'

'They're still fascists. His son, and the son of his son. They think Villa Rosa should belong to them. He stalked Alessandra.'

A bang came from the cistern as if the house had something to say about its ownership ... or, I mused, the house was not the property of any man, Nationalist or Republican. It would still be here when our era's drama was over. Would our words seep into its walls and collect in the cellar too?

On that cheery note he went upstairs to get his swimming things.

'Hurry up! The sun's cresting the mountain.'

'I can't find my swimming shorts.'

'It's in the drawers.'

Why does he need his bloody trunks when he's an exhibitionist? He never swims without them in the Cala. No flashing on his own doorstep, perhaps? I was still annoyed he'd not warned me about the naturist spot – it was his deception, which I was beginning to see was an unattractive part of his nature.

We rounded the drive and walked out into the tiny lane. Once past the well, Miguel's anxiety rose. He stopped talking and his lips set in that familiar frozen line.

'What's with you?' I laughed.

'Shush, Cariño, this is the neighbour's land. I don't want to disturb him.'

'But you have a right to cross his land as he does yours.'

'I don't want to see him.'

As if he heard our whispers, the neighbour appeared, rake in hand like a magician's staff, barring our way to the olive groves through the gap in the crumbled down stonewall.

After an uncomfortable delay he moved aside, glaring at us.

I was not sure whether it was my fear I felt or Miguel's.

We walked through the olive grove in silence. I sensed something dark, a simmering fury coming from Miguel. His shadow cast long in the morning sunshine, winding through the ancient olive groves, over the stile and down the gravel path, across the rickety bridge over the torrent, which gushed so loud it blocked out the twitter of morning birdsong. His dark mood did not lift until we were in the icy cold water.

The Cala was deserted. Either side of the tiny bay sheer rock loomed up. There was no beach, just rocks. The clear water was so calm it looked like a pool today. Deep and turquoise, you could dive in from the high rocks either side. This was the only way to enter in the winter as to go in gradually was a more drawn out torture. A quick dive and fast strokes and you acclimatised. The flag post where the restaurant on the cliff raised the medusa flag in the summer was naked.

We climbed onto the high rocks just below the restaurant, undressed in silence and pulled on our rubber swimming hats. We must have looked like aliens, wormlike and white, as we plunged into the icy cold water. Me first, him laughing as he surfaced.

'You're crazy, Cariño.'

'It's wonderful, isn't it!'

He went under and looked around, goggles on, for Medusa then resurfaced.

'Medusa?'

'None.'

We swam cliff to cliff. It was too cold in the winter to swim all the way out to where the cliffs parted and the Cala met the open sea. Our limbs were heavy within ten minutes, fifteen if we kept moving. My head started to clear as if the crystalline clarity of the water had infiltrated my being. But my nose was still blocked.

'It's heaven, isn't it!'

We both laughed. There was such a lightness of being in that moment. Perhaps that was the lightest we ever were, there in the sea. My merman and his mermaid and not another soul in the world.

One side of the high cliffs glowed pink in the sun.

We both cleaned our noses. This was a ritual of his and that was the morning he taught me. He liked to play the teacher.

'What are you doing?'

'Cleaning my nose, Cariño.'

It was a disgusting thing to do, the sort of thing a child would do. I trod water and watched as he dipped his face into the water, one finger on one nostril and blustered and blew into the water.

'What on earth are you doing Miguel?' I was laughing like a child. It was hilarious to watch.

'Cleaning my nose. The salt dissolves.'

I tried to copy him but just got a mouth full of sea water and spluttered into the sea.

'Watch me, Cariño. Like this.'

'Do you inhale with your open nostril all the way up?'

'Yes, until the water reaches your mouth.'

I tried it. Sucked water up one nostril then blew my nose into the sea through the other one. Afterwards both nostrils were completely clear. Amazing, it was as though for the first time in my life I could breathe through both nostrils equally. It made the whole world seem clearer. The sun was higher now and twinkled on the water around us. So different from the day I'd first come here alone, waiting for Miguel. The shadow of disappointment at being stood up still lurked. The cliff to the left threw a shadow over us.

Miguel looked in the same direction.

'That's where the mirador is.' His expression lost its light. 'Let's get out, Cariño.'

'A few more lengths.'

'You'll catch a cold, Cariño.'

He was right, but I didn't want to let go of this moment. I wished that lightness of living could last forever, could be the personality of our relationship, and just that one swim gave me hope.

Miguel was up on the rocks, towel around his shoulders when I turned from my backstroke, looking up at the big blue canvas sky.

'Come on, Cariño, that's enough.'

That phrase rattled me. *That's enough.* His order stunted my swim, but I obeyed as my arms and legs were heavy with the cold. It had entered my bones. Plus breakfast would taste so much better after a swim.

We walked back carrying the lightness with us, laughter making our steps light and present like mountain goats.

'You see, isn't a morning swim a good idea.'

'Yes, you are right, Cariño. I feel fantastic!' He had adopted my vocabulary. Strange this exchange of learning.

'I want to speak in Spanish – or I'm never going to learn.'

'But I want to improve my English.'

'How about you speak in English, I reply in Spanish? Si hablo en Español, tu hablara en Inglès?'

His face changed.

'Hablaría.' He corrected me.

'Hablara.'

'No, there are more syllables. Listen to me, Cariño. Hab-bla-rí-a.'

'Habla ...' Nerves set in at getting it wrong, at my mistakes changing the atmosphere. We wouldn't get anywhere if he didn't allow for my poor grammar for a while. I wished he had the patience to persevere with my pidgin Spanish, but instead it irritated him when I made mistakes. I fell silent.

He marched on, his gaze to the cliff that was still shrouded in the shadow of the night. He waited for me at the stile, offered his hand and helped me over.

'How are your articles coming along?'

Miguel had encouraged me to write travel articles about the island and send them to the English-speaking world press. Instead I'd found myself unearthing story upon story as I sifted through the internet about the plight of Mallorcan families during the Spanish Civil War. Not exactly an enticing draw for tourist readerships seeking sunshine and tapas.

'Despathio.'

'What?'

'Des-path-io.' I tried again, trying to pronounce every syllable, more to please him than myself. I was satisfied with finding the right word for slow and not bothered about its pronunciation. I'd polish my accent after I got the basics.

'You sound like an Andalucian maid.' It was a mumble but I caught it. Did he even care how my travel article was progressing?

'Slow.'

I reverted to English, changed the subject to regain the lightness of the Cala. The lightness had gone. In its place were dark thoughts about General Franco's Dragons of Death. Miguel said the neighbour's grandfather had been one.

16

Mirador

A Deià evening closes in like a drawstring duffel bag. All the lightness of the morning swim had dissolved and the mountains closed in around the valley. A cloying claustrophobia, the press of silence cumulated during the day, anticipating approaching darkness, the damp, fingering its way into my bones as I sat at the dining table facing the Juliet balcony.

My laptop screen had switched itself off. I'd decided to write an article about Palma as a winter break destination, got as far as describing the sign for Can Mir prison in Plaça de España and my imagination spun off of its own accord and pictured the parlours of houses like this one all over the island with plaques commemorating the site of Can Mir hanging from the walls. Those thieves of the night, were they the little old ladies dressed all in black like the ones singing the Lord's Prayer in the Santa Eulàlia who hobbled along with step ladders under their arms to reach the sign as Palma slept? Reservoir Grannies. Or more likely Falangist attempts to delete memory. Either way suggesting Mallorca is an island of nocturnal thieves might not sell it to the travel sections of English speaking newspapers.

Miguel was working in his library. Every so often I could hear him get up, walk to the en suite and flush the loo, followed by the clank of ancient pipes. Even his footsteps above my head aroused me.

He came downstairs, put his hand on my head, moved it down inside my top and stroked my breast, that familiar constantly warm, dry skin.

'How's the article going, Cariño?'

'Slow and stuttering. Do you have any books about the Spanish Civil War?' What I'd read up to that point was just from the internet and as he didn't have wifi I had to ask to borrow his phone for his hotspot, which he timed. *Next time we go into Palma I must find a way to have my own internet connection out here in the sticks.*

'In my library but most are in Spanish, Cariño.' He looked at me with interest as he gently played with my nipple. 'If you're really interested, I dare say Palma library has a few in English.'

Palma, the thought of the city slightly lifted the weight of claustrophobia.

He looked at the table. The 1950s recipe book was still next to the fruit bowl, untouched. The small thin volume dragged us both into its pages.

'Have you decided which cake you will bake me, Cariño?'

'I don't bake cakes.' My heckles were up.

'But I like cakes, Cariño.'

'I've never baked a cake in my life.'

'Well, now you have a recipe book you can learn. My grandmother's recipes are in here.' The claustrophobic fear of turning into my mother rocketed me up from the chair and swiped his hand out of my jumper in one swift motion.

'We have to get out of here, Miguel.'

'It will be dark soon, Cariño.' That teenage whine again. My husband never irritated me like this.

'Then let's go.' I marched past him down the stairs with the focus of the morning swim.

He frowned, then laughed. 'I like your London determination. We are learning each other. Ok, let's go. There's something near here you might find interesting.'

Long shadows stretched across the olive groves. It was warmer outside than it was inside the house.

'Miguel, is this how you usually live?' I didn't wait for an answer. 'It's not healthy. We have to move, do something everyday.'

'There's not much to do in Deià, Cariño. I told you, people run from Deià. Even I need to escape sometimes.'

'We're in the middle of the most idyllic countryside on earth and we sit all day in the house!'

'It's cold outside, Cariño. We'll catch colds.'

'I'm beginning to suspect you're a hypochondriac, Miguel. It's sunny outside. We should soak up the sun everyday. In New York and London people hit the parks as soon as the sun comes out. My chest needs heat to absorb all this damp.'

'I dare say you are right, Cariño.'

This felt like his way of shutting me up. It worked. He broke the silence.

'There was a painter who lived just there.' Miguel pointed to a small stone house with a big new double-glazed window (which meant it had likely been bought by rich Northern Europeans as a holiday home) across the valley. 'He had weak lungs, but he painted outside all day, even in winter. My mother told me that during the War Civil, Franco's men would not allow him to paint and so he painted inside the house. He contracted tuberculosis and died.'

So he does realise the risk to people with respiratory conditions!

'What's wrong with the heating, Miguel? Villa Rosa is like a fridge.'

'Heat is jolly expensive, Cariño.'

Across the valley chimneys exhaled thin plumes of smoke into the clear blue sky.

'What about the fire? Why not light it?' When I'd first seen the old-fashioned open fireplace I'd imagined evenings snuggled on the sofas in front of the fire.

He made old man noises in the back of his throat, reluctant grumblings that I had learnt meant he was thinking about it.

'We need fuel for that, Cariño. Fuel is expensive.'

'Heat is essential. We need a solution. My hands are numb. I can't even type my fingers are so rigid.'

'Ok. Ok, Cariño. We will collect some firewood, but we have to wait until it's dark.'

'Why?' Maybe Mallorca was an island of nocturnal thieves after all.

He didn't answer. Instead he put his gloves on my hands and marched on ahead of me. We crossed the neighbour's land in silence, through the hole in the wall and into the olive groves. When we reached the stile, we took a left instead of following the path down to the Cala, and started a steep climb upwards, towards the cliffs to the left of the cove. The side that had been in shadow as we took our morning swim was now lit up pink as the sun began its descent.

'Do you see the face in the rock?'

'Oh yes! I do. It's like the one in the cliff on the other side. Guardians of Deià.'

He squeezed my hand. 'You have the eye of a writer, Cariño.' This made me smile coming from him and I remembered how much I admired his writing. His words, his imagination had drawn us together in the first place. 'But this one you can only see the features – large nose, overhanging full lips and the high wrinkled brow, the brow of a thinker – you see, Cariño? You can only see it for an hour at sunset. As children we used to call him the shadow *caballero*, how do you say? Shadow knight.'

It seemed that we were the only people alive in Deià, an Adam and Eve of a couple.

'I used to walk at this time in the summer with my book. I didn't have many friends. Nobody wanted to be my friend. And so I made friends with books. I was happier in my books than anywhere else.'

'What did you read?'

'Enid Blyton – the Famous Five.' I nearly laughed, but stopped myself. 'Then Orwell, you know he joined the War Civil?'

'Yes, I remember reading *Homage to Catalonia* years ago.'

'That's a book I dare say you can find in English in Palma Library. I read everything. I wanted to be a journalist, a serious journalist. But I ended up writing stories, won some awards and maybe I am better suited to fiction. Fiction is a lie parading as truth.' He echoed the line of our interview.

Do you even know what the truth is? But I didn't interrupt him as he carried on telling me about the books he read as a boy growing into a teenager. Most of them were British writers – Dickens, Eliot, Lawrence.

It was the most he'd revealed to me about his past. He seemed innocent, not guarded for a change. Maybe the relationship could work. It takes time to get to know someone.

'I miss the boy I was. There is a part of me that is trying to return to him. I was happy in those summers climbing up here.'

'What happened to that boy?'

He didn't answer. Maybe it was the shadow of the evening, but I sensed there was a reason he lost a connection to the boy who walked and read in this wild paradise.

The land became steeper and the path disappeared into thorny shrubs, rocks and trees. We were close to the cliff edge, above the face in the rocks below now, walking on the top of the guardian's head and I wheezed as damp clung to my lungs. It was not the first time I thought of him as a mountain goat – like Pan, that hooved Greek devil of a god – he climbed effortlessly. Twenty-five years my senior, it was testament to how if you exercise certain muscle groups all your life they never abandon you.

'Hurry up, Cariño. It will be dark soon and I want to show you something.'

I liked that he was thinking of me, but my lungs hurt. I puffed as I followed, some way behind him.

His agitation increased as we got closer to a rough viewpoint carved from the rock. Here he stopped.

'This mirador is where my grandfather was murdered. They came in the night, took men from their beds and walked them here. If they did not jump, I dare say they were pushed.'

Shocked at learning I was standing on a murder site, I held my breath and I looked over the edge, imagined the broken bodies smashed on the rocks below and washed out to sea.

Miguel took out his polla.

This startled me. Surely it was disrespectful at the place where his grandfather had been murdered. Confusion muddied with my lust.

'Do you want to suck it, Cariño?'

I did not but my body told a different story. Every cell, every pant vibrated with my need to draw him into me. Why did he think of sex now? It was the last thing on my mind. Might it be his exhibitionism? Couldn't be. There was nobody to see us but the possibility excited me. I knelt, aware how it would look to a Peeping Tom, my head bobbing as Miguel looked out at the red sky turning the sea a shocking fluorescent scarlet.

He stroked my head when I'd finished. I wiped my mouth and face with a tissue. I always carried one in my pocket when we walked around Deià.

'I used to come here to read my books as a boy, under this tree. I'd stay for hours in the summer and daydream about a girl, a blonde girl. And then I would wank. You are that blonde girl, Cariño. Finally you have come and found me. I love you, Cariño.'

The L-word. It jolted me. It all seemed so incongruent – the murdered grandfather, the blowjob, him declaring his love to me. I was confused. Most incongruent of all I was the depth of contentment that filled my soul as I lay in his arms under that tree – as if I had been waiting for an embrace from a man like this since I was a child too. A Rumi quote went through my mind: *What you seek is seeking you.* Had we found each other? As I lay next to him on gnarled roots grown above ground, looking into a scarlet sea, another voice, a quiet intuition nagged in my gut: *Leave or you will die here.*

For the second time that day I thought how tourists only see one side of Spain. What's hidden in the shadows when the sun goes down is too dark for travel articles.

'What happened to your grandmother and mother afterwards?'

He pushed me off him. I wished I'd not asked, not disturbed our brief intimacy.

'Let's go, Cariño. I dare say it will be dark soon and we have fuel to gather.' He looked at the sea. A desolate feeling consumed me, and the voice in my gut whispered: *He will never escape the tragedy of this island's past.* The thought weighed heavy with generations of sadness.

We walked back a different way and passed a house with a large driveway. A sneakiness came over him and he put his finger to his lips, a furtive look around and he indicated for me to copy him. There was a stack of thick chopped branches by the gate and he took some plastic bags from his jacket pocket, held them open while he pointed at the logs for me to fill the bags with them.

Vegetable soup again. We sat opposite each other at dinner in our usual places, me facing the window.

'Are we on rations?'

It was a joke but after our walk on the cliffs I wondered whether the poverty mindset of the Spanish Civil War had somehow been inherited and imprinted on his psyche and had merged with his reality. Miguel was an extremely wealthy man. This frugality was crazy.

He laughed with me.

'But I cook it well, Cariño?'

'Yes, it's delicious.'

'Spanish men can cook.'

'That's true.' *So you keep reminding me.*

'Deiàns were lucky during the war. They could live off the land. I was surprised there are still madroño fruits on the tree. The summer was so long this year. Even the sheep are pregnant again.'

'Climate change. It's screwing up the natural pace of things. Poor sheep.'

He picked up the Fifties recipe book, still on the table. It had become like an ornament along with the vase of wildflowers and the fruit bowl, like one of his phallic sculptures, a symbol of his desires.

'I like desserts. There's probably a madroño cake recipe of my grandmother's in here.'

I dipped a chunk of homemade bread into the soup. I felt pressurised to bake, but baking cakes wasn't me. I flicked through its greasy yellowed pages. Scrawled down the side of one page was what looked like a recipe – madroño something.

'Whose handwriting is this?'

'I dare say that's my grandmother's writing.'

'What does it say?

'It says ...' he walked under the bare low voltage lamp bulb, squinted, then got impatient. 'Something about putting more sugar in madroño jam.'

I wanted to ask again what happened to his grandmother after his grandfather was killed, but I didn't dare.

17

Madroño Jam

Villa Rosa exuded its deceptive peace in the evening's soft shadows as I entered the front door. December lambs baa'd and birds twittered in the olive groves. The mountainside was a deep emerald green. Layer upon layer of pine trees circled the rock crags at the tip of the Teix. The four-thirty sun tipped its rocky peaks in fluorescent pink light and the huge grey face in the mountainside stared down on me like a silent king with pink Mohican hair. Bright red fruits hung high up at the top of the madroño tree directly outside the lounge window, lit up like bulbs on a Christmas tree – the high ones I'd not managed to reach when Miguel sent me out to pick them for madroño jam-making.

I joined him in the kitchen. It was the room in the house where most our arguments started, so I found myself avoiding it.

'Are you certain there were no more fruits higher up, Cariño?'

'Not that I could reach. Too high or too hard.'

He faffed about with the scales getting increasingly stressed about the weights.

'¡Uf! It's not 1 kilo. I only know the right measures for 1 kilo. I dare say I don't know …'

He mumbled something unintelligible, then asked me again, as he did when life didn't do what he wanted it to do.

'… are you sure, Cariño?'

Does he think I can magic madroños out of thin air?

'Yes, my love, they were too high, or too hard. Maybe you can reach them.'

His usual panic started.

'It's a disaster! I dare say I don't know the measures. Oh no!' He tried to read the instructions on the bag of *gelitino* under the low voltage lamp that hung over the oven.

'I don't understand this. Can you read this, Cariño.'

That bloody Fifties recipe book again. It lay open like a book of law, condemning me.

And I did my usual too – tried to keep a level head for both of us.

I took the bag of gelatine from him and held it up to the bare bulb. I had to squint. Dinner was always cooked in a twilight as he was obsessed with saving energy. Not for ecological reasons. *I'll be in glasses within months at this rate.*

Even with my basic Spanish it was easy to understand: '250 kg. It's a 500g packet, so half the packet.' *Why does he get so panicked by such a small thing?*

'Here, Cariño, read what it says in the recipe book.'

He thrust the book towards me. I put my hands behind my back, petulant as a little girl. The book fell on the floor. He did not notice my irritation, or he ignored it.

'You're so clumsy, Cariño.'

As I bent down to pick it up a Vesuvius of emotions erupted. I held them in as I gathered the loose pages and stuffed them back in. One page had broken loose from the binding altogether. When I picked it up I realised it was not a page, but several pieces of letter paper folded and compressed pressed flat between the pages. I stuffed the letter into my pocket with a strange urgency as if I were stealing something and it wanted to be freed.

'Cariño, can you read it to me?'

I read out the instructions in his grandmother's handwriting as best I could, but stuttered and stumbled over the unfamiliar Catalan words.

'Cariño, your pronunciation is better than that.'

'This is Catalan. Or Mallorquín. I'm guessing.'

It was only a recipe for jam, but there was something powerful in the strong shapes of the letters, something deliberate, determined. She had gone over each letter several times with the ink.

'¡Uf! Do I have to do everything, Cariño. Why don't you help me?' Miguel's impatience was irrational. The kitchen became oppressive. One of us was about to explode. I put the book back on the work surface.

'Finish it on your own.'

The letter wanted to be opened too. I walked into the lounge, sat on the sofa by the open fire – at least we had heat after stealing firewood. That was another thing I didn't like about him. Why couldn't he just buy wood?

I unfolded the letter. It was old. The pages were splashed with oil, translucent in areas from decades of grease.

'Cariño, can you help me please?'

I jumped, stuffed the letter in the pocket of my oversized cardigan and walked back into the kitchen.

'Cariño, do you want to make the jam? I dare say it would be good practice for you.'

He doesn't want to make the jam either! The deal was I collect the fruit; he makes the jam.

'I think it's better if you make it.'

Both of us in the kitchen wasn't a good idea. The stress of dozens of dinners was stacking up. Like the washing up he insisted I left and only washed once a day to save water, the balance of another plate precariously placed on top of dirty bowls with spoons and forks left in them looked like it was going to topple over. I tried to make room for the strainer to clean the little red fruits. I'd have liked to know how to make madroño jam, but sensed I should leave the kitchen before he went into one of his mad anxiety panics when things didn't go exactly his way (which changed like the wind so you never knew from one minute to the next what to expect).

'You can help me, Cariño?' He was going to delegate something else for me to do. I could tell by the patronising tone in his voice. 'Can you wash this?'

He handed me the saucepan (I didn't comment on the fact he was wearing his fingerless gloves for cooking) and put it in the sink. A stack of plates wobbled as I brushed them with my hand. I felt his irritation, his panic behind me. What am I not doing in the way he wants it done now?

It reminded me how my father used to hover behind me, directing me. Eventually I would do something wrong – drop a knife, cut my finger – and he would snap. But Miguel was not violent. He didn't shout and rage at me, but the control, the micro-management of every small task felt like an attack. Familiar – that anxiety of his. And mine. Was it his, or was it mine? It was impossible to know. It started as his, but emotions are contagious, they travel like a virus from one person to another.

'No, no, the other one.'

What difference did it make what sink I washed it in?

'No, Cariño. Not like that.' His energy was a tight coil of anxiety behind my back as I hunched further over the sink.

'I can wash up a saucepan without your direction.'

'No! Do it like this …'

I handed him the saucepan.

'I think it's better if you make the jam.'

I walked out of the kitchen, took a breath and went back in.

'I think we should make a rule that we don't use the kitchen at the same time. I can't stand being directed about how to do things basic I do every day of my life.'

He ignored me, as if I'd not spoken. This was something I found disconcerting. If I said something that did not fit with the focus of his direction, he would ignore me as if I had not spoken at all.

'Can you take the garbage, Cariño?'

He handed me the bag. My irritation burned hot in my face. I'd been trying to write my travel article all day and he kept giving me small jobs to do around the house, interrupting my flow.

I took the bag. At least it was an excuse to get out of his presence. I collected the rubbish bags from both bathrooms and marched up to the top of the hill to the communal bins. On the way back I passed another madroño tree. The oldest one in Deià, Miguel had told me once, and the fruit was perfectly ripe, ready to fall. My annoyance dissolved and I reminded myself to enjoy this country life. Deià had worked her magic on me once again.

I used the bottle bag to collect the little fruits. As I picked, looking up into the leafy branches, something sharp fell in my eye. I kept picking as I wanted to return with a big bag of fruit for the jam, but the pain! It stung like a needle. The face in the mountain lit up bright red for a moment in the last shock of sunlight. The king of the mountain looked cross with me.

When I took the bags back to the house my eye was red and very painful. The panic that had been rising in my chest – his panic, now mine – flamed into a fire. Now I'd not be able to write this evening. A whole day lost to housework and doing odd jobs Miguel assigned to me. He used to pay a maid to clean, but he clearly saw me as an opportunity to save money.

'Are you ok, Cariño?'

Now that I was in a panic his voice was calm … as if my panic had calmed him.

'Something fell into my eye.'

'I will prepare a camomile eyewash. Dr Miguel will wash it.'

Rage burned silent and ferocious inside me. It reminded me of the time he had insisted on taking the magnifying glass to my sore vagina to inspect it (I had refused this ridiculous intrusion – he was not a gynaecologist).

I went into the bathroom and cried. The anger fell away with the tears. In its place was claustrophobia. I had to get out of Villa Rosa. Immediately. I took my coat from the peg by the front door and in my hurry to escape marched fast through the gates and ran up the steep lane.

Night had arrived, the day was lost, my productivity was at a low and my deadline loomed. I needed that pay cheque. I'd taken the brunt of the divorce – a combination of my guilt and being married to a New Yorker with a prenup meant I was broke. I would walk away from my marriage with nothing but the clothes on my back. At least I still had my freelance client, but that would not last long if I missed deadlines.

The moon was bright and Deía rested picture perfect beneath it. I crossed the road and kept running until I reached a gate. *We'd walked through this gate on my birthday two weeks before, when I was still living in a fantasy, still had hope in the dream of a new life.* As I stumbled over fallen branches and chalky rocks on the path I reflected that even my birthday was all about him. The walk had been about him living out his fantasy of having outdoor sex with a blonde foreigner like his teenage fantasies at the mirador.

For a birthday gift he gave me one of his novels wrapped in a teacloth. The main character (there were always male exhibitionists from Mallorca now I thought about it) had sex outside with his ex-wife in Deià at the mirador.

At the time it felt liberating compared to the stuffy expensive restaurants my husband took me to. But at least they were restaurants that served my favourite food. What had Miguel said about the cake he baked? *I dare say chocolate is my favourite, Cariño.*

My legs felt weak. I had to sit down. What a fool I'd been! I lay flat on my back as all the energy drained from my body into the cold rocky earth.

The sky was bright with stars. The smell of pine washed away the cloggy, claustrophobic atmosphere of Villa Rosa and my head cleared a little as I lay there. What was I doing here? It was close to Christmas and I was with a Scrooge, sitting in his million Euro house huddled in one room for heat, fingerless gloves and all!

Deià was a beautiful prison. I wanted to go home, but I had no home to go to.

This is your home now, Cariño.

Pain seeped through the pores of my skin. My grief was not new. Miguel was another version of my controlling father. I lay on my back until I could feel my body again, until the numbness had gone, and I could feel the damp from the earth seep in through my skin. When the damp reached my bones I pulled myself together and walked back. Disappointment bit at my heels as I walked along the curved, decked walkway that skirted the road.

I walked slowly, gathering myself. There were no cars that night, no breeze. Stars sparkled just as they had done those first nights dining on the balcony when I thought I'd found the man of my dreams. Nature's immutable constancy calmed my hysteria, but a silent snake of fear churned in my gut, its black tail whipped my groin. From the place where lust first drove me, fear and despair now mingled.

My walk back down the steep alley to Villa Rosa was ambivalent. I knew I should be walking – running – in the opposite direction, but a powerful compulsion led me back, and my mind revolved on thoughts of how I could explain to him his selfishness, how I could inspire the love I craved from him. My awareness was eclipsed by my loud thoughts so I didn't see him until it was too late.

Rake in hand a man barred my way. The neighbour! Miguel's ravings about being attacked by the neighbour with a rake drowned out everything else.

'Fuig, fuig, fuig.'

His hoarse angry voice made me freeze. The white-haired man blocked my way in the middle of the driveway. He stood, legs grounded and banged his rake on the ground. He was shorter than me, wide and stocky.

Adrenaline pumped in my ears. I could not think. I just stood there and stared at him. I should not have left the house. Perhaps Miguel's stories about the crazy inbred locals were true. The neighbour raised his rake and launched into a frenzied babble of Spanish – perhaps it was Catalan or Mallorquín ... I caught stray words.

'FUIG ... LOCO ... PERILLÓS ... FUIG, FUIG.'

My tongue was a lead weight in my mouth.

He waved the rake in the air.

I took a step back.

He pointed the rake towards the road.

'GO.'

Was this a racist warning? Miguel had told me how the locals only tolerated foreigners due to the positive economic impact they had on the town.

'Cariño, who are you talking to?'

Miguel called from a window inside the house. It was a relief to hear him.

It took everything I had to find my voice, like finding your scream in a dream.

'Here.' It was more of a scream than a word.

'Come inside.'

The neighbour made a noise. It came from deep within him, a snarl like a dog might make, and he stepped backwards into the bougainvillea, still waving his rake.

Why hadn't Miguel come outside? Did he remain in the house out of fear for his safety, or did he not realise the neighbour was there? Surely if he knew it was the neighbour, he would have come to my rescue – after all, he had been attacked by him. Hadn't he?

When I opened the gate, hands shaking from the shock of the neighbour's threatening outburst, Miguel was standing at the front door with a torch.

Before he could say anything, I said, 'I'm angry and sad,' and walked straight past him into the bathroom. The childishness of the basic words I'd chosen shamed me – but I'd learnt that in order to communicate my feelings I had to talk to him as if I were talking to a very young child. He would not pick up on my distress unless it was spelt out to him. Either he couldn't pick up on emotions (and I wasn't exactly hiding them) like someone with Asperger's … or he didn't care, I thought as I looked in the mirror at my eye trying to locate the sharp object which was causing me so much pain.

The tiny madroño thorn had worked its way into the inner corner of my eye.

'Don't touch it,' Miguel said. He was by the door.

'Please, stop directing me. Unless you have a cotton bud, you cannot help.'

I improvised with a toothpick wrapped in cotton wool and removed the madroño thorn.

When the pain receded, I went into the lounge. It was lit by a single lamp. Miguel sat on the sofa. He looked like a little boy.

'Cariño, I felt you'd abandoned me. Please don't leave without me again. I didn't think you were coming back. It felt like eternity, like I was waiting for you forever. I was afraid of the neighbour – what he might do if he found you.'

I apologised for not telling him I was leaving the house. How could I tell him I'd feared I'd made a huge mistake leaving my husband to come to live in this tiny town? Miguel was right – the natives were hostile. And although he clearly took the same stance as the forty lawyers who set out to prove George Sand an 'immoral' woman, he was clearly in cahoots with the author when it came to her opinion of the locals. However, since borrowing *A Winter in Majorca* from his library, I imagine Sand would include Miguel as a local on account of his kleptomaniac tendencies for lemons and firewood.

He hugged me, although part of me held back from him, did not submit to his embrace. I was relieved to be safely inside the house and to have strong arms around me, but the shock of the thorn and the neighbour was still in me along with so many unanswered questions. Something didn't add up.

He poured me a glass of red wine and we sat in silence and watched the fire. George Sand was right – in Mallorca the silence is deeper than anywhere else.

With the silence harmony descended. A rare peace I wished would last for eternity.

Miguel broke it and got up to go to bed.

'Are you coming to bed, Cariño?'

'You go ahead. I'll be up soon.'

I took the letter out of my cardigan pocket and unfolded the paper thinned by time, deadened like a flower pressed between pages for decades. It was written in Catalan. An act of rebellion in a time when Catalan was banned, surely? A domestic rebellion. I would need a dictionary. Apart from a few words which jumped out from the page, I could not read it. It was signed *Sofia Valentina Nadal* in large confident letters, so heavily written that the nib of the pen had spurted too much ink for the S of Sofia and left a little explosion like an emoji ink bomb on the tail of the S. Sofia. Was that his grandmother's name or his mother's?

An ancient floorboard creaked on the landing.

'Goodnight, Cariño.' That was his way of saying *hurry up*.

When the flames died to red ash in the grate, I walked upstairs to the bedroom, put on his grandmother's nightdress and got into bed. He was reading.

'Miguel.' He hated being interrupted when he was reading. 'What was your grandmother's name?'

He peered at me over the top of his glasses.

'Sofia.'

'The writing in the margins of the recipe book, did you say it was your mother's or your grandmother's?'

'I don't know, Cariño. It could have been either of them. You do ask jolly silly questions, Cariño.'

He didn't want to talk. His hand moved to my breast, cold and dry, and the letter was forgotten.

18

Debris

Over breakfast I was quiet. Although I never got the impression that Miguel was listening, oddly it bothered him when I wasn't talking. He poured the tea. Black Assam. As one week disintegrated into the next, I found myself eating what he ate and enjoyed it as if I were acquiring his palate.

'I dare say you're quiet this morning, Cariño. Are you jolly ok?'

Yellow sunbeams stretched over the chequered tablecloth, glistened in the fruit bowl on the skin of pomegranates and persimmon (the *kaki* trees he'd pointed out in the hermitage when everything had seemed exotic and possible now appeared ordinary) and lit up the delicate fuchsia petals of the flowers Miguel had picked and put in a vase (he never bought flowers). I'd thought it sweet initially. It was simply part of the seduction.

This could have been any Villa Rosa breakfast. As usual he was agitated to shovel it down as fast as possible and start work. I was yearning to connect and enjoy the short period we had together before the day started. Did I savour each moment together because I knew deep down it would not last, that this sham of a relationship would go the same way as Miguel's previous relationships? This realisation was the reason I was quiet that morning.

My mind was turning over the items at the back of the down-stairs bathroom cabinet. I'd been looking for some Aloe Vera to soothe my eye, which had ballooned up again sore and inflamed as it had done on and off since the madroño thorn incident, and had come across more Italian beauty products with the logo of the naked woman covered in flowers. Same logo as in the en suite. Shampoo, body cream, massage oil – women's possessions. The oil triggered thoughts of intimacy shared between Miguel and his ex, but that was not what disturbed me. It was the debris of a failed relationship – the bottles were the surviving remnants of the fall-out. Would my selection of bottles and potions neatly stacked in front of the mirror go the same way? Would the next woman find my things in the cupboard? Would she see the labels in English, Walgreens and Dr. Hauschka and wonder what favour of intimacy we had shared? Disappointment, increasingly familiar, muted me. That quiet voice of the intuition, the deep knowing that our days as a couple were numbered, that my things would have the same, sad fate, stuffed at the back of the bathroom cupboard. Debris of my disappointment.

How did their relationship end? He'd never been clear. The remnants of Alessandra (the debris and the bits and pieces he'd told me, or let slip) seemed to construct the shape of someone quite lovely in my mind. Beautiful (I'd seen her photo, a screen-saver on his computer screen, which he'd since changed to a photo of me). Talented (although he played down her musical accomplishments), I'd listened to one of her CDs I'd found in the rack. The face on the cover matched the screensaver. Kind (he said she turned cold).

I reached for the jar of madroño jam (a reused mustard jar).

'What happened to her, your ex?'

'She went back to Italy.'

'Why?'

'Do you really want to talk about this, Cariño?' He got up, walked round the back of me and started to touch my neck, kiss my ear. 'What shall we do today? Do you want to swim?'

He's avoiding my question. Why does he do that?

I let it go.

Miguel walked to the window. The beauty of the olive groves always struck me like the first time.

'Graves once said Deià is already-painted.'

I ignored his repetition. He was like a broken record sometimes.

'Did you meet him?'

He carried on looking at the Cala. 'Today is not a good day to swim. What do you think, Cariño?'

'Why not? The sun is out and it's already warm.' Coming from a cold damp island I couldn't see what the problem was. I noticed Mallorcans didn't swim in winter, but it wasn't properly cold.

'I dare say I see fur on the surface of the sea.'

His accent was sometimes so thick it was difficult to understand him as he'd learnt English from reading books. Although he seemed to think he spoke the language better than I did. He had no self-awareness that his Enid Blyton diction was antiquated. His idea of himself was young and hip.

'Did you say fur?' I couldn't help laughing as I said it.

'The Sirocco is coming. Graves wrote a poem about the Sirocco. I will find it for you.'

He became agitated and started mumbling to himself. He mumbled when he didn't want to talk about something.

This little thing he was doing for me made me glow inside – how wonderful to be with a man with poetry in him. Miguel dashed upstairs to the library. Then ran back down. I imagined him running about the place when he was the boy who read voraciously in Deià's hillsides, learning English from books.

'Here it is.' He opened the book and showed me the poem.

I took a breath and readied myself to read Graves' poem out loud … 'Sirocco at Deya' … but Miguel's rising impatience stopped me in my tracks. He started to mumble again. This time I caught the meaning of the Spanish: his editor needed a quote for the opening of his new book. The disappointment I'd felt in the bathroom looking at the Italian product labels echoed painfully through the chambers of my heart. His frantic search for the quote was not for me. Miguel grabbed the book from my hands.

'Yes, yes, there is too much fur on the surface of the water for swimming.' A pinch of envy – how I would have loved to have that knowledge in me, for to acquire it would have meant a lifetime watching the sea from this house and learning the signs of the winds on the surface of the water. That was the moment, standing beside the window, that I realised I had fallen in love with Deià. And like all moments in that house, the feeling was tarnished by disappointment.

'Then let's swim now before the Sirocco arrives.'

'Cariño, we must work. You spend too long at breakfast. It is nearly 10:30.'

His impatience was at fever pitch. He snatched the book from my hands and walked back into the living room, flicking through it, oblivious to me. 'She needs a quote … I do not know which one.'

I followed him upstairs to the library, still disappointed that the quote had not been for me but a ruse to divert the conversation to what he needed … but then I had never published a novel and perhaps he was under huge stress from his editor.

'Can I help you?'

Engrossed in stressing about the quote, he did not hear me.

I looked at the shelves. Bottom row devoted to yellow hard back bound dictionaries. Catalan – English, another Catalan – Italian, another – and another. How many broken relationships had he had? The dictionaries reminded me of the letter. I'd forgotten about it. I put my hand in the deep pocket of my cardigan. Still there. I held my breath and removed my hand slowly as if I was afraid he might sense the secret folded in my pocket. I looked up the rows – a lot of fiction, just as much history, so many languages. As I started to take the poetry books from the shelves to help him, I made a mental list of the Spanish Civil War books I would return to, the books about Catalonia. I'd start by re-reading Orwell's *Homage to Catalonia*. I'd learn the culture of my new home from books as he had learnt English from them, walk Deià's hillsides as he did as a boy and read in the winter sunshine. By Spring I'd speak some Catalan – *and I will have translated his grandmother's letter.*

'What sort of quote do you need?'

He looked at me angry at first that his mutterings were interrupted, then a blank expression fell over his face as if I was a stranger and he was bewildered as to why I was there at all. I felt as though I might be a shadow, a ghost. I clenched my nails into my palms to bring back the feeling of being real. Then, sudden as a lizard darting across a wall, his whole demeanour changed.

'Thank you, Cariño. Yes, I dare say you can help me.'

With the sun streaming in, we sat together, and I consoled myself that the sea would still be there tomorrow and at least he was aware of my presence now.

'I dare say my editor needs a quote about relationships and the sea. Two themes of my novel.'

Miguel dumped Robert Graves' book on my lap. Then abruptly snatched it back from me and in a sort of mania started to thrash about on his bookshelves talking to himself in Spanish in an angry voice. I carried on looking for sea related quotes, eager to please him.

I held up the book, opened on the page with another Graves quote.

'What about this?'

'No, no. That's nothing to do with the theme of the novel.'

It struck me that he had been vague about what the book was about.

'What's the book about?'

An agitated shiftiness came over him. His head practically went in the book in his hand like he was trying to avoid the question.

'A relationship between a man and a woman.'

'It will help me focus on what to look for …'

He frowned, walked back downstairs and started talking to himself, walking in circles around the living room table. 'Exposure. That's what I need to be careful of.'

'What are you worried about?'

'It's the ending. Maybe I have given away too much.'

'How does it end?'

'He kills her.'

The sentence sent a shockwave through my body that made me freeze.

Miguel stopped in his tracks and stared at the fruit bowl. The same yellow sunbeam illuminating the skin of the fruit lent a jaundiced shade to his olive skin. His brow creased and the shadows beneath his eyes were tinted dark purple as if he'd been punched. He looked like a tired old man. I reminded myself he was sixty years old after all, but there was a dark intensity to him as if a thick cloud surrounded him and I was on the outside and the morning light could not penetrate.

I felt afraid and I did not know why.

'Tell me the story,' I heard myself say, but part of me didn't want to know. I remembered the murders in his other novels – all crimes of passion, all unnecessary wastes of human life, and even more disturbing, all justified by the narrator who suggested that the murders were the fault of the victims.

As if surrendering – to my question or burnt out on the anxiety that had driven him all morning – he slumped on the sofa, stared at the polished wood floor in front of him and let out a sigh that sounded like a suffering animal.

'She deserved it, the woman. She had to go, but it was difficult to kill her. I think I made her too much like Alessandra.'

The name lodged in my throat.

'You based the female character on your ex you mean?'

For the first time he looked at me, then looked away.

'Does that bother you, Cariño? All writers do it.'

'No, I'm just trying to understand the story. Getting it out of you is like getting blood from a stone.'

'What did you say?'

This was probably too colloquial.

'So what happens, what's the story? There's a murder at the end, but where does it happen, what's the motive?'

My light-hearted tone sounded strained in the heavy atmosphere clouding the sunny room, making it seem as if we were in an oppressive bibliographic microclimate different from the wide horizon with the sea in the distance on the other side of the library window.

'You really want to know?'

My heart skipped.

'Why wouldn't I?'

'My editor said she couldn't see the female character but that she got a good idea of the man. The man, he's from Mallorca. And the woman, she's Italian. They meet, fall in love, have lots of sex … outdoors. You like sex outdoors, don't you, Cariño?'

He started to touch me. I became aware of his skin, of the hair on his legs, of a strange low-level fear humming inside me mingled with my rising desire. But I had to know.

'This story, it's fiction, but is the sex in it autobiographical?'

'Autobiographical? No, well some of it. Some of it happened. Not all of it. It took me a long time to decide how to end it. And when you arrived I knew. You are my star, my lucky shamrock. You gave me the ending. It was you coming to Villa Rosa that first day when you opened the gate and walked up the path. I knew then she had to die.'

'Nice to know I inspired a murder!'

He laughed.

I laughed.

We needed to laugh to break the atmosphere. There was something disturbing in it the remnants of which still hang in me like laundry that refuses to dry in a damp climate. A disquiet at this talk of murder and lust. Debris of a broken relationship. And fear. I ignored it. I was becoming accustomed to brushing off so many little things. He's a writer. They're odd, all that time they spend in their heads making up stories.

He stood up, a sudden change in his energy like he was feeding off my fear, fuelled by the confusing electricity in the atmosphere, took out his polla and offered it to me. What was it about his cock that I found so fascinating, so irresistible, unnerving and so unsettlingly familiar at the same time?

19

Agony

Moonbeams cast striped light through the shutters of the bedroom giving Miguel the appearance of a naked convict. He liked to break and enter. Foreplay wasn't his thing. We were compatible in that respect I guess. His hunger made me feel desired which nurtured me somehow, made me feel like I existed. After being ignored all day and his agitation and preoccupation about finding a quote for his novel, which went on for over a week, it was a relief to feel solid again.

'You want it from behind, Cariño?' There was not an ounce of tenderness in his haste. Coquettish, I pushed him away playfully, but he did not take the hint. That was Miguel. When he wanted something, my desires were irrelevant.

'No, I don't.' My voice was small, endeavouring to maintain intimacy but there was only him in the room now. Only his overshadowing desire.

'You want anal sex, don't you Cariño. Yes, you do.'

'Miguel, stop. I don't want it.'

He kept thrusting.

'You like it.'

I moved forward on the bed and he fell out of me. Damn him and his fantasies.

'Cariño, what's wrong?'

'I said I don't do anal.'

'But it is for your pleasure. I dare say you will like it.'

His Enid Blyton speech tick lost its charm.

'*I dare say* I don't want to.' My sarcasm killed any intimate pretence.

'But Cariño, don't be like this. I know you will like it. Come here.' His smell engulfed me again. 'The Lover made his bed between agony and pleasure.'

Agony and pleasure? Oh, he's quoting Ramon Llull. Like he did at the Hermitage. It reminded me of my silent vow and how I was ready to say, *I do.* It was different then. I longed to return to that mystical sense of magic on my first visit when everything seemed possible.

We fell into each other again and he started to tell me a story, one of his fantasies. Like the sex it started off mutually pleasurable and then became all about him and his solitary fantasy world.

'… and in the sex club I allow the man to fuck you up the arse. You want his polla. It's not as big as mine is it, Cariño?'

I was just a hole. I could have been any hole. Part of me dissolved, disintegrated and from nowhere a rage rose up inside me and challenged him.

'If you want to have group sex so much put your cock where your mouth is and let's go to a couples club.'

He'd been pestering me about swinging for weeks.

'You want to, Cariño? Si, si, si …' The idea delivered his climax.

I was left dissatisfied. He couldn't be present. Always drifting off into one of his bloody stories. The idea of being in a relationship with a novelist had been appealing, but I hadn't considered the negative consequences of him bringing his work into the bedroom.

I finished myself off in the en suite. The little window looked up towards the Teix and the outline of a lonely olive tree against the clear ink blue sky made me sad. My climax left me with a yearning like winter branches reaching up, begging the moon for sunlight.

Tomorrow I would swim in the Cala no matter how much he protested. How could I go from a husband who gave me all the freedom in the world to a man who made a big fuss if I wanted to swim alone?

He was sitting up in bed watching me as I walked over to my side. The painting of the woman nursing her baby was still on the wall above the dresser despite me telling him it gave me the creeps, like he was enforcing a silent message.

'Have you ever wished you had bigger tits, Cariño?'

A cruel comment but I had that strange déjà vu feeling again which made it sort of comfortable and intimate.

'When I was young, yes, but now I'm glad they're still pert and don't sag.'

'I am looking forward to some big tits at the club. I dare say I am a man who likes big tits.'

All of a sudden his carefully groomed beard and tash made me think of drawings of Pancho Sanchez and Don Quixote on the front cover of his edition in Villa Rosa's library.

'I was joking. The club's a bad idea.'

'But you said you'd been to clubs like that before. You liked it.'

'I liked it at the time, but I was young, exploring. It's a bad idea to go with someone you love.'

I'd explored my sexuality briefly in my teens before I settled down with the naïve belief that I knew myself. Miguel had sent everything I thought I knew about myself out of the window.

I married for love, but had I really been in hiding, playing it safe?

That Friday night we drove down the mountain to Palma, past the Cathedral and up to an elevated residential neighbourhood overlooking Palma harbour. The car pulled into a small car park in front of a converted house. Miguel was nervous. I was not. I knew what to expect.

Miguel paid without complaining about the price. That made a change. A dark passageway separated the real world from the club proper and my heels echoed in the silent tunnel of a corridor. We turned a corner and the throb of bass from the speakers made the anticipation in my belly pulsate to the same beat.

The bar was modern backlit glass so that the bottles of alcohol glowed like multi-coloured church candles. Blue shone through Sapphire gin. Vodka glowed white and Cava and Champagne bottles glistened absinthe green. Black walls and tables were lit by little red lamps, mini-lightsabers that gave the place a sci-fi feel like being in a spaceship. Two large screens played silent porn.

Three couples sat naked in pairs.

The barman's friendly smile put me at ease. He was young with tattoos on his arms and made me think of baristas in trendy coffee shops. Inked for fashion, no deeper meaning I speculated as he had a lightness about him.

'Hola, how are you guys?' He had that relaxed way like you were old friends typical to the Spanish (with the exception Miguel).

'Great, thanks.' I returned his smile.

Miguel mumbled.

On the bar was a sweet jar full of plastic wristbands. Miguel and I had discussed the rules over breakfast – for a change he'd sat at the table with me instead of eating in the kitchen standing up.

He'd looked up the club online – they had a strange way of coding preferences using wristbands. Green meant anything goes, pink women only, and black was partner only. I chose pink. Miguel chose green.

I felt out of place and uncomfortable as, other than the barman, we were the only people wearing clothes. Rather than listen to Miguel mumbling at me to hide his anxiety while attempting to look without looking (an art men rarely master), I suggested we explore. I'd already checked out the clientele with discretion. All the women wore black wristbands.

'Shall we go inside?'

'But Cariño, we get a free drink.'

Of course, Miguel must have his pound of flesh.

The barman pointed in the direction of another dark corridor. His tattooed bicep made me impatient to hit the club. Miguel kept me aroused but never satisfied me.

'You can change through there.'

Miguel had said he didn't care if I played with women. I had prepared myself that I might witness Miguel having sex with someone else, but now I was in here I just felt angry at him and at myself for putting up with the crumbs he threw me.

I left my drink (along with Miguel's frustration at his failing to control my movements without losing his temper) at the bar. The women's changing room resembled those at old-fashioned swimming pools with its wooden benches, hooks and lockers. The smell of chlorine was replaced by musky essential oils burning in alcoves decorated with ornate Asian style furniture.

I wanted to be naked, but Miguel insisted I wore a corset, which had belonged to his ex. I'd chucked it back at him and told him to wear it himself. After persuading me that she'd never worn it as it was too small, I agreed, but was uncomfortable wearing her seconds. My husband used to buy me made-to-measure lingerie when we first met. I'd worn the corset partly to shut Miguel up and partly as I couldn't be bothered to go shopping in Palma. It wouldn't be on me long anyway.

The bed was enormous. A red glow from the hallway lights saturated the mattress. We were in one of the six rooms leading off a main corridor. Miguel had been attracted to a woman in her forties. She was with a short man. Miguel followed her in.

'They look jolly interesting.'

It was not the man he was referring to, but I was aware that the man had zoomed in on me, a predatory eagle look that spotted its prey from a distance. That look reminded me of something else, something I did not have the sight to see at the time. I whispered to Miguel. 'Remember, you need to protect me. I don't want to have sex with any man except you.'

'Yes, yes. Of course I will protect you, Cariño.'

We were on the bed, all four of us. Neither of them wore wristbands. The woman and I kissed, touched, played with each other's nipples with coyness. I remembered this too – how women did not assume like men that other women were game, but tiptoed one step at a time. Even with my pink wristband she was sounding me out. Miguel looked as though he was going to move in on the woman, but he was not ready. It was small conciliation that his dysfunction was not only with me. His droop was accompanied with his usual air of both arrogance and self-conscious anxiety.

Miguel whispered in my ear. 'The people in this club are not beautiful enough to turn me on.'

I did not say what I was thinking: *What on earth do you think you are, some young stud? You're the oldest man here by a long shot! Do you think those young women look at your sagging arse and swoon?*

To hell with him. He's spent over a month wearing me down, nagging me about going to a couples club. He knew I didn't want to come here. Now I'm here I intend to enjoy myself.

I relaxed into the couple giving me their undivided attention. Miguel fiddled with the woman's nipples, his gaze constantly on his own cock. I closed my eyes and sunk further into the pleasure of more than one pair of hands expertly caressing me.

All of a sudden I felt a thrust from behind. It took me by surprise. I gasped, looked behind me and saw the short, broad man. It added to my surprise to hear him speak English as previously the couple had spoken in Spanish – 'Sexy pussy, sexy pussy.'

I clenched, entry barred. Looked to Miguel. He did nothing. There was a moment in which I could have resisted, but the inertia of my heightened arousal overcame me and I relaxed. To hell with Miguel. I didn't want to come here anyway. I removed my wristband and relaxed.

What a relief to feel properly devoured by a man. Although I felt tricked – him and the woman had worked together to prepare me.

'Are you ok, Cariño?' He sounded like a lost boy.

What could I say with a sturdy lusty man inside me and a woman who kept me rising to climax with her hands?

Afterwards we talked. The man was a captain from Plymouth. His girlfriend was Portuguese. They lived together in Palma, but he was at sea a lot. She was nice and attractive. After they'd gone I asked Miguel why he'd not had sex with her.

'I did not fancy her. It's late, Cariño. Let's go.'

'We've only just got here.' There was no way I was leaving. He'd made such a fuss about the club, manipulated me and run circles around all my protestations. I didn't want to go to a sex club with a man that I loved, but as usual I submitted to his desires. One orgasm was not going to satisfy me.

'I'm tired, Cariño.'

Four tanned, toned young bodies bounced playfully into the room. The women jumped on the bed next to us giggling and the men stood at the side of the bed, their young erections ready. The women started to give them fellatio, swapping every few sucks. One of the women was extraordinarily beautiful with pert little breasts.

I moved to leave. Miguel followed me, his face distressed at his droop. I didn't have the heart to insist we stay in the presence of those fine young erections.

As we left, he hardened and took me into the nearest empty room and began to focus on me. It was so very pleasing to feel him, just me and him, the sounds of other people's pleasure coming from the adjacent room. Just as we were getting somewhere, he stopped and insisted we went back into the room next door.

Two tight buttocks with the girls' heads bobbing. Miguel stood next to the young men, a row of three. I knelt next to the girls, and for a brief moment the phalli statues in Miguel's garden and those in the secret room at the Naples Museum formed a collage with those belonging to the men. The beautiful girl stopped momentarily and smiled at me. She demonstrated on her partner and nodded for me to do the same – with sanctity as though we were performing some ancient rite. I followed suit. Then she swapped. I felt Miguel soften in my mouth. What was it that triggered his loss of arousal? She took him in her mouth. We swapped back, she lay on her back with her legs spread and told me to do the same.

I did so. She screamed as her partner made love to her. People crowded into the small room to watch this free young woman take her long, enjoyable journey to orgasm. I wanted so very much to journey with her, our pleasure feeding off each other, mounting, making the final outcome even more intense, everyone's hands helping, supporting us to climax. But Miguel wasn't up for the task. He kept looking down, saying,

'It was working earlier!'

Nobody took any notice of him.

'It was working earlier, wasn't it, Cariño?'

I couldn't see the point of answering him, but as he kept saying it louder and louder, I agreed like a mother pacifying a child.

'Yes, darling, it was.'

We left.

When I got to the car I looked behind me. Miguel was nowhere to be seen.

I went back inside and found him in the bar talking with the Portuguese woman who was explaining to him where she lived. There was something about the way he had tuned into her that I found unsettling. We'd not discussed talking, but this felt like more of a betrayal. Sex would have been part of our agreement. Charming her address out of her was not.

As we sat stationary in traffic alongside Palma harbour I stared out over the ocean.

'Did you like it, Cariño?'

I was a mess of contradictory responses. On the one hand it was a relief to have sex. It is one thing to abstain entirely as I had done for years, but to constantly have a man arouse you and then disappoint without making any attempt to find another way to satisfy you is beyond frustrating.

'Did you?'

'No. I dare say I thought I would, but I was wrong.'

'What didn't you like about it?'

'I was not in control.'

My heart pinched at the word and my mind expanded into comprehension. In his fantasies about group sex he was always in control. In the club, we worked as a group, as a team, and Miguel was unable to collaborate. It was all about him. I'd initially thought that Miguel was just a selfish lover (which he was), but as we sat there in the traffic and the twinkling harbour lights I wondered if he purposefully kept me in a permanent state of arousal as it was easier to control me that way.

'The clubs are about other people's pleasure.'

'I don't care about other people's pleasure.'

'How do you feel about watching me have sex with another man?'

'I didn't like it.'

'But you fantasise about it.'

'In my fantasies I decide who fucks you.'

'Then why didn't you protect me from him?'

'I was confused, Cariño. You looked like you wanted to.'

Nausea and confusion silenced me all the way back up the mountain to Deià.

20

Scrooge

From Deià to Soller, the neighbouring town over the other side of the Teix, the drive was breath-taking. We passed Lluc Alcari. That walk down to the rocks seemed tame now and a lifetime away. We'd not spoken about the club again, but I sensed it brewing inside him.

I'd got used to the hairpin bends and did not look over the edge of the cliffs as the car swung round sharp corners. Miguel caressed my bare leg. Whenever he didn't need both hands to drive we held hands. We acted like lovers, but it felt like a pretence. I pushed the thought aside and colluded in our game and stroked the hairs on his leg trying not to touch the skin, pacifying him, hoping the storm that I sensed would not break.

You're living in your shadow. That voice again, a man's voice with a German accent, the voice from my dreams. They were becoming more frequent and Carl Jung in his wire-framed glasses was now haunting my daylight world too. Rationalists would say I had an active temporal lobe. *I'm drinking in my present,* was my inner reply and I melted further into the idyllic landscape, into the sensation of the hairs on his tanned leg under my palm, and listened to Miguel's voice. He didn't mumble when he lectured.

'Soller was totally detached from Deià during its medieval heyday. The Kingdom of Mallorca traded with Italy and France rather than the mainland. I dare say due to the mountain – there was only access on foot. ¡Joder!'

I grabbed the handle above the window. He swerved a group of cyclists as we rounded the bend. One of them shook his arm in anger at us.

'I fantasise about driving them off the road.'

'We missed them. Carry on – I want to understand everything about Mallorca.' My encouragement for him to continue was to calm his nerves. I didn't hold his hand again.

'This road. It is quite new. During the War Civil it was more of a track. Women used to have sex with soldiers in exchange for sugar on this road. The black market was rife in the War Civil ...' he continued, but his tone had changed. A silent rage simmered and vibrated on his vocal cords. It put me on edge for the rest of the drive, and I found myself wondering if his grandmother had sex for sugar. It must have been hard for her after her husband was murdered. The morning after my first night at Villa Rosa he'd told me about the black market trade in sugar when we took this road to Lluc Alcari. He didn't mention the currency of exchange then.

'I cannot see you the same way again, Cariño. You are not the woman I thought you were. You are a different sort of woman.'

So here it was. The fallout from the club. It felt like I'd been stabbed in the heart.

'We went there for your pleasure.' My lips pursed.

'You are a different woman to me now.'

He might as well have called me a whore.

'There is only one type of woman,' I snapped.

I was enraged. The bloody Catholic virgin-whore thing. He'd better not suggest I go to confession. This insult ran deep. I wanted to explode, but I knew this would come. The tension had been building over the days since the visit to the club.

I breathed, pushed it aside. Told myself to ignore him. This was meant to be a nice day out away from Villa Rosa. I wasn't going to let him spoil my day.

We parked in Soller harbour and walked through steep narrow streets. Miguel was an elastic band ball of impatience and agitation, grabbing me by the arm with unnecessary pinches to move me this way and that through the crowds. I wanted to stroll and enjoy the scenery, saunter through the streets as a couple in this little fishing town turned tourist haven. He wanted to get to the fish market before all the best fish had gone.

The fish market was undercover. It smelt like fish markets all over the world. The wet, briny smell chilled my nostrils. Miguel made a show of asking me what I wanted. When it didn't match what he wanted he convinced me otherwise. I took his view – he knew his native fish best.

Why's he buying so much?

'We won't eat all this fish! I leave for New York before Christmas.'

He mumbled something.

We'd shared food money in a kitty. That had been my idea in an attempt to dissolve the awkwardness when we reached supermarket tills. Miguel liked the idea and had stuffed all the notes into his wallet before we left Villa Rosa. We wouldn't need all of it, but I said nothing.

'I like this kitty idea, Cariño. I paid for everything with Alessandra.'

Was it my imagination or did he pronounce her name extra slow and with feigned longing in his voice every time he said it?

'To begin with I liked it – I'd never been a provider before. My ex-wife paid for everything. I was spoilt. So I thought, why not? It would be good for me to do that for a change. But after six months I didn't like it anymore. It began to bore me. She got a job as a cleaner as her Spanish wasn't good enough for an office job.'

There was something odd about it. Money is a difficult subject in a relationship, but surely he could have supported her until her Spanish improved. She'd left Italy to live with him after all. And surely he was loaded. Villa Rosa alone must be worth at least two million Euros. Every book he published was translated into twenty languages and were instant bestsellers – some had even been adapted for film. I knew writers only earned pennies per book, but surely he had money.

'So what happened after that?'

'Well, she didn't speak Spanish. But she learnt quickly.'

I didn't like the judgemental tone in his voice.

'Then she thought she spoke Spanish better than me!'

Hypocrite. He thinks he speaks fluent English! Half the time I struggle to understand him. I didn't tell him he sounded like a character in a Famous Five novel.

Never rely on this man. That faraway voice, the voice from my dreams. It drowned inside me. What happened to his ex-girlfriend anyway? I still wasn't clear.

'You never explained how the relationship ended.'

'Well … you know, these things. In the end she turned cold.'

'But what was the last thing you said to each other? When was the last time you saw each other?'

His face changed. The familiar darkness descended as if the fluorescent lights had been dimmed over the whole market. The airy height of the ceiling and clean, icy smell was replaced by a claustrophobic overwhelm of fish guts and nausea. I want to get out into the fresh air.

'Let's go.' He was abrupt, snatched me by the arm and led me out.

He weaved me through the cobbled streets in and out of the crowds, his grip clenched my upper arm like a parent dragging a badly behaved child away from the playground. I felt sad as I watched the stalls pass me by – the grief of missing out on Saturday morning market life we might never live again. And a deeper grief – of losing my soul.

We passed a cake shop. I asserted myself.

'Let's go in. The cakes look delicious.'

'We can't afford it, Cariño.'

Did he spend all the money from the kitty on fish? We had fifty Euros in the kitty this morning.

'How much was the fish?'

'I bought polpo and Sobresada.'

'Why? I'm leaving in a few days. And what's Sobrasada?'

'You've never tasted Sobrasada? You will love it. Come on, let's go, Cariño. It is for you – for our special Christmas dinner.'

'Oh, that's sweet.'

'Come on, Cariño.'

'But I've not seen the town.'

'I dare say we'll return. You live here now.'

'I've not had a coffee for days.' Miguel only drank tea. 'I'll pay.'

And then he did that thing I never got used to. He creased up his face, dropped his left shoulder and slouched into the exasperated stance of a teenager.

'Cariñooooo.' His wining tone matched his stance – as if I was his mother preventing him from doing something he wanted to do.

'I'm getting an espresso. You can wait here if you want.'

He followed me into the café. As soon as we were inside his demeanour changed and he started to behave very strangely, looking around to see if anyone was looking at him, tilting his chin and holding his expression for way too long like I used to do as a young girl posing for a photo. In a sixty-year-old man it was embarrassing.

'Cariño, would you like cake?' He said it loud as if addressing an audience.

Was there anyone in particular he was parading himself for? The only other customers were a well-dressed German couple seated by the window who were far too busy flirting with each other to pay any attention to us.

The girl behind the counter smiled as she placed the coffee and cake on the counter and waited for me to work out which coins to give her.

'No, Cariño, please.' He pushed away my hand with the ten Euro note. It gave me a head spin. Didn't he say only a moment ago that he'd spent all the kitty money?

We sat at a table in a cosy alcove that looked like it had been designed for old-fashioned courting couples, but we were far from that. I watched as Miguel spooned the sugar, heap after heap with the greed of an addict.

'Sugar is carcinogenic.'

He ignored me. Sipped, clattered his cup in its saucer, pulled a face and added more sugar with such nervousness granules splattered across the table like shrapnel.

I tried to ignore him.

I like coffee shops. I work in them, read in them, zone out in them. And the coffee here was good, but with Miguel's agitation and strange, loud projection of his voice in English about odd subjects he didn't have the vocabulary for, I couldn't relax. I drank my coffee and let him finish the cake (he'd ordered one piece to share). His version of sharing meant one quarter for me and the rest for him.

Dinner was another story. Miguel knew how to create an atmosphere of seduction. He lit the candles on the table. The Juliet balcony doors were closed, but the church was lit up and we sat and watched the twinkling lights of the village. It was an unusually mild night so close to Christmas, but Miguel's hypochondria made him so fearful about catching a cold that I didn't bother suggesting sitting outside in hats and scarves.

'Sobrasada is made with minced pork and spices.'

I had expected it to be a sausage, but instead Miguel put a side plate in front of me with a tiny piece of stale bread (toasted and burnt at the edges) with a bright orange paste and a drizzle of honey.

'Um, delicious!' I hadn't expected it to taste so good. I didn't like eating pork as pigs are more intelligent than dogs. I hoped they had at least led good lives until the Mallorcan festive season. In Sand's time they didn't.

Miguel had several pieces of toasted stale bread, two of which I saw him stuffing into his mouth in the kitchen before he came into the dining room.

Then he brought in the vegetable soup.

'I really like the sobrasada.' Surely that was just a taster to see if I liked it.

'Good, Cariño.' He kissed my neck.

'Can I have some more?' I felt like Oliver Twist in the workhouse. Difference was I'd paid for the food.

'Cariño, it is not good to eat too much sobresada. We won't have any left.'

'Won't have any left for what?'

He stroked my neck. 'Come on, Cariño. You don't want anymore.'

'Yes, I do. A bowl of soup and a stale crust of bread isn't enough. What happened to all that fish we bought – the octopus and all that seafood?'

'It's in the freezer. Come on, eat.' He kissed me and I felt a strong urge to chuck the bowl of soup in his face. I tried to keep my voice level, but the anger was difficult to control.

'Why did you put it in the freezer? I leave for New York the day after tomorrow.'

'Tut! We bought so much. We won't eat it all.'

'Did you tut?'

'Cariño, what's wrong with you? I didn't know you wanted it now. We have all those vegetables to eat. They'll go bad if we don't eat them today.'

'I thought this was our Christmas dinner. You are like Scrooge!'

'Scrooge, Cariño?'

'Charles Dickens' character Scrooge.'

He knew the reference. He laughed.

'Do you think I limit myself? Maybe you are right, Cariño. Maybe I should not limit myself.'

The image superimposed over Miguel of him stuffing his face with sobrasada under the dim single bulb in the kitchen, licking the knife quick so as not be caught like a thief. He was a Scrooge.

I ate the soup and looked out across the valley. I didn't say anything more about it, but a silent rage smouldered inside me. *Thank God I have a ticket out of here ... but when I've tied up the loose ends in New York, I have to return. What have I done? That this was now my home made me feel sick. What am I doing here in this deserted town in winter? Two days until I am out of here.*

'Come on, Cariño. I want something sweet. Let's make a hot chocolate and rum. I have something that will make you happy.'

Miguel went upstairs and I heard him open a drawer in the desk in the library with a key, then close it again.

He came back down and put his hands over my eyes. The feel of his dry skin excited me.

'Inhale.'

I inhaled. Grass.

'Where did you get that?'

'A friend. I don't like to take it myself. It makes me paranoid, but maybe we should try a little together. Would you like that, Cariño?'

He crumbled a tiny amount into the hot chocolate. I grabbed the grass from him and added more. He protested. I ignored him. I needed to get trashed, relieve myself from the anxiety of being around him. I needed to escape.

What the fuck is he doing with that teaspoon?

I don't believe it! He's going to ration the rum too.

'Give me that. I'll add my own rum.'

'But I'm the director, Cariño.'

'You can control the sobresada rations, but you're not rationing my rum. You really are a bloody Scrooge!'

He laughed.

'¡Cariño!'

I knocked back the rum, grass and hot chocolate and made another one ignoring his protests, put on some dance music and started to sway in the lounge. My fingertips were still numb, but the movement and the rum warmed the rest of me.

Miguel had the rhythm of a Thunderbirds puppet, all arms and legs. Graceless. He was no Spaniard in that respect either. As my anger, anxiety and frustration at his control and stinginess melted into a mellow glow we danced in front of the open fire. Then we made love.

For once he remained hard without falling into his preposterous fantasies, which I had lost all patience with after the sex club.

'Cariño, it's like being an adolescent again. Can you feel it?'

'Yes, darling. I can.'

His pleasure increased. I lost myself to that rare moment. Just as I was close to climax, he got up, frantic, ran off, left me there on the rug, cold without his body to warm me. I turned my head and watched the flames. An orange spark jumped out of the fire and landed on the plastic cover of a book he'd stolen from Palma library. A momentary fizz, then the spark was gone, a black hole in its place. It was a Graves book, the one he'd taken the quotation from and sent to his editor.

Miguel was back, excited with his laptop.

Surely he's not interrupted our lovemaking – and my orgasm – for porn!

The way he walked in, with a stoop, he really did remind me of old Scrooge from the TV adaptation of *A Christmas Carol*. Naked, he was a cross between Scrooge and a Teenage Mutant Ninja Turtle toy (cartoon lizards with long forward reaching necks that resembled old men). The initial repulsion I'd experienced towards Miguel during our first kiss returned, just for a moment.

Was it his age that had repulsed me or something deeper in his soul: his selfishness?

When he knelt in front of the low coffee table to set up the laptop, my emotions congealed in confusion: that old disappointment that he fetched the laptop just then, just at that moment of real connection, a dark curiosity about his need for porn, my humiliation that I was not enough to arouse him – and rage that my pleasure was ignored. Rage that our lovemaking was all about him.

When I lowered my gaze to his erect polla I was overcome with desire again, walked towards him on my knees, desperate. I no longer cared that he was stingy with the sobresada – as long as he shared his polla with me.

Grunts came from the laptop. Miguel masturbated in front of three men and a woman having group sex.

'Do you want one of them inside you, Cariño?'

'If you want me to, darling.' I remembered his need for control in the club.

'You like my polla, Cariño?'

'Yes.'

'Now I want you to suck one of their pollas and I will watch.'

'Ok.'

'You like it?'

'Yes.'

He rode me from behind watching the porn intently. Then he came.

Afterwards I felt the same as I always did. Dissatisfied, disappointed, hungry for the connection we'd shared on the rug. Or perhaps it was just me who felt it. Maybe his mind was solely in his laptop fantasy.

He went upstairs to bed.

I wrapped myself in a blanket and watched the fire until it went out. I stayed alone in front of the fireplace, in my own fantasy world where this was my home, our home. What was wrong with me to hanker over a man who would half starve me, ignore my existence most of the time and is selfish in bed? It was as if something inside me had split in half. One part had the good sense to message Miranda to ask her to recommend a therapist. The other half wanted to stay and submit to him.

'Cariño, come to bed.'

I went upstairs.

Miguel got out of bed, went to the chest of drawers and took out one of his mother's jaundiced ivory nightdresses.

'Here, put this on. You will get cold.'

The heater was not on that night. The temperature in the bedroom was so low I could see the steam from my breath.

'Cariño, stay for Navidad. We will make love like teenagers again.' His cold, dry, old hand reached over to caress my nipples.

'Your nipples are erect, Cariño. You are excited?'

I did not answer. I was cold, aroused and disappointed. He would do nothing to alleviate my sexual frustration. I was now convinced he liked to keep me hungry.

I turned onto my side, but did not sleep. I wondered if his grandmother had done the same with her husband before he'd been thrown from the mirador. Did he love her? Had he been cruel or kind? I imagined the tears that had been cried into the ivory linen after he'd been taken by Franco's men. I resolved to make a start on translating the letter in the morning. I didn't know why, but I sensed it held a clue, a key perhaps to Miguel's heart.

The numbness moved from my freezing feet to my heart.

21

Euromillionaire

Women. They're all the same. Sugar whores.

A tug on the duvet and my left leg is bare to the chill of the night.

Again, my fingers reach out. Her back is porcelain to the touch; there is moisture in her skin from years wrapped in jumpers, hidden from the sun; it surprised me that she's not made of alabaster, but a far rarer thing that transformed under the sun. She has not burnt as Celtic skin does, but taken on a rich olive colour like my own, like she is part of me.

I reach out again to touch her nipple, but it's the cold shoulder for me tonight. The games lovers play. Why are women so difficult? ¡Uf! It would bore me if she yielded too soon, but how to convince her to sign over her divorce settlement? She insists there's no money. That's a lie. Why do women lie? I like the kitty approach. First, I need her to stay.

Another tug. The pull-push game.

Villa Rosa has seduced her. What is this house worth now? Two million Euros? One short high street and six estate agents. Deià must have one estate agent for every ten inhabitants out of season. A rich American might pay three million. With my inheritance and royalties I could live a different life. If I were another man, I would sell it, travel the world, be free of its ghosts. Escape Deià.

Her skin is ice. She wants the heater on. ¡Uf! We Mallorcans can't afford central heating like rich Northern Europeans. A shard of anger, a bolt of Olympian thunder. The Teix. I see the iron mountain, feel it looming over the thin walls of the house. The old prison feeling. *Save, Miguel. Do not waste your money. We are poor people.*

She wants to bleed me dry, trap me, humiliate me. Make a fool of me. I'm a poor Mallorcan man. At the club. She humiliated me. I am a man who likes to be in control. I understand that now. And she must yield to me. The man must control the finances in a relationship. That is how it must be.

The duvet moves like a swan, graceful with her movement. A small sigh, a sexualised yawn. A slight swish of her buttocks against my polla. I imagine in the darkness her tanned terracotta skin, which retains the oiled sheen of porcelain even in the summer.

I will not give her what she wants.

She must pay for that.

Sugar whores, all of them.

22

Bloody Lip

Wednesday was market day. We stood on the driveway to Villa Rosa in the morning light. Lemon sunbeams criss-crossed through the branches of olive trees, the torrent gushed with new violence down in the valley, and when I breathed in the winter air the cold stabbed my throat. A bird swooped overhead. I looked up at the wall of rock. That's why it's so damp. The Teix.

'I dare say it's better you go shopping now before all the best vegetables are gone, Cariño. I'll be home by nightfall.'

Miguel handed me the rest of the notes and coins from the kitty. I leave tomorrow. I was exhausted from too little sleep and cold to the bone from being in that freezing bedroom and there was a tight warning in my chest that my asthma might set off if I didn't warm myself up. Palma was warmer than Deià. I tried again.

'I could just sit in the sun on a bench while you have your appointment.' It would dry out my lungs.

'We talked about this, Cariño. We decided it's jolly you stay in Deià.'

He'd decided. The conversation had been with himself as if I were invisible – worse than invisible, for even Villa Rosa's ghost, real or imagined, had some impact on him and could make its presence felt.

Miguel made such a fuss about me not going to Palma. The mysterious pull he exerted over me had me anxious at the idea of being separated from him. Why had I become so clingy? *What's wrong with me?* This was the question I would ask a therapist. Tomorrow I would fly out of Palma airport. Miranda had replied to my message and said she'd get back to me.

My mind was made up: I would not be coming back. Not for the first time, I felt like a dying man savouring the pleasure of his last cigarette. I inhaled the look of him, along with the lemon light of a Deià morning.

'I still don't understand why you are seeing a psychiatrist, Miguel, and not a psychologist? Psychiatrists are only for nutters – locos! You're not a loco pretending to be just slightly cranky are you?' I was being playful, but the humour was forced and he wasn't in the mood for jokes either.

'I dare say I don't know what you're talking about.'

In his black polo neck and with that dark expression he looked like the baddie in a Bond movie. He looked evil. *What a terrible thought! The grass we smoked last night must have made me paranoid. He's probably just worried about the appointment. His downturned mouth made his jowls sag more than usual this morning and his lips looked purple.* Since the sobresada episode, in my imagination the image of Scrooge was superimposed over Miguel. I still didn't understand what those pills he'd been taking when I first met him were for.

'Miguel, please explain to me why you are seeing a psychiatrist. I am worried about you. Doctors don't prescribe pills for no reason.' I said it with serious concern in my voice. Concern for him or myself? Perhaps both.

'¡Uf!' He sighed like an impatient teenager. 'Do you really want to know, Cariño?'

Something in my gut cringed. Did I? I nodded and held my breath.

'I told you about the neighbour being violent?'

'Yes.'

'I reported him and we went to court. The neighbour accused me of attacking him. I lied to the psychiatrist because my lawyer advised me to plead mental illness. It was my only defence.' He mumbled something in Spanish about the neighbour being a son of a whore.

'What …? But you were the victim. I don't understand.' It didn't ring true. And why hadn't he mentioned the court part before?

'Yes, I was the victim, Cariño, you know, but he twisted the truth, said I attacked him, got a man from the village to act as a witness – they stick together these peasants.' Miguel laughed incredulously. 'Can you imagine me being violent, Cariño?'

I did not answer. My heart was racing. I swallowed hard and the cold cut my throat. My head spun in confusion. His story didn't ring true. Hadn't he said the drugs were for depression … something to do with his agent? That story hadn't made sense either.

'Cariño, that is why I don't want you to talk to him. Don't go near the neighbour. I dare say he's a dangerous man. I want to protect you, Cariño.' His emphasis lingered on the word protect. He didn't protect me in the couples club. I wanted to believe him, but there had been too many lies.

'But why take pills if there's nothing wrong with you?'

'I wanted it to look convincing.'

'But you could have lied about taking the pills too.'

'¡Uf!' Miguel's eyes darkened with rage at being quizzed.

'Cariño, you asked me to tell you. Now I have to keep seeing the psychiatrist as I don't want to go back to court.'

'Well why not tell the truth?'

'Cariño!' He took my face in his hands, his fingers over my mouth, gently at first, then harder so my lip, slightly chapped from the cold, cut into my teeth. Nose to nose, my face cupped in this grip, he looked into my eyes forcing me to look back as unless I closed my eyes there was nowhere else to look.

'When I look into your eyes I only see peace, Cariño. I thought I needed those pills. I dare say I was very stressed, depressed even, but now you are my pills. You are all I need.' He continued his hard Paddington stare. I searched his eyes for softness, a hint of love but all I could see was darkness. Like looking into an abyss. I wanted to look away, but even after he released his hands from my face I could not as I was trapped in his gaze which had an irresistible hold over me.

'What do you see when you look into my eyes, Cariño?'

'An abyss.' Fear caught in my throat and I had a sensation of falling, falling into a black hole.

He laughed. 'Cariño!' And he held me out at arms length as if he was considering the size of a new suit on a hanger in a shop.

'I have to go. Don't worry about me, Cariño, ok?'

I nodded. It felt like I was in some sort of trance when I recall it now. Gripped by a combination of fear and irresistible compulsion. In that moment I would have agreed with anything he said.

Perhaps to normalise things, I said, 'Shall I take the octopus out of the freezer for dinner?'

'No.'

He kissed me, got in the car, slammed the door and reversed out of the drive. His black car screeched and spat gravel like an angry hearse.

I walked up the path with the granny trolley to buy the vegetables. At least walking would get the circulation going, although

I had to go slow as my breathing was catching my chest. I thought of George Sand's experience and how Chopin's tuberculosis suffered in the damp. There was a metallic taste in my mouth. I wiped my finger inside my lip. Blood.

23
Graveyard

The shopping trolley bumped behind me as I dragged it over gravel to join the queue for the vegetable stall. Although Forbes branded Deià one of the ten most idyllic places in the world to live, and to the eye it is indeed a paradise, Deià had taught me that naïve eyes can be deceived. It's no longer the village Robert Graves spoke of in 'Sirocco at Deya'. Since Richard Branson built La Residencia hotel, the rich have flocked to the dead poet's 'insupportable Arcadia'. In summer it was overrun with coachloads of Northern European day-trippers and in winter the village appeared deserted. Except on market day. On Wednesday mornings hibernating inhabitants venture out to fondle vegetables, nod at each other, and exchange pleasantries about the weather.

'Buenas dias.'

It took me a few moments to recognise the tall man with turquoise beads plaited into his grey beard. I think Miguel said he was an artist. If Gandalf were an artist he would have looked like him.

'Buenas dias! The temperature's dropped.'

'Cold …' His speech stumbled and he searched for words in the sky. 'Might snow this winter.'

Words often falter in winter as if Deiàns are speaking a foreign language. Often they are as many of the residents are foreigners – artists, musicians, rich Americans and Europeans – but the locals stumble over words too, like prisoners who haven't had visitors for months.

'It snows in Deià?'

He cleared his throat.

'Sometimes.'

There was a pause. We looked down over the olive groves and then up at the mountain. It seemed bigger in winter.

'A friend visited last year. He intended to stay all winter, but he ran away and missed the snow. Good timing – when it snows in Deià there's no escape!'

We both laughed. It was a shared joke between hard-core Deiàns that some people flee before their intended stay is up.

'Why do you think people run away?'

He cleared his throat again.

'I don't know. Perhaps they run from the mountain. My friend talked of an overwhelming claustrophobia and oppression.' He looked up at the Teix then continued with the tone of a sage. 'Two types of people come to Deià. Those seduced by her beauty who run when she shows her shadow, and those who remain forever under her spell. It took me a while to work out which one I am. Have you decided yet?'

He looked me in the eye for the first time. His eyes were the same turquoise as the beads in his beard and the Deiàn sky.

I licked my lip. It still tasted of blood where Miguel had gripped my face.

'Yes, I think I have.'

'Well, have a good winter.'

He waved as he walked off, giant leeks peeking out of his canvas shopping bag.

From the vegetable stall queue I looked across the valley at Villa Rosa. My plan had been to read by the pool in the winter

sunshine, pack and take some photos to remember Deià by …
and to satisfy my curiosity by finding the key to the cellar. It was
bugging me what Miguel was so secretive about down there. He'd
taken to going down every morning and most evenings before he
locked up the house. But now I was away from the house, I did
not want to return.

On a whim I asked the vegetable man if I could leave the trolley
and my shopping list with him – 'volvo pronto' – I'd be back soon.

'Si, No problem.' He had that soft Spanish ease Miguel lacked.

I took the route I'd taken the first day I arrived, the day I'd been
seduced by Deià and bitten by medusa in the Cala – before I'd met
Miguel. Would I ever get back to that version of me?

I sat on a low wall by the torrent until my temples thudded
from the pounding water and the noise drowned out the thoughts
biting like medusa in my head: *Don't trust him, his story doesn't add
up, stay and you'll never leave, you'll be a prisoner here forever.*

A shadow in my peripheral vision gave me the creepy sensation
of being watched. I gasped. The neighbour! Holding his rake.

He took a step towards me.

Don't talk to the neighbour. Miguel's order echoed in my mind.

I jumped down from the wall and walked as fast as I could back
up the way I'd come. I walked blindly up and around. And around
another corner to escape the crazy neighbour. Breath short, sweat
broke on my top lip.

At the top of the lane next to an old stonewall, I stopped to
catch my breath and looked back down the lane. The neighbour
was gone.

A sound so loud and close it made my bones shudder vibrated
through my body.

What was that?

I was standing beside the church. The bell tolls every hour on the hour, but I was used to it being a far off sound. Here it felt like I was the bell.

The church is near the hostel I'd booked into months before. It was a crumb of comfort that I was near the place where I had last felt myself. That was the last night I'd slept properly, felt like a whole human being, not this half-life existence, nerves crackling from lack of sleep and anxiety, clothes hanging off me I'd lost so much weight. I looked up at the church door, but did not want to enter into another damp Deià space, so I sat on a bench in the overgrown churchyard.

Too unsettled to sit still, I wandered around the gravestones pulling away overhanging shrubs as I read the tombstones. The old excitement of exploring Deià reignited when I saw Robert Graves' gravestone beneath a cypress tree. Under his name was inscribed, poet.

Maybe Miguel is dramatizing the thing with the neighbour? Maybe novelists confuse the boundary between fact and fiction. I walked away from the scruffy grave. Another tombstone caught my eye. This one was as ill-kept as Graves', but it was recent, just two decades old. It was the name that drew me in: Maria Isobel. Maria Isobel, Maria Isobel … why did that name make my heart feel like a clenched fist? I don't know any Marias, let alone a Maria Isobel. I could not read the family name. It was as if it had been etched out. It was too new a stone to have crumbled away. The stone next to it was older. NADAL. SOFIA VALENTINA NADAL. Oh my God, is this his family plot? A surge of fear swept up me, my head spun. I have to get out of here.

I turned abruptly and froze in shock. The neighbour. Just steps away from me. His face was fierce and weathered.

I swallowed. *Don't show him you're afraid.*

We looked at each other.

He began to shake his head, slowly at first. He lowered his eyes to the gravestone and his head shook faster, pointed his rake at me and gabbled in Spanish or Mallorquín, I do not know which. If he'd been speaking English I would not have understood as a ringing in my ears like tinnitus stunned my brain.

He stared at the gravestone as though he'd forgotten I was there.

Run now while you have the chance, I told myself, but I couldn't move.

'Ell la va matar. Me entiendes? Él la mató. Él la mató.' Then he waved his stick shooing me off like a mosquito. 'Fuig. Vete. Go.'

I legged it back to the house without stopping. On the way I remembered the groceries, but I wasn't going back. George Sand was right. The locals didn't like strangers.

When Miguel got home I was sitting on the sofa staring out the window. He sat next to me.

'Cariño, you're trembling.'

He took my hand and I felt myself fade into him, relieved to nestle into his black polo neck, the familiar smell of his skin.

'I don't have the vegetables.'

He tilted his head to the side like a dog.

'The neighbour cornered me in town.' I was reluctant to mention the graveyard.

'Did you speak to him, Cariño?'

'No, not a word.'

'Good girl.'

'What did he say?'

'I did not understand.'

'Good. Good girl.' He nodded. Then laughed. He seemed genuinely amused.

'I'm sorry he followed you, Cariño, but what were you doing walking around? I told you to come straight back, didn't I, Cariño?'

I nodded. The confusion was overwhelming. Why was he so relaxed? Why wasn't he angry with me for leaving the vegetables?

'Don't worry, I'll collect the vegetables in the car. Have you packed?'

'No.'

'Pack while I'm out. I'm taking you for dinner tonight, Cariño.'

I looked at him blankly. Dinner out? That's what normal people do. I was so surprised I felt even more confused. He kissed me as if he were auditioning for a role in a cheesy B-rate romance.

When he left I went upstairs and opened my empty case. In the side pocket was Miguel's novel that had brought me to Deià in the first place. It reminded me that I was a journalist and had another life outside this spooky valley. I flicked through the pages thumbed at the edges. As I was about to put it back my heart did a double-take. Sirens rang in my ears as they had in the graveyard.

For Maria Isobel

The name on the gravestone. He'd told me he'd dedicated the novel to his ex-wife, but he hadn't told me she was dead!

Mato. Mato. The word mato had lodged in my brain. Mato. I must look it up. What did it mean? I ran into the library and pulled out the Spanish-English dictionary, hands shaking as I frantically leafed through the pages: ma, ma, mat, mató: past tense of matar … ok, matar … I flicked back a page and passed my finger down: *kill; slaughter; murder.*

I gulped. That was his wife's grave. His neighbour was telling me she was murdered. Then who was she was murdered by? By the neighbour? By someone else? ... or by Miguel? Was he warning me off for my own safety or was he threatening to kill me too?

I slammed the dictionary shut. At the same time the car door slammed.

'Cariño, can you help me with the shopping?' As he called upstairs from the lobby Miguel's voice had its usual impatience.

'Coming.' My voice quivered.

Right, I reasoned with myself. *Your Spanish is rubbish. The crazy neighbour could have said anything. All you got was one word and that might not be right. So chill out. Murders don't happen in tiny Spanish villages. Stop with the conspiracy theories, go to dinner and simply ask Miguel what happened to her.*

In my haste the books had fallen at my feet. I shoved them back onto the shelves. One lay open at the title page: Bluebeard. I rattled back in my memory. The story of the wife killer. It was in Charles Perrault's *The Complete Fairy Tales.* I pushed the book right to the back out of sight.

Just a coincidence. Just a silly fairy tale. Just breathe.

24

Dinner Out

The next time I walked down the staircase I'd be leaving. I took in the detail, the aged wood, the hollow clop my footsteps made; the old stone of the last flight that led to the lobby, the scuff of my shoes. Before I reached the bottom step I felt Miguel's anxiety. Hat in hand, I scooted into the downstairs bathroom to push my hair up under my hat. My body was fighting off a cold and I didn't want to let the night air near my scalp as it was still damp from washing.

'Cariño, are you ready?' He sighed.

I listened for tapping. My imagination travelled to the cellar. Miguel had been down there under the house all day and came up covered in dirt and stinking of shit. He said he'd been cleaning out the sewage. When he went into the cellar was the only time he didn't want my help. My imagination conjured a woman tied up, tapping the pipes in her desperation to draw attention to herself. Other nights I imagined the regular, rising impatience of two people having sex, one of them banging against the cistern. But the pipes were as silent as the Deiàn night. I berated my imagination. Miguel could be cruel, but he's not a psychopath and I'm not a character in one of his creepy novels.

His exes were. Why not you?

I pushed the thought away and forced a cheery voice. False cheer America had taught me. Ignoring my inner voice was an older habit.

'Coming!'

Miguel wore a woolly hat and thick-soled, old man shoes. He thought he was stylish, whereas I was well aware what a dishevelled picture I painted in my layered jumpers and misshaped woolly hat. His perception of himself was distorted. I'd had enough, but he was taking me out for dinner and so I was ready to start afresh from tonight. Maybe this dinner would make amends. Or was I being delusional?

'Cariño, can you give me money for the kitty? We've spent it all.'

So, he's not taking me out for dinner – I'm paying for it! The realisation brought back the disappointment, the emotional leit motif I wanted to escape, a feeling that knocked on the door of some lost memory. As I ran back upstairs I thought of the *pulpo* in the freezer. If I was leaving why had he packed the freezer with all that fish? But I took my last fifty Euro note from my purse anyway. Although he didn't know it, it was our farewell dinner.

'Cariño, what are you doing up there? The table is booked for eight.'

'I can't imagine there'll be a queue in Deià in the middle of winter.' The words snapped sharp like medusa stings in the cold air.

As I gave him the note I half expected him to say it was a misunderstanding, but he shoved the note into his wallet as if it were his right. There was a feeling of disbelief – as if at any moment Miguel would change and was just acting like a Scrooge.

Surely he didn't invite me and expect me to pay?

'What's all that fish for? I leave tomorrow.'

'Have you packed, Cariño?'

'Yes.' I wanted to scream at him for not answering my question, but more than that I wanted our last night to be a beautiful memory and so I held my tongue. This was my last night in Deià. I could sulk or make the most of it. And dinner out in this little village in winter is a treat in itself so whether I was paying or not I resolved to enjoy my last supper.

The town was silent, the church in the distance lit up the houses that hugged it on the hillside, lights in windows like choirboys each holding up a little candle. As we neared the town snowflake lights hung between the houses. The only sound was the torrent which got louder, deafening as we approached. The air was a clean cold that in Northern Europe would indicate snow.

'Come on, Cariño. We're late.'

He raced ahead dragging me along. I wanted to go slow, to remember. He had no idea that I was savouring my last Deià n night. I made myself become present to the mountain. This would be the last time I'd see it in this electric blue light just before dusk ends. My grief added to its beauty, for grief is in sync with a Deià n winter; grief aligns with the shadow of Spain, the undercurrent that gushes like the torrent through the generations, unseen by tourists, forgotten, trapped in the rocky face in the mountain.

Hidden under an enormous tree at the bottom of one of the town's labyrinth lanes was Sa Cova. The homemade sign above the door raised my spirits – a hand painted polished hunk of wood that kept the shape of the tree: *Sa Cova, oriental home cooking.*

The internal stonewalls, low ceiling and six wooden tables packed tightly together created an intimacy against the cold outside. So many empty tables. What on earth was the rush? I'll never make that walk again and he ruined it by his anxious haste.

'Hola.'

An Asian woman greeted us like old friends. The girl who made up our table for two said she was from Andalucia when I asked her. Miguel was preoccupied with the wobbly table leg.

'There, perfect,' said the Andaluz girl as she put a napkin under the table leg.

I spoke to her in Spanish.

'You have an Andaluz accent!'

'Do I?' My old Spanish teacher had been from Malaga, but it was funny to think I'd learnt something I'd not been aware of learning and I could not hear myself.

Miguel wasn't pleased to hear this, but he forced a smile.

'It is because you forget your past participles and don't pronounce words properly.'

'Well you don't have the patience to speak to me in Spanish and I'm not allowed out the rest of the time. Aren't you going to accuse her of sounding like an Andalucian maid?'

Even though the question was rhetorical any normal person would have said something to my mini-rant. Not Miguel. And I was left yet again wondering whether I'd spoken at all.

'What would you like, Cariño?' Miguel insisted on speaking in English, even though everyone else was speaking in Spanish – the owner, the waitress, the cook who had come out in her white pinny when I'd asked what went into the Chinese stew.

'Me gustaria Hoisin ribs and Beijing spicy noodles, por favor.' I emphasised the sibilant s's softly in the way she did and enjoyed hearing the soft accent in return as Valeria (I was already on first name terms with the waitress) took my menu from me.

As we chomped into the ribs, people began to arrive with the news that it was snowing.

'Snowing! In Deià!' Although the artist had mentioned this at the market I didn't quite believe it.

'Yes, it sometimes snows here in winter,' said the waitress and fetched photos from some years earlier with the Teix white like a Swiss postcard.

The restaurant was full and everyone was in the mood for socialising – except Miguel who frowned every time I responded to the Germans and Americans at the adjacent tables. After so long in isolation it was a relief to be with other people.

'Are you enjoying your dinner, Cariño?' Miguel's question incensed me. He asked as if he was taking me out when I was the one paying, and the way he said it was as if we were in a play and he was acting his part, but he acted it like a wooden toy. Not for the first time his movements reminded me of Thunderbirds puppets, every gesture unnatural. Despite my irritation, I found myself pushing him to engage again in what next.

'Miguel, tomorrow I leave. We have no plan. You say you want to spend the rest of your life with me, but I don't have the means to support myself here. I've spent all my money. I must return to work after I've sorted out things in New York.'

Miguel looked distracted and then put on a wide grin.

'Cariño, do you really want to talk about this now?'

'Yes, or I wouldn't have brought it up.'

A shadow fell over his features – or had they dimmed the lights?

'I dare say I like the ribs, but the sauce needs more sugar, don't you think, Cariño?'

'Why are you avoiding my question?'

'Cariño!'

Although Miguel did not want to engage with the other people in the room, like in the café in Soller, he was acting as if he were the centre of their attention. I wanted to scream at him: *They have given up trying to engage us – we're now just part of the furniture.*

'We have no plan.' A quiet voice inside me said, *let it go.*

'Let's talk about something else, Cariño.'

I looked at my food.

A squeal of delight came from outside as a group of diners left to go and look at the snow. A blast of cold air came in as the door closed behind them. I looked at the group of three in the window seat, ordering hot chocolate brandies. Miguel had refused me another glass of wine. Laughter was missing from our table.

'Can I get you anything else?'

'Just the bill, thank you.' Miguel didn't ask if I was ready to leave. It was so cosy in Sa Cova I could have sat for hours in its intimacy observing other people having fun. The thought of returning to Villa Rosa made me shiver. It was warmer outside in the snow.

'No dessert?' Valeria looked surprised we were leaving.

'Yes. Lychee ice-cream, please.'

'Cariño, do you really want dessert?'

'Yes, that's why I ordered it.'

'I dare say we should go home. We need to be up early to drive to the airport.'

What's the point? His sulking will just give me indigestion anyway.

'Actually, just the bill. Thank you.'

Valeria went to fetch the bill in her good-humoured way.

Miguel reached over to take my hand in his. This was his way of telling me he was pleased with me. 'Thank you, Cariño.'

His gesture of praise unleashed a sudden, sharp wave of hatred which I'd never experienced towards anyone ever before.

'How did your wife die?'

'Cariño, I told you.'

'You didn't tell me she was dead. I found out as I came across her gravestone.'

His frown was rockier than the forehead of the face in the Teix. Being away from Villa Rosa and with normal people gave me courage.

'How did you and your ex split up?' I couldn't bring myself to ask him, *and where is she now?*

Miguel tried to disguise his anger and direct it at the waitress.

'Why is she taking so long with the bill?'

'Valeria is the only waitress with all these tables. Are you going to answer my questions?'

Suddenly Miguel's face lit up like a boy who has been asked to pose for a school photo. He looked at the painting on the wall next to us with excitement.

'Look, it is Villa Rosa.'

Indeed it was, but I was not interested. He was changing the subject again.

Valeria returned with the bill. Miguel paid with my fifty Euro note. She was swift with the change as if she sensed a domestic brewing.

'What are you doing?'

'I'm leaving Valeria a well-deserved tip.'

'I told you we don't tip in Mallorca.'

'Well I do. She's been run off her feet all night.'

I left a ten Euro note on top of the change on the little stainless steel bill plate. I put on my coat and left Miguel staring at the tip.

I marched back up through the town to Villa Rosa, resolved that I would never return to Deià, the small hope that he might redeem himself extinguished. He had no idea what I was thinking, not because I didn't tell him, but because it didn't fit his version of events – which was that I had infinite resources and I would keep spending my money to return to him. *What on earth is wrong with him?*

By the torrent I stopped. Its wild rush was the only sound. There was peace in the air. Snowflakes landed on my forehead. I tilted my face to the sky and felt my anger drift away as snow melted on my nose, my left eyelid, another on my cheek.

'Cariño, don't spoil our evening.'

Me spoil it!

'Stop avoiding my questions and stop spending my money.' I marched out of the town, along the road and up the drive in a fury, the snowy peace forgotten. I took the key from under the plant pot and let myself in.

Ah, a thorn scratched me. I sucked my hand. The metallic taste of blood for the second time that day! A sign to get the hell out of Deià. The snow had better not settle.

He sat up reading under the glow of his bedside table lamp. I lay next to him, duvet up to my nose, eyes closed. Sharing a bed with someone I was in the middle of an argument with was something I didn't want to get used to. All our married life my husband and I had a habit of resolving disagreements before we slept. I thought of the divorce papers; copies had been sent by email from his lawyer. In a few days he would be my ex-husband. I couldn't go back to that life – as calm as it was, I was hiding from something in the relationship and I wanted to find myself. In the safety of my marriage I'd lost myself. Neither could I stay with Miguel.

I looked up at him in his reading glasses and held back the tears. I loved him. How could I love a man who ignored me at best and drove me half insane the rest of the time?

When he thought I was asleep, he got up and went out the back door. I crept down to the kitchen. Below the kitchen window

I saw him go to the door that led to the cellar. The snow was falling fast. He clanked around under the house for a while. When he came in I crept back into bed.

'What were you doing?'

'Nothing, Cariño.'

'What do you do in there everyday?'

'Do you want a hug, Cariño?' He never hugs me. Another diversion.

'I *saw* you go into the cellar.' I felt a twang of fear saying the forbidden word.

He laughed.

'You *saw* me, Cariño! I left some things in the laundry. What else would I be doing?'

My head spun. *Am I going mad?*

25
Cellar

We lay in bed, him one side and me on the other. Miguel started to speak, gently at first. I do not recall exactly what he said – he painted pictures of an imaginary future, an insupportable arcadia in Deià, happy and content, him writing, me doing I do not know what, but he was an expert at painting imaginary pictures. I had to draw a line under the excruciating pain his impossible fantasies caused me.

'Miguel, I will not be returning. When I leave tomorrow we will say goodbye as lovers. We are not a couple. You do not understand partnership. Partnership for me is about writing the script together. Your idea of partnership is that I am a character in one of your novels. I am a real person.'

He leaned over and tried to touch me. I craved his touch, but his dry fingers caressing my breasts was pacification. I pushed his patronising hand away.

'Miguel, it's over.'

He flopped back on the mattress and tutted like a teenager. Then he took tight hold of my wrist, too tight.

'You're hurting me.'

He let go and flew into a rage. The sharpness and suddenness of it frightened me.

'So you want to leave me. You don't care about me. You just care about yourself …'

Lying there in the bed next to him as he ranted on, I was deaf to the words. I fell into a sort of fearful, paralysed state. The temperature had dropped so much that when my tears trickled under my earlobes and down the sides of my neck they were cold.

Miguel raged on.

I lay frozen.

At some point Miguel slept.

I could not sleep. My brain was working overtime trying to piece together snippets of conversations with Miguel, the incongruent dates, incongruent stories, searching for the truth. I know he's lying to me, but about what – and why lie in the first place? I listened to him snore long enough to satisfy myself that he was asleep, then peeled the blanket off me.

Downstairs was colder. The fire had burned out. How nice it will be to have central heating again. A deep sadness swam inside me, my blood circulating it around my body so that I felt its weight in my limbs as I tiptoed downstairs towards the cellar.

Why was it so painful to give up, to leave a selfish, stingy man? There was no point trying to talk to him. It was as if I did not exist at all. He'd heard me but he didn't seem to care that I was leaving him – or was it that he did not believe me, was it that he thought I was just making a fuss and would be back as soon as I'd signed the divorce papers?

Being with him ungrounded me as if I were an insubstantial ghostly apparition, an avatar, his avatar. I must get away from him. The same magnetic attraction that had me drop my life in New York now repelled me from him. Is this what happened to his ex?

Did she too run away, stifled by his need to control, leaving her clothes in the wardrobe?

Dinner growled in my stomach and chilli fired my belly. I crept downstairs to the bathroom. It was a relief to lock the door. A deeper relief followed as I sat on the loo and expelled the indigestible anxiety I'd swallowed with each mouthful of food. Dinner passed straight through me. The stench was real. Should I pull the chain? Miguel might hear it.

Tapping.

Tapping on the pipes.

I sat motionless, stuck to the cold seat, and listened. It was coming from the pipes. I knew that hollow metallic noise that travelled along pipes. When I was at school we used to tap codes at night as a way of communicating with girls in different dorms.

My fear linked me to the cellar like a magnet. What the hell had Miguel been doing down there all day? *Cleaning out the sewage.* I didn't believe him. My speculation went haywire as I remembered the neighbour; matar: to kill, murder, slaughter. What if he wasn't cleaning out the sewage? What if he was digging a grave, his ex-girlfriend's grave? I needed to know what happened to her and I was certain the answer was in the cellar.

I pictured Miguel in the bedroom two floors above me, asleep. Could he be a murderer? What if the neighbour was accusing Miguel of killing his wife? Then might he have killed his ex too? The sheer floral dress in the wardrobe, all the clothes that were there when I met him, gone three weeks later when I returned … and what would stop him killing me?

His rage when I said I was going. Anger is one thing. Murder is another. *I'm losing my mind. I just need to get out of here, back to normality.* But the tapping continued.

Clink, clink, clink, clink.

And then it stopped. It was not consistent like water dripping from a tap, or a cistern filling up after a flush. What if someone was down there? What if she were alive, tapping in hope someone might hear?

Don't be crazy. There's no way she could have survived down there that long. And if he buried her and that was what he was doing, not clearing out the trough as he'd said, then what was I going to do – dig her up?

I gasped aloud at the thought of it – scary cellar scenes from horror movies flicked through my muddled brain: *Misery, The Silence of the Lambs.*

I have to go down into the cellar and satisfy myself that my suspicions are unfounded. It is the only way to rid myself of these crazy thoughts, put my mind and my memories of Villa Rosa to rest.

The forbidden key to the cellar was on his key fob in the lobby. I gently picked up the bunch of keys and crept barefoot out the backdoor past the swimming pool. It was so cold in the house, I was surprised it was colder outside even though it was snowing. The ground was wet underfoot.

My hands shook as I fumbled to fit the right key.

The rustiest key on the fob sprung the lock.

The door creaked. I stopped and looked up at the sky. Snowflakes fell gently and the landscape glittered in the light from the terrace. For the umpteenth time I wondered how such a paradise could be so deceptive.

I hesitated. *Go back to bed, forget the cellar, get up in the morning and go back to New York,* instructed the voice of reason. Instead I walked down the steps into the cloying damp. A musty stale smell made me wrench.

I should have brought a torch. Only four steps down and too dark to see my feet. I walked back up and stroked the wall for a switch. The walls were slimy and cold. Found one – a dim yellow glow lit the bottom stone steps.

It felt as if I were walking into the history of the house and I imagined his grandfather, who'd martyred himself in the Spanish Civil War, being marched up these same steps when the house was searched by Franco's Dragons of Death. If doom had a smell, this musty stale damp was it.

The dim glow came from a bare bulb hung low over an ancient desk. On the desk was a laptop. It was too dark to see much else. Somewhere in the dark at the back of the cellar the cistern tapped with its irregular beat.

I've never gone through anyone's email before, but I had to know the truth. I sat on the wooden chair and opened the lid. I tapped in the password Miguel used for his internet hotspot: Villarosa. To my surprise his email instantly opened up. Like most people he used the same one for everything.

I searched for Maria Isobel.

Nothing. Odd that he had no emails from his ex-wife.

In the email search I tapped Alessandra.

Hundreds of emails appeared dating back years. I clicked randomly to begin with. She wrote in Spanish. It appeared they had periods apart when she'd returned to Italy. I didn't understand everything but enough to work out she was angry with him most of the time. She accused him of being a liar, a bastard, not delivering on his promises. Bloody hell – he'd proposed and kept postponing the wedding. He gave her the same thin excuses, the same manipulation.

So it was not just me.

Oh God!

A photo of Alessandra gagged and tied to a chair looking like a torture victim. Above her head hung a bare lightbulb. I gasped. That was the lightbulb above my head. The photo was taken here. She was down here. And that chair – it was the birthing chair, the one he told me his grandmother gave birth to his mother in ... and Alessandra was wearing the corset. He told me she never wore it. Did he kill her in it? Her large breasts hung over it. Nausea added to the shock as I realised I'd worn that same corset. The photo was attached to an email. I scrolled down ... Miguel had sent the photo to Alessandra the week before I'd arrived in Deià to interview him.

Oh God! *Él la mató* – the neighbour's words beat in my skull: He killed her!

My heart thumped so fast I thought it might stop dead in my chest.

Did Miguel kill his ex? Did he take photos of Alessandra before he killed her? Did I wear a dead woman's corset? My hands shook and I forced myself to read on. I had to know the truth.

Wait. Breathe, I ordered myself. This is an S&M photo, but maybe that was their thing. Miguel certainly had tried to get me to do that: the slaps, the control. He liked playing the master. Maybe they dressed up and played sex games – the cellar made an ideal S&M dungeon. The thought calmed me a little.

I looked back to the emails, searching for dates. The next one was sent in reply to the photo:

> I do not want to play your games anymore.
> Not your sex games, not your mind games.
> We have nothing together except broken
> promises. Leave me in peace.

I looked up at the lightbulb and exhaled violently. In the thin light the bulb gave off I watched the dust particles blown by my sigh. Thank God! He did not kill her. They were just playing a game. I remembered his suggestion that I sat in the chair, the night he tied my wrists together.

Rage replaced fear. He lied to me about the corset. He said she never wore it as it didn't fit her.

I scrolled back to the most recent emails. She'd had enough. She was leaving him.

Her last email was dated three days after I arrived in Deià!

The betrayal made me want to gag.

What happened after that? Where was she emailing him from? She can't have been in Villa Rosa if she was emailing him.

I should have stopped. I'd seen enough to satisfy myself my intuition was right about him being a big, stinking liar. But I wanted more. I wanted to leave for New York with enough dirt on him I'd never ever want to come back.

The emails continued while I'd been in New York. Possibly the same days he'd been persuading me to the return to Deià, to start a life with him, the bastard had been emailing her:

```
If you return I will marry you.
We will marry in the church in Deià.
Come, Cariño. I love you.
```

Argh! Cariño, he used it for her. If I hear that word again, I'll scream.

When I was here, he was begging her to return to Deià to marry him. I had to read the emails again to believe it. My belly fired, but not on chilli. If I'd had any food left in my stomach I'd have puked. Even if I'd not been lied to, reading love letters between your partner and his ex is not a sensible thing to do.

A floorboard creaked above my head.

Miguel was up?

I was stunned, the shock of betrayal. I held my breath and listened.

Silence.

Must have been my imagination.

I had to know more. I returned to his inbox – this time more methodically.

There were emails from his psychiatrist, lawyer, publisher.

The lawyer advised Miguel to continue with the psychiatry. Why? There wasn't much else. The psychiatrist's latest email suggested another session:

```
Remember what we discussed last time.
Make the unconscious conscious.
Your family's history, your shame
does not need to define you.
```

This must have been the psychiatrist he attended yesterday in Palma. It was in response to Miguel's email about him masturbating over me wearing his mother's nightdress.

Wow! This is too fucked up. I looked down at his mother's nightdress. I wanted to strip it off me, run up the stairs naked and out into the street and free myself from this house, its history. I didn't want to know any more. My head was spinning. I felt sick and dizzy.

'Cariñoooo,' Miguel's voice echoed through the house above my head.

My heart pinched.

My hands shook.

I quickly quit Email, shut the laptop and walked back up the stairs.

Replace the keys on the table in the lobby, go into the bathroom, flush the chain and return to bed.

I moved like a zombie, performing the basic instructions I gave myself.

The clank of the ancient plumbing was still tapping as I slipped under the duvet.

Miguel turned over as I got into the bed.

'Cariño, I told you not to flush.'

'Sorry.'

Miguel reached out to touch me.

'Why are you so cold?'

He turned, his cock hard against me and broke and entered in his usual way.

I was rigid with fear. But far, far more disturbing, I was wet with excitement. He slipped in. This time he sank his teeth into me, bit me like teenagers do. It terrified me that I took pleasure from this.

Just go along with it, leave Villa Rosa tomorrow and never come back, instructed the voice of reason which pushed its way through the nausea, confusion, fear and paralysis. The ingredients of disaster mingled in me. I lay there, too numb to throw off his mother's nightdress, too frozen to clean the inside of my leg. It irked me like a straightjacket but I just had to get to the morning and to the airport.

Lay still, be quiet and I'll be gone in the morning. The voice was mine, but it was distant, far off, as if it were talking to me, pacifying me from somewhere in my past, somewhere long forgotten. I did not sleep. At points during the long night the truth of betrayal cut through the numbness like medusa nips and stings.

When the church bells tolled and the cockerel crowed I was numb again.

26

Goodbye to All That

Last night's snowfall had not settled. The face in the Teix winked with a deceptive orange-pink twinkle. I thought of the artist with the turquoise beads in his beard. The emails, the cellar, the sleepless night seemed unreal. The truth was so far from the lie I'd lived for months.

This was goodbye to Deià, goodbye to Miguel and his lies and goodbye to Villa Rosa. A trinity of betrayal. Goodbye to all that. I looked across the valley to Graves' house – how ironic that his refuge had been my prison.

I waited by the low stonewall overlooking the olive groves for Miguel to drive the car up the narrow lane. I hoped he'd take a long time. He'd sent me on ahead to throw the garbage in the big bin by the road. I knew better than to interrupt his routine and a dull bewilderment at his lack of emotion at our parting muted me. He'd robotically got out of bed to the alarm, jumped into his impatient rhythm as if today was any other day and ordered me about in his usual snappy manner. Was it that he did not understand what I'd said to him about me not coming back? Or was it that he didn't care? Surely some sign of sadness would be normal.

Stop wondering what he's thinking. All that matters is that I get out of here.

House lights dotted the hillside and I felt jealous of Deiàns who got to wake up as if today were normal. Just like Miguel and Villa Rosa, Deià exerted a mysterious hold over me. I'd fallen in love with all three of them, inextricably linked in a dark trinity. Goodbye to Miguel was goodbye to Deià and tearing myself from Deià stung like cutting out a part of myself, like amputating a gangrenous limb.

A shuffle below the wall startled me. Looking up at me was the neighbour. He had a scowl on his face and started shooing me off as if I were a donkey blocking his path.

Don't worry, I'm going.

And there it was again, that doubt – is he shooing me off for my own good? It made no difference now.

Miguel's hearse rolled slowly up the hill towards me. My heart pounded and I backed away from the wall so Miguel would not be able to see I'd been interacting with the neighbour. An intuitive fear instructed my movements.

'Cariño, come on, we will be late.'

His sharp tone made me jump as he rolled down the window and the way he looked at me made me think of psychopaths in horror films. I wanted to hit him for calling me Cariño.

I dared not speak as we drove. Holding back the tears was painful as if behind my eyeballs were razor blades ready to slice if I as much as let a single tear flow. So I remained silent and focused on slowing my breathing.

Miguel was oblivious to my suffering. The whole forty-minute drive to Palma airport he talked incessantly. I tried to shut out his voice and to focus instead on photographing the landscape to memory. This was a breakup from the island too, for Mallorca had seduced me, beguiled me and tricked me. The shadow of Spain lurks behind every door, echoes in the caves below miradors, rattles its unresolved grief through terrace wind chimes when the Sirocco blows in.

I held two cups of tea in jam jars. Miguel insisted we needed tea in the morning. Tea splashed and scorched my hand as he took a hairpin bend. I felt nothing.

'So what do you think? I dare say you can work from Deià when you return. You'll love that life, writing your articles from home, won't you, Cariño? Or you can get a job in Palma or Barcelona and fly back to Mallorca weekends.'

He darted from one impossible topic that included me as a fluent Spanish speaker (my broken Spanish was little better than when I arrived, although reading and the dictionaries had helped a bit) in his imaginary universe of our future and ignored Spain's economic crisis.

As we passed the prison Miguel sped up as he always did.

'Cariño, drink your tea. It will get cold.'

I drank the tea although I didn't want it. He'd worn me down, rendered me spineless. He'd not hear me anyway if I spoke. What I wanted was irrelevant to him. The torture of my voice not being heard was unbearable sitting right next to him. Trapped in the car. My breathing shallowed.

Claustrophobia brought with it a memory of sitting in my father's car as he accelerated at lightning speed late for a golf match. It became harder to breathe. An old knowledge that if I stayed still, closed my eyes and held my breath I might just make it to the destination alive and then my mother could take over driving and I'd be safe. My mother's voice was in my head as he took the lights on red, *your father is a safe driver*. The fact he'd had several accidents due to dangerous driving in mad rages did not seem to register in her mind.

This feeling of being trapped and holding my breath, desperate to arrive at Palma airport and be free of him, was exactly the same sensation as I'd had in the car with my father as a child. Although Miguel did not speed, it was like I was reliving it, emotionally. Emotionally Miguel was dangerous.

We arrived early. I was desperate to get out, but he would not open the car door.

'Cariño, look at me.'

He turned my chin towards him, his grip just a bit too hard. Could he see where he'd split my lip?

'I'm sorry for my anger last night. I dare say I understand what you mean about me spending the kitty money, but I thought it was our money, Cariño.'

I couldn't be bothered to argue. I was exhausted.

'Don't worry about it.' I turned and forced my jaw from his grip.

He insisted on sitting with me on a seat in the airport and continued to talk about our future together.

What's wrong with him? What's wrong with me?

'Will you miss me, Cariño?'

'Yes, I'll miss you.' This was true. Razor-blade pain behind my eyeballs stopped the tears.

Miguel leant over and whispered. 'What about my polla? Will you miss my polla, Cariño?'

An older Mallorcan couple walked by and gave us a disapproving look. The humiliation made me assert myself.

'I'm leaving and all you can talk about is your polla!'

'Cariño, what's wrong? Us being together is destiny. Fate. When you opened the gate and walked up my driveway the day we met it was as if you had lived at Villa Rosa all your life. You love our home.'

The word home set off the tears. Where would I go? When I signed the divorce papers, I'd have three weeks to remove my stuff. My husband's lawyer had wrapped it up: I'd leave with nothing. The apartment was in my husband's name. Homeless at thirty-five. This was not the life I'd envisaged as my fate.

'Cariño, I know you love me.' He started to kiss my neck (it was bruised where he'd bit me in the night) and made his way to my lips.

I kissed him. It was a farewell kiss, but I was the only person who was experiencing the pain of separation. I was processing two heavy loads of pain. His and mine.

'Remember the sailor wives' Jesus, Cariño? You will be back.'

I watched him wave as I went through the barrier with my transparent plastic bag of toiletries to freshen up on my Madrid – JFK flight and thought of the products with the New York labels I'd left in the cupboard, debris for the next woman to find. It was the most disconcerting feeling, saying goodbye to someone forever and them smiling back at you as if it was just goodbye until the next time.

How did he know I'd be back? It still irks me that he could predict me.

PART 3

Flight 705 To JFK

I'm in a house. It's by a lake. Switzerland. I'm in Switzerland. The lake is like glass. I want to walk into the lake. The shore reminds me of a beach the way it slopes into the water. I am wearing a long green dress like a woman from Ancient Greece. I start to walk into the lake, each step deeper, the water rising up my dress. I feel the dress hang wet and heavy on me, coaxing me onwards like a lead weight, pulling me down. There is just me and the water in a sort of serene togetherness, each ebb of the lake on the shore is perfectly in tune with my breath and I long to be the water so completely that I am the soft shish on the shore. I yearn to be the water.

Suddenly there is a commotion behind me. A man from another era is shouting someone's name. I do not turn at first as I have forgotten my name. I am irritated by the interruption as if shaken from a deep sleep. I stop and turn. The man is wearing an old-fashioned suit from the turn of the century. There is something dishevelled about him and neat at the same time. He wears wire-framed glasses and throws them off as he splashes into the lake. He lifts me up and carries me out of the water through the garden being tended by gardeners, up to a grand old house. It is his house.

Then I am in a sort of office-cum-library. The feeling is like in my old childhood living room. I am breathing North London air, but it is not North London. It is Switzerland. I know this. And I know I have not been born yet. This is before I am born. The man is Carl Jung and I have the feeling I've met him before somewhere. This is Carl Jung's bureau in his home. His wife comes in with tea. I know it is his wife and I know that she is afraid that I might betray her. I want to tell her she has nothing to fear – I am not born yet, but he ignores her and so do I.

We wait in silence until it is night and the household, his wife, the servants have gone to bed. Time passes quickly as we breathe in the North London air in the house by the lake in Switzerland – which I exhale and Jung inhales as he gets up to speed on my life, my childhood; my case.

Jung makes notes and every so often he passes me a pot of Indian ink and indicates that I should draw. Every so often I draw. Strange shapes and circles appear like mandalas on the page as if they paint themselves. He picks up one of my pictures, of a boat on blue water and puts it on the wall. It is instantly framed and he writes his name on the page. I don't like this, that he has signed my work as his own, but I know all comes from the Great One and so I hold my tongue.

Jung clears his throat, puts his glasses down on his writing desk and looks at me. Those intense, hollow blue eyes hold my gaze. I cannot look away. It feels as if I am falling into them, like falling into a bottomless pit. I gasp. It is the only sound I have made using my vocal cords, for we were communicating with our minds as he interrogated my personal history (this reminded me of Miguel's interrogation the first day we met after the interview). His eyes are Miguel's eyes and then my father's eyes and a sharp pang of fear makes me stand up. I want to scream and run out of the room and back to the lake and carry on with what I was doing. What was I doing in the lake? I begin to shake. I do not exist yet. But I am here. The incongruence makes me very, very fearful. But I sit as if I am paralyzed in the old-fashioned wooden chair and continue to share the North London air that hangs like a mist in the space between us.

There is a sexual tension in the room and a fire burns in the hearth. Neither of us have spoken with words, but Jung knows all he needs to know – and he is struggling within himself not to use this knowledge to destroy me.

Then Jung nods his head towards the window, and although we are in an era before television, it is as if the large window, which looks over the lake, black with the night, is a screen. On the windowpane rides a red figure on a horse. A man all dressed in red, hair a mass of red flames, rides on to the screen. Jung begins a silent dialogue with him. I do not understand what they are saying, but I know that they are talking about me – and the things Jung wants to do to me.

I want to run from the room as it heats up, hotter and hotter, but I cannot. I am trapped in Jung's house. Although nothing binds me, I cannot leave until Jung decides it is time for me to go. A tiny, barely visible girl is in the windowpane screen. She is dressed in a pale green Ancient Greek dress and gold bracelets of snakes are winding up her arms. She has no mouth. She becomes gradually brighter and I am transfixed, as if I am seeing my own reflection in the glass for the first time. The fiery Red Rider wants to kidnap her and carry her away. I look to Jung. He is silently crying.

He points at the figures in the glass and says in German: 'They are our shadows.'

I do not understand.

Jung points again as if his very life and perhaps mine depend on it: '*Unless you make your inner situation conscious, it will happen and you will call it fate.*'

The gold snakes on the girl's arms get bigger and wind up and around her like a throne of protection.

It was Jung himself I needed to protect myself from. I heard his inner battle, his desire to control me, his battle with the Red Rider. Jung filled me with the terror of being trapped.

I woke terrified on the descent into JFK with a jumble of words in my head: *make the unconscious conscious … call it fate.*' That's not right, but the more I tried to recover the words, the further they receded. I knew it was very, very important that I remember. I typed the dream in my mobile phone notes as fast as I could, straining into the shadow of the dream for every detail.

'Coffee, madam?' The flight attendant looked impatient behind her smile.

A voice in my mind said, *Cariño, you don't want coffee, do you?*

I sipped the coffee. After tea for weeks, airplane coffee tasted like a good brew. I began to cry again. How could I miss Miguel, a man who was so controlling, who wouldn't let me choose whether I drink coffee or tea for breakfast?

What on earth's wrong with me?

Coffee, the knowledge that the Statue of Liberty was below the clouds, and the first real sleep I'd had since arriving in Mallorca two months earlier made me feel real. I had to pull myself together and forget him. Whether Miguel accepted it or not, that was goodbye.

27

Christmas Eve

Sunset is a perfect time of day to arrive in New York City. Big orange rays have a clear stretch down wide, straight avenues. New York is a series of crossroads that extend from one side of the city to the other. Crossroads – the city's layout mirrored my life. After Deià's jumble of lanes and corners that hid surprises it was a relief to have so much space. The bigness of it hit me like it had when I'd first arrived from London nearly two decades ago.

A plastic Yoda swung on the mirror of the taxi. The taxi driver, who I'd hardly noticed when I got in at the airport, had a shaved head and a gold earring.

'What number?'

Mexican accent. His gold earring glinted in the orange evening as he took my case out of the trunk and set it down on the side-walk. I'd naturally adopted a few American ways of saying things, although after all these years I still sounded British and had to edit British English out of my articles, but being back in NYC I noticed that my silent internal words had changed. Trunk, rather than boot. Sidewalk, rather than pavement. I thought of Sofia's letter written in Catalan. I couldn't imagine a world where it was dangerous to speak British English.

A message from Miguel: *Cariño, please call me as soon as you arrive at your apartment.*

I reminded myself of my resolve as I took the elevator up to the twenty-second floor. *I'm not phoning him. Miguel doesn't listen to a word I say. He'll lie when I ask about Alessandra and why he's seeing a shrink. There's no point talking.*

When I stepped into my apartment reality hit. It wasn't mine anymore. There was an empty feel to it. Neutered tones once stylish now felt soulless. It had a bought feel. Someone else's vision of home. Not mine. Not anymore.

As my husband told me, freelance journalism isn't a proper job. I had no savings (I'd spent those on transatlantic flights) and no pension. Nothing was in my name. I'd be homeless. My husband had gone out of state on vacation with his family (who understandably now hated me) and when he was back in town I had to be packed up and out. In the meantime, he'd wiped the joint current account and told me I could only have my share after I'd signed the divorce papers. After splitting the joint account, I'd have $9000 to my name.

I sat in the cream armchair by the window and looked down over criss-crossing wrought iron fire escapes. I usually loved the run up to a New York Christmas, the buzz of shoppers, the smell of roast chestnuts, dodgy Santas on street corners that made me think of the Eddie Murphy film *Trading Places*. How long would $9000 last? Christmas was off. Not that I was in the mood. I felt lonely, sad, guilty, a failure. I'd tried to get my husband to go to couples therapy for over five years, but he wouldn't do it. If only I'd broken it off before I cheated.

My face crumpled. I tried to hold back the tears as after the betrayal I didn't feel I had a right to cry. I despised myself for it. The distortion of my pain split my lip again.

My phone beeped incessantly. Miguel, Miguel, Miguel.

I ignored it without reading his messages.

The first snow began to fall. My vision did a strange thing and confused the narrow alley at the back of the apartment block with the lane that led up from Villa Rosa to the road. Just last night I'd walked back down that lane as snow fell over Deià. How strange it is to hurtle one's body through the air, across continents and land in another place altogether. My body was in NYC, but my heart and soul were still in Deià.

It's over. You had a lucky escape. Stop thinking about Miguel, I told myself. But I couldn't help it. It was like picking a scab. The shock of the emails, the S&M photo in the cellar, the letter I'd scribbled before leaving for the airport in an unthinking rush and left in the library on his desk. I wanted him to know I wasn't the fool he'd taken me for – that I knew he'd betrayed me as well as his ex.

My phone pinged with the tone (Abba's *Fernando*) Miguel had set for calls and messages so I knew it was him. It still surprised me Miguel was an avid Abba fan. He was a mix of so many contradictions. I couldn't resist reading it.

Another message: *Cariño, I miss you. Villa Rosa is empty without you. Please tell me you are safe.*

Miguel must have read the letter by now. I imagined him reading the letter when he got back from the airport, breaking down, realising he'd lost me, catching the next flight to New York City to come and sweep me off my feet. I fantasised that my letter might ignite an epiphany and turn an old Scrooge into a generous, kind person with integrity who admitted his infidelity as I had done with my husband, had remorse, and begged my forgiveness. Chose me. Fat chance of that, but those were my foolish fantasies.

How sad we could not find a way, I'd signed off at the end of my letter. I gulped and let out a sob. Surely it would touch Miguel. Will anything reach him? I don't think he even understood that I was leaving him. It was as if he was just playing his own script and in his script I'd return to Deià after Christmas.

The phone interrupted my sobbing. My heart jumped with hope – maybe it was Miguel calling to put things right? Wrong ringtone. And how could he put things right? I'd be a fool to forgive him after his lies.

It was Miranda.

'Hello Gorgeous! Had enough of chasing your cunt across the world?'

'Miranda! God, I've missed you.'

'Right, postpone jetlag. There's a Christmas dinner at The Greenwich and you're coming. Gladrags on. 5pm Aperitifs. No ifs, buts or maybes. I'm paying.'

She rang off. Is that how she sees it, that it's just about sex?

The Greenwich is one of those five star hotels that does Christmas better than Lapland. Red berries and holly hung over the fireplace of the lounge bar and a huge Christmas tree that looked like Christmas stylists had been at it stood in the corner of the room. Grand as well as cosy.

Richie waved me over to an oversized sofa. He'd grown a handlebar moustache. He was no longer an advertising exec. He'd reinvented himself as a ringmaster in an animal-free circus.

'Here she is!'

'Love the tash, Richie!' I tried to be chipper as I kissed them all, but the sight of their concerned faces made me want to cry. I held back the tears.

'You look terrible.' Miranda, honest as ever.

'Did he starve you?' Shiva looked genuinely concerned.

'Size zero is so last year.' Richie hadn't lost his sense of humour.

'Yeah, a month in Deià with Scrooge is all you need. Don't worry. I've left him.'

'Thank God for that! Told you he was a shit.'

'You did. Wish I'd listened.'

'It was just because you hadn't had sex for so long.' Miranda's rationale for everything involved sex, but maybe she was right.

'So tell us all about it, Sweetie. But first you're having a burger.'

Richie lifted his hand and a young Italian-looking guy came over within seconds.

'But we're having Christmas dinner in under three hours,' I protested.

'And you're a turkey who needs fattening up.'

'I could kill for some fries.'

'That's our girl.'

Richie called over a gorgeous waiter. *Why couldn't I have fallen for an inappropriately young man instead of a complicated old Scrooge?*

'Mojito, darling?' Without waiting for my reply, Richie turned back to the waiter, 'Mojito for the *single* lady.'

He winked at the waiter.

'She's far too beautiful to be single.' He leant forward and looked me in the eye as he put fresh white paper doilies on the low table.

That's my Richie – set me up with an inappropriate antidote. A toy boy didn't interest me.

While I waited for my Mojito, Miranda shoved her cocktail into my hands and made a show of putting on her glasses on the table (her corporate boardroom weapon to distract people and interrupt their thread). She frowned, opened her Prada handbag and passed me her lipstick. I hadn't worn makeup for months. Miguel didn't like it.

It felt like an act of rebellion to apply *Rouge Coco Noir* in the mirror above the fireplace.

'That's better.'

'It matches your eye bags.' Shiva put her hat on my head – which meant I was in the talking seat.

'I haven't slept since the fifth century.' I felt my sense of humour return as I munched on fries and let the whole horrid experience flow out to frowns, looks of horror and rolled eyes.

'Oy Vey! It wasn't even good sex! Is there anything you like about him?'

I stared at them. All three stared back at me on the opposite sofa waiting for an answer. I scrambled about in my brain for a logical explanation.

'At first he seemed like the perfect man. We talked about literature and he seemed genuine, but ...'

Shiva couldn't keep it in anymore and swiped the hat from my head. 'The guy's not only an old meanie who can't keep it up. Miguel's abusive!' I'd never heard Shiva drop her gentle Asian diplomacy. She was furious. Abuse! The word stunned me.

Miranda swiped the hat from her head and put it back on mine. I suspected dinner had been planned.

'Abusive? That's a strong word.'

They looked at each other, confusion and shock on their faces. I felt like a child and the humiliation made my armpits sweat. I'd avoided their messages in Deià, avoided their judgements, their common sense. I'd had my phone switched off most of the time. I realised now I'd wanted to fall into that enchanted world behind the wall of the Teix. Reality's painful.

'He sounds like a narcissist to me. He lies, doesn't listen to you, leaves an asthmatic to wheeze in bed all night, feels entitled to spend your money. Not that you have any now due to the least strategic divorce ever. How could you live in New York City for eighteen years and divorce so badly?'

Richie faked a cough. 'Let her finish, Miranda.'

But it was too late – that started Shiva off. She didn't even bother taking the hat.

'He's a sociopath. They can't relate. How many times did you tell him you needed space before you left your husband? He hounded you to go back before you were ready. He just wants control. He couldn't care less about your needs. That's what sociopaths are like.'

I hadn't told them about his ex-girlfriend … let alone the neighbour.

'The sobresada thing. Meanness is so unattractive.'

'Our girl's home now. What are you going to do about getting a job?'

'No point looking over Christmas vacation. I'll let my network know I'm available as soon as the holidays are over.'

'You've got a good reputation. You'll find something.'

It wasn't finding work I was most worried about. It was the feeling of sitting in The Greenwich lounge, thousands of miles away from him, under his gaze. I'd had this feeling before. As a child. And all through my teens until I met my husband, I'd felt under my father's gaze. Now I had that feeling again. I hadn't escaped him. He was watching me.

My phone vibrated in my bag. I knew the ringtone. I switched it to silent without looking at the message.

'Was that him?'

I nodded.

'He's a predator. Delete it. Don't read it. He'll only try to persuade you to go back.'

'That's the problem. Although I've left him and I know he's a shit, I have this urge to run back to him.'

'Stockholm Syndrome.' Miranda said it with a serious look on her face.

'What's that?'

'Don't Google it now. Look it up when you're over him – but basically there was a bank robbery in Stockholm in the seventies and the hostages developed positive emotions towards their abusers.'

'He hasn't hit me.'

'Come on, you know abuse is not just physical. He's taking advantage of your vulnerable state. He's manipulating you.' Shiva sat forward. 'Listen, darling, just see him as a catalyst that made you realise your marriage was a sham. You're strong. You'll get over this.'

My phone vibrated again. This time I couldn't resist looking. *Feliz Navidad!* The second message was a photo of him and two women grinning at the camera, a lavish Christmas feast laid out on the table. A fish feast!

'Doll. Hello, is there anyone in there?'

'It's from him.'

'Turn your phone off. Block his number.'

I looked up, jaw dropped, heart palpitating. The phase Stockholm Syndrome spun in my mind. I hadn't felt this disorientated since I left Palma. Miguel ungrounded me, spiralled me into confusion.

I held up the photo for everyone to see. On the table was the sobresada, the octopus – all the fish we bought at the market.

'And who are those women? Do they know you paid for their Christmas dinner?'

They passed my mobile along the sofa. The humiliation of having been taken for a fool made me feel sick. I took a deep breath and bit my bottom lip. The pain stung like medusa.

'No tears on Christmas Eve.' Miranda squeezed my hand.

'Bastard.' That's what his ex-girlfriend had called him in her emails.

'Well darling, sometimes it takes being made a fool of to realize you are one.'

I zoomed in on Miguel's face. He looked happier than I'd ever seen him. Had he read my letter? Did he understand that I'd left him? Did he care?

'There's something else.'

They all leant forward on the sofa opposite me.

'He did the same to his ex. I read his emails. I know it was wrong but I needed to know for certain.'

'Darling, he's a narcissist. He'll have a string of women he's used and discarded. Once he's sucked one victim dry he'll move on to the next.'

'Shiva's right. Let him go. Rebuild your life. My spare room's yours until you sort yourself out, ok?'

Miranda was right. I mouthed *thank you*. I needed to let him go, but like a pitbull with lockjaw, another part of me just couldn't let go of the bone. I'd left everything for him, he'd persuaded me, made promises about a life together in Deià. Along with the pain and anger when I looked at the photo, a deep yearning arose for Villa Rosa, for nights by the fire. A yearning for home.

Villa Rosa will never be home. The voice was distant, a quiet knowing. A battle raged inside me and good sense was losing.

28

Disintegration

By the time I dragged myself from bed and switched on the TV, New York City snow was grey sludge. I marvelled at the efficiency of the city snow clear up (as I did every year). Giant snow machines had started sweeping the streets before dawn and the news commentator gave a neighbourhood-by-neighbourhood progress update. London would come to a standstill in this much snow ... and Deià? Deià was already at a standstill, locked in a time warp. My head throbbed from another sleepless night. The afterglow of being with friends had been extinguished by Miguel's incessant messages. His words got into my head, planting himself deeper with each thought and my brain had been spinning all night unpicking his web of lies.

I put the Alessi coffee maker on the hob. My husband and I had bought it in Rome. We'd been happy then. He'd never have stopped me drinking coffee. A fresh wave of grief caught in my throat. *What have I done? Just focus on making the coffee. Where's the coffee?* An empty packet of Lavazza rested on top of the garbage bag.

As if the universe was conspiring in my gloom, my phone beeped. My heart jumped in case it was another message from Miguel. He'd sent twenty-three messages since I left Mallorca. Must be strong, must follow Shiva's advice and delete all messages.

The bank. Shit, I'd exceeded my credit limit! My innards felt like they were being strangled.

What was I thinking, running away to Deià for months? I should have stayed in NYC, sorted out my shit, got a job. Why did I listen to Miguel, why did I trust his promises? He'd said not to worry about money – he'd cover my flight, the moving costs. He had money, but he never reimbursed my flights. Miguel didn't contribute a penny. Instead he spent my money on some Christmas bash with two women I'd never met ... was the older one his French publisher of the intimate emails? Come to think of it, he'd not introduced me to any of his friends. How had I ended up in this mess? How could I have been so stupid? *Miguel's invisible leash – I'd submitted to it.* Was Miranda right, was I so starved from being in a sexless marriage I'd run after the first guy who showed any interest in me?

My foolishness runs deeper than that.

I rummaged through the cupboards. Just tinned food, two rotten carrots on the top shelf of the fridge and a box of PG Tips at the back of the cupboard. No milk.

'Builder's tea, it is.' That's what we called strong tea in London. My voice sounded small and frightened. The London slang and the smell of PG Tips stewing in the mug reminded me of home. *Home? I'm homeless.* I knew that feeling. When I'd left home at seventeen I'd resolved never to go back. The sinking feeling of defeat made me dizzy. I was skint. My last paid job had been in the Autumn – the fateful interview with Miguel. *It's fate, Cariño. Fate.* A fate as bitter as black tea. I took a sip too soon and burnt my tongue. As I stuck out my tongue under the cold running tap I remembered my dream. Jung had spoken of fate ... and home. I had to go home ... but I don't have a home. I had a sharp niggle of intuition.

I have to go back to London.

London. I'd sworn never to return. It brought the memory of my father. The last time I saw my father was the day I left for New York. No, there was one brief visit to NYC, dark and blurred in my mind. My mother lived in a care home. *Maybe dementia is kinder than the truth.*

Londoners dream of escaping to the seaside. My old friends had fled for Brighton, Margate or the West Country. London wasn't home anymore, but I had to go back. It was like that feeling when you forget to pack something when you go on holiday and it's not until you get on the plane that you remember what it is. I'd forgotten something and I had to return to retrieve it.

I looked around me at all the beautiful paintings and tapestries my husband and I had bought together. There were white squares on the wall where he'd taken the expensive ones. Statues from Asia, wall hangings from Africa. I couldn't bear the task of packing that life up into boxes. *I'll phone one of those charities that clear out people's houses after they die. Just two cases for clothes, laptop and camera. That's all I need.*

Aghh! I'm a bloody fool. I chucked a cushion at the TV and the plant on top fell to the ground; the pot smashed and soil sprayed across the wood floor. We chose the oak together: *Whatever wood you prefer.* My husband had gone with my preference. Miguel would never do that. I stared at the soil, the exposed roots of the plant. My legs gave way and I had a sensation of my body folding, falling in slow motion to the floor. Pieces of ceramic stuck to my palms and the tears came, hot and fast. I was grieving the loss of two men at the same time. After the Christmas holidays I would sign the divorce papers and my marriage would be over. My kind husband at least gave me closure.

Miguel on the other hand did not accept closure. Instead he stalked me as if I'd not broken it off with him, as if I were returning to Deià. There was no point answering. Shiva was right. He's a sociopath. I told him countless times I don't have the money for a return flight.

That was the thought that made me panic.

I don't have the money.

My breath stuck high in my throat.

Sharp, desperate gasps for air.

Must stay calm.

Mustn't panic.

Need fresh air.

As I threw open the window a crisp layer of snow fell off the window ledge.

The city bombarded me with a wall of noise.

I closed the window immediately.

Shower, I'd have a shower.

I jumped.

Abba ringtone again.

Miguel.

This time I read the message: *Cariño, please, I'm worried about you. Call me.*

Hit delete.

Shower.

Let the hot water run over me.

Jesus! I still had my socks on. I wished I could run down the plughole with the water, be the water and escape the pain of dissolving, of not existing. What's happening to me? I felt like I was disappearing. What worried me most was the desire to be nothing. It was not violent. I didn't imagine cutting my wrists or taking pills. I saw the Cala in my mind and imagined Deià, its winter glow, saw myself leaving Villa Rosa and walking down to the Cala, into the water as I had walked into the lake in my dream and never coming out again, the medusa swimming past me without stinging as if we were fellow water creatures and they could not hurt me now – and I saw Miguel, for the first time with real feeling in his dark eyes. In my suicidal fantasy, my death woke his compassion.

Pull yourself together. It's Christmas Day. It's normal to feel shit being alone on Christmas Day. Just get through the next two days. Switch off your phone. Arrange to meet Shiva, borrow some money until the peanuts from my divorce come through in January. In the meantime, tinned food. It's not the first time you've eaten like a student.

My quiet voice spoke sense.

As I sat on the lounge floor wrapped in two bath towels, hair dripping, my phone beeped. *Who's that? Nobody close, no programmed ringtone. Who could be messaging me on Christmas Day?*

Drew Eddison: *Dear Friends and Colleagues, Seasons Greetings from the Eddisons.* And a family photo of the New York News Culture Editor grinning with his family under a card-worthy Christmas tree. Family. I'd met enough New Yorkers to know that the happy family image often masked dysfunction. I'd heard the rumours about Drew snogging the temp at last year's Christmas party. But it did remind me of my article. Drew had given me a chance as a freelance writer and I'd turned my article in late. It missed the print run.

I picked up my phone: *Sorry for the late arrival of the Nadal Interview. Thank you for the opportunity. Have a magical Christmas.*

Drew Eddison: *Deadline's a deadline. Where the hell are you?*

My fingers tapped the screen with hope: *Sorry, Drew. Have I blown it?*

Drew Eddison: *Will run in next issue. Good article. Got under the skin of the writer. You've never missed a deadline. What the fuck's going on?*

Damn, he deserves an explanation: *I'm going through a divorce. No excuse. I'm really sorry.*

Drew Eddison: *Sorry to hear that. If I throw you another job I need to know you'll meet the deadline.*

I felt ashamed of letting Drew, the paper and myself down. I'd been so consumed with my emotional world, with Miguel, I'd slipped out of time. I recalled the shock at the date when I sent off the article that Friday afternoon. I lost a week! Time was different in Deià. The wall of the Teix, it created an artificial bubble. Only now I was away from it could I start to get some sense of perspective, feel myself in reality again.

One Week Later

29

Coffee Me

One week later I ventured out. January in any city in the Northern hemisphere is depressing, but particularly in New York City. Americans go so all out for Christmas that the streets look dull and depressed when the festive masks are pulled off. People rushed past on the other side of the floor-to-ceiling pane of glass to jobs, families, things that bound them to life. Sirens and the drone of the city sounded far off like I was receding. I felt like I wasn't really there, like the bigger part of me was in Deià, watching the NYC street from the stillness of Villa Rosa.

Shiva sat next to me in the window seat of *Coffee Me*, in the same hat she'd worn the day after Christmas Day when I met her to borrow some money to tide me over. It must be new. She'll wear it to death then give it to Richie. The fact I could predict this gave me a small sense of security. Why couldn't Miguel be consistent?

'I'll get the coffees.'

'What with? The money I lent you last week? Sit down, I'll get them.'

Shiva put the tray on the table between us and arranged her sales bags.

'You look worse than last week.'

'I feel it. I can't sleep and I'm out of Lavazza! It's like post war rations in my apartment – and I can't rent a room unless the bank extends my overdraft.'

Shiva didn't laugh at my attempt at a joke.

'Why do you need rent money – you're going to stay at Miranda's when you move out your apartment, right?'

A screaming baby in its buggy put me on edge.

'I'm going back to London.'

'What?'

Shiva wasn't expecting that. Neither was I, but now I'd said it, I realized that was exactly what I'd been planning all week as I disposed of my old life, keeping only the essentials packed in two suitcases.

'Why? You don't have anywhere to live in London, no job. It will be like starting from scratch.'

'I can rent a room if I can come to an arrangement with my bank. London's not quite as extortionate as New York and I know a little nook in North London that's escaped gentrification. Built on an old plague pit.'

Shiva put her hat on my head. 'Ok, talk to me. What's going on inside your head? Tell me everything.'

I told her about the strange dreams, Miguel's messages, the way his refusal to acknowledge I'd broken it off made me feel as if I was dissolving, receding into the trauma of my childhood. I'd run from London escaping an abusive father, and unlike my American friends, I'd never addressed the trauma, never seen a therapist. It had been stiff upper lip for me. The past was over and I wasn't digging it up.

'… but I feel as though the past has found me, caught up with me. Miguel makes me feel like I did when I ran away from London to NYC at seventeen – like I'm still running from that feeling of not existing, of not being heard, still escaping the pain. I have to go back – like I have to return to the scene of the crime.'

When I'd finished I put her hat back on her head.

She wore a sad look.

'The past won't be there anymore, honey. It's gone. The only way to dig it up is to see a therapist and you don't have to go to London to excavate your memory.'

'I have to go back.'

'God, you're stubborn. Then see this guy.'

'Miranda recommended someone already.'

'Miranda only sees sexperts!' We laughed. 'Shop around, honey. Speak to them before you decide. You need an expert in narcissism in families … and someone who will go deep.'

She picked up her phone and shared her therapist's contact details.

'Jeff Monroe?'

'He's a Jungian psychoanalyst. I saw him when I was a student in London. He's hot on dream analysis. Take him your dreams – especially that one about Jung.'

I did not tell Shiva about my suicidal fantasy in the shower.

Just need to get to London.

Maybe Jeff Monroe could help me.

My NYC apartment felt foreign. Two suitcases stood in the lobby. That's all I had to show for sixteen years of marriage. I still had my Green Card so I could return to NYC to work, but I had to return within six months or I'd lose that right.

Miguel's name in my inbox startled me. He never emailed. He only used apps to call when I was in NYC. I guess he thought he'd find another way to stalk me. I'd read the preview lines:

> Cariño, I'm sorry. I dare say I've been
> a fool. Can you forgive me? I'm worried
> about you. Please send me your bank
> details. I want to deposit …

I knew I shouldn't read on. My gut twanged and my intuition screamed at me: *delete it*, but my heart fired with hope. It was everything I wanted to hear.

30

Therapist

The Edwardian bay-fronted houses differed only by their front doors. Messy front gardens tended to lead to the original doors with a small pane of stained glass at the top. Neat gardens led to new doors. The pavement was grey and wet from polluted London rain.

When I was a child I used to stare at the stained glass window of home from my usual spot at the top of the stairs, wishing I was on the other side of the door and far, far away. Ca n'Alluny, Far Away House – that's what Graves named his house in Deià. He didn't look back. A swell of fear gathered in my belly. Maybe I shouldn't either. This was not the road of my childhood, but it could have been any road in the villages meshed together that make up North London. When I'd left home at seventeen, I'd vowed never to return to North London. It felt like defeat to be back. Everything was different, yet the same.

I'd got off the bus opposite an equally familiar kebab shop sandwiched between a chippy and a Jewish Deli. Do they clone North London High Streets? *I'll pick up a tub of chopped liver and gefilte fish balls on my way back. I don't want to be late for my first appointment.* Jewish deli food was the only thing that gave me any sense of nostalgia. A shadow had descended like a Medieval tapestry, heavy with dust and survival, as soon as I stepped off the bus. Did everyone's therapists live in neighbourhoods that resembled the streets of their childhood? Or was this just a depressing coincidence?

Suburban North London makes me feel small, trapped, mute and as grey and meaningless as the paving slabs of stone beneath my feet. Add to that January's slit-your-wrists grey sky and the lingering terror of last night's dream (Jung had made another appearance; his need to control me still haunted me like he was inside me, a terrifying part of myself I could not escape). The world hadn't felt this bleak since I was a child. Jeff had asked me to write up my dreams. I wondered what he'd make of the famous psychologist's appearance.

I had loads of questions for my first session. I repeated them over and over as if they were the only things separating the grey of my being from the grey of the paving stones. *Why am I with a man who makes me feel like I don't exist? What's wrong with me?* I was certain that my nightmares held a clue.

Jeff Monroe's garden had the original door with the stained glass window. Jeff's door was painted gloss black. I was nervous and occupied my mind with remembering what colour our family front door had been. I waited with a patience only prisoners know. I couldn't remember the colour. On the other side of the door I heard a floorboard creak. My shoulders clenched at the sound, a flush of heat surged through my body, sweat cooled above my lip and something inside me contracted, and I had an urge to hide and curl into a foetal position. Someone was walking down the stairs towards the front door. My hearing painted a picture of the inside of Jeff's house. It was my own childhood staircase I saw in my mind's eye. I stood, motionless on Jeff's doorstep. In the black gloss of the front door I could make out the faint shadow of my body, upright, tall. *What's wrong with me?* I repeated the question like a mantra. It calmed me.

Somehow I always knew I'd be back here. Here, on the other side of the door, knocking to be let back inside. The weight of unfinished business was heavy on me as I waited for Jeff Monroe to open the door.

'So. Hello. Come in.' Dublin accent. I could trust that. My grandmother's Irish tones only ever spoke the truth. But still I was nervous.

Jeff's white hair was remarkably thick for a man in his seventies. He didn't smile but I took to him straight away. There was something no nonsense and real about him. After American service smiles it was a relief to be greeted by an honest look.

We sat in his front room, which served as his therapy room and library. Jeff on one couch, me on the other, face to face. Me, facing the bay-fronted window.

'So, can I get you some tea?'

Tea.

'I never say no to tea.' I relaxed back into Britishness.

As I looked around, I was catapulted back to my childhood. I'd sat in a front room this exact shape and size looking out of a bay window planning my escape. My earliest memory was of me as a terrified five year old in the same grey London light. Twelve long years of imagining myself big enough to leave, listening to the distant source of the hum of life and traffic of central London, wishing the curse of childhood away. Hour upon hour of imagining different methods of escape … I would be a lawyer in New York, nurse in India, journalist in Sydney, archaeologist excavating the ruins of Pompeii.

Bookshelves lined the walls. I focused on reading the spines to avoid the familiar light coming through the bay window and shut out the familiar drone of the city in the distance.

A book with a bright red spine caught my attention and my thoughts wandered off to Jung's office-library in my dream.

I can't remember now how we started. Jeff opened the session in a professional way and I found myself telling a seventy-ish year-old man intimate details about my life. Jeff listened.

'So, if I can stop you there. Miguel has lied to you, more than once, blocked you – and by that I mean that he ignores you, denies your reality, and you have evidence that he is intimate with another woman. He treats you like a slave to his needs without any regard for your needs, like an extension of his being. How does this behaviour make you feel?'

Thank God he's not one of those annoying therapists who listen like a leech and don't say a word.

'Confused, angry, desperate.' I did not add suicidal. It had only been a fleeting thought in the shower.

'Does he have any good points?'

The question shocked me. What did I like about Miguel? Now I thought about it, not very much.

'Well, to begin with I was enchanted by him … I admired his writing. He said he wanted to make a life together, tried to convince me to live with him in Mallorca. I said no, but he convinced me. And I believed him.'

'So, if I can stop you there. Is he attractive, physically I mean?'

'Not really. He's twenty-five years older than me. I find him attractive, but …' I thought back to the first time we kissed, how repulsed I'd been by his age spots, his sagging skin, by his disgusting exhibitionism.

'But?'

'But I made myself kiss him, forced myself to have sex with him like it was something I had to get over and done with, like the repulsion was a wall I had to get to the other side of. The first kiss made me feel sick, sick to the pit of my stomach. I closed my eyes and thought of something else, a vague hope of what was on the other side of the kiss. I made myself do it. Although I found him physically repulsive initially, now I desire him.'

Voicing this to a man old enough to be my father made me feel ashamed, but therapy requires honesty.

'How do you feel about that?'

I had a strange sensation as if the space between our sofas widened and bulged and in the jaundiced haze of North London light that hovered over the rug between us all the emotions of my childhood manifested. Invisible, but present.

'Shame. Shame that I got myself into this mess.'

'And does this shame remind you of anything?'

The North London yellow-grey light bulged further. I felt as though it might swallow me whole.

'My father.'

'Did your father ever interfere with you?'

'Interfere?'

'Any unwanted advances?'

'My father beat me. I've dealt with that. There was no sexual abuse if that's what you mean?'

'Did he ever humiliate you?'

'Yes, all the time.' I felt a repulsion creep up my spine as I remembered my father's naked body pulling me into bed with him, laughing and joking and his tongue licking my face and ear like a dog licks, but in slow motion leaving a snail trail of saliva. The memory ignited the same repulsion I'd experienced the first time I kissed Miguel.

'What did he do?'

'He used to pull me into bed with him naked, make fun of my breasts when I was developing, call me names: slut, cow, whore. My mother would just lie in the bed and read a book, say he was joking.'

I took a breath. I could taste the pale grey-yellow light – it was the flavour of pain.

'Even when I was thirty years old, just a few years ago before their NYC visit, I had to beg my mother to ask him not to lick my face in front of my husband. It made me so ashamed.'

To say these things, finally, to hear myself say them and not to be ignored was numb relief. I gulped the North London air and continued.

'I'd told my husband, but he sort of ignored what I said like my mother did. I felt like I was talking to myself, like nobody ever listened to me and wondered if I was making a fuss over nothing.'

'What you have just described amounts to interference. It is not ok to pull a young girl into bed, nor to make comments about her body – and licking a woman's face is disgusting. It amounts to sexual abuse.'

My brain froze. Sexual abuse! I was about to defend myself, my father, but asked a question instead.

'What's the definition of sexual abuse?'

'So.' Jeff started most of his sentences with so, then paused, like the word was a sentence. There was something reassuring about the decisive, abrupt way he said it as if each *so* marked the pulling away of some old dusty tapestry. I knew sitting in the yellow-grey light from the bay window that I needed Jeff, that I could not reach up and pull away the tapestry myself, but that perhaps we could do it together. 'Sexual abuse is anything which humiliates a person and distorts their natural growth. It does not need to include penetration to distort the psyche, to cause trauma and for the psyche to split as a result.'

Nausea pounded my throat: the memory of that first kiss with Miguel, disgust at my father, confusion at how I got to my thirties before anyone defined sexual abuse for me. I felt like I was going to puke. I needed a brandy. Instead I reached for the tea. It was cold. I downed it anyway.

'I was sexually abused?'

'Abuse is anything which distorts the psyche. What your father did to you amounts to sexual abuse.' He repeated himself and let it sink in.

Why hadn't anyone told me this? Why am I only finding out now? Why did my mother just lie there and read a book?

'How old is Miguel?'

'Sixty.'

Jeff nodded. His face was not like cardboard therapists who hold their gaze steady. Behind his watery blue eyes, his quick mind was building a picture, piecing together the jigsaw puzzle of my life. I sensed that he was going to put the jigsaw back together better than I could. But there were missing pieces. And the more we spoke, the more I remembered fragments, confused, hazy fragments and I felt as if I were standing at the edge of a bottomless pit. I felt like I did when I looked in Miguel's eyes.

'One summer when I was fourteen or fifteen, I can't remember which, I was in the playground and I said to Mel Rose, 'I had sex this summer.' She looked shocked and asked me who with. My head spun and I replied I did not know. That memory still makes my head spin in confusion. Why did I say it? That summer I'd been on holiday with my parents in Mallorca. I do not remember what happened, but I returned hating my father and something inside me had broken.'

There was a lull. I did not cry. I was too stunned for tears. I just sat there on the sofa, my hands cold and clammy. Breathing the air in Jeff's front room was like breathing the air of my childhood, as if the last exhalation before fleeing had loitered there in North London, stagnant, waiting for my inevitable return.

'Does Miguel remind you of your father?' Jeff's voice sounded very, very far away as if he were on speakerphone.

I'd become a statistic, one of those who repeats the pattern of child abuse again. And again. A grey staleness clogged my lungs. It was an effort to find my voice.

'Yes, in many ways.'

'What ways?'

'He's selfish, a narcissist, he's right about everything, it's his way or the highway, he's cruel, he's not violent like my father, but he has mad bouts of rage if he doesn't get his way ... like my father he has made comments about my breasts which humiliated me ...'

I did not mention his polla, how similar it was, the way it mesmerised me.

'That's enough. So he's like your father in those respects. And there is something sociopathic in the way he does not listen to you.'

'That reminds me of my mother too.'

The room was still, silent, but a clash of cymbals overwhelmed me as if the source of the sound was inside my eardrums. My breathing was shallow, clogged with grey-yellow light and tears threatened.

'He's my mother and father rolled into one!'

'Correct!'

I appreciated Jeff's straight-talking, but I'd leave here soon and walk those same North London streets I had not trod for years. I pictured my father raging like a rabid dog, spitting, saliva dribbling down his chin when I was five years old and could not reach the doorknob. Trapped in a room just like this. My thoughts became speech.

'My whole childhood was simply waiting, waiting to be big enough to reach the doorknob and walk away with a purse of my own like mummy.'

'So. You are independent. You walked away. In other aspects of your life you are confident, assertive, but here you are again with a dark abuser, playing the role of the victim.'

Confusion changed to panic.

'Abuse? That's a strong word. Is Miguel abusing me? I mean, he doesn't hit me.'

'Abuse is anything which distorts the natural psyche.'

I repeated Jeff's words as if I were back at school and learning something for the first time. 'Abuse is anything which distorts the natural psyche.'

There was a lull, but the silence between us was full.

'You say you were celibate for years. Did you desire your husband?'

'When we first met, but in the end I didn't feel like a sexual being.'

'When children are abused, their sexuality can develop so that they require some form of danger to excite them as adults.'

Jeff discretely checked the clock.

'I'm afraid we run to Freud's fifty minute hour and that has almost past. But I'd like to look at your inner world next time.' Jeff picked up my printouts. 'I have your dreams here. Shall we go through them together next time?'

'Yes.'

I wanted to run out of the front room, get back to the city, breathe in the fumes of New York rather than this stifling, pain-polluted North London air.

'So. Same time next week?'

I needed to get to the bottom of things faster than that. Jeff was the only thing standing between me and taking Miguel up on his offer to fly me back to Deià.

'Can we meet sooner, Friday?'

'Yes. In the meantime, you might want to give the relationship some space, come back to yourself. This will not be a fast process and therapy offers no guarantees.'

'How long?'

After what he'd just explained I knew this was a ridiculous question.

'Six months, possibly, if we meet regularly, if you do the work. It might be wise to stay in London so we can meet in person for at least two or three months.'

'Yes.'

When I stepped back into the Edwardian street I switched on my phone. Nine missed calls from Miguel. *Does he sense I'm disconnecting myself from him?* Delete, delete, delete. *Why hesitate? Why is it so difficult to delete his messages?*

As I waited at the bus stop and looked up at a grey stone gargoyle on the church I fancied I saw the face in the Teix in its gaze and felt home sick for Deià. *Why after escaping do I yearn to return to Villa Rosa?* These questions would have to wait until Friday.

31

Therapist

The red spine on the bookshelf caught my attention again as I sat on the sofa and Jeff Monroe poured the tea. His sharp gaze followed mine.

'Extraordinary that you single out that book. It is the red spine you are looking at?'

I nodded.

Jeff handed me the book. *The Red Book* was embossed in gold letters on the front cover.

'What a coincidence! Carl Jung.' I looked at Jeff who had picked up the printed pages with my dreams on. 'Jung wrote this?'

'Yes, remarkable in the context of your dreams. Jung wrote extensively about synchronicity. He did not believe in coincidences.'

As I flicked through, the pages of *The Red Book* parted and fell open on a page that described a red rider.

'Oh, my God!'

'The Red Rider?'

Jeff's eyes were closed. He was smiling as if extraordinary coincidences were usual in his life.

'Yes, the Red Rider, one of the manifestations of Jung's shadow.'

'What's the shadow? I mean I have a sense of what it is but I'm not entirely clear.'

'So. The shadow is that part of us we keep hidden, that causes shame.'

I wanted to ask, *what's my shadow*, but Jeff continued.

'Jung wrote *The Red Book* over the years he had a mental breakdown. Based on his behaviour at the time – his letters to Freud, his treatment of his wife, his affair – psychotherapists today suggest Jung experienced a period of what we would now call Narcissist Personality Disorder. *The Red Book* was written when he removed himself from the world, went inside to do the inner work. Jung attributed his most important theories to the period when he wrote *The Red Book*. In particular his shadow theory – the Red Rider represents his shadow, that part of him that he could not accept.' *Jung was a narcissist?* 'But today I want to focus on your first dream, your nightmare about Miguel's house, and the dream you had last night.'

'So. Would you like to remind me of the dream you sent me – the nightmare you had last night?'

'Yes.' I had a copy of the dream I'd tapped into my mobile phone notes, but I didn't need to refer to it. I pretty much remembered it word for word.

'I am at the gate of Villa Rosa – Villa Rosa is Miguel's house in Mallorca. I'm locked outside the house. I want to go inside. The garden is overgrown, a mess. I can't find Miguel. I look for him. The walls of the house are made of his skin, covered in age spots. Then the house changes and it is my old family home, very much like this house, in North London. My father chases me into my bedroom and beats me with a golf club. I am afraid. I am desperate to get away. My mother enters and tells me, *Daddy loves you*. I see the sea in the distance, the Cala, but the neighbour, Miguel's neighbour, stands in my way. He's threatening me with a pitchfork. I run around the back of the house intending to escape.

Red police tape is strung across the cellar door, the type in murder scenes. I am afraid, but drawn like a magnet towards the door. I have to know what's inside. I have to know the truth. I start to walk down the stairs to the cellar. I woke in a cold sweat, screaming. I can still feel the terror of the dream.'

'Dreams speak to us in symbols. Houses usually represent the psyche. The overgrown garden alludes to the confusion of your inner world. But it's Miguel's house made of Miguel's skin. It is as though you are sharing the same house, sharing the same skin, sharing his psyche. In relationships with narcissists – and I am not diagnosing him, I cannot do that from a distance and he's not my client, but from what you have told me, he presents narcissistic and sociopathic traits – boundaries are violated. Narcissists do not have boundaries. He treats you as an extension of himself. As his victim he feeds from you. Psychology calls victims narcissist supply. You realize the danger and have a positive impulse to escape. That is good. However, you are blocked by the neighbour. What does the neighbour represent for you?'

I think about the neighbour's warning, the word I found in the dictionary. Matar: to murder. For some reason I did not tell Jeff about the event in the graveyard. I shrugged my shoulders instead.

'He has a neighbour. He told me never to speak to the neighbour, that he's not a nice man.'

Jeff frowned and looked pensive. 'Ok, we can come back to that. Sometimes dreams speak to us in ways that reveal themselves over time. Have a think. At any rate, he represents a block for your escape. And then you have a compulsion to go into the cellar, your subconscious, your shadow. This can be seen as a healing impulse too as the psyche seeks healing. To heal we must confront our shadow.'

'Is that why I've ended up with Miguel?'

'Correct. In an attempt to heal your psyche has lead you to a dark abuser like your father.'

'But there's no healing with Miguel. All I've experienced with him is pain.'

'That is the message I think your dream is trying to tell you. And you realize it in your dream. The sea represents a healing impulse within you to be free. You believed that the life Miguel painted for you would offer some healing, a new life in Mallorca, but instead it is a lie. He is not the man you thought he was – inside the body of the sixty-year-old man is a child. His psyche is diseased – represented by the cancerous skin on the walls of his house. A relationship with someone with Narcissist Personality Disorder, or if that is not his diagnosis, someone who we know denies your reality, is a sort of murder. Victims of narcissists undergo a murder of the self, they are engulfed in the needs of the narcissist sometimes to the point they feel they no longer exist. We established last time that Miguel resembles your father. Your dream confirms this. In psychology we call this transference. You have found another version of your father and are hoping he will change. Miguel has not at any point demonstrated empathy. He is wholly concerned with his own needs.'

Jeff sat back on the sofa and stared at his bookshelf with a gaze that reached beyond the books.

'Why are they like that, my dad and Miguel – why are they so cruel?'

'So. In narcissists there is usually some trauma in childhood. It can be difficult to address as unlike you they often lack any memory of the abuse, of their needs not getting met. And so they compensate. If they go into therapy, which is rare, they usually leave as they do not respond well to being challenged.'

'Yes, they are always right.'

'Correct!' Jeff had a serious look on his face. 'And they only relate to their own needs. How does it feel when your reality is denied, when your needs are disregarded no matter how many times you appeal to Miguel?'

'I feel like I do not exist.'

'Have you ever had suicidal thoughts?'

I remembered my thoughts in the shower.

'I feel invisible, desperate with Miguel, very similar to how I felt as a child. On Christmas Day I wanted to disappear with the water down the plughole in the shower. Yes, I wanted to die.'

Jeff gave me a long stare.

'Dissolving into water. That came up in the Jung dream too.' Jeff shuffles through the pages he had printed my dreams onto and put on his reading glasses, then took them off and looked me in the eye.

'Miguel makes you disintegrate, like the house in the dream, if we see it as your psyche showing us the extent to which Miguel has infiltrated your inner world – the walls of your psyche being covered in his skin covered with age spots, as if he is a parasite on your house feeding off your psyche. That is the effect of narcissists. There is nothing in either of your dreams that suggests any healing will arise through relationship with Miguel, but they're only two dreams. We've come to the end of this session. Would you like to book another?'

'Yes.' My voice is small.

'Next week, same time?'

I do not know what week it is or what time, but I say, 'Yes.'

'Please continue to document your dreams and email them to me. When we have a series, we'll have a better picture.'

'Is there anything you want to ask me?'

'Should I return to him?' I knew this was an insane question in the context of the session, but they were just dreams and back then I did not value them as I do now.

Jeff eyed me intently.

'There is nothing good about Miguel's effect on you. He makes you disintegrate and your dream has confirmed what you already know. The question is can you prevent yourself from returning to him? You seem to be driven by a compulsion.'

Compulsion. I knew the word, but I did not remember its meaning – as if my internal dictionary had deleted the definition of the word which so accurately described my impulse to go back to Deià.

I got up to leave. *The Red Book* was sweaty between my palms.

'You can borrow *The Red Book* if you like – have a read, see it as homework in preparation for our next session.'

I do not remember saying goodbye. As I waited for the bus I felt like an open wound. I sat on the red plastic seat of the bus stop with *The Red Book* in my hands and stared at the bare branches of an oak tree. And as I stared, red madroño tree berries superimposed themselves on the winter branches. Did the berries hurt when they burst open? I felt like red madroño berries. Raw, unprotected, violated.

32

The Red Book

North London February drizzle. There's nothing greyer. Sandwiched between Camden Town and Belsize Park, my bedsit window faced a tower block with smooth concrete walls. On the single shelf above a hob with two rings was *The Red Book* and a defiant air-tight packet of Lavazza.

Deep down I knew that I would not be in the bedsit for long. It would have been cheaper to take a room in a shared house, but I couldn't face strangers. I was back in North London with one purpose: to uncover the invisible force ruling my life, compelling me to love a man who abused me. To know myself.

I made coffee with the dented Italian coffee maker I'd bought from a second-hand stall at Camden market, took *The Red Book* down from the shelf and flicked through, looking for mentions of the Red Rider.

Jung's voice was not what I expected it to be. His words had the pace of a storyteller, not a therapist. But perhaps that's what therapists are – experts at unpicking the narratives of our lives.

I stopped at a chapter entitled *The Red One*. It was a dialogue between Jung and the Red Rider. The similarities between my reoccurring dreams and Jung's narrative shocked me. I read with increased speed. Jung wore a green garment ... I wore a green dress in my dream. *Must ask Jeff what that symbolises. Feels relevant.* I closed the book and opened it again.

Jung watches from his castle as a horseman in a red coat approaches. Jeff said that houses represent the psyche in dreams, so Jung's castle is his psyche. I guess a narcissist couldn't be satisfied with a North London semi-detached.

I read on. I expected *The Red Book* would use some psychology jargon eventually, but it didn't. More like a fantasy novel with mythical characters set in ancient landscapes of Medieval Romance. Jung built drama like Stephen King builds suspense, using emotion. He described being overcome by a strange fear as the Red One, with red hair and shrouded in red, confronts him and Jung suspects the Red Rider is the devil.

Jung's vision continued with a dialogue between himself and the Red Rider (who berates Jung for judging him to be the devil). It had the rhythm and pace of the conversations I'd had with Jung in my dreams. Spooky – spooky like a horror movie where you don't want to look, but you have to carry on watching from behind the pillow to find out how it ends.

Dim February yellow-grey light peaked through the clouds. I'd been reading non-stop for three hours trying to piece together Jung's visions, searching for insights into my own dreams. I needed another coffee.

I picked up *The Red Book* again, its pages now stuffed with torn-off pieces of newspaper and re-read the sections about the Red Rider. The Red Rider was the character that grabbed me most – perhaps because he had shown up in my own dreams. What a mysterious coincidence. I'd never read any of Jung's work before.

Jung's narrator mused whether the Red Rider was his own personal devil. So was Jung saying that the devil was part of him?

I remembered Jeff saying the Red Rider was Jung's shadow and the shadow is the part of us that we don't accept. Why did the personification of Jung's shadow show up in my dream?

Jung answered my question. A sentence jumped out at me – 'If ever you have the rare opportunity to speak with the devil, then do not forget to confront him with all seriousness. He is your devil after all.'

The phone rang. Number Unknown. Normal ringtone and Miguel was far too stingy to pay international rates. It might be the bank.

'Hello?'

'Cariño!' Miguel sighed like he was relieved to reach me at last. Just this one word made my heart fire from its deepest chamber and his sigh conjured an image in my mind of the Red Rider. The Red Rider represented my shadow too, my desire to be controlled by men like Miguel, like the Jung of my dream, like my father. Was that it? I would have to ask Jeff. I knew I should hang up but I couldn't.

'Cariño, I know you are disappointed with me. Please, Cariño, I love you. Please let's talk. At least to have closure if that is what you want. I've been a fool. I have money. I dare say I should have given it to you when you gave up your old life to be with me. Please. Let me transfer the money to your bank account. Whatever you decide to do I want you to take my money. I can transfer 25,000 Euros today, now. Just send me your bank account details. Cariño, are you ok? I'm sorry, Cariño.'

It was everything I'd hoped for. Miguel acknowledging my need for closure, delivering on his promises. More than that – being prepared to let me go. And he still wanted to help me.

But what about the emails? The ex-girlfriend calling him a bastard, the flirtation with the woman in the sex club – and who were those women eating the fish I'd bought?

'Cariño, are you there? Talk to me, please, Cariño.'

His voice, the familiar frequency of it penetrated deep into me like water flowing into water and logic melted away.

He sighed again.

'I want a fresh start. To have a life with you in Deià, or wherever you want. I'll come to New York, anywhere. We'll find a way.'

The voice in my gut shrieked at me to put down the phone, to not listen to his promises, not engage in conversation, a voice like nails clawing the dirt at the sides of a well I'd started to slip down.

'I'm in London.'

When I spoke my intuitive voice dissolved in my belly, its protests disappearing like darkness falling into darkness.

'London?' He was silent. 'Cariño, shall I come and take you home? Just ask. I won't come if you don't want me. Whatever you want. I'm listening to you now. I heard everything you said. I was just a fool, an idiot, a Don Quixote. I've been fighting my own windmills, Cariño, invisible windmills. When you left I went to see the psychiatrist. She told me to consider your needs. I wrote down everything you said. From now on it's your needs first. I dare say I've been a fool, Cariño. Can you forgive me?'

His Enid Blyton speech made me laugh and cry at the same time.

'Who were those women in the photo? I went through your emails. I didn't trust you. I'm sorry for not respecting your privacy, but I knew you were hiding something from me. You were intimate with her.'

'It's ok, Cariño. I don't care you went through my emails. I was secretive, afraid. She is my publisher. Intimate?'

'You talked of stroking her hair as she read your poetry by the fire in Villa Rosa, in a language only lovers would use.'

'Not intimate, Cariño.'

'Would you talk to a man like that?'

He was silent.

'Yes, it is true, I have kept it open, kept the fire kindling. She's useful to me – but it's just a professional relationship. I don't want her. I don't even fancy her. I promise, Cariño. I'll stop interacting with her if you like.'

'That's not it. I just want to know you only use intimate language with me.' With that sentence we both knew I was won over, but that voice in my gut, the one falling away rose up from the darkness.

'I have to think about it. I'm seeing a therapist too. I want to talk it over with him before I make a decision. Until then I stand by what I said. It will not be easy to trust again. You lied to me about Alessandra. I don't care about the S&M photos. You asked her to come back to you *after* you met me.'

He sighed.

'I was confused, Cariño. You were such an unexpected light in my life. It was fate, I knew it, but I was afraid, I was slow to react to my heart. I called her after you left, she'd gone to visit her mother in Italy, finished the relationship with her officially.'

It was true that the emails stopped after I left, but it still felt incongruent. I didn't speak. The different voices within me were locked in a tug of war, one with my left ear and one with my right, pulling me apart, splitting me into two parts – one submitted to Miguel's voice, the other resisted, fought for autonomy.

He'd lied to me.

'I bought you a coffee machine, Cariño, an Italian one like the ones you told me you use.'

'This call will be costing a fortune. Shall we talk on a data call instead?'

'I don't care about the money, Cariño. I only care about you …'

I was melting, melting into him but the voice of reason rose up again. I interrupted him.

'And what about the corset? That was a lie too – Alessandra was wearing it tied to the birthing chair.'

He was silent.

'Well?' Any softness had gone from my voice. The rage I'd felt when I saw the photo under the bare bulb in the cellar the night before I left Deià returned. Miguel changed his tone too.

'¡Uf … just a jolly silly game!'

I sucked in my breath to hold back the tears at him justifying betrayal.

'I'm sorry you saw that, Cariño.' His voice changed.

'I dare say I lied about many things, Cariño. My limited mind-set is the reason for the corset idea. I was thinking of saving money, always thinking of saving money. We Mallorcans, we believe we are poor. I have spoken to my therapist about it. I am sorry for this. Cariño, please believe me. I will never lie to you again.'

'I'll call you back on data.'

It was late afternoon by the time we finished talking. I looked at the screen of my mobile: 4 hours and 34 minutes. I left it plugged into the electric socket beneath the sash window, loose in its frame with gaps in the putty like the windows of seventies London. The walls of the buildings outside the window transformed. Red sun-beams lit up dirty windows and I thought of how the last beams of sunlight make the face in the Teix wink before it falls into the shadow of dusk. Not even Jeff's sage advice would prevent me from returning to Deià.

33
Miguel's Therapist

I dare say I feel like I'm waiting outside a courtroom for my sentence every time I come here. The sign outside her door has changed. Gold, engraved with her name and qualifications: Melissa Tordera. Expensive looking. I'm paying her too much. ¡Uf! The neighbour. ¡Joder! The neighbour. How I hate him.

Her office door opens. She smiles in that patronising way therapists have and I follow her in. Mesmerising, the way her hips swing in that tight skirt, the sort my mother might have worn, or my grandmother. ¡Uf! I should be leading her to the couch.

I take my usual seat on the couch opposite her. She crosses her legs and pulls her long skirt further over her knees. She's not beautiful but she arouses my teacher fantasy. I picture her taking off her glasses, pulling up her old-fashioned skirt and pulling down her panties. Does she wear panties? Her face squashed against the upholstery of the couch, arse in the air, me pumping her. Ah! I'm hard. I am healed. She has healed me, my British muse. She will return. I need her. I just need to convince her. If she doesn't, I'll go to London to fetch her.

'Miguel?'

'Yes, sorry. What did you say?' The light from the window is in my eyes. I squint and she gets up to close the blinds. I dislike being interrupted.

'How have you been since we last met?'

Melissa looks intently at me. She's trying not to look at the bulge in my trousers. Does Melissa fantasise about my polla? Her voice comes back into earshot.

' … how are you finding the pills since we changed the dose. Are you less anxious?' She has such a gentle way about her, so caring, so trusting. She was a good choice. My lawyer was right. She believes anything I tell her. It's a joke, this therapy business. And there was me thinking they could read your mind or something! Therapists are as gullible as everyone else.

'Yes. They're working.'

'Good, we'll continue on that dosage then. Your libido is not affected? No side effects?'

'None.'

My thumb keeps moving against my hand. Melissa looks at my hands … or is she looking at my trousers?

'You seem agitated. Have you seen the neighbour again?'

'He still disturbs me when he crosses my land with his rake. Could we ask the court again that if he has to cross my land he leaves his rake at home. It re-traumatises me every time.' I am learning the language of this therapy business. It's money for old rope. I could do it myself.

'We know the court's answer to that. He said he needs it for his work and he feels he needs to protect himself from you.'

'¡Uf! It's crazy. The witness lied. I told you.'

'Yes, you did. Breathe. Just focus on your breath.'

Good, the hyperventilating is convincing. She writes in her notebook. This will all be used as evidence – in case I'm ever called to court again.

'How are other things? Your work? Your relationship?'

'Good. I've finished my novel. My girlfriend inspires me. She went to New York to divorce her husband. But now she is in London. She should be here with me. It is incredible. Like destiny. Like we have known each other forever. And the sex! And we talk for hours and hours. All night long – isn't that incredible? I need her with me at Villa Rosa. That house, I'm not happy in that house alone. I want her here. I'm anxious because she is not returning my calls – as well as because of the neighbour provoking me with his rake.'

I might as well get something out of this. And I dare say Melissa was quite useful last time when we talked about the relationship. I dare say! I'm even thinking in English now.

'Did you talk about your girlfriend's needs before she left?'

The question seemed odd. I stared at Melissa.

'Her needs?' My mind drew a blank.

'Yes. Did your girlfriend communicate what she wants from the relationship?'

'She said she needs space to think.'

'Can you give her that space? Can you respect her needs?' This irritates me. My thumb rubs fast against my palm.

'Yes, of course. I can do that.'

'A relationship is a two-way thing. You write the script together.'

'Yes, that is clear, but my girlfriend wants the same as me.' My thumb starts to move quicker. I feel the dry skin of my other thumb against my palm. Melissa watches my hands.

'Lay down on the floor please Miguel.'

I lay on the floor. I like it when she does this.

'Close your eyes. Now focus on your breath. Allow your thoughts to drift away, release your hands, put them by your side. Relax. That's it.'

As I listen to her voice and try to focus on my breath I get excited. I imagine Melissa opening my flies.

'If any random thoughts or images manifest in your mind, please tell me.'

'My grandmother. Although I know who you are, I picture you as my grandmother as you sit next to me, I see her in the bed as she used to do when I stayed with her at Villa Rosa in the holidays.'

'How old were you?'

'Very young. She was not like my mother. My mother was cold. My grandmother carried a great sadness in her, but she loved me.'

'Yes, she loved you in a good way.'

I see my grandmother's nightdress, feel my boyhood shame at the cruel words of the boy next door.

Your grandmother was a whore. She fucked my grandfather for sugar by the side of the road. Son of a sugar whore. Son of a sugar whore.

The old rage fills me along with the neighbour's peasant dialect; he still speaks rough like he did as a child.

'Now you are her. She is talking to me in the bed, my grandmother. She should be in my bed, not in London. Two months she's kept me waiting. Always waiting.' My breathing is shallow.

'What are you feeling now, Miguel? Your girlfriend is not your mother, not your grandmother. Remember what we discussed last time? What feelings does she provoke in you?'

'She brings out the tormentor, the aggressor in me.' I shouldn't say that. I don't want any court thinking I have violent tendencies. 'I would never hurt her. I love her. I just want to be with her so much, it's such a strong love it's a violent need, that is all. I love her.'

'Keep breathing – now slow the breath down. Breathe into the present moment.'

I breathe. It calms me. I don't like that Melissa is in control. I go soft.

'Good, that's better. Can you give your girlfriend the space she needs to make her decision?'

'Yes.'

As I said it I felt the rush and urgency in my chest to get back to my computer to draft the letter that would win her back, pull her back to me.

'Thank you, thank you. I know what I must do now.'

'Good.'

Words of persuasion started to form the sentences in my mind. Her needs. She wants security, a home, she wants Villa Rosa to be hers. I will promise her all of that. These shrinks aren't such a waste of time after all. A ring. I will give her a ring. Women love rings. It reminds them of marriage.

34

Therapist

Jeff Monroe's watery blue eyes were pensive after he'd read my dream, which he'd printed on crisp white paper. I stole the moment to look at the spines of the books in his North London living room. I couldn't think of it as anything other than a living room as I'd spent so many hours associating those big bay-fronted windows with home as a child. But this was a room for business, the strange business of unlocking the secrets at the heart of human behaviour. Did I understand my own behaviour yet? I understood that I'd chosen a man like my father. What I did not understand was why I would do such an illogical thing. All I'd ever dreamed of was being free of his control, his rage, his gaslighting, his neglect, his letching – and what I was slowly coming to accept: his abuse. Like returning to North London, to a living room almost identical to one I'd spent twelve years dreaming of escaping – from the age of five when I looked up at the unreachable door handle as my father raged, until I cut loose at seventeen. It made no sense.

'Remarkable dream.' Jeff's gaze moved from a point in the middle of the room where the yellow-grey North London light hovered between the two couches and looked at me. 'As we have established, dreams are full of symbolism and houses usually represent the psyche. Does Switzerland mean anything to you? Do you know anything of Jung's life?'

'Only that he's the reason we are sitting here now – that Jung and Freud were the fathers of psychotherapy – I thought he was German. Was he Swiss?'

'Yes, he was Swiss. And the Ancient Greek dress you wore in your dream … what does Ancient Greece symbolize for you?'

'Ancient Greece brings to mind the Greek Myths, philosophers, beautiful statues, naked statues which did not shame or hide the human body. But I wouldn't have wanted to be a woman in Ancient Greece – from what I know women were kept indoors for breeding.'

'So. You are dressed as a Greek woman, the woman whose only escape is to suicide – I assume that is what you are intending to do in your dream? Or to disappear, submerge yourself in the subconscious – that is what you are doing in this work.'

'Yes, there was a sense that I was going to disappear into the water, but I was not afraid. The lake was inviting me to share its dark serenity. I knew that was my only way of escape. I've tried meditation, various forms of healing approaches over the years. I've always known I was screwed up.'

'Meditation will take you only so far. The only way to transform is to re-experience the darkness. The lake is a symbol of your subconscious. There are no guarantees in this work.'

'Jung was dressed in green when he met the Red Rider in *The Red Book*. Why green?'

'Yes, green – it is different for everyone, but it could be seen as a healing impulse. All the characters in dreams can be seen on one level as different aspects of the psyche. Your green dress is a healing impulse as well as a potentially destructive impulse. Jung concluded, like the Buddha, that bringing the light to the darkness was not enough, meditation was not enough – one must confront the negative emotions, return to the original trauma and by so doing, the hope is that healing will follow, that the negative emotions will transform through love and acceptance.'

'You're saying that's why I'm with Miguel, to relive the emotions of my childhood?'

'Correct. The psyche seeks healing. The word heal comes from whole. The psyche seeks wholeness, to unite the fragmented aspects of self, to bring together the splits in the psyche. At a young age you split sex from love. Our job is to unite your personality split. Your psyche seeks to return to the original trauma in order to heal.'

We both stared at the rug between our sofas. At the centre was a mandala pattern which glowed in the dim North London light. Jeff looked up and focused his sharp blue gaze on me.

'So. Can I ask you, have you ever felt suicidal?'

The question made me hold my breath. Yes, when I was seventeen. I couldn't take any more of my father. I begged my mother to listen to me, just to listen. It was after he'd gone on one of his rampages, smashing every plate in the kitchen – it was like being at one of those gimmicky Greek restaurants living in our house. He came for me with the golf club – I can't remember if he hit me or not that time, but I couldn't take anymore. My mother kept telling me he loved me really. I was hysterical. I threatened to jump out of my bedroom window unless she listened to me. I just wanted her to listen to me. I screamed at my mother, *He's a nutter, he's mad, can't you see?* My mother was angry at me, no, you're the mad one. And I realized she was right – I had the window open and I was threatening to jump. I had no intention of doing it, but my behaviour was definitely mad. After that I stopped being able to cope. I was suicidal then. Instead of killing myself I left home.'

'And have you had any suicidal thoughts since then?'

I think about it. I felt desperate at Christmas in New York, when I'd received Miguel's messages in which he ignored everything I said to him, ignored the pain I'd expressed in my farewell letter.

'Narcissists do not relate. They only care about their needs. Denial of your reality is a form of psychological abuse. How does it make you feel?'

'I feel as though I do not exist. My head spins. I am confused by how he twists what I say when I remind him that I cannot come to Mallorca to live with him. He tells me I am mad. He ignores me and gets angry if I disagree with his version of the way our life will go. This makes me panic and I feel like I'm losing my mind.'

'So, you disintegrate. Your sense of self is denied. Does this remind you of anything?'

My heart gallops like wild horses. I feel like I'm about to be trampled to death by the charge of energy racing through my body, by the realisation. 'It reminds me of the night I just described to you – of my mother telling me I was mad.'

'Denying someone's reality is a form of psychological abuse. What you experienced as a teenager was what psychologists call a Double Bind, whereby the victim of abuse may be sane, but is driven to insane behaviour by the environment they are in. It seems that you maintained your sanity until your teens when your mother's denial of your reality drove your psyche to disintegrate and out of desperation you sought, or contemplated the only way out of the pain. Suicide.'

I was struggling to breathe. The air we shared between us, the intense yellow-grey North London light from the Edwardian bay window was overwhelming. We'd been at this for weeks, replaying, revisiting, circling back to the past I'd spent a lifetime forgetting. My shoulders started to heave. Tears fell on my lap.

Jeff nodded towards a tissue box. I dried my eyes. Jeff waited. His gaze darted to the clock on the mantelpiece. For a moment I thought it was the clock in my childhood home. I used to stare at it, willing time forward. He picked up the page with my Jung dream again.

'So. Do you feel ready to continue looking at your inner world?'

'Yes.'

Jeff leaned forward, his elbow on one knee and looked at me very intently.

'Jung, the psychologist who invented shadow theory is in the dream. His Red Rider character is also in your dream. Had you read Jung's *The Red Book* before our previous session?'

'No, I'd never heard of it.'

Jeff sits back and looks pensive again.

'Extraordinary.'

'I read it at the weekend. The Red Rider – is he Jung's shadow?'

'The Red Rider certainly seems to be one of the numerous representations of Jung's shadow in *The Red Book*.'

'Jung says in the Epilogue that it took him sixteen years to write.'

'Between 1914 and 1930 Jung worked on *The Red Book*. The Jung family finally allowed it to be published seventy years later. The synchronicity with your dream and Jung's visions is extraordinary … and the concept of synchronicity also came from this period of his life. You knew nothing about Jung; however, you have in your dream created what sounds very much like a description of Jung's house on Lake Zürich. More pertinent to your case is the fact that during this period, Jung exhibited behaviour that many psychoanalysts today would describe as Narcissist Personality Disorder. He had an affair, exhibited grandiose attitudes and lived solely in his fantasy world. He tried to rein in his narcissistic behaviour and struggled with this for the rest of his life. Jung considered these decades the most important of his life. He attributed all his subsequent theories to the period he retreated – the shadow, transference, and so on were derived from this pursuit of the images and fantasies of his inner world and stories and visions that spun out of it. His shadow concept in particular. As we have discussed, the shadow is the part of us that drives compulsive behaviour, the part we often repress and label as bad, unwholesome, the aspect of self that we do not want to own.'

Compulsive. Compulsion. That word again.

'In this dream you and Jung are in his house by the lake. He takes on the role of your therapist and on the windowpane you play out your shadow selves together.'

'What is my shadow?'

'We've discussed that your shadow is the victim.'

I don't remember discussing this, but then as I think back to our previous sessions, my shadow was the only thing we were discussing. As with the word compulsion, I was blind to it.

Jeff looked at me and as if he sensed my confusion, my not remembering this, my blind spot. Like the best teachers he repeated it in another way.

'A part of you is assertive, confident, but a part of you seeks to submit to controlling men like your father. Like Jung in your dream. Jung's shadow was the narcissist. The red-cloaked man in your dream, the Red Rider as you call him, is almost exactly as Jung described in *The Red Book.*'

This coincidence should have spooked me out, but it didn't anymore. The realisation that I was somehow caught in a pattern of replaying the pain of my childhood through my relationship with Miguel was far more unnerving. I felt out of control. As I looked back over my scant relationship history I realized that every man (except my husband) had been controlling to greater or lesser degrees.

'You're saying that Carl Jung was a narcissist?'

'Yes. He did not consider himself fit for practice and refused to take patients during most of the period he worked on *The Red Book*. He would lock himself in his room and go into his inner world. When the shadow is kept hidden, not accepted, we act out. Jung sought to bring his shadow into the light.'

'What does act out mean?'

'Act out means we are driven by unconscious desires.'

'What are you saying? That I have an unconscious desire to be abused?' My voice was wobbly.

'In the dream you and Jung are both struggling not to fall into your patterns. He is trying not to control you. You are trapped, chained under his gaze, under the gaze of the dark abuser. His face changes to your father, to Miguel, and back to Jung. It is as if this desire to be controlled by a dark abuser is rooted in your childhood abuse by your father. Our early parental experiences become branded into us and drive our behaviour until we free ourselves from them. That is the work we are doing here. We seek to free you from your compulsions.'

We contemplated the mandala in the middle of the rug.

'To answer your question, yes you are driven by an unconscious desire to be abused. The psyche seeks healing.' Jeff repeated this phrase again. 'In this dream there is a glimpse of a healing impulse. You have sought out a therapist – the man who founded shadow theory – Carl Jung.'

'But I've sought him out in his narcissist phase. He controls me in the dream.'

'Correct! Jung represents your shadow, the dark abuser you have internalised, as well as an impulse to liberate yourself from its grip. Your inner world is showing us your shadow very clearly. You seek out men like your father, dark abusers, and you try to change them.'

'Oh God!' I groaned. 'You're right! I see it. I'm trying to change Miguel. I mean why not just choose a nice guy, right?' The penny dropped. As if mirroring this lightbulb moment the rug took on a slightly less jaundiced glow.

'Correct! If it had not been for the abuse by your father – and your mother denying your reality – you might have been satisfied with your husband.'

'We can't know that for sure.' I say it slowly as the dawning happens, but I know this to be true. I remember thinking when I said *I do* at the alter in Las Vegas in front of Elvis that a safe barrier had been drawn between me and my lust for dangerous men. 'It's true. Somehow I always knew this.' I was ashamed to admit it.

Jeff's voice was soft. He knew the truth was painful for me.

'Yes, and more amazing are the words at the end of the dream. They call to mind Jung's words … I can't remember exactly, but something to the effect of until you make the unconscious conscious, it will drive your life and you will call it fate. No, that's not quite right. Hold on, I have it here.' Jeff got up and took a book from the shelf, passed his finger down the index and flicked to a page near the end of the book. 'Yes, here it is. *When an inner situation is not made conscious, it happens outside, as fate.*' He replaced the book, returned to his sofa, sat down and looked me in the eye. 'The hope is that by bringing the shadow into consciousness, the victim, the part of you who wears the Greek dress and cannot assert her needs, who disintegrates if she is ignored, if her reality is denied, who desires to be controlled by abusive men – by making that part of yourself conscious it will no longer control your choices. In this work there are no guarantees and you may always find those types of men attractive. But the snakes on your arms do not allow the Greek green-robed victim to be controlled by the fiery red-cloaked rider. Snakes represent wisdom and the gold bracelets, female accessories traditionally used to beautify, to seduce, transform into powerful protectors.'

My heart sped up. I understood this. It was as if I had always known this and the wisdom of dreams.

'But I love him.'

'Yes, you confused love and abuse at an early age. In the first dream we discussed, your mother tells you *Daddy loves you* after he beat you with a golf club ...'

'That happened.'

'Yes.' I felt the compassion in his voice enter me as he nodded his head. 'That's a very confusing message to give a child. We will work together to try to bring that confusion into the light.'

'It makes me so angry. My father made me like this.'

'Yes, it is an extraordinary thing that our romantic desires and sexual fantasies are forged in childhood.'

I had not talked of my sexual fantasies, but it was true that the Jung dream had been infused by a sexual tension.

'So. We are coming to the end of our session. How do you feel?'

'Numb.'

'Remember the snakes, the green dress – they represent a healing impulse for self-protection in your psyche. There is hope in the dream.'

Jeff walked me to the door as I wrapped myself in my coat and scarf. I was shivering from my cold epiphany.

'When would you like another session?'

'I'm returning to Deià.' I should have told him this earlier in the session. Was I afraid he might talk me out of it?

Jeff did not look surprised, but a very serious expression made his jaw appear locked.

'Are you ready to die for this man?'

Jeff's question shocked me. I wanted to tell him not to be so dramatic, but I knew what he meant – by returning to Deià I faced the very real danger of disintegrating and falling into madness. And then another realisation.

'You mean that if I am triggered to act out that I might make real the feeling of not existing?'

'Correct.' Jeff said it gently. 'The pain of not existing may be matched by an impulse to suicide.'

I knew it was unsafe to return, but I was driven. It was as if I had never really left. Deià was inside me, Miguel was inside me. I had to give him one more chance. What if he delivered on his promises this time? What if he adjusted his behaviour, what if he loved me enough to change? He'd said that he was seeing his psychiatrist and talking to her about us. That she had asked him to consider my needs.

'I have to return.'

'Can you agree a time limit – book a flight back so that you can return and reflect on your time together, take it slowly?'

I stared at Jeff and his voice grew distant, like I was already gone. Miguel had booked me a single flight. And where would I return to – the bedsit? I'd not be renewing my lease. All I could think of was Deià.

Jeff tried another tack.

'You must tell Miguel what triggers you.'

'Tell him I have suicidal thoughts you mean?'

'Yes. You must tell him that when he ignores you, blocks you, lies to you that you disintegrate, you are triggered into suicidal thoughts.'

'Yes, I'll tell him.' The thought of admitting my weakness to Miguel was daunting – what if he used it against me? But I knew Jeff was right. If we had any chance of making a go of the relationship, I had to be honest.

I pulled on my gloves and tried to hold myself still. I was shaking.

'Thanks for your advice, Jeff.'

As he opened the Edwardian front door, he added, 'If you need a session, we can do it online.'

Like I used to do as a child on my walk to the bus stop, I avoided stepping on the lines between the grey paving stones. The grey North London streets seeped into me and I longed for big blue Mallorcan skies and Miguel's arms around me. And hope. My phone beeped when I turned it on. An email from my husband's lawyer. He wanted an address to post the divorce papers. Nausea gagged my throat. I felt faint. I'd lost my husband's protection … from myself. I was alone, but at least I was free from denial. The paltry sum I had to show for sixteen years of marriage was pathetic, but I felt grateful to him. What we had was wholesome. It was me that wasn't whole.

My yearning for Miguel's arms was intense. Maybe Miguel could change now he was seeing a therapist?

My mind rolled back to the Hermitage, to my silent vow.

How can I dream about marrying a man I've just spent an hour discussing as a 'dark abuser' as Jeff calls him?

I coughed as the February fog hit the back of my throat.

PART 4

A Bedsit, North London

My nights became silent. No Villa Rosa. No Jung. No Red Rider. No me in a green dress.

The condensation on the windowpanes made it impossible to work out what the weather was like, but the atmosphere in my bedsit clung to me like the damp London Februarys of my childhood. I rolled over in the single bed and the broken spring groaned.

Abba's *Fernando*.

Morning X

I was dissatisfied by Miguel's message. The ringtone triggered anxiety, but there was some comfort in it too. I imagined him getting out of bed, eating his breakfast standing up in the kitchen as he threw me a crumb of a message before he started work.

The week before I left London felt like the week before I left home at seventeen. My fairytale future distracted me from my emotional state. I knew that developing a relationship with Miguel would not be easy. I was resolved to be honest with him. At least then, if it didn't work, I would know that I had tried, taken Jeff's advice and voiced my needs and told Miguel what triggered me.

Abba's *Fernando*. Miguel's tone made my breath catch high in my chest.

I have listened to what you said, Cariño. I understand you. I understand that you need security.

Abba's *Fernando*. My heart beat faster. Anxiety increased.

A photo. I could not make out what it was. I dropped my phone on the bed. It rang again.

Abba's *Fernando*. Breathe, must hold myself.

The deeds for Villa Rosa, Cariño. We have an appointment in Palma with the lawyer. I dare say you will need to sign them. Come home, Cariño.

Abba's *Fernando*. This time my heart filled with hope.

Another photo. A selfie of Miguel in the church of Santa Eulàlia standing in front of the sailor wives' Jesus.

Since our conversation, my days were punctuated by Miguel's morning messages, his night-time calls. The consistency of it, the regularity, like clockwork, 7:30am and 10:30pm, lulled me into a false sense of security. These crumbs of attention, coupled with Miguel's promises, were sufficient for me to feel safe to return to Mallorca.

Are you ready to die for this man? Jeff's warning echoed in my head as I stood under the shower in the shared bathroom and violently lathered the shampoo into an old lady white bouffant. *You must tell him what triggers you.* Jeff was right, I mustn't forget how low I became. I rinsed off the shampoo and watched the suds being sucked away with the water. Death by plughole. I would never let myself get into that state again. Christmas had been tough. I still felt guilty for betraying my ex-husband, but at least he had the chance to start a new life. And so did I. *To free yourself from your father's abuse, you must not act out your shadow. Do not play the victim.*

I had returned to London and discovered the mystery of my behaviour. Was it possible to change?

35

Grandmother's Ring

The plane was only a third full. Early March isn't a popular time to travel to Palma. I looked around at my fellow passengers. It was a comparatively short hop on the Gatwick-Palma flight compared to the trek from New York. Two teenage boys with dark hair and blue eyes, possibly visiting grandparents, and several formally dressed Spanish men and women, likely returning from London on business. An older British woman with dyed red hair and white roots, a huge diamond ring on her middle finger, returning to her second property perhaps.

A steward passed me wearing so much chemical perfume it lingered in the stale air around me for a few breaths. I coughed and clicked my phone back on. The screen opened at the page of the book I'd been reading in the departure lounge. I found my place. Mallorca's surrender had been brokered by the British consul in Mallorca in collaboration with Franco's Nationalists on 7 February 1939. Did the British fear communism more than fascism or was it more simple? Trade. Wasn't it more likely the British wanted the war over to free up international waters for trade? Perhaps both.

I carried on reading for a bit, but it was difficult to concentrate so switched to another book and scrolled to the section on the

Balearic Islands. More than two thousand executed. Men being taken in the night; family members who brought food to the jail were told that where they'd gone, they wouldn't need it. Miguel had told me a similar story. My neck ached. I rolled my shoulders back. A vertebra in my spine cracked as I stretched. My ears were so blocked that I had a locked in feeling.

As the plane circled the North West of the island I added a red bookmark on the page and closed *The Spanish Holocaust* on my phone. I squinted through the window to single out the Cala among the secluded turquoise coves. How many men were forced to jump from those cliffs in the night?

On the surface it might seem that Mallorca got off lighter or with less of a fight than parts of the mainland. But reading between the lines I speculated that Mallorca's soul had undergone a slower, more insidious torture. Franco had been appointed Captain General of the Balearics three years before the civil war started.

The plane tilted to the right and I looked across to the windows on the opposite side. All I could see was the sea. The man sitting across the aisle had a moustache like General Franco. That little Hitler clump of facial hair must have been the fashion during the 1930s. He had the same fat oval face and black Franco eyebrows. I felt cold all of a sudden, looked away and picked my phone up again from the empty seat where I'd placed it.

Franco took a similar approach of inflicting terror throughout Spain as he had during his time in North Africa. His entire battalion in Morocco stuck decapitated heads on sticks for his approval. He appeared to be one of those merciless military nutters who enjoyed inflicting unnecessary harm. I suspected Mallorca's soul had been eaten away by fear before the Civil War even started. Franco's pathological control must have been felt deep in the souls of Mallorcans before the island's surrender. There is something powerful about putting up a fight. I knew this. I did not take my beatings lying down. Child though I was, I'd resisted, called my father a wanker when he raged at me. Was that why Miguel's grandmother wrote in Catalan – was it her personal revolutionary act of defiance? My father could beat me, he could terrorise me, but he would not silence my soul. The day he conquered me was the day I surrendered. I'd been surrendering to men like him ever since. My ex-husband was a place of safety, a place to hide, a celibate landscape without passion or danger. Maybe my affinity with Mallorca was nothing to do with the seduction of its fertile valleys and sunny coves. I identified with its silenced soul, its buried pain. Spain's shadow was well hidden in Mallorca, in stark contrast with its paradise veneer. Mallorca's shadow mirrored my own.

The sight of Palma Cathedral on our descent extinguished my dark musings; its sandstone elegance brought back that sense of possibility and expansion I'd experienced months before at the Hermitage. The last conversation I'd had with Miguel had given me hope that we could make it work, that I could make this island home.

When I switched my mobile back on, Shiva's name pinged on my screen: *NYC to London. How's it going with Jeff?*

My face flushed. How do I tell my friends I'm back in Mallorca? The last video conversation I'd had with Shiva I'd promised her the relationship was over.

Our hotel was tucked away down Carrer de Can Brondo, a tiny street off the wide leafy Born. The Brondo Hotel website described its decor as New York loft cum Bohemian chic. Miguel wanted to book a cheap hotel the other side of the Avenida. I wanted to be in the magic of old town. Brondo was made up of several buildings:

eighteenth century Mallorcan townhouses and a factory. Before and after Franco, I thought. It retained the high ceilings and mixed opulent elegance with cement floors and walls of glass that invited natural light.

As it was low season and the manager was a hospitable Mallorcan (I'd concluded that Mallorcans, with the exception of the crazy neighbour and Miguel, are nothing like what Sand experienced in her *A Winter in Majorca*), we were upgraded to a suite with a terrace.

The manager showed us to our room. I looked up the modern steel staircase and bare brick walls.

'Follow me please.' He spoke in English rather than reply to Miguel in Castilian Spanish. Why on Earth did a Mallorcan man insist on speaking Castilian Spanish? Was it because of being in the presence of a foreigner? I'd noticed Catalan people switch to Castilian Spanish when foreigners are present. Miguel would not care about that. Perhaps a leftover of the Civil War years when Mallorcans would have been punished for using their Catalan dialect? Surely not. Although the more time I spent on the island, the more I noticed the influence of the war. Is it possible that terror is passed down through the generations, a sort of emotional DNA so that we are shaped by the trauma of our ancestors?

As my suitcases were crammed with all my worldly possessions the manager was some way behind us.

'Miguel, go and help him with the cases. They're heavy.'

'Why did you bring so many things, Cariño?'

'Two suitcases are not a lot.'

'I dare say you're right.'

Has his therapist told him to agree with me? Better not to question it. He's gone to help.

'And remember to tip him.'

'Why would I tip him if I'm bringing the luggage?' Miguel looked genuinely confused. *Jesus, this was not going to be easy. I guess this is what they call 'working' on a relationship.*

My ex-husband would never have questioned a tip, especially not if we were upgraded! My ex-husband was American. It's a different culture. I resolved to stop comparing.

The manager opened the terrace floor-to-ceiling doors for us.

'Bonic.' I said beautiful in Catalan to compensate for Miguel's rudeness.

'Where are you from?' he replied in Catalan.

'Sorry, I only know a few words in Catalan.'

'He asked you where you are from, Cariño.'

I understood; speaking is harder.

'London originally ... but I live here now.' I looked at Miguel then hesitated.

Miguel answered in Spanish. 'We live in Deià.'

This time the Manager answered in Spanish – for my benefit. I understood a little better why Deiàns might dislike Miguel. He refused to speak the local dialect. It was like he was saying, I am different to you, better.

'Ah, Deià, I ride my bike there at weekends.'

That won't go down well with Miguel – he fantasises about running cyclists off the road.

'How wonderful ...'

Miguel spoke over me. 'Next time I see you I'll run you off the road.' This he said in Catalan (I was picking up more). Language in his mouth could be used as weapon and communication tool within the same sentence.

I laughed, gabbled in a combination of English and broken Spanish to make up for it. 'The views are so incredible. Graves, you know the poet, he said Deià is already-painted.'

The manager laughed and chose to take Miguel's comment as a joke and smiled at me.

'Yes, but we need to keep an eye on the murderous drivers!'

Good answer! We both laughed from the gut. Miguel joined in although he had that lost boy look on his face like he didn't understand the joke.

'Well I'll leave you to settle in. Please do not hesitate to call reception if you need anything. Will you be dining with us?'

'We will dine out tonight.'

Wow! Miguel's booked a restaurant for dinner. How lovely! He's really making an effort.

Miguel's expression darkened as soon as the manager left the room.

'Why were you laughing at me, Cariño?'

A twinge of fear made the muscles in my left eye judder. I stepped towards him, put my hand on his arm to pacify a simmering rage I sensed inside him.

'We weren't laughing at you, Miguel. Why don't you speak in Mallorquín? You grew up here, right?'

'My mother insisted on Castilian, Cariño. My mother tongue is Spanish. I am different, Catalan does not come naturally to me.'

He switched his demeanour in his sudden way. The switch didn't calm my twitching eye.

'Cariño, you returned. That is all that matters. You love me.'

'I do love you.' I said it with the knowledge that I had tried not to love him, that I was holding on to the thin hope Jeff had unintentionally given me: *It's rare with narcissists, but healing can happen with love.* Miguel was trying.

I followed him outside onto the terrace. The high walls either side created a sort of vacuum shutting out the city. We sat on the sofa next to each other like any ordinary holidaying couple might.

'You like it, Cariño? Anyone could see us out here.'

Something in his energy changed. I knew he was thinking of sex outside on the terrace. As if the invisible sexual leash jerked around my neck I walked on my knees across the sofa towards him. We both looked up above our heads to the other terraces. When I looked back at him his polla was out and ready. The risk of being seen which had excited Miguel was contagious (although moments before I only wanted to enjoy the silence and his presence). I dropped my knickers on the stone floor and climbed on top of him. He opened my blouse and sucked hard on my nipples. My short shriek joined the caws of seagulls in the turquoise blue square of sky above the inner courtyard.

As usual he needed to take control of my leash and positioned me on all fours on the sofa. He wanted something I had previously refused. I would compromise as long as my needs were met too, I had resolved within myself. In cat pose, back arched, neck stretched up to the sky I came again and this time the square of turquoise transformed into night and I felt as though I were all the galaxies in the universe for a brief moment and I became nothing in my personal galaxy of pleasure.

Miguel was happy.

'I dare say I told you that you would like it, Cariño.'

I could not argue. It had been the most intense orgasm of my life.

Miguel got up swiftly without holding me as I'd asked him to do. It made me feel like crying, but maybe that was the shock of the orgasm and losing my anal virginity. It was a more intense, forbidden (in the Catholic hemisphere of my brain) penetration, and I was a little in shock.

'Miguel, can you hold me please.' My voice was a plea. It made me feel pathetic.

He stooped, back to the terrace with a blanket, which he put round both our shoulders.

'Be careful of your lungs out here, Cariño. The plumber is coming the day after tomorrow to fix the heating in Villa Rosa.'

'Thank you.' I stroked the whiskers on his cheek and smiled. He was growing a beard.

'I have something for you. I hope you like it.'

He gave me the blue velvet ring box to open myself. It was a pearl on the thinnest band of gold. That would bend out of shape after a single bowl of washing up, but the pearl was beautiful.

'It belonged to my grandmother.'

Was this an engagement ring? His grandmother's ring. That's a big deal. My mind wandered to her words, pressed between the pages of her recipe book – they'd been in Catalan. My gut danced in a confusion of hope and fear.

'Which finger should I put it on?'

'This finger.'

He put the ring on my marriage finger. I imagined this same smooth motion of his hand over the fingers of his dead ex-wife and ex-girlfriend.

'Does it fit?'

'It's a bit big.'

'I dare say we can have it made smaller tomorrow.'

He gave Alessandra a ring too, but he never married her. I pushed away the soft voice of intuition. I'm not spoiling a night at the opera with my doubts.

36
Opera

We showered together in the Brondo's minimalist wet room, prepared for the opera and walked into the night like any Palma couple might. The sky had turned electric blue and the stars were out as we sauntered hand in hand down the narrow cobbled street on to the grandeur of the *Paseo del Born*. The dryness of his palms reminded me of my father's hands. I was aware of that now. Transference, Jeff called it. *He's not my father. If I want this to work, I must interact with the present, not my past,* I told myself.

It was a honeymoon evening. Hats-and-coats weather but mild after icy London drizzle.

'So where are we going for dinner?'

Miguel mumbled something. 'We are on a budget, Cariño.'

Instead of dinner we ate empanadas on a bench opposite the opera watching the beautiful people file in through the glass entrance doors of the Teatre Principal.

I enjoyed eating al fresco under the sky without Miguel's restaurant anxiety. And the empanadas were delicious. They tasted like home after exile. How I had missed being close to him. Gratitude is a wholesome feeling.

Our gaze locked onto a beautiful woman, heavily made-up, cleavage low, dress skin-tight in red stilettos. She fawned her partner as they walked past us and crossed the road to the opera.

'Some men like their women to dress like that. So he can show her off – look what I have. Look what a big polla I have. I don't like women who dress like that. I dare say I prefer the Arab way, your tits for my eyes only.'

Why's he telling me this? It made me feel uncomfortable. I brushed the empanada crumbs off my lap.

We were like teenagers in the box. It was not like going to the Met with my ex-husband (how strange to now be divorced, a woman with a history, a new identity). No ice bucket, no Champagne.

When an old couple entered the box next to us, Miguel started to behave in the self-conscious way he did around strangers. Old – they must have been in their sixties – so Miguel's generation.

'I bet they haven't had sex for years. I dare say he is jealous of me, Cariño.'

I laughed.

Miguel picked up my foot, took off my shoe, put my stockinged foot on his leg and started to massage my foot.

'How are your feet in those high heel shoes, Cariño?'

Miguel moved his chair so that my foot massage was in full view of the couple. This was embarrassing. I pulled my foot away wishing I had a programme to stick my head into – but Miguel would not buy a programme. Instead I leant forward over the balcony and watched the opera-goers below in the plush auditorium of the Teatre Principal.

'This is so exciting. I haven't seen Carmen for ages.' The last time was at the Met with my ex-husband. We'd sat with our gaze in the programme or binoculars to avoid talking to each other.

The hush of the audience drew my focus to the stage and the curtain opened on a square in Seville. On the right, a door to the tobacco factory. At the back, a bridge. On the left, a guardhouse.

A factory bell rang and the cigarette girls ran on stage tittering and gossiping.

The old couple next to us lifted their binoculars. Maybe theirs was a sexless marriage like mine.

Carmen entered. Black hair, faded red dress. She bulged, skin glistening with sweat, over her corset strung tight with stereotype. An off-white rag of a petticoat above her corset threatened to reveal her nipples on each inhale as she sung her first aria about the wild nature of love. She was the most provocative Carmen I'd seen. Her voice, the vibration of mezzo-soprano notes, transformed the atmosphere of the auditorium, which buzzed on the frequency of sex. I indulged in the afterglow of sex on the terrace under starlight and avoided looking at the couple next to us (who were probably equally embarrassed by Miguel's earlier foot rubbing attempt).

In the interval we went to the bar and Miguel bought one glass of Champagne to share. 'You didn't want a whole glass to yourself, did you Cariño?'

'Yes, I did.' *He can't change into a generous man over night,* I told myself.

'Shall I go back and get another glass?'

We looked at the hordes of people pressing against each other like refugees, desperate to be served. I thought of the book I was reading; the description written by Julián Zugazagoitia, a socialist ex-minister handed to Franco and shot. The human mass scattered across the winter countryside that slept huddled around fires fuelled by wood from carts and branches. In the morning, mothers refused to let go of babies dead from the cold. These were perfumed opera-going Mallorcans, but even so, how can a whole nation transform from one version of itself into another in a matter of decades and forget? That harrowing description was imprinted into me just from reading it and the glorious Mallorcan sunset bled a little that evening. Within this crush of bodies were decedents that carried the frequency of loss in their souls. The opera, the bullfight, the sunset as it bleeds into the ocean that skirts Spain like a petticoat, is where that grief is held.

'Cariño, I dare say we will get crushed in there, but I will buy you one if you want.'

'No, let's enjoy this one together.'

We passed the glass between ourselves and I tried to not feel that old disappointment. It was a small thing. Was his stinginess a symptom of the trauma of this island? The German couple next to us were laughing and joking, so free and easy together. It made Miguel's uptightness more obvious. I had a vague sense that I recognised them. Then the memory came back to me. They were the same couple we'd passed months before when I first walked with Miguel in Palma's streets. I smiled at Miguel. There was a scowl on his face. He was trying and so was I, but could we change ourselves at a fundamental level when the trauma that had forged us occurred so young? Perhaps the best we can do is to become aware of who we are. Would self-awareness give us choice? At times I felt like an addict in relation to Miguel and addiction dissolves choice.

'There was a recent production of Carmen by an amateur acting group here in Mallorca who used the metaphor for the War Civil. Anachronistic, of course and too simple. I did not like it. As Orwell pointed out in *Homage to Catalonia*, the war was morally muddy. It was totalitarianism on both sides.'

Listening to him speak about his history reminded me how I'd fallen in love with him. Although his insistence that there was no such thing as truth was a problem in our relationship when it came to his lies, it felt appropriate in the context of the Spanish Civil War. But it annoyed me that as he spoke he raised his voice, so his opinion could be heard by the couple next to us, rather than lowering it so that we were in intimate conversation. Why did he always have to put on an act in public?

'Let's go back to the box.' It was impossible to relax with him in public.

He took off my shoes again and picked up my foot and massaged it balanced on his knee. This time I allowed him as nobody was watching. Our neighbours (and everyone else) were in the bar. Maybe now was a good time. We had forty-five minutes of the interval left.

'My therapist told me that I must tell you what triggers me. This is embarrassing but Jeff insisted that I must tell you that I might become suicidal when you ignore me, change the subject without acknowledging what I'm saying, when you massage the truth, and when you get angry if I remind you of real life.'

Miguel put my foot down and pulled me towards him. I looked into his eyes, desperate to find compassion in them. His eyes were dark mysteries to me.

'Focus on the present, not the past, Cariño. On our future togetherness. My therapist said this is the best way forward for us. Please don't punish me for my mistakes.'

I kissed his cheek. Then looked at the pearl on my wedding finger.

'Is this the ring you gave to Alessandra when you proposed to her?'

His eyes darkened. Maybe this wasn't a good time.

'You want to talk about this now, Cariño?'

'I want to talk about it before we return to Villa Rosa. On neutral territory.'

Miguel nodded and looked at my stockinged foot.

'Alessandra killed herself rather than live without me.'

I was stunned. *But she called it off with him. I read her emails.*

'When? When did she kill herself?' My voice quivered, my heart raced, my head spun. It didn't add up.

'My grief has nearly ruined our togetherness as a couple. My therapist says this is the reason for much of my behaviour.'

Was this possible? The floral dress, the emails – they stopped when I was in New York over Christmas. So when did she do it? Did she move out when I was in New York after my first visit and then kill herself when the emails stopped? But he was asking her to come back. She finished it. Not him. I stared at him, stunned.

'I read your emails. She finished it with you.'

He looked like I'd slapped him round the face.

'You read my emails, Cariño?'

'I told you and apologised.'

He cleared his throat and continued. 'I do not care. I have no secrets from you. It is true that she left me, but she wanted to come back. While you were in New York at Christmas she returned for her things. I had stored them in the cellar. When she saw another woman had moved into Villa Rosa she changed her mind, wanted to try again. I said no. I told her that I was in love with you.'

Was this possible? Why didn't he tell me Alessandra had returned for her things? Too many secrets. Was this credible?

'I'm sorry, Cariño.' He massaged my foot. I pulled it away from his pacification. It reminded me of my mother telling me daddy loves you really after a beating, the incongruence of it, my wanting, needing to believe in the words even when the reality couldn't be further from the truth. He took my foot back. I allowed him to continue, massaging me with his words, setting the story straight.

'Forgive me, Cariño. I thought it was better that you were not exposed to this. There were so many problems between us already. I knew you would not return if you knew. I know I did the wrong thing.'

'When were you going to tell me?'

'I don't know. I'm telling you now.'

Crocodile tears, I thought.

'It is true I limit myself, I worry about money, but we Mallorcans,' (that was the only time I ever heard him call himself Mallorcan), 'we believe we are poor. We were poor for many years, for generations after the War Civil. But what am I trying to say?' He kissed my foot and looked as if he might cry. 'I am trying to say that I love you, Cariño. Alessandra, her mind was unhinged. She was not happy for a long time. I tried to help her, but she ...' His shoulders slumped forward. 'I'm sorry, Cariño. I did not want to give you this burden. Alessandra. My therapist tells me not to blame myself, but ...'

'It's not your fault,' I heard myself saying. Did he ignore her? Deny her reality too? This time the voice in my gut woke me up.

'I do not want that to become my fate. I take full responsibility for my actions, but I'm sorry to tell you that I have had suicidal thoughts – when I was in New York.'

'I told you not to be there alone. I wanted to go with you, to support you, Cariño, but you would not allow me.'

That was sort of true – in as much as I'd left him.

Miguel grabbed my foot, stopped my thoughts in their tracks and broke down in tears.

'Cariño! Thank you. Thank you for telling me. Thank you for loving me. Thank you for returning. I went everyday to the Jesus of sailor wives and I begged for your return. Thank you for believing me.'

Don't trust him, screamed my inner voice and my belly rumbled.

'I believe you. If we are aware we can avoid falling into our patterns. You can avoid making me an extension of your fantasy world and denying my reality and I can avoid my own – my panic and disintegration when you deny my reality. We can do it if we stay conscious.'

'Yes, yes we can, Cariño.'

His face was wet with tears.

'When I saw you open the gate and walk up the drive to Villa Rosa that day I knew it was fate. I had no choice. I was confused, Cariño. Finishing a long relationship is not easy.' That much I agreed with. There were days I'd considered running back to the safety of my ex-husband, tearing up the divorce papers, not signing them. 'I do not want that to become your fate, Cariño. I failed to see the signs. Thank you for seeing a therapist and trying to make our togetherness work, Cariño. Thank you for telling me your triggers – I will not fail this time.'

This last sentence worried me, but I couldn't work out why. I was swept away with grief. His and mine.

'I want to understand you, Miguel. Why do you lie?'

'I have to be innocent, Cariño. My therapist says that is why I bend the truth. It's like adding anachronism to a historical novel aimed at historical accuracy. The reader will lose trust in the story if all of a sudden you have Franco call Mussolini on his mobile phone.'

The music began, lights dimmed and the velvet curtains opened on a square in Seville. At the back of the stage were the walls of an ancient amphitheatre with posters advertising a bullfight.

Jeff's voice cut across the voices of Carmen and her new lover, the bullfighter. *Narcissists always have to be right or their fantasy world will crumble. They need to believe their own lies.*

I get it. I understand him.

'Thank you for your honesty, Miguel.'

I squeezed his arm and carried on watching the love story ramp up to its tragic finale. The old couple were seated in the box next to us. How long they had been there I do not know, we were so sucked into our own drama.

Carmen was alone on the stage with José, her old love as he pleaded with her to return to him. She wore a black dress with a slash of red silk for the final act.

'No! No!' Carmen belted out.

My belly rumbled in unison. Truth has a frequency and Carmen's truth soprano'd in my belly.

Carmen threw José's ring across the stage.

The theatre held its breath as José followed her, knife in hand.

He grabbed Carmen by the wrist; she leant backwards, her black dress off one shoulder, hair loosened from its fastening and held the knife close to her neck as she struggled. Carmen freed herself from his grip and with one swift movement José stabbed her in the stomach.

I gasped. I knew the ending, but Carmen's plight had entered me, her voice vibrated in every cell of my body. Her tragedy felt as though it were mine too. When Carmen slumped dead into José's arms, he placed the ring she'd thrown at him on her ring finger.

As we shuffled downstairs towards the exit in the crush of the mass exodus, Miguel mumbled a line from the first aria in my ear, 'Si je t'aime, si je t'aime, prends garde à toi.' His breath was hot and a low vibration of sex still hung in the air, heavy now, with the darkness of tragedy.

Miguel

37

Transaction

The jewellery shop is in the old town. It irritates me the way she walks like a German tourist, so delighted by everything. She's nearly in my pocket. At least this old wooden door's been oiled. When I brought Alessandra here, it squeaked on its hinges.

The owner's eyes light up as I approach.

'Señor Nadal ...'

I like that he knows me by name, and smile as he fawns pleasantries over me.

He was a friend to everyone with jewellery. My grandmother's voice; her words still bubble up inside me from time to time. *His father melted more wedding rings than a priest melted candles during the war.* He never got your ring though, did he grandmother.

'What can we do for you today, Señor Nadal?'

I pass him the blue velvet box with my grandmother's pearl ring in it.

He recognises the ring of course, but he doesn't show it. He smiles and asks for the lady's hand. His ring of ring sizes jangles as he waits.

¡Uf! The shame she gives me. She looks like an idiot, that blank stare.

'Show him your hand, Cariño.'

She holds out her hand.

'The wedding finger?'

I nod.

'Congraulations, Señor.'

I can hear him. *How long will this one last?* As long as I choose. That old thunderbolt of rage shoots through me. But this is part of it, part of the game. The ring. It will bind her to me. A warm, woolly expansion in my heart? It surprises me. The idea of her being bound to me, perhaps?

'This one's a bit loose.' She looks down at her ring finger with the jeweller's tool on it.

'Let's try this one.' He's smiling.

'Oh, not in English, please. I'll never learn otherwise.'

'Prueba este.' Still smiling.

Whether she understands the words or not – he's speaking in Spanish. As he knows I will not speak in Catalan? Probably because he assumes she will not understand Catalan. I'm being paranoid, but I know they don't like that I'm different from them, that I'm special.

'Eso es una K. Bueno. Podemos cambiar el tamaño del anillo en unas pocas horas.'

He is polite. He speaks to both of us, as a couple, when he tells us he can resize it today. She likes this. I feel her body warm as she snuggles in closer to my bare arm.

'They can resize your ring as we wait or we could return, Cariño.' I play patient translator. My voice conceals my irritation. I add as if it's an after-thought, 'or I dare say we could go to the bank now, Cariño, and your ring will be ready when we return.'

'The bank?'

'To transfer your divorce settlement.'

'Oh, open a bank account you mean?'

Her expression. The distrust. I need a different tack.

'Into *our* account.'

Her frown. She has a ring. What more does she want? That usually does it.

'Into *our* kitty, Cariño.'

'Open a joint account, you mean?'

The rage is in my face. The jeweller is hovering. I feel his discomfort. She's humiliating me again.

'Regresaremos hoy, más tarde.'

I dismiss him.

'Gràcies, Senyor. Estará llest per tu en breu.'

Yes, that's it, back off, you peasant shopkeeper.

'Let's discuss this outside, Cariño.'

She's not going to give in without a discussion. ¡Uf! She's hard work.

Tourists and lunch-goers bustle past us. How I hate the city on days like this.

'Let's walk and talk, Cariño.' I don't like an audience.

She takes my hand. Good, she will yield to my will. If not, the ring will do it when she puts it on her wedding finger.

'Your money is no good to you in dollars, Cariño.'

'It's been so emotional, so fast, I hadn't thought about it, but yes, I should open an account here. In my own name.'

'We are going to be married, Cariño. Joined in all ways. A couple. A real couple. I'm so happy. It makes sense to deposit our money together.'

She pulls away as I reach with my lips for hers, stops in the street.

'I'm not depositing my money in your account.'

¡Uf! All this fuss for $3000. It's the least I'm owed – for keeping me waiting, tormenting me, making me suffer. I'm not going through that again. A joint account. That could work too, for now. I'll make sure I'm the only one with a card and access.

'Of course not, Cariño. A joint account is what I mean.'

'Your idea of fifty-fifty is eighty-twenty.'

'$3000 is not a lot of money, Cariño. I'm a poor Mallorcan man, but I have more than that. Together we are richer. Together we can do anything, Cariño.'

For a moment I believe it. A vision of a future off this island starts to form. Her gaze is on me. I take her arm, keep us walking. She pulls away from my arm, but walks with me.

'I know how I was about the sobresada, Cariño. I limit myself. I'm sorry for that, Cariño. I was thinking as a single man, not a couple. But that has all changed now. I understand what you need.'

'What do I need?'

'Security, Cariño. You need to feel safe.' This was something my psychiatrist had told me. *What does she need? For a woman to leave her home, she needs to feel safe there will be a home for her with you.* Therapists are good for something it seems.

'I'm here. I'm prepared to try. Is that not enough?'

'It's give and take, Cariño. I do not want to be going to the sailor wives' Jesus to pray for your return every time you leave Mallorca. I need security too, Cariño, please. Will you meet me halfway?'

She takes in a gulp of air, looks up to the sky. Her eyes are the same wide blue. She sighs. She's letting go of her resistance. I'm nearly there. The house will convince her.

'We will share everything. Deià, Villa Rosa, the bed …'

I kiss her, move in towards her. Feel her yield to me.

'I love you, Cariño. I want to share everything. You are part of me.'

'But what if it doesn't work? What then? Until I learn Spanish I'm dependent on the odd job I get from the New York News, and after the messages from my editor on Christmas Day I doubt I'll be top of his freelance writer list.'

'It will work, Cariño.' Shift to her logic, shift to her thoughts of another divorce – as if that could ever happen with us. 'Then the law will decide it, Cariño. I have no children. No family, except for you. Legally you are entitled to fifty percent of everything I own.'

I take her arm, gently this time, as if we're on an aimless stroll through Palma's dry streets, enjoying the shade of the palm trees – and walk in the direction of the bank.

38

Jewellery Shop

Desde 1926. The jewellery shop survived the Civil War. The signage – swirly gold calligraphy – looked different when we returned, as if I were in some unreal dreamscape. I felt the cobbles, painful under my feet. I carried the weight of a mistake inside me. It was one thing sharing a kitty. Another entirely to transfer the $3000 left – after flights, London bedsit rent, deposit (lost), living expenses, paying back Shiva and therapy fees – into a joint account. *Together we are richer*, Miguel had said. There was a look in his eyes then – was it hope? Was it sincere? Whatever, he'd convinced me to trust him.

Inside, old-fashioned luxury gave it a timeless quality. The glass in the carved polished wooden cabinets sparkled clean, but there was a dusty feeling of something worn trying to be new.

The jeweller greeted us. The ring was nearly ready, just being polished. Miguel was more chatty now, more relaxed. The visit to the bank had given him security. It had the opposite effect on me.

As they talked, I walked towards the door. I needed to be alone for a moment, to take in the reality of what I'd just done. The ring did not bind me to him. It was the joint account that did that. We'd found a compromise. Not his account. I'd have my own bankcard.

I pulled open the door to step outside into the sunshine.

'Cariño, where are you going?'

I felt the leash again and stepped back inside and continued looking at the rings and Mallorcan pearl necklaces.

As Miguel paid the young girl at the cash register, who insisted on wrapping the box again, I pretended to browse the glass cabinets.

The owner was in front of a mirrored area behind the counter talking under her breath to the shop assistant.

'I wonder how many times that ring has been sized!' Is that what she said?

Why would Miguel have his grandmother's ring sized many times? Had he gifted it to his ex-wife too? Had he taken it off his dead wife's hand? The thought made me shiver.

I couldn't be certain and my language was poor, but there was no doubt about the look in the woman's face, like she knew something I did not. *It's my imagination*, I told myself. I'd learn Catalan. Then I wouldn't have these paranoia trips. It's impossible to be part of a culture without language in common. It struck me again how odd it was that Miguel chose not to speak the local language, despite his explanation.

'Can I wear the ring now?' He had the box wrapped in gold tissue paper in his pocket.

'It's a pearl, Cariño. You can wear it, but remember to take it off when you do the washing up, ok?'

The ring, the opera, Alessandra's suicide, Carmen's murder, the bank transfer, the overwhelm of being in Miguel's presence again was so disorientating I forgot – until we were waiting at the reception desk to check out of the Brondo – about the house deeds and the lawyer.

'Didn't you say we have an appointment with the lawyer?'

Miguel ignored me, rubbed his thumb against his palm, looked impatient and hit the old-fashioned brass bell on the desk with the palm of his hand.

He's blocking me. I could name it now, but having a psychological explanation didn't make it feel any better. And I didn't want to feel like a gold digger, but it was his idea; it was what he said we were doing. He even mentioned *Villa Rosa* on the way to the bank … didn't he? I felt like I'd been drugged, my brain was so foggy.

We will have a meeting with the lawyer as soon as you arrive, Cariño.

Those were Miguel's exact words.

'Miguel. You said we had a meeting with the lawyer for me to sign the deeds.'

It was my sanity I needed to assert, not ownership of Villa Rosa.

Miguel looked around avoiding my gaze.

'Miguel.'

'Lawyer, Cariño?' He frowned as if he didn't know what I was talking about.

'You said I needed to sign the deeds of the house.'

'Yes, yes, Cariño. I dare say we will, but not today.'

My head started to spin again. He definitely said when I arrived in Palma. That's today. That's why we stayed in Palma last night.

'Did something change since we spoke?'

'No, Cariño.' I felt his impatience mounting. His countenance changed like he was greeting an old friend when he saw the receptionist.

He gabbled in Catalan and peered down the bill like an Old Scrooge. Why did it always take him so long to pay? We hadn't had any extras, nothing from the fridge. It was just the room rate. And why was he now talking in Catalan?

As we walked to the car he receded into his own world.

'Miguel, when will we see the lawyer?'

'Soon, Cariño.' He laughed and kissed me. 'Don't worry, I know, I remember everything we agreed. Just don't take me so literally. We'll see him another time.'

I wanted to ask, then why did he tell me that? I thought that was why we were staying the night in Palma, because of the appointment.

39

Plumber

One of the conditions of my return was that the heating was fixed. The plumber arrived early the next day. Miguel suggested I stay in bed, but I was so happy to be back in Villa Rosa I jumped out of bed and walked around the house throwing open the shutters.

Miguel had laid the table with madroño jam, toast and a steaming pot of tea. For a change he joined me at the table. We both laughed at the jam.

'No dramas this morning, Cariño,' he said as I spread it. A dart of rage shot inside me at this remark. He started the madroño drama – how dare he imply it was my fault. Let it go, I told myself. It was easy to let the remark slip away as I got up, opened the window and hung out of it. The morning was perfect. The Cala. Something inside me relaxed at the sight of it. I felt as though the turquoise triangle in the distance had been waiting for my inevitable return.

Miguel got up and put his arms around me.

'Welcome home, Cariño.'

I snuggled into his worn winter jumper. Like Graves and his second wife, Beryl, who were stompers of the Deiàn hills too according to a biography I'd dipped into, we put away our posh Palma clothes and pulled on jumpers and jeans which we'd wear for two, maybe three weeks without washing. This was Deià life. I was catapulted back into my own fantasy of living a poet's life (to use Graves' phrase and reason for settling in Deià). Environments can change the identity of a person, or bring out some latent aspect of their psyche. Like a dangerous muse, Deià brought out the worst in me.

'The Cala looks so inviting.'

'It's too cold to swim, Cariño.' Why did he dislike me going to the Cala without him?

'I used to swim in the Atlantic on the Kerry coast near Killarney as a child.'

I'd not returned to Ireland since my grandmother died. It was too painful. She'd been the only person who acknowledged my father's abuse. Sometimes my mother packed me off to her. It must have pained her. *I know what he does to you. He's a wicked man,* she used to say. She kept me sane. Until she died, Ireland had been my only refuge. There was another memory, a guiltier one, of sunny swims, siestas and humiliation. What happened that summer my family went to Mallorca? My memory is murky like swimming through a muddy lake. Where did we stay? There is nobody alive to ask now. And my grandmother wasn't there to witness. Jeff said memories can remain buried if they're too painful.

'I dare say the plumber will need my help. I have to direct him. There are areas it is dangerous to dig, down there beneath the house.'

The thought of the cellar made me shiver.

'Are you cold, Cariño?'

This new caring Miguel was what I wanted, but I didn't feel safe.

'I'm fine. Thank you for getting the heating repaired, Director del Mermalada.'

He laughed at the joke, the dig at him directing me around the kitchen when he got in a panic about making madroño jam and throwing the water outside instead of down the sink and anything else that wasn't precisely as he wanted it.

'I dare say it is very good jam! I feel like I'm in a Famous Five novel of my childhood eating an English breakfast!'

I laughed too.

He added some more jam to his toast, like he was demonstrating that he wasn't limiting his rations, not being a Scrooge.

Don't trust him. I batted away the small buzzing voice of doubt that stung like medusa, whipping away hope.

'What will you do today, Cariño?'

'Walk to the Cala.' He didn't need to know that I intended to swim.

'Yes? And maybe bake a cake?'

This comment would have irritated me, but instead it jogged my memory. The letter. His grandmother's letter I'd stuffed between the folds of her nightdresses in the antique chest of drawers. Was it still there? What if he'd found it on one of his mad reordering sprees? So what if he found it? What did it matter? My gut told me that letter held some knowledge I must uncover. I must translate it as I'd intended to. No matter how long it took me. Why not just ask Miguel to translate it? My intuition was telling me to translate it myself. It belonged to him, but I did not trust him to give me truthful translation. Trust. We had none. What hope did the relationship have without that foundation? Like Villa Rosa, our relationship was built on secrets and lies in the darkness of the cellar.

'I've booked an online session with Jeff this afternoon.'

Miguel's silence made me nervous. He sniffed.

'Cariño, you don't need Jeff now you are home with me in Villa Rosa.'

'Miguel, I was suicidal a few weeks ago. I've just been through a divorce, I've moved country and our relationship is triggering painful memories from my childhood. I feel I need his support a while longer.'

'He's expensive, Cariño. We can't afford it.'

His attitude confused me.

'But the other night at the opera you said that you were happy I was seeing a therapist.'

Miguel looked at me and smiled.

'You are doing it again, Cariño. I dare say you have the imagination of a novelist.'

My head spun. I thought back to the conversation we'd had when he massaged my foot in the box. No doubt about it. He was committed to my therapy. And his own.

'You thanked me for working on my stuff in therapy and wished that Alessandra had done the same.' My tone was incredulous.

'What has Alessandra got to do with this?'

'You wished she had worked on herself.'

'I didn't say that, Cariño.'

'I told you my triggers – that I disintegrate when you lie. Please, Miguel.'

'I don't lie, Cariño.'

'You admitted that you lied about Alessandra, that you were still with her when we met.'

'No, Cariño, you misunderstood me. It was not black and white.'

My heart began to beat fast. I began to sweat. I reminded myself that this was a trigger, that it was hooking into the confusion I felt when my mother denied my reality, that I could walk away. But the compulsion arose, along with the desperate need to make Miguel tell the truth, the feeling of being trapped. I started to panic.

'Why can't you ever just tell the truth? Why do you have to lie about everything?'

'Why can't you accept me, Cariño?'

I got up from the table and ran upstairs, away from him. My mind shot to my mobile, stuffed under clothes folded in the chest of drawers in the bedroom. I'd not switched it on for a week. I should call Richie, get a dose of reality, let Shiva know I'm ok.

He followed me.

Fear propelled me forward. I ran for the en suite, but Miguel reached the top step before I made it past the bed. He grabbed my arm.

'Cariño, please, don't run away. My therapist said we need to talk things through like adults.'

He pulled me more gently and led me to sit next to him on the bed.

I sat. I sensed that if I struggled he would exert his strength over me and I'd learnt at a young age that a woman's strength is no match for a man's.

'Cariño, listen to me, you are not well. You're acting out.'

That phrase he learnt from his therapist. He's using his therapy against me. My heart juddered with fear.

'Miguel, I need to talk to Jeff today. The money in the joint account is our money.'

'You are so ungrateful. I support you. I paid for your flight; I am jolly generous with you. Everything you eat here I pay for.'

'What about the fish feast you had with your publisher? Who paid for that?'

He got onto the bed on top of me and pinned down my arms over my head. His eyes darkened to two black coals and the skin on his face sagged so much that for a moment I glimpsed him for the old man he was. That sobered me. I closed my eyes for a moment, imagined breathing in golden light, forced calm into my voice before I spoke.

'Darling, I am grateful for your generosity, but I really would like to speak to Jeff today.'

He flew into a rage – more of a tantrum the type a two year old would have – pushed himself off the bed and ran downstairs. I followed and watched, terrified as he threw himself face down on the breakfast table and pounded it with his fists. I stared at the madroño jam jar as it rolled across the floorboards. A tantrum is more frightening and absurd in a grown man. My gut pinched and I was suddenly afraid. I told myself that he was not my father, he was not violent, but he was out of control. In that moment the words of the neighbour returned to me, chanted like an evil, silent mantra – *mató, mató, mató.*

'Hola? ¿Tot be?'

It was the plumber. He must have heard the banging and come into the house.

Miguel stopped as suddenly as he'd begun, slid off the breakfast table, straightened his jumper and went downstairs without looking at me.

I cleaned the madroño jam from the floorboards, put the lid on the jam jar and did the washing up. When Miguel came back inside he acted as if nothing had happened and so did I.

'Thank you for washing up, Cariño.'

He stroked my hair and kissed the back of my neck. Now was not a good time to talk about what had happened. I needed to talk to Jeff before I spoke to Miguel. It annoyed me. His kisses had the usual effect on me. My fear and anger transformed to sexual excitement, which in turn made me feel powerless.

'It is better you don't come downstairs, Cariño. The plumber will help me with the heavy work and then I will finish the job alone. I dare say it will take until night-time.'

'I'm going to walk down to the Cala.'

'Alone?'

I laughed.

'Yes, I walked New York City streets alone for eighteen years. I think I can manage a stroll to the Cala without getting mugged.'

'Wrap up, Cariño. Your asthma, remember. I prefer to go with you, but today I must be here with the plumber.'

'My asthma is more at risk in this damp house. What are you so afraid of?'

'Be careful when you cross the neighbour's land, Cariño.'

Today he wanted me away from the house. Away from the cellar, perhaps? I tried to banish my suspicions, but it was not like him. Usually he tried to talk me out of going to the Cala alone or insisted on coming with me.

I felt like a criminal as I pulled the towel from my bag on the rocks. The Cala was deserted. I'd not packed my swimming costume as there was no way to dry it without Miguel knowing.

In winter no flags warned of medusa. Mallorcans don't swim in winter. I gasped as I lowered myself off the rocks into icy turquoise water as clear and still as a pond. I pulled my goggles over my swimming hat and propelled myself into a fast crawl towards the narrow inlet that led out to the Mediterranean, scanning the clear water left and right for medusa. There were none, but I remained alert as the thought of being stung on my vagina made me hypervigilant.

Miguel would not come down to the Cala – he was too focused on getting his money's worth from the plumber – but a low hum of fear in my chest meant I ended up surveying the cliffs instead of watching underwater for medusa. The sliding cold, briny water moving against my coño as I swam along with the pulse of the fear between my legs (in the energy point Jeff had called the root chakra), made me aware of what Jeff had drawn my attention to – fear aroused me. Was this what Miguel's exhibitionism was about too – this low ebb of fear and excitement?

Water had got under my swimming hat. I dried off, dressed as fast as I could, hung the towel on the rocks to dry and lay behind a rock in a suntrap for my damp hair to dry. The Cala was my peace. I resolved to swim everyday. It had cleared my head and my intense desire that Miguel acknowledge my needs. Miguel had already fallen back into his pattern of lying. He had to be innocent. I must not let his pattern trigger me. Two mental people would not work. I must keep my head, but how could I maintain my sense of self if I let him get away with his lies all the time? I couldn't join him in his fantasy world.

By the time I returned home it was lunchtime. I watched the plumber drive off with a lorry load of dirt and rock and rubble. Was all of that under the cellar? Looked like a full scale excavation!

A chunk of frozen soup from the freezer was defrosting in a saucepan on the hob. Miguel looked up from cutting the bread (he had to hunch over the bread board and put his strength into it – stale as usual). He looked almost happy as he put the knife down to kiss me.

'Cariño, I missed you. Don't go without me to the Cala again. I will come with you in future.'

I smiled back at him, took spoons from the drawer and started to lay the table for lunch.

'Cariño, the wifi is down.' He said it as if it were the most normal thing in the world. I did not make a fuss about it being a coincidence that it happened the afternoon I had a session booked with Jeff. 'I dare say I can postpone my work this afternoon abajo and drive you into Valdemosa. You can have your session in a café. I know one which will be deserted in the afternoon.'

I exhaled with relief that he'd not ignored my therapy session. I couldn't face another meltdown if he pretended he didn't remember me telling him about my session at breakfast.

'I can reschedule my session.'

He kissed my head. It was a patronising kiss, the type fathers give to well-behaved daughters. A twang of anxiety pinged in my gut at the thought of Miguel finding out about my swim in the Cala.

We sipped carrot and courgette soup in silence. The sunshine lit up the yellow tablecloth. Miguel had put some flowers in a jar.

'These are nice.'

We smiled at each other and I was overcome by a sudden paralysis at the horror of this lunch scene, our future getting old in Villa Rosa, creeping down to the Cala for my short moment of private freedom every morning during our lonely winters. It made me feel old and dead, like sleeping in one of those jaundiced nightdresses. I thought of the letter again, tucked into the folds. Was it still there?

40

Memory

For dinner we finished the remains of the carrot and courgette soup. The tablecloth took on a jaundiced yellow-grey glow from the distant lights on the church and the low wattage energy-saving bulbs that reminded me of the light in a North London bay-fronted sitting room.

'The plumber fixed the tapping, Cariño.'

'I thought you said you didn't hear any tapping.'

'I dare say I didn't want to worry you. You were afraid of your ghost.'

My heart started to beat. I smelt a lie.

'But you told me about the ghost. I never even thought of ghosts before you told me Villa Rosa was haunted.' I didn't add that I had been imagining his ex locked in the cellar, tapping for help.

'Cariño, there is no ghost in Villa Rosa. You made that up in your imagination. I dare say you should be the novelist with an imagination like yours.'

Miguel's laughter was slightly wicked as he laughed at his joke.

I struggled to inhale.

Don't panic, I told myself.

Just walk away.

I walked upstairs to the bedroom and into the en suite and closed the door.

Miguel followed me.

He was in a rage.

'Cariño, I was talking. You walked away when I was talking. It is you who are projecting onto me. You do not listen to me. You ignore me.'

I was more afraid than I had ever been. I knew this type of rage. Their eyes glaze over. When my father lost it, he disappeared, he no longer recognised me. I did not exist. And as Miguel stood there barring my exit, his mouth opening and closing like a Thunderbirds puppet, the bombardment of accusations became unbearable. He came into the bathroom towards me.

'Get out, please just leave me in peace for a short while. My head is spinning.'

'You don't respect me.'

He walked into the bathroom.

I fled past him to the door.

The bombardment of accusations continued.

I ran past him into the bedroom, got into the wardrobe and closed the door from the inside. I crouched down in the furthest corner in the dark and burst into tears. I could not stop sobbing. And in the darkness I was transported back in time. It jogged a memory. Jeff had warned me that once we took the lid off Pandora's Box, forgotten memories may come back. I remembered this feeling of absolute fear and desperation, battling to make sense of what had just happened to me, crouching in a wardrobe. What was I afraid of? My father. My father was on the other side of the wardrobe door. It smelt like this. It was the summer I turned fifteen. The summer my family went to Mallorca. I was back there. Or else I'd never really left. The smell of perfume, the scent my mother wore.

'Please, leave me alone,' I was begging now. All the fight had gone from my voice.

'Cariño, please.'

Miguel opened the door and got into the wardrobe with me. He was suddenly calm. As the moonlight from the window in the bedroom caught the side of his face I thought I saw a smile. He looked genuinely relaxed, peaceful even, as if my panic had calmed him. He stroked me like a pet and took my shaking hands and led me out of the wardrobe to the bed.

His polla was hard.

Another flashback. My father, naked and hard in the bed next to me.

'Let's get into the bed, Cariño. Let me hold you.'

I just followed him, raised my arms like a child, let him take off my clothes and pull his grandmother's nightdress over my head.

I fell asleep in his arms, exhausted.

I do not know how long I slept, but the Teix was a black shadow against an orange sky outside the window when I woke to Miguel forcing himself on me.

I was shocked.

'What are you doing? I don't want to have sex.'

'Cariño, it will make you feel better. It is good for us.'

I lay motionless as he entered me. Tears were cold as they trickled over and into my ears. Like waking from a nightmare to realise the dream was real. I was living a nightmare. I may have escaped my father, but here I was again.

As Miguel moved inside me I closed my eyes and recognised the smell of my father's skin, the dry touch of his hands on my breasts, the nausea and the blood red shame of my silent orgasm.

Afterwards he got out of bed. For a change I was glad he had gone. A familiar numbness descended as I took off my nightdress and went into the en suite to wash.

As I folded the nightdress and replaced it in the pile of thick cotton in the chest of drawers I remembered the letter and felt methodically into each fold. There it was, near the bottom of the pile of cotton. That would be my work over the next few days, even if it was simply a distraction until I could work out how to speak to Jeff. I had no creative juice to write travel articles, but I needed some focus to keep me sane.

Miguel cooked dinner the following night.

'Do you like it, Cariño?'

'Yes, thank you.'

'Are you feeling better?'

'A little. I want to book a session with Jeff. I need to talk to him.'

Miguel rolled his eyes. There was only a flicker of fight left in me.

'Why did you roll your eyes, Miguel?'

'You know, Cariño, nobody does psychotherapy these days. I dare say cognitive behavioural therapy is better to adjust your behaviour.'

'But I explained, my issues run deep. I want to get to the root. I've started to have memories and they are difficult to deal with.' I stopped myself from telling him about my memory while we had sex. He'd used the information about my triggers (ignoring me, blocking, gaslighting) as ammunition and upped his game, increased the gaslighting, the denial of my reality, twisting my memory.

'Then talk to me, Cariño.'

'Miguel, please. I need professional help.' It was not the first time that I regretted transferring my meagre divorce settlement to the joint account. What a fool I'd been.

'Why don't you try these?' Miguel took a packet of pills out of his trouser pocket. I recognised the box – the pills he'd been taking when I first met him.

'I don't need drugs and you're not a doctor.'

I pushed them back across the table towards him.

He smiled at me.

'I love you, Cariño. We will get through this together.'

He took my hand. His dry skin, I remembered so clearly now. No wonder he seemed so familiar.

This is not fate. He just reminds me of my father. Every cell in my body juddered in repulsion.

You have confused love with abuse. Jeff Monroe's words started to make sense. Miguel was not my father, but like my father he did not love me … although they might think they do in their confused minds.

This torture is not love. My quiet voice shouted from my gut and some fight came back into me.

As I sat there, my hand in his, staring at Deià's church floodlit, a golden glow in the distance, another old pattern emerged within me. The determination to escape.

A tear hit Miguel's leathery hand and he stroked my hair.

I'd read a magazine article when I was in London. A psychologist stated that there is tenderness in S&M relationships. Clearly they are not speaking from experience. Miguel's caresses were a form of torture. I never knew when the next psychological twist of the knife would hit. In these lulls after the madness, Miguel was at peace as his control was complete. I was on tenterhooks, the constant hum of fear strumming in my gut. This was why Miguel was so familiar to me. This was the constant reality of my childhood. I knew Shiva's New Age past life stuff to be utter rubbish – in my world at least, the sense of inexplicable déjà vu

I experienced when I opened the gate to Villa Rosa was an opening of Pandora's Box. I'd simply walked up the drive to another version of my father. But why, why recreate the pain of the past? I needed to talk to Jeff.

41

The Letter

Miguel took to waking me up during the night. He'd stand at the end of the bed, naked, accusing me of lying, of not respecting him, not listening to him. What hurt most was that this excited him. Jeff would have called his accusations a projection – I knew that was the case, but in the middle of winter in the silence, Jeff's words were thin protection.

I began to doubt myself. Increasingly I locked myself away in the library. I did not have the energy to flee. I'd only just arrived and the invisible noose tied me to Miguel.

Every time I heard Miguel's footsteps I slipped the letter between the pages of *The Forging of a Rebel* by Arturo Barea or *The Book of the Lover and the Beloved* by Ramon Llull. My skin was constantly alert to him as I sat on the varnished floorboards in the library with the Catalan-English and Spanish-English dictionaries opened. The hairs stood up with *piel de gallo* when he came up the stairs and my body – my heart, my gut, my lungs, my coño convulsed with his footsteps.

False alarm. I took out the letter again. Each time I slipped it randomly into another page of one of the books, I would read what was written on the right hand side of the page when I took it out again. Jung might call it synchronicity. A rationalist would call it superstition. I knew in my withering soul that it was an act of madness, as if I had been flung from the rocks overlooking the Cala and clung to the caper bushes for support.

The Spanish book, a memoire about the Spanish Civil War, was in three parts. The first part was narrated in the author's boyhood voice.

The boys from the orphanage came down too and played in the procession. They were children without father or mother who lived there in the Home and had to learn music. If one of them played their trumpet badly, the teacher would knock it up with his fist and break the boy's teeth. I had seen a boy who had no teeth left, but he blew the trumpet beautifully.

Translating random chunks of Arturo Barea's novel served to give a context to the letter. Through the words of the little boy in Madrid and this woman in Deià in Mallorca, I plodded on at a snail's pace deeper into the memories of two victims of the Spanish Civil War. Their voices joined the others swimming inside me.

Footsteps?

I stopped, folded the letter and again slipped it between two pages.

Another false alarm. The hyper-vigilance of my childhood had returned. I heard things that were not there, misinterpreted the sound of birds walking on the roof for the footsteps of a man. I returned to Arturo's story.

At each end of the viaduct was a policeman on patrol, to keep people from throwing themselves over. If anyone wanted to do it he had to wait until late at night, when the guards were asleep. Then he could jump. The poor men must have got terribly bored, wandering round the streets until they could kill themselves.

Reading these words my breath caught high in my chest, would not reach my diaphragm, followed by a gush of pain. I knew what it was to be a prisoner, desperate for escape – not a prisoner of Villa Rosa, not Miguel's prisoner, but a prisoner of my own psychology. We are all prisoners of our own minds. I looked out of the window of the library at the cliffs either side of the Cala, at the mirador that had been the exit for so many Deiàns.

Arturo's voice had captured my interest. His voice, and Miguel's grandmother's, stood between me and panic, their words were a rope thrown across the decades. I grabbed it as my soul hung from the caper bushes on the cliffs. Arturo's words vibrated with truth. I flicked ahead in the book, to the Civil War, wondering if there was anything about Mallorca, but it seemed that most of the book was based in Madrid where he lived. I gasped at a chapter entitled *Villa Rosa*. Jung would call that synchronicity.

The Villa Rosa was one of the best-known night establishments of Madrid.

Villa Rosa was Arturo's escape from his lonely marriage. I was shocked by the similarity with my own life. I too saw Villa Rosa as an escape from the loneliness of marriage. He lost himself in wine, whereas I lost myself in a man. I'd hidden from my addiction to dangerous men in marriage. My ex-husband was safe. But before him there had been a string of men, different versions of my father. Jeff had helped me to identify a narcissist, but unlike alcohol, which comes with labels – Vino, Jerez, Manzanilla – narcissists walk among us in disguise. And like the devil, they smell sweet. Miguel even smelt like my father. I shivered at the bite of memory that had surfaced that day. I must speak to Jeff.

The back door handle clicked. I held my breath and was quick with my hands. I checked the corners of the letter were completely hidden inside the book. I'd not got far with it today, but translating Arturo's story was helping my Spanish.

It was also my cover in case Miguel demanded evidence of my activity. I secretly wished he would, but like my father he had no interest at all in what I was doing unless it benefitted him.

I'd have to wait until Miguel went into Palma to see his psychiatrist. I couldn't have an online session with Jeff while he was in the house. I couldn't trust Miguel to give me privacy.

It wasn't just the letter that drew me back to the library. As I slowly unravelled the language of Ramon Llull's book – a mystical dialogue between a human soul and God – I had the sense it was feeding me. Each time I slipped the letter from the book and read the right hand page, I wondered if the Medieval mystic, who founded the hermitage where Miguel had taken me on my first visit to Deià, was sending me messages, appealing to me to undo the silent vow I'd made to Miguel in the hermitage. *The Lover sat captive in the prison of love. Cares, desires, and memories guarded him in chains so he could not escape. The Beloved breathed life into him and saved his soul.* Llull's ancient words offered a hush of wholeness.

The furthest I ventured from Villa Rosa that winter was to the Cala. Those cold, naked swims cleansed me each morning, kept me sane. Each day I risked being seen but this small rebellious act was all I had to separate me from complete submission.

One cold morning in March my heart numbed when I looked up at the cliffs and saw the shadow of a human form in the bushes. Miguel? I trod water too long and my limbs became heavy with the cold. Eventually I pulled myself back up on the rocks to dry off.

As I walked up the road that Graves had funded the construction for – perhaps to make his own daily walk down the steep slope of the mountain to the sea easier – the neighbour stepped out of the trees and on to the road, rake in hand as usual.

I stopped.

We stood watching each other.

So he was watching me. Dirty old man. I was relieved it had not been Miguel.

'Bon día.' My voice quivered on the Mallorquín greeting.

'La mató. La mató.' This time I understood the Mallorquín: He killed her.

'Who killed who?' I answered in Spanish as my Mallorquín was not good enough to speak, although I understood a little more from eavesdropping on locals at the Wednesday market and from my translating.

'Go,' he said in English with such force that my legs reacted and I ran as fast as I could up the hill, over the little bridge and through the olive groves. I did not stop until I reached the gates of Villa Rosa where I gathered myself before entering the house.

Miguel was still in the cellar working on his new novel. He had taken to working down there as if he was playing gatekeeper.

There he stood, staring at me. I knew he listened out for my return.

'Cariño, what's wrong with you?'

He came towards me, stroked me, looked genuinely concerned.

'The neighbour,' I panted.

'I told you not to disturb him. Cariño, what happened? Tell me.'

'He shouted at me to, told me to 'go'.

'I dare say him and his family think they own Deià. This house is mine. Ignore him, Cariño. I told you … did you speak to him?'

'No.' I was still trying to catch my breath. My asthma was not good after such a damp, cold winter.

'Good girl. I don't like you walking alone, Cariño. I told you this before.'

I pulled myself together. He would not stop my morning swims.

'I'm fine. He just surprised me, that's all.'

My heart beat fast at the thought of Miguel discovering that I had been swimming.

I made a pot of tea and sat on the terrace and told myself the neighbour is just crazy. Just ignore him, had been Miguel's advice. That was easy enough. He seemed simple but harmless. I was disturbed by the thought that he was spying on me when I took my morning swim. It was my only freedom. I'm not surprised people flee Deià. It's true that the mountain creates a microclimate; it is a trough of damp in winter, but it's not the weather or the mountain. They run from Deià's control. Those who remain during the winter are victims of its groping seduction.

Miguel joined me for a change. I had that familiar feeling, déjà vu as he drew me into his embrace. Now I knew it for what it was. It was what I always yearned for from my father, to be held. But this was not love, this temporary contentment. It was the inconsistent calm before the inevitable storm.

42

Therapist

By the time Miguel had his next session in Palma it was the 1st of April. He was surprised I didn't want to join him. I nearly postponed my online session with Jeff as I was so desperate to escape Deià.

I set my computer up in the library as the mobile signal was strongest in there. As Miguel had cancelled the wifi, I tethered my computer to my mobile hotspot.

In my eagerness to speak to Jeff, I was set up early, so I returned to Arturo's book. Although he was a man of a different era, and although I despised his generation for teaching him, as his new wife's father had lectured him, that *a woman is either married … or she's a bitch and a street walker,* and hated him for becoming a product of his generation, I understood that I was partly irritated with him as he was not so different from me. I too did what was expected, married a suitable man and compromised my ideals.

I still believed that somewhere there existed a woman with whom I might have a contact beyond the physical, with whom I would have a complete life of mutual give and take.

I considered myself braver than Arturo. More honest. And this I also knew was a conceit that my looming session with Jeff Monroe would likely squash. But I did not systematically betray my ex-husband and plan a life to both juggle wife, mistress (who he complained wanted to '*absorb me*') and other sexual freedoms as did Arturo. I put all of my being into making it work with one man while I let the other go free to find love. I knew I had less hope than Arturo while I remained *absorbed*, as Arturo put it, by Miguel. For I felt he sucked from me. Despite rationally acknowledging this, the irrational part of me schemed in endless, exhausting circles about how I could make Miguel love me.

The video call rang, the screen flickered and there was Jeff Monroe sitting on the same sofa he used for our London sessions. The dim, depressed quality of yellow-grey North London light even travelled across the binary code into the library at Villa Rosa and entered the invisible field between us.

I exhaled like I'd been holding my breath since the last time I'd seen him over a month ago and now it was safe to let it go. The connection wasn't great and now and then the screen froze, but I could see him and that gave me an instant relief.

'So. Let me get a good look at you.' Jeff looked serious. 'Can you update me? How are you?'

'I'm in a constant state of anxiety – it is exactly the quality of fear, hope and disappointment, the feeling of being trapped, paralysed that I felt as a child in my parents' house.'

The words exhaled out of me in a rush. Most of all I needed to tell him about my suspicions of rape. I could talk to my friends about the gaslighting, get feedback that it was Miguel, not me who was being insane, but more and more I was withdrawing from that life. Miranda, Shiva and Richie all advised me what any sane person would: Leave him. But I couldn't do that. Reading the 'Villa Rosa' chapter in Arturo's book had made me realise that I was in some way addicted, chained to the iron gates of Villa

Rosa in some awful inverted-suffragette-submission. Where was the independent woman I'd been?

'And your inner world, your dreams?'

'No dreams. It's not like me. What does that mean?'

'The inner world can go silent when we are disconnected from our unconscious – if there's something you don't want to see.' Jeff closed his eyes and the screen froze so that he stayed that way for a while. But his voice was as level and clear as it ever was. His Dublin accent calmed me.

'Rape. It makes sense, but I can't remember properly. I cannot condemn my father without knowing for certain, but the memory is murky.'

'Whether or not there was penetration is inconsequential to a large extent. We could dig deeper into the memory, attempt to uncover it, but that may not be wise or necessary. We know that your father's interference has hardwired you to seek out men like him, dark abusers that bear a resemblance to him. Do you need to remember?'

It was true that the damage had been done. What difference if there was penetration in addition to all the other abuse? I'd prefer not to know.

'You said the process required we go back into the pain – I'll do what is required.'

'You're doing the work. You are remaining emotionally aware. You are aware of your emotional state.'

'It makes my head spin when Miguel lies, twists the truth, ignores me. '

'How does that make you feel?'

'Like I don't exist. It wasn't my father that made me feel like that. The golf clubs were real. I had bruises to prove it. It was my mother. When Miguel changes his story, it gives me the exact same feeling as when she'd tell me that I was the mad one, denying the beatings. Thank God for the bruises. They kept me sane.'

'Yes, she denied your reality. Miguel does that too.' He paused. 'So. You told him your triggers?'

'I did. It's like he's using it to dig the knife in – it's got worse – like I gave him the ammunition to destroy me.'

Jeff looked serious. 'I need to ask you this as I need to assess your current state. Do you have suicidal thoughts?'

I thought of Arturo's childhood memories, the men jumping from the viaduct in the famished years before the war, the men being pushed from the mirador overlooking the Cala ... and my thoughts of joining the wives who threw themselves from the same spot and followed them to their grave in the icy water of the Cala.

'Suicide. That's what you meant when you asked me at the end of our last session if I was prepared to die for Miguel, isn't it?'

The tears were hot as they rolled over my cold cheeks. My voice was a crack of a whisper. I was so ashamed to admit this weakness.

'Yes. It's so painful.'

Jeff's voice softened. 'Yes, I know. Many survivors of child abuse cannot withstand the pain.'

'It is a pain like nothing I have experienced. I know pain. I have a high pain threshold. But this feeling of not existing, it's an eternal fire, like I'm in the fire, burning from the inside out, everyday, with just momentary moments of relief when he touches me, throws me a crumb of attention. But then he withdraws it and I'm back in the inferno. It's a living Hell. And I know there is a way out of this pain, but I will not take it. I can withstand it.'

'Yes. You are resilient. You are brave, remarkably so.' There was respect mingled with the compassion in Jeff's voice, the sort of respect warriors receive in epic dramas and I understood I was in a battle and the war was hopeless. I had no choice but to surrender. The enemy was inside me. The enemy was not Miguel. It was my own damaged soul.

'You have tried. He hasn't kept his part of the bargain. I am very concerned for your safety. I suggest you return to London.'

'I know logically that's the only solution, to walk away, but it's so hard. This must be how addicts feel – I can withstand the burning, but I don't know if I have to strength to leave him.'

'Yes, that's a good way of putting it. Addiction removes choice. Choice was taken away from you by your parents. But now you can choose. Can you reconnect with your seventeen year old self who packed her bag and left home, got on a plane and created an independent life for herself in New York City?'

In the top right of my screen a notification from Shiva appeared. Then Miranda. Then Richie. Shit! I'd been avoiding them, kept my phone off, not logged into my messages. Like an addict, I'd cut myself off from my friends.

I felt myself exhale. I'd gone unconscious again.

'Can you reconnect to her?'

'I can't leave him. I'm nothing without him.'

'Yes, when the parents don't support the child, the child cannot feel supported. I understand, but I believe you have the strength to leave him. I don't usually do this, but I'm concerned for you alone out there and how your state has deteriorated. Call it a break if that's easier.'

'What will happen if I don't leave?'

'You will unravel, disintegrate. You've fallen into a hole. You look diminished. I know you are strong, but people with Narcissistic Personality Disorder, if that's what it is, are dangerous to live with. It is very rare that they recover. Just because he's in therapy doesn't mean he will improve. It's a long journey. We have a joke in my profession that it is the people in relationship with narcissists who end up in therapy. He'll chew you up and spit you out.'

I thought of the dark abyss of Miguel's eyes, how I had once feared looking into them and now I felt as though I was swimming in a black bottomless lake filled with burning, biting medusa. I knew Jeff was right.

'Ok, I'll leave.'

It was silent for a while. Jeff's gaze darted to the clock above the mantelpiece, out of frame of the camera.

'Can I ask what triggered the memory of the rape?'

'His smell. Miguel smells like my father.'

'Yes, smells don't lie.'

I didn't mention the smell of the dress. That was impossible. The dress was gone. I was very afraid it was too late and I had gone mad.

Miguel

43

Hardware Shop

Ferretería. That old sign is orange with rust. I like the Arab quarter. I dare say it makes me feel like I've travelled back in time. I do not feel I was destined for this era with its mobile phones and wifi … I hope she's not spending time and money talking to her friends. ¡Uf! She makes my blood boil the way she smiles, her happiness, her pain, her, her, her. My psychiatrist says she triggers the aggressor in me. It's her fault, her fault I feel like this. I'm hard again. I'll resolve that after I've done what I came here for. I was surprised she wanted to stay in Deià. I dare say it's better she's not with me, dragging her heels, gawping like a child in wonder at the buildings, wanting to go into churches, wanting to waste my money in cafés eating ice-cream.

What's this in my pocket? I pull out the bankcard with her name on it. At least she won't have access to my money. The benefit of the postman not coming to Villa Rosa – I collect my mail from my mailbox in the village. Fold it in half, one way, then the other so the plastic breaks and I throw it in the bin opposite the hardware shop.

I like the smell of metal, oil and wood.

'Señor. Señor.'

The old man again. His son has opened another shop across the street. Entrepreneurial, these Arab shop-keepers. His crow's feet have deepened, from grinning too much I suppose. Idiot.

'How are you today, Señor? Very good to see you. We have not seen you since the summer. I heard there was snow in Deià this winter.'

¡Uf! I'm not in the mood for chit-chat. Smile, Miguel. Act like you're interested. It's a struggle to force the corners of my mouth up.

'Good afternoon. Sorry, I was thinking about all the chores I have to do around the house after the winter. Problems with the heating, problems with the damp, with the plumbing, the list goes on.'

'Ah, yes, Señor, the trials of being a property owner. My son has just bought a new apartment on the Avenida himself. Always something to do. How can we help you today?'

He always speaks in the first person plural, as if his son is also present. Lonely. That dark pain again. I know lonely.

'The plumber …' (yes, say the plumber suggested it), '… the plumber recommended Sodium Hydroxide to unblock the pipes.'

He nodded with that serious look on his face, like he was a high paid government advisor and needed to look the part, and shuffled in his open toe sandals which he wore winter or summer to the back of the dusty little shop.

'Yes, yes, Sodium Hydroxide, the best chemical for drain clog because most drain clogs are formed by hair and human bio-gunk.' He laughs at his own joke.

'I know.'

He smarts at the impatience that seeped into my voice. Must give him a reason for why I know that. ¡Uf! I hate justifying my actions.

'I'm a novelist.'

He laughs again, nods his head with disguised relief and pats my arm.

'Yes, yes, I remember, Señor the writer. Stories are important in my culture. Literature. We are made of stories.'

He's still laughing the fool as he reaches up, takes the bottle and hands it to me. I let him do it although I could reach far easier than him. I'm far taller. But he likes to serve and I like to be served.

'Much better than hydrofluoric acid, which is often naïvely used in crime films to dispose of human remains. It would dissolve a body. Of course you would still be left with a brittle, insoluble calcium shell of a skeleton.'

'You can use that in your next novel.' He's still laughing as he hands me my change.

I force laughter too. It sounds foreign in my lungs. Never natural, not like hers, so free and so easy. The old irritation burns inside my brain.

I'll find myself a whore before I go back to Villa Rosa. Might as well make the most of being out of the house.

44

Mirador Murders

Deià life, the slow pace of it was still foreign to this city girl despite the aching familiarity of its shadows and rocky creases. The evening walk was the high point of our days (my personal high point was still my morning swim which I suspected the neighbour continued to witness from the cliffs). We would leave for our walk an hour before sunset. That day in April, Miguel and I walked to the mirador.

Neither of us had mentioned the episode in the wardrobe weeks before. My session with Jeff lingered in me, his appeal for me to leave Deià. I couldn't face another scene with Miguel and so I had taken to avoiding any subject that might lead to him throwing a tantrum or me having a meltdown.

We took the coast path on the opposite side of the valley from the Teix. It was overgrown and as I tried to keep up with Miguel thorns flicked in my face and scratched my hands. I looked back towards the Cala and wondered who else might have seen my naked body climb from the sea onto the rocks in the mornings. The thought of being watched and Miguel's invisible noose tugging me after him aroused me. I was beginning to understand Miguel's exhibitionism. My behaviour was driven by a low groin hum of excitement, fear, danger and shame (rather than the initial problem of hiding and drying a wet bikini).

A thick mist hung in the evening air and my lungs struggled as we climbed higher. Head down like a soldier on a war march, Miguel was locked in his own world.

'Miguel, slow down.'

I thought of the letter. Now the words were knitted together well enough to start to piece together his grandmother's story. I shivered at the thought of it.

'What happened to your mother and grandmother after your grandfather's death?'

'I told you, Cariño.' He didn't want to talk about it. Then he kissed my hair and said, 'You really want to know, Cariño?'

'Yes.' And as I said it, I knew that I would regret pushing it.

'War is another world, Cariño.' He looked out to sea as if it was his memory, as if he were there, but then perhaps my speculation about hereditary trauma was correct and his emotional DNA had been triggered.

'One day, when I was reading in the olive groves, the neighbour – we were both young then, he a few years older than me – he cornered me with some boys from the village. I was not like them, fighting, playing football. They took my book, called me names. Said my mother and grandmother were whores, that after my grandfather – the bourgeois traitor they called him – had taken a swim in the Cala (I dare say they laughed at this joke), my grandmother and other whore widows had been force fed castor oil and made to walk through Deià's high street soiling themselves.'

The shock of this information, the emotional vibration of his DNA, shuddered through me, thrashed and stung like medusa, and I felt I was sinking in a kaleidoscope overload of whirling images – the broken bodies of men floating in the Cala where I swam every day, the humiliation of those women made my skin burn like hot wheals, the taunts of the boys in the olive groves, and something else, something not from the past, but here and now, Miguel's silent need to inflict pain on me. His faraway look changed, just for a second, to satisfaction at the obvious discomfort he was causing me.

'It was systematic humiliation. Terrorism was Franco's speciality. Women were marched through high streets humiliating themselves in towns and cities all over the country.'

Had his grandmother soiled herself in the nightdress Miguel made me wear to bed? Why was he telling me? Why did I want to know? Please stop, I wanted to shout, but the words would not come out. I'd asked for this. His hereditary trauma was contagious and had infected me like a virus and my mood was changed, aligned to his grim oppression and again I was overwhelmed by desperation to flee Deià.

We stared out at the sea. The mist was a sickening glow like cheap orange squash tanked with chemicals that rot guts and hook children into a lifetime of addiction to sugar.

'The boys tore the pages from my book – it was my favourite Famous Five novel – they said my mother begged the soldiers to fuck her for sugar.'

His face was expressionless, his voice matter of fact, as disassociated as a newsreader, his eyes inkwell black as the orange light disappeared into their bottomless darkness.

'Is that what the Pact of Forgetting is for?' I knew it meant serious crimes committed during the Civil War would not be investigated, but I wanted to hear it from him rather than books written by foreigners.

'The Amnesty grants both sides impunity for crimes during the War Civil. Whatever it was. Murder, rape, theft. I dare say it was the only way to unite the country after war.'

I nearly mentioned the letter. Fear prevented me; the glazed look in his eyes, the fathomless abyss made me hold my tongue. In that moment he was further from me than ever. I knew that soulless look. It was familiar to me. I was sitting on the roots of the same trees his grandfather likely stood on before he plunged to his death, I slept in a nightdress his grandmother must have wished she could die in, be swallowed up by Deià's high street rather than live with the humiliation and I knew I had to leave or I would be swallowed up by Deià's shadow. Sitting in that sick orange mist I understood what made people run from Deià. An equally strong force held me there, some invisible traumatic thread strung out taut between me and Miguel. I yearned to cut it, but first I must finish the translation of Sofia's letter. It was a compulsion, a duty almost, stronger even than my need to reach him, to reach out and hold Miguel.

I held myself instead, distant from him. On the gnarled roots of that old tree that had witnessed the mass executions of so many innocent men, I knew that Miguel would swallow me up. I knew that I would not be able to withstand the pain of being invisible, of not existing, of being a mere extension his tortured soul. So I sat, silent, muted by pain and resolved to escape.

Miguel stood up suddenly.

'Let's go.'

I was relieved he did not take out his polla. I don't think I could have stomached it.

'Cariño, let's go.' He held out his hand to help me up from the roots of the tree. A sudden paralysis made it difficult to move, like my limbs would no longer respond to requests from my brain.

That night we ate like an old married couple. In silence. Deià's church glowed gold on the hill, a focal point for me to gaze at as I sipped my steaming soup. He watched me eat. My silence disconcerted him.

'I am jolly glad you like it, Cariño.' His Enid Blyton English sent a snap of rage through me. I had an urge to punch him in the face.

'Yes, thank you.'

'Are you ok? I dare say you are very quiet this evening.'

'I'm tired. I can't sleep.'

'Why don't you take these?'

The pills again. Miguel put the white cardboard box on the table next to my soup bowl. It was dented from being in his pocket.

'They will calm your anxiety, Cariño.'

He said it softly, like he cared. A murderous stabbing fear made my heart pound uncontrollably.

'I don't need drugs. I've told you that.' I pushed the pillbox back across the dinner table towards him. What a fool I'd been depositing all my remaining money into a joint account. 'Did you check the mailbox today? Any post for me?' *It's odd my debit card's not arrived yet.*

'No.' He mumbled it.

I don't believe him.

'Next time we go into Palma, I want to visit the bank and find out what's happened to my debit card.' He refused to register for online banking, said there was too much fraud.

'They are slow in Mallorca. It's not like New York here.'

'I don't want to ask you every time I want to pay for something.'

I knew that this statement was pointless.

He smiled at me.

'We will get through this, Cariño. Our love is strong.'

I stared at the church and imagined myself out on the mountain, free from Miguel's control.

But escape eluded me. I was trapped by the same control that kept my mother glued to my father, denying not just my reality, but hers too, baking cakes from her own 1950s recipe book, cooking for a man who threw his dinner back at her in one of his tantrums. Deià had trapped me in the landscape of her picturesque lies. Beneath the houses on the hillside, under the olive groves, in cellars and swimming pools were thousands of skeletons: men, women and children murdered and buried under skies lit by shooting stars.

Mallorca is a sunny graveyard of secrets and sin. Like me, Deiàns had buried their trauma. A dark secret lurked in the cellar of Villa Rosa and the letter was beginning to throw some light on what it might be. The letter. Finishing the translation into English had become my irrational excuse to stay.

45

Letter of Forgiveness

The cellar door was locked. I'd taken the keys from the key hooks in the lobby. I flicked the light switch and the bare bulb glowed a dim yellow over the writing table Miguel had set up near the cistern – he took his laptop down there sometimes, said being locked away helped him concentrate. Miguel had gone to the market. He'd walked so I was in peace for a while, although I imagined the walls of Villa Rosa had ears and were an extension of Miguel so he could hear every move I made through his connection with the house. This time I'd brought a torch with me. I took a breath and shone it into the far corners, half expecting to see the ghost of Sofia standing in her nightdress beside the cistern. The damp air clung to my skin and smelt of sewage. A scuttle of tiny feet. That dart in the darkness, close to my own feet, was probably a rat.

I took both copies of the letter from between the pages of the novel, the original Catalan version and my English translation, and laid them out on the table. I wanted Sofia to bear witness to her own words so I'd decided to read the letter out loud in the cellar. I had considered reading it at her grave, but I felt her presence in the house and did not want to risk being disturbed again by the neighbour.

As had become my practice, I opened the book and translated the page on the right hand side of Arturo Barea's novel (my literary alibi) where I'd randomly slipped in the letter. I squinted in the dim yellow glow to read it back to myself when I'd finished. As usual it seemed synchronous with the events of the day, the meanderings of my mind.

Then, at a quarter-past two in the morning, I went to the microphone in the blanketed cellar room and described the trench in Carabanchel which our men had wrestled from the Civil Guards, the stinking shelters through which Angel had guided me, the rotting carcass of the donkey wedged in between burst sandbags, the rats and lice and the people who fought down there. The secretary of the Workers' Committee, that acidulous man from the Mancha (I thought of the gaunt, black-dressed women in the market square of La Ronda), smiled thinly and said: "Today you've almost made new literature." My old Sergeant blinked and snuffled, and the engineer of the Vallecas control room rang to say that for once I had spoken as if I had guts.

I closed the book with ritual reverence and stroked its cover as if it were a sacred text, breathed in, cleared my throat as I imagine Arturo had done that morning in front of the microphone. I was intimately aware of the letter's contents. I'd suffered over the choice of every single word, switched one word for another like a novelist, or wartime journalist, like Arturo perhaps had, or maybe like Miguel's grandfather had sweated over the best choice of words when he wrote the letter to General Franco that sealed his watery fate.

12 July 1987, Villa Rosa

To those I forgive,

The others I forgave years ago, nameless faces, disembodied members. They saw only a leftist widow, a leftist whore. The enemy. You, I have struggled to forgive. I have tried many times to write this letter, but failed. Today is my 87th birthday. A decade since *The Pact of Forgetting* silenced Spain. But the inside of a human mind is never silenced. Marta Alma Llobet (may your sweet soul rest in peace) – I try to remember you prancing around the olive trees in the garden before the war – but I cannot push away the image of your face, a crushed paper ball of pain, hair pulled back and used like the reins of a horse as those men raped your sweet innocent soul, one by one, in the cellar that stormy night.

It was a night when the Sirocco had blown in with such hot fury and those Saharan winds snatched away our screams for help and pleas for mercy. But who would have come? Who remained to hear them? They'd taken the men. They, Franco's men. And marched them to the mirador. We knew what fate awaited them. We knew that in the morning we would go with baskets like our neighbours had done, to collect what was left of them on the rocks. I secretly wished that if we women made it through the night alive that the sea would give their bodies a grave, so sick was I of the flesh.

When they arrived, I'd been with my husband, Mateo Julio Nadal. The house was different then. What is now the library was an attic and I told my daughter to hide there, shooed her up the ladder. We'd heard them in their truck pass the road by the house before they came down the lane. There was time to hide her. Up she went on her father's strong shoulders.

Brave, they called him. Foolish, I'd said, when he refused to follow orders, spoke out against Franco's bidding. A hero, some still say now. But where did his loyalty lie? With his politics or protecting his wife and child? I was angry too with you for many years, my dear, darling washed away husband. I forgive you. And although I raged at you for decades for speaking your truth, for standing up for all that is right in this god-forsaken country, for fearlessly facing those young, directionless fascist thugs that night, I would not respect you more than any man who has walked the earth if you had not. You spoke for me too, and for the millions too afraid to speak out against the Falange. I forgive you, my husband. May your soul rest in peace. For the peace of my own soul is why I write this letter. How my shoulders yearn for your strong arms around me, just once more as I sit on the floor of this cellar. Now a storage space for summer patio furniture, hats and the junk of our daughter's young family. You would love Miguel, thoughtful, just like you.

This is my second attempt at this Letter of Forgiveness. The first time was the winter of 1977, just after *The Pact of Forgetting* was passed. Miguel was in his early twenties; he'd come down here into the cellar for something and disturbed me. But it was still too raw. Now the wound is old and calloused over. Now I have the strength for it, dear, brave, foolish husband. I feel you by my side now as I hold this pen steady in my aged hand. How cheated I feel that we did not watch the wrinkles etch deeper year on year in each other's faces. At least our daughter was spared. I could not have watched her as I was forced to watch Marta Alma Llobet (bless her soul). Here they come again, the tears. I thought there were none left. Maybe after I write this letter the old wound will heal once and for all. They had their fill with us, drank what wine they found down here, stole what food we had left for the winter and drove off singing,

> *He's Franco, Franco, Franco*
> *We have a leader*
> *The passages of honour*
> *We will deliver*
> *With no fear of adventure*
> *The mandates of your voice*
> *Maker of our new history*
> *He's Franco, Franco, Franco*

That song, the light tone of their slurred words (like school children singing Christmas carols) still wheels in my mind. At least your brother was not among them. Although I might have forgiven him sooner had he not hidden behind his words and come to take you to the mirador himself.

Franco, I forgive him for unleashing his monstrous shadow over our country. Fascism is the shadow-half of Spain's broken heart, the soul of our nation split, itself splitting souls as the war wheels rolled away from Villa Rosa.

Marta and I did not dare move for what seemed like a very long time. I see the exact spot, there, by the pipes of the old cistern.

I remember the flick, flick, flick of a soldier's pocketknife by my right ear. I still hear it sometimes, always in my right ear, when the Sirocco blows in from Africa. *The Pact of Forgetting* could not silence that. I thought he was going to slit my throat with it. When he was finished, I silently begged him to as the next one took his place. And the next. I do not remember how many there were. Maybe *The Pact* has started to do its work on my memory, but the flick of the knife in my ear, the pain on Marta's face as she scrunched up her eyes, her mouth, as they pissed on her. And the rest.

You should have gone into hiding, held your tongue after your refusal to send those prisoners of Can Mir to the firing squad. That sealed your fate. A soldier, no matter his military status, has no say. What difference that your brother condemned you a traitor? What difference? You should not have fought with words, dear husband, for those who lack the skill of arming themselves with words will use cruder weapons. Marta and I paid for your clever rhetoric that night. Your appeal for leniency, for a fair trial for those men and women, your pleas for justice to General Franco and his baby snatching doctors became our pleas for mercy.

I forgive you, my husband. And I thank you. Maybe one day when the people of Palma tell me that you were a brave man, I will not want to scream at them: *In his bravery, he abandoned his wife and daughter to a lifetime of torture.* For she may have escaped rape, but she suffered through me. Forgive me, my daughter, for every dark look and every harsh word. They were not aimed at you, but came from my own shame, my own hatred of those singing fascists.

I forgive each one of you. As I sit here now I force my heart to send you, my rapists, love. For that is the only thing I have found in this long, torturous life of mine that can dissolve the pain and the raging beast within me.

And you, Juan Pablo Llobet. Finally, I come to you. You who knew me as well as my brothers, all rounded up in the night, all dead by then too. You, who had laughed and played with us in the summers, who'd eaten at our table when the winters were harsh. You, who I had kissed, just an innocent kiss, just once beneath the two twisted olive trees, the Lovers (followed by a giggle) we called them as children. You must have hated my husband when I returned with that rich, educated Palma man, but could you not find it in your heart to be happy for me? I stared you in the eye afterwards and you kicked me in the stomach and told me never to look you at you again. All these years I never have. All these years you pass through my land with your rake in your hand. Do you think I'm afraid of you, you little man? You killed me a very long time ago. It was only my daughter and now my grandson that gave me the will to live. Otherwise I would have thrown myself off the mirador onto the rocks like your sister Marta did and gone to a watery grave with my husband and best friend.

You took a piece of my soul. And now I want it back.

I forgive you, Juan Pablo Llobet, most of all. For it is you I have hated all these years and in doing so I have been diminished.

I, Sofia Valentina Nadal, forgive you for raping me, and your sister, that night in the cellar and again and again with your eyes every time you passed my house. There is no such thing as forgetting. I will not forget. I do not accept what you did as acceptable, even in war. It was evil. And I, Sofia Valentina Nadal forgive you Juan Pablo Llobet because I will not go to my grave with this hatred in my heart. After all these years, I want peace more than I want revenge.

I forgive the tears I was made to shed.
I forgive the pain and the humiliation.
I forgive the betrayal and the lies.
I forgive the slander and the shroud of shame, under which I was forced to walk the streets of Deià.
I forgive the hatred and the torture.
I forgive the violation of my home and my sense of safety.
I forgive the punches, the beating, the branding and the raping.
I forgive the terrorising and emotional abuse that continues to this day every time you glare at me and rape me with your eyes, and smile with that toothless smile of yours that opens my scar afresh, again and again.
I forgive the wrecked dreams.
I forgive the stillborn hope.
I forgive the lust, envy and jealousy.
I forgive the injustice carried out in the name of war.
I forgive the cruelty and the aggression,
I forgive the rage and the contempt,
I forgive the world and its sins – for they are many.
I forgive Spain, El Padre, for forsaking its people,
I forgive the theft of my husband,
I forgive the destruction of my friend,
I forgive the loss of the sons and daughters I might have had,
I forgive the theft of my soul – and today I take back what is mine. With these words, with the power of the truth of an individual soul, for an emotional truth resides inside me that no jury, historian or god can deny.
I forgive you.

Sofia Valentina Nadal

Her signature was strong. Confident loops and strokes much larger than the words in the rest of the letter, the stamp of her soul on the page.

When I'd finished reading I let out an enormous breath. And silently thanked my voice for not breaking before the end, for allowing the grief to flow through me like the torrent into the stale, musty air of the cellar.

For a long time I sat there, her letter in one hand and my typed English translation in the other. And I knew that somehow the magic of catharsis had occurred like after watching a harrowing movie. Her voice had spoken through the page, through my tortured translation because she had in her 87th year found the courage to speak her truth and feel her pain. I did not doubt that she had healed her wound and gone to her grave with a peaceful heart. I also understood something, a mystery I'd mulled over for a long time. Without realising or intending it, Sofia Valentina Nadal had spoken directly to my own soul in her letter. I was drawn to Spain because my own soul was wounded. Sitting there by the cistern on the dank floor of the cellar, a thin boundary between my feet and Deià's bones, all the sessions with Jeff Monroe converged into a personal epiphany. The split in my soul mirrored Spain's broken heart. My silenced victim knew what it is to be forced to forget, to sweep pain and trauma into shadow.

Spain is home because Spain mirrors my own, raped soul.

As my tears fell beside the cistern where Sofia's had once fallen, I knew I must muster the strength to sever myself from Miguel. The trauma in his family, the shame and the silence of the Civil War fuelled the emotional abuse he subjected me to, perpetuating the circle of shame. No matter where his trauma began and Spain's ended, I knew if I stayed that I would live a life of torture like his grandmother and become a mere shadow of what I once was, or what I might become.

But on reading the letter out loud, witnessed by the shadows and the tapping ghosts of the cistern, compassion swelled in me, and my incurable love for Miguel, my compulsive need to heal him so that he might return my love, made it impossible to put wisdom into action. I was bound to him as he was bound to Villa Rosa. We shared the same skin.

46

Housewife

The tattered recipe book was open on the work kitchen surface. I liked how the page where his grandmother's faded handwriting had scribbled the recipe for madroño cake in the margin was splattered with the ingredients of a cake baked years before. It made me feel like I belonged, like I was part of the family, another daisy in the chain of Villa Rosa women. I imagined Miguel's grandmother standing in front of this window beating eggs, flour, sugar. Sugar. Miguel added it to everything. Did he think of his grandmother, of the taunts of the boys in his youth – *sugar whore* – when he sprinkled sugar in his tea, his soup, on toast, spooned it into his mouth straight from the packet?

I followed Miguel's grandmother's neat instructions to the letter and I imagined her standing beside me as I recreated her cake mix for her beloved grandson. It deepened the feeling of belonging, of family. Arturo's novel improved my Spanish. Sofia's letter taught me a splatter of Catalan as I translated Nadal family recipes. Catalan was banned in January 1939 after the fall of Barcelona. Speaking the language was a punishable offence. Sofia must have written this recipe before the 1936 occupation of Mallorca. Was that why Miguel chose to speak Castilian? They must have been so afraid. Did fear prohibit the local language long after the ban had been lifted? Her letter was a revolutionary act. Her recipes, a domestic rebellion.

How silly it now seemed that I'd rebelled all my life against cake baking. I love cakes and I loved how tender Miguel became when I baked for him. This thought grated, like some part of me still fought the charade. *It's no charade – this is my life now.* I wiped my hands down the apron and cracked another egg on the edge of the fifties mixing bowl.

Now the sugar. I weighed it on the old iron scales and added it to the mix. The thought of women bartering their bodies for sugar with Nationalist soldiers, Franco's Dragons of Death, on the road between Deià and Soller. My stomach rolled with a sickly, saccharin nausea as the sugar tipped the scales with a click. What had those stories done to local souls? Unlike Deiàns, living side by side with neighbours who'd murdered, raped, stolen, I'd only been here a few months and already my own mind was heavy with the darkness buried in the earth beneath the tourist magnet Mallorca had become. So many bodies in unmarked graves all over Spain, its European neighbours descending in droves to touch the sunny surface, unaware of nameless ghosts that lurk beneath their feet and haunt the olive groves.

A thump outside jerked me from my thoughts. What's Miguel doing down there? I craned over the sink and peered out of the window. He was carrying the birthing chair across the patio and down to the cellar.

In he comes.

'Miguel, what were you doing?'

'Nothing, Cariño. Rearranging the bedroom, giving us more space.'

That chair gave me the creeps even before I'd seen the picture of Alessandra tied to it in her corset. I was glad it was going to the cellar.

I returned to my mixing. The wooden bat of the spoon against the bowl was soothing, but domesticity could not prevent my mind from running over the latest information I'd gathered from my reading. The death toll was massive. Spain's neighbours danced around the edges of the Spanish Civil War. The French reluctantly set up camps for half a million refugees who walked, freezing and starving across the Pyrenees from Barcelona. Britain wanted a swift end to the war to resume international trade. Hitler's Germany took the condemned for their own holocaust camps and sold guns to Franco; the Italians sold Franco more guns. And Stalin's Russia sold men and artillery to the Republicans – and pocketed a vast sum of gold bullion. Both sides bankrupt Spain.

Spain had successfully buried its past under palm trees and sunshine. Spain and I had something in common. Neither of us had confronted our ghosts. Jeff's warning rang inside me like a siren: *The only way to heal is to confront your shadow.* And Sofia whispered, *an emotional truth resides inside me that no jury can deny.*

I folded in the eggs. Mixing was hard work. The women of Villa Rosa must have had strong arms to make cakes without a food mixer – perhaps beating eggs prepared them for the work of their men. It's the same everywhere. Women take up the jobs of men during wartime. I was grateful to have been born in a rare blip of Western European peace, but I was beginning to understand the weight of the task that fell on the shoulders of my generation to heal the dirty wounds of the past. The battle rages on, perhaps until the last soul has spoken their truth.

The sun would set in an hour or so. Just in time for Miguel when he finishes his work. He'd taken to writing longer hours in the cellar. I looked out over the olive groves to the Cala in the fading light. I no longer yearned for the sea, for escape. That urge had dissolved since reading the letter. I did not have the strength to leave him. Compassion divorced itself from wisdom. I was content to stand at the kitchen window and melt into the beauty of the olive groves in the late afternoon sun, settled, greedy to stay in Deià's abundance.

That comforting thought reminded me of something I'd read in El País. In the face of the economic mess, which the author referred to as the hungry years, following the fall of Catalonia, Franco declared Spain self-sufficient with no need to import: *Spain is a privileged, self-sufficient country. We have everything that is needed to live and our production is sufficiently abundant to assure our own subsistence.*

Franco's words triggered a feeble, mute rebellion inside me: *Do not become dependent on Miguel.* I battled the voice back into the trenches of my awareness and beat the cake mix faster.

As I beat, I stared at the olive groves and imagined Miguel's grandmother beating the same mixture in those last years before she died. Giving birth to Miguel's mother in the birthing chair and imagined myself in that same chair. The Mallorcan pearl on my ring finger, covered in cake mix, a glint in evening sunbeams and I saw myself giving birth to Miguel's child in that chair, screaming with the pain of childbirth but safe within the walls of Villa Rosa. No sterile hospital but wrapped in the resilience of generations of women, willing my child out of the birth canal. Then the voice rose again with a sharp snap: *I forgive the rape of my soul.* The photo of Alessandra tied to the birthing chair, her head lolling to one side snapped into my mind with a sudden fury and a disturbing twang of arousal. I pushed the S&M image of their sex games away with my anger. *Focus on the present, not the past,* I told myself. But my mind was agitated. The letter. The neighbour's cruelty. *Did Miguel know that his neighbour's grandfather had raped his grandmother?*

I slopped the cake mix into the baking tin, licked the spoon and in a sort of trance found myself walking upstairs to the bedroom carried on a low hum of arousal. I opened the drawer beneath the picture of the African woman nursing her child, pulled out Alessandra's corset, walked into the en suite and ran a bath. I took my time shaving my legs, rubbing in my creams and made myself up like a prostitute, red lipstick and black kohl so thick I did not recognise myself. In the same trace I took one of his grandmother's nightdresses from the drawer and wore it over the corset, walked back downstairs to the kitchen, opened the oven and placed the cake on the ancient cooling rack, all the time aware of the leash that connected me to my fiancé in the cellar.

I did not care that Alessandra had worn this corset, did not care about anything but seducing Miguel. Although we'd had sex only once since the night in the Brondo hotel over a month ago, he'd kept me in a state of arousal, topping it up each night, caressing my breasts, touching me until I was wet and panting. Then turned over to read his book. I would pick up Arturo's book, alert to any sign of desire from him. More than once I'd masturbated next to my fiancé after he fell asleep.

Tiptoeing barefoot on the cold stones of the patio, nipples erect over the top of Alessandra's corset, brushing against the nightdress, I balanced the cake in one hand as I hooked the index finger of my other hand under the iron latch on the cellar door. I'd not been down there since the day I'd read Sofia's letter. The stench of earth and shit overpowered the smell of freshly baked cake as I gently pulled open the cellar the door. The plumbing must be broken again.

47
Cellar

The bare lightbulb in the cellar gave off a yellow-grey jaundiced glow as I walked barefoot down the dusty stairs cut into the rock of the Teix, breasts out over the top of the corset like Alessandra in that photo, but hidden under Sofia's nightdress. Careful not to drop the cake, still warm and smelling wholesome from the oven.

Miguel looked round from where he was bent over the birthing chair, dark eyes wide and furious.

'What are you doing, Cariño? I told you not to come down here.'

What on earth's going on? The cellar was a mess. His desk, the one I'd sat at, had been moved to the other side of the cellar, his laptop unopened in its pouch on top of it, along with tools caked in earth. A spade stood upright against the stonewall next to a hole, freshly dug in the ground.

The cake wobbled on the plate I balanced in one hand like a cocktail waitress. We watched it bounce down the steps and smash on the floor.

Silence hung between us as our gazes locked into each other.

My feet froze to the cold rock step as if I had become stone too. I dared not take my eyes from his as if the longer the stare lasted, the longer I would be allowed to live.

I had caught a glimpse of what was on the chair.

I did not want to look at it again.

A flash of bone and skin on skull, balanced on top of a canvas bag.

Run. The voice was urging me. *Run for your fucking life.*

I turned and made a dash for the door.

Miguel was behind me.

As I reached the door he yanked my hair back with such force I nearly lost my balance.

I gripped the iron door handle with all my strength. He pulled me back by my hair, his teeth scraped my ear as he talked.

'Did you dress up for me, Cariño?'

I dared not move. He had me in his grip. Must find my voice.

'I told you not to come down here while I'm working. It's not what you think, Cariño.'

I tried to speak but my teeth chattered and I stuttered.

'I'm sorry. I w-wanted to surprise you.'

'Thank you for the cake, Cariño. I recognise the smell. Madroño cake. Clean up the cake and we'll have some tea together.' He kissed my ear. 'Good girl.'

He dragged me out of the cellar, nails deep into my forearm, the other holding back my hair. We walked past the swimming pool towards the house, our steps in sync, my neck yanked back.

Suddenly, there was a thud, his grip released.

Turn around, I told myself.

It was the neighbour.

Rake in hand.

Miguel was on the ground. He shook his head, ignored the neighbour and reached out to grab my ankle.

The neighbour was quick. His heavy boot came down on Miguel's hand. Miguel's movements were uncoordinated as he tried to get up.

The neighbour shook the rake.

'GO!'

I stared at Miguel stunned on the ground. *He killed his wife!*

'GO!' The neighbour's gruff English shook me out of my hesitation.

I ran, barefoot.

The neighbour shouted after me.

'No talk. No police.'

I turned to see him kick Miguel again. Miguel looked confused and said something in Mallorquín. 'I'm innocent.'

Miguel was no longer aware of me. Pity tugged on my invisible leash and made me stop. I should help him. What if the neighbour killed him? He killed her. *La mató.* The neighbour's warning in the graveyard came back. I knew what it meant now. *He killed her.* This time fear pumped power into my legs. Repulsion and fear surged through me as I looked at Miguel on the ground. Those bones were Alessandra!

'GO! GO!' The neighbour shook his rake at me in a rage.

Run.

I ran.

48

Escape

The fastest way to the road was through the house. I shut out Miguel's muffled pleas of innocence coming from the back patio, dashed to the lobby, threw on my coat and pulled on my boots in a panic. *Money. I need money.*

The kitty. The kitchen. Bowls and flour on the work surface from my baking struck a sharp shock of truth – Miguel was turning me into his mother! My hands shook as I stuffed two fifty Euro notes from the kitty into my coat pocket. Just about enough for a one-way flight to London. *Shit, shit, shit. Passport.* In my bag.

I grabbed my bag from the lobby and without looking back ran out up the drive to the road. The Teix was hidden behind the pine trees that overhung the curve in the road, but I felt its presence behind me. I kept running until my lungs burnt and I thought I'd have an asthma attack.

Should I go back? Should I give a statement to the police? The neighbour's warning: *no police.* Why not? The voice of reason was loud and clear now: *It does not matter why not. Keep going. Never look back.*

As I walked in between sprints my mind darted from one memory to the next trying to piece together the elusive truth. Not looking back takes you forward, but you cannot escape the past. The shadow of my past was what drew me to Miguel and the past was playing out on the patio. I prayed the neighbour would not kill him.

The fear of Miguel's car driving up behind me kept me moving and alert.

Did survivors of the battle for Barcelona who marched to the French border feel that dark tug back to the hell they'd fled from? I knew this feeling of escape. I was seventeen the day I packed my suitcase and left home. I was back there again, a teenager escaping the torture of my childhood. Defiance, determination, the idea of a better life, of safety drove me on as I fled from my father's control. *That's the last time he hits me.* The half a million refugees who crossed the Pyrenees that winter into the refugee camps must have felt this mix of sadness, defiance and faint hope, this fear of being pursued. 600,000 people never made it. I would make it.

Coat buttoned up to the neck and his grandmother's nightdress below the line of my coat. I kept looking back. *Did he kill her?* But he dedicated his last novel to her: *For Alessandra.* Did he dedicate his novel to a dead woman? Was I to be his next victim, his next literary dedication so he could rewrite the story of our love affair and write himself as an innocent character in it?

As I approached Valledemosa I saw headlights in the distance. My heart contracted. I stepped off the road and clambered into the trees.

A motorbike. Thank God!

I waved at the moped. It stopped.

'Palma.'

He nodded, looked at my boots and the long nightdress below the hem of my coat and passed me his helmet.

49

Mallorcan Pearl

As I sat on the plane trying to slow my breath, I imagined Miguel running across the runway to stop me leaving. What frightened me most was that I found myself yearning for another of his explanations, more lies to convince me to stay.

The flight attendant took my unopened box of food.

'Finished madam?'

'Thank you.'

If she opened the tinfoil lid she would find a pearl ring in the mash potato. One of the old black and white Civil War photos was imprinted in my mind's eye – a French officer who'd prised open the fist of a refugee to make him drop the handful of Spanish earth he carried into exile. It was sensible to let the ring go, along with all my unanswered questions, all the unfulfilled fantasies of the married life we were never destined to live.

Who loves a murderer?

A victim. My rebel voice said it loud and clear and I felt the shame of it. All the mistakes I'd made, leaving my ex-husband, loving a … a murderer? I don't know for certain that Miguel killed Alessandra. I don't know who that skull belonged to. But I know deep in my soul that he was murdering me. A slow, insidious murder of the self.

Narcissists create such a web of lies it is often impossible to find the truth. Jeff's words punctuated my thoughts as we belted up and prepared to land.

I half expected to see police cars on the runway to take me in for questioning as the wheels bounced on the ground at Gatwick Airport. There was a skull, a grave in the cellar. Some crime had been committed.

No police. The neighbour didn't intend bringing the police into it. Perhaps I would never know the truth. Perhaps it was better I didn't. All I needed to do was to stay away.

I've never been so relieved to see a grey British sky and feel the bite of cold drizzle on my face.

My nerves started again as I reached UK Border control. Queuing with other Europeans, we moved quickly, a union of neighbours.

My ePassport opened the gates as soon as I scanned it. I walked as fast as I could to the exit, holding my coat around my nightdress, bare feet numb in my walking boots. Thank God I did not have to remove my coat to be searched at Palma airport.

Now to disappear. Miguel would come after me. I knew him. He would stalk me. Only the narcissist chooses when it's over. He'd come after me.

When I got out of the airport I took my phone out of my bag and dumped it in a bin.

Epilogue

One Year Later

That strange trick of memory obscures the view this morning. Deià overlays itself on the grim terrace of converted Victorian houses and I feel the shadow of the Teix as I stare out of the kitchen window of my attic studio, through grey North London drizzle.

The snap of the letterbox, the thud of the post hitting the mat three floors down shatters my vision of Deià.

Damn, I was doing that thing again. I told Jeff I'd stop it. Deià is fantasy. This grey view is my reality – and real life is good, or getting better bit-by-bit. The nightmares have stopped and I have a small writing job for a local paper – locked to London, the odd cultural event, but mostly reporting on Bingo nights for the over 60s and cats rescued from trees by firemen. I'm lucky to have escaped Miguel. And to have Jeff – we work on my pattern, my addiction to playing the victim with controlling men like my father. It is the strangest work. Perhaps it is the only work.

I'd made an anonymous phone call to the Palma police when I returned to London. For weeks after my return I'd scoured the pages of *El País* and *El Diario de Mallorca*. Why couldn't I find anything? Surely murder was front page news. Eventually I concluded that there could not have been a murder. And if there was, there must have been a cover up. That was a small relief.

For months I was haunted by questions. Whose skull was it? Alessandra's? I had no way of finding out and so I'd resolved to forget, but Deià had got into my bones and on grey mornings like this I crave it. Jeff helped me understand that it was an ancient wound, an old addiction to a childhood pain that drew me to Miguel, but the shadow of the mountain still looms over me in my converted Victorian attic.

9am. Let's log-on. I check the weather while I wait for Jeff's call – looks like this afternoon will brighten up. Must resist the urge to check the Mallorcan press.

Jeff's white hair appears on my laptop screen in the glow of the yellow-grey light from the bay window behind him, the same North London light that lingers outside my own window.

'How are you today?'

'Ok. I know it's crazy, but I still miss Miguel, still keep trying to understand why he was so controlling and why my father was like he was.'

'We do not know why Miguel or your father are like that. People with Narcissist Personality Disorder rarely seek therapy and when they do they usually leave as they don't respond well to being challenged, or lie as they confuse the boundaries between the truth and their fantasies.'

Jeff repeated the same things in different ways every session. Therapy was like school and although I'd considered myself a good student, unlearning my childhood conditioning made me feel like I had a learning disorder. The truth did not want to stick.

'What disturbs me most is that I was attracted to such a cruel person. When I told him what triggered me, Miguel upped his game, twisted the truth until I became so riddled with doubt I believed his lies, believed I was the one with the problem.'

'The psyche seeks healing. You gave Miguel many chances. You told him your triggers and he used that as ammunition to control you. So. Through Miguel you have faced your shadow: the victim who colludes with the abuser.'

'But I still feel so ashamed for falling so low. I was such a fool to believe his lies, his gaslighting. It seems so obvious now. He was a rotter. I should have left much sooner.'

'If only it were that easy. *If the fool persists in his folly, he will eventually become wise.* It's a quote from Blake. You had the courage to do the inner work, to understand how the pattern was forged in your childhood as a result of abuse imprinted onto your psyche. Very few people follow it through because the pain is so intense. You have awareness now and your intuition is strong. So. Listen to it.'

An hour later we say goodbye. I always feel clearer after talking to Jeff. I boil the kettle for another coffee.

The coffee tastes good this morning. Grey skies don't lie like Deià sunshine. My smile at my new independent life as I sip is real too. With Jeff's help I'm letting go of the past, forgiving myself for betraying my husband, for betraying myself.

My footsteps feel substantial as I walk down the staircase and flick through the post for my flat number: 4C (looks like a bill), 4C (another bill), 4C (a jiffy bag with a typed label). What could that be? Feels like a book … don't remember ordering anything from Amazon.

I rip open the jiffy bag with childlike curiosity.

A book! My heart dives at the publisher's logo. And the title. *THE SILK PAVILION by MIGUEL MATEO NADAL.*

My hands shake. Head spins. Legs lose their strength. I crumple on the bottom step, watch the book fall out of my hands. I see the cake again, falling in slow motion down the cellar steps. Sit down, breathe. I can almost feel the stone of the Teix through my jeans.

Just breathe like Jeff has taught you. In ... and out ... In ... Miguel's not here, he can't hurt me here.

How does he know where I live?

The dedication.

I rifle the crisp virgin pages. Ouch! Paper slices skin. I suck the blood off my finger and I thumb to the dedication:

For Lucy

I touch the print, half expecting the letters spelling out my name to disappear as I stroke them. My blood stains the page.

Beneath the dedication is a quote. Miguel always adds a quote – what had he said when I'd spent the morning looking for one for his last novel? *I dare say the ideal quote sums up the core of the story – like a clue, it adds a layer of depth but does not tell the whole story. It can be a jolly red herring.*

He still stands ready,
With a boy's presumption,
To court the queen in her high silk pavilion
(Graves)

Need to hide. I run upstairs. Slam the door shut. Lock it. I'm back there, shutting my father out of my bedroom. I need Jeff. No, I need the truth.

I scroll down the search results, clicking through the pages of *El Pais* and *El Diario de Mallorca*.

What's this?

Body Found in Deiàn Cellar.

I click the link to the article dated three months ago.

There was a photo of the *mirador* where Miguel's grandfather was forced to jump to his death. Miguel's face in another photo, and the caption: *Spanish Civil War Victim buried after seventy-six years.*

I had been bothered by a smell for months and eventually I went down to the cellar to find out what it was. I expected to find a sewage blockage, a constant problem in the house, but instead I found the body of my grandmother's best friend.

Miguel's grandfather was heralded a hero for trading his life to protect innocent villagers from the Nationalists. The article ended, *Miguel Nadal is writing a novel inspired by the murder of his grandmother's best friend and neighbour (Marta Llobet) during the 1936-9 occupation of Mallorca.*

My head spins.

This is a lie. I spent long enough with Sofia's letter to know it was dated 1987 and Marta was raped with Sofia that night in the cellar when the Dragons of Death came. Marta jumped off the mirador rather than live with the shame. Shame of rape. And incest? I thought back to the letter. There had been so much in it. Her brother Juan had raped both of them. Miguel's neighbour's grandfather had raped his sister.

Breathe into the truth. That was not the body of his grandmother's friend and neighbour. She'd jumped from the mirador.

I read on. There'd been a burial. *At last we can put the pain of the past to rest:* a quote from the neighbour.

Whose body had really been buried?

The Amnesty meant there would have been no investigation, no autopsy.

What had happened between the neighbour and Miguel that day on the patio after I fled from Deià? What pact had they made to maintain their family secrets?

I'll never know.

But I do know I have to get out of this flat. Miguel must have found me through my articles, through the local newspaper. Escape. I'd disappeared once. I can do it again. But my identity will need to change.

Would I live in the shadow of the Teix for the rest of my life, just as I live under the shadow of my father?

Despair and fear, the monotonous wheel of my psychological pattern turns in my gut. Perhaps the best I can do is make the unconscious conscious. Or I can stay where I am and write down the truth as Sofia did? Miguel didn't come after me. THE SILK PAVILION will likely be a defence of his innocence. Miguel lost control over me when I woke up.

He can kill me in fiction, but he can't kill me in North London.

A rebellion rises inside me with all the strength and defiance of Sofia's words: *I forgive the theft of my soul – and today I take back what is mine.*

I'm staying.

Miguel won't tie me to a birthing chair in London. He can't shuffle around in his cellar here. He'll find another victim, a more compliant one.

I choose to stay.

I will my legs to walk to the window. They feel like jellyfish look, like all the strength has seeped out of them, but there is a sting in my heart. A fight in my soul.

The old sash window scrapes and wobbles in its putty casement.

My hands shake as I tear the pages filled with twisted lies and warped words aimed to gaslight me into self-doubt and submission.

I crush the pages of his book into a ball and chuck them out the attic window. His words are poison. I'm not reading them.

I watch the torn scrunched-up pieces of paper fall like confetti onto grey North London pavement.

The scrunched-up part of me wants to flutter down to the pavement with the book, but there was a bigger compulsion at work in me now and I feel my London determination, a drive for independence kicks in my chest.

Right, back to work. I have an article to finish for the Finchley News. I sit at my multipurpose desk-dining-breakfast table and open my laptop. My screensaver of Richie, Shiva and Miranda in The Greenwich Hotel at Christmas makes me miss my friends in NYC, but I'd lost my Green Card. Nevermind. I have this freelance job at least.

As if by that strange magic Jung called synchronicity, there's a ping on my computer. The first line of an email notification from Drew Eddison glows in the top right hand corner of my screen: *Hi Lucy, how does a trip to Hawaii sound? The writer Diane McDonnell lives on Kauai island ...*' A new assignment for the New York News. Drew is giving me another chance. A bolt of freedom cuts through the noose of pain and my breathing frees up.

Kauai Island. Another island. Another reclusive novelist. Diane McDonnell must be at least eighty. I've read somewhere that she'd been banished from Ireland in her twenties for writing the sort of everyday truth about women's lives that annoyed the Catholic Church; went to India, trained as a yogi and now writes bestselling spiritual novels that fly off the shelves in their millions. Kauai sounds lighter than Mallorca. Maybe I *can* travel the world as a freelance writer after all? Not escape. Freedom.

THE END

Historical Note

The Spanish Amnesty Law (1977) A law promulgated by the Parliament of Spain in 1977, which freed political prisoners and permitted those exiled to return to Spain with guaranteed impunity for those who participated in crimes during the Civil War and Francoist Spain. The law is still in force, and has been used as a reason for not investigating and prosecuting Francoist human rights violations. The Act institutionalised Spain's *Pact of Forgetting* – a decision by Spanish political parties, during and after the Spanish transition to democracy, not to address atrocities committed by the Spanish State. *The Pact of Forgetting (Pacto del Olvido)* can be seen as a political decision (by both the leftist and rightist parties) to avoid dealing with the legacy of Franco, who remained in power until his death in 1975.

Spanish Civil War (1936 – 1939) The different names given to the two sides may require clarification.

Franco was a Nationalist and on the right. Nationalists were also called fascists and included Franco's Dragons of Death. People who sided with Franco were called Falangists and referred to collectively as the Falange. The Falange were right-wing conservatives and supported by Nazi Germany and Mussolini in Fascist Italy. The Catholic Church in Spain supported Franco and portrayed it as a holy war against the godless communists.

The Republicans, the government that Franco sought to usurp, was the left. The Republicans were the democratically-elected government of Spain. People who sided with the left were referred to as Republicans, Leftists or Reds, and were often considered communists. In Spain at this time anyone who opposed Franco was grouped under this banner and there were many liberal scholars who, condemned as intellectuals by Franco's regime, had no other political choice but to join one of the Republican groups (of which there were many). Russia was the only significant military power prepared to sell the Republicans weapons.

Acknowledgements

I thank Spain for being my teacher and my healer in so many ways.

I thank Barbican Press for believing in this book and breathing life into it.

I thank Dr Alan Mulhern for his sense check of the psychoanalysis and valuable feedback.

I thank Filiz Rezvan for her sensitivity and generous feedback, and filmic vision for the book and for seeing its film potential.

I thank D.D. Johnston for his reading suggestions, keen historical eye and his brilliant book of the Spanish Civil War, *The Deconstruction of Professor Thrub*.

I thank my friend Manuela Gonzalez for her help with the Spanish, and her continual support.

I thank my friend Marisa Tordera for her help with the Catalan, and for a wonderful dinner in Valencia.

I thank Romy and Miguel Bunn Bellamy for their help with Mallorquín.

I thank Marta, for her family's story, which is not referenced in the book, but which gave me an emotional lens through which to view a patchwork of stories.

I thank Philip Ayckbourn for all those Nero conversations, which helped develop the characters.

I thank Grace Nichols for her deep sensitivity, empathy and support.

I thank Mick Jackson for his feedback and support.

I thank Tony Leonard (R.I.P) and Liz Brooks for their tips on building narcissistic characters.

I thank my friend Sonia and her family who first took me to see Franco's memorial in the 80s.

I thank my Catalan flatmates, Ima and Rosa who told me stories and taught me so much about Cataluñya. If you ever read this, please contact me – I would love to see you both again (I lost my Filofax in the 90s and moved around a lot).

I thank countless Catalan friends at parties in Barcelona who gave me stories of their families, while Barcelona was bombed in the 90s and I conducted my code-switching research between Castilian and Catalan at the Universitat Autònoma Barcelona.

I thank friends whose families supported Franco and showed me another side to war-torn Spain.

I thank the people of Deià and Palma who shared their stories and the stories of their families so generously.

I thank Tony, Julio, José and Angus Cameron for the conversations about politics and the Civil War.

I thank Roy for his encouragement.

I thank my dear friend Hayley for taking the photo of me swimming in the Cala – we didn't imagine then that cold February dip would inspire the cover of the book.

I thank Patricia Walton and my brother, Miles Walton for so much love.

I thank my dogs, Blue and Moon, who are part of all that I do.

I thank Dr Sono Shamdasani, Editor of *The Red Book* for his kind permission to quote from the book.